Books by Walter Winward

THE MIDAS TOUCH
SEVEN MINUTES PAST MIDNIGHT
HAMMERSTRIKE

THE MIDAS TOUCH

Walter Winward

Simon and Schuster
NEW YORK

This novel is a work of fiction. Names, characters, places and incidents are either the product of the author's imagination or are used fictitiously. Any resemblance to actual events or locales or persons, living or dead, is entirely coincidental.

Copyright © 1982 by Walter Winward
All rights reserved
including the right of reproduction
in whole or in part in any form
Published by Simon and Schuster
A Division of Gulf & Western Corporation
Simon & Schuster Building
Rockefeller Center
1230 Avenue of the Americas
New York, New York 10020
SIMON AND SCHUSTER and colophon are trademarks of Simon & Schuster
Designed by Ed Carenza
Manufactured in the United States of America

1 3 5 7 9 10 8 6 4 2

Library of Congress Cataloging in Publication Data
Winward, Walter.
The Midas touch.

1. World War, 1939–1945—Fiction.   I. Title.
PR6073.I58M5   1982   823'.914   81-18533
ISBN 0-671-42569-2   AACR2

FOR MALCOLM AND JANE

THE
MIDAS TOUCH

Prologue

September 28, 1943

There were more uniforms than usual in the boarding area and a handful of men in plain clothes who were unmistakably Gestapo. He shivered involuntarily and felt beads of cold sweat break out across his forehead and in the small of his back. Something seemed to have happened to his legs and it took all his will power to continue walking forward.

Logic told him that, under ordinary circumstances, it would take them a while to know where to look, a few hours to figure out in which direction he'd run. But these were no ordinary circumstances. The fragment of intelligence he carried in his head was enough to change the whole course of the war, and they would know it. No effort would be spared to track him down and kill him.

He held out his boarding pass and priority travel papers and tried to ignore the fact that he was being scrutinized by the nearest of the Gestapo officers, a heavy-set youngster with piercing blue eyes. It was a routine check, that was all. He was imagining that there were more of them than usual, that they seemed more alert than on other occasions. Anyone taking the civilian Lufthansa flight from Berlin to neutral Stockholm was bound to get a good going-over.

Satisfied that the documents were in order, the airline official franked them and pushed them back across the desk. But before the traveler to Stockholm could pocket them, the Gestapo man was at his side.

"Bitte," he said politely, holding out his hand. He flicked through the papers, checking for inconsistencies. Twenty seconds passed. Thirty.

"You are Herr Joachim Seidemann of Frankfurt?" he asked finally.

"I am."

"And your business in Stockholm?"

"It's all written down."

"I should like to hear it from you."

"I am the Scandinavian representative of Reutlinger Draht-Hanfseilfabrik, ropemakers, of Offenbacher Landstrasse 190, Frankfurt. I'm traveling to Stockholm to negotiate a contract with members of the Swedish Maritime Agency."

"For ropes?"

The man known as Seidemann swallowed heavily. Keep it simple, they'd always told him. Never offer more information than a situation demands.

It would take just one telephone call to establish that Reutlinger Draht-Hanfseilfabrik, a genuine Frankfurt company, had no Scandinavian representative named Seidemann, no employee named Seidemann at all.

"For ropes," he said. "Ships need ropes," he added sarcastically, "and the Reich needs the foreign exchange."

"It must be a very important contract."

"It is."

"To send a man in your state of health, I mean. You look ill, Herr Seidemann."

"A touch of flu, that's all."

The cold blue eyes studied him. They saw a man in his early thirties, above average height. He was considerably underweight, however, his narrow face pinched enough to suggest it was a long time since he'd seen a square meal. Give him a decent set of clothes and feed him up and he wouldn't be a bad-looking fellow, but, as it stood, there was not much danger to the Reich here and precious little chance of such an unprepossessing individual successfully closing an important deal.

The Gestapo officer handed back the documents.

"I wish you a pleasant trip, Herr Seidemann. Perhaps the Swedish weather will clear your flu."

"*Danke.*"

The rope salesman, known to British intelligence by his correct name of Eric Peterson, walked out to the waiting aircraft, the first hurdle crossed but more than aware that he was still far from safe.

Twenty minutes before the Lufthansa flight was due to touch down at Bromma Airport, Stockholm, a flash signal was received in Prinz Albrechtstrasse, the Berlin HQ of the Gestapo. It originated from Bürgerstrasse 22, home of the Frankfurt Gestapo, and ordered the immediate arrest and detention of Joachim Seidemann, understood to have taken a plane earlier in the day for the capital.

It took ten minutes for Prinz Albrechtstrasse to get through to Tempelhof Airfield and a further ten to establish that Joachim Seidemann had boarded an aircraft for Stockholm.

A quick check with Lufthansa revealed that their Bromma flight would now be on the deck, on Swedish soil and therefore subject to Swedish law. Even if a priority message was sent to the captain of the airplane ordering him to take off immediately and return to the Reich, this would not be possible without refueling, which could not be accomplished in safety with passengers aboard.

Interception would have to be made the hard way, though in this respect the Gestapo had one thing in its favor, that being the notorious slowness of Swedish customs and immigration. If they moved fast . . .

A description of Seidemann was wirelessed top priority from Prinz Albrechtstrasse to the German Legation in Stockholm, where, because of the signal's eyes-only prefix, it quickly found its way to the desk of Helmuth Falck.

A giant of a man and a one-time professional wrestler, Falck's cover in the diplomatic list was that of special assistant to the cultural attaché, though the closest he'd ever come to culture was burning a few books way back in the 1930s. In reality he was the local commander of the SD (Foreign Section) —the Sicherheitsdienst or Security Service—and held the rank of Unterscharführer.

Sixty seconds after decoding the message he was in his car and racing for Bromma, a fifteen-minute journey, where he arrived just in time to be told that the last of the Berlin passengers had cleared the airport and that no one remembered Herr Seidemann. He might, however, try the taxi rank.

The first port of call for Eric Peterson, alias Joachim Seidemann, on reaching the center of Stockholm was an address in Garvargatan, a street in the residential area west of the Old Town and the Royal Palace. There he asked the taxi driver to wait and spent ten minutes in the apartment of a girl named Kirsty Gottmar, who was shocked by his appearance and more than a little angry at not having seen or heard from him in two months.

He placated her as best he could and, to get her out of the room, confessed, without revealing his point of departure, that he had traveled a long way and could use a cup of coffee laced with something stiff. While she was away he scribbled a brief note on a scrap of paper and looked around for a place to hide it. It didn't take long, though he had to work fast when he heard Kirsty returning.

She had a thousand questions she wanted to ask, including the important one of when precisely she would see him again. He told her he could not answer that, but if she had not heard from him by Friday—today being Tuesday—he gave her a number to ring and a name to ask for.

Before leaving he borrowed fifty kronor from her in small notes.

If the taxi driver thought it strange that this somewhat scruffy, cadaverous individual who had flown in via Lufthansa from Berlin next wanted to be driven to the British Legation in Strandvägen, he was a Swede and therefore far too polite or disinterested to pass comment, even to himself. Sweden's neutrality extended down to its hacks. If a man could pay, that was all that mattered.

Strictly speaking, Peterson had no connection, official or unofficial, with the Legation, even though he had used Stockholm more than once as a staging post for clandestine trips to Germany. But as the Swedish capital was a hotbed of intrigue, worse even than Lisbon, his masters had always warned him to steer well clear of Strandvägen. Which for the most part, except for arranging transportation to and from the United Kingdom, he had. But now it didn't matter who was watching, taking photographs. His usefulness in Germany was undoubtedly at an end.

His contact for the UK flights was the AMA (assistant military attaché), a youthful major by the name of Browning. As with any embassy or legation throughout the world, past or present, assistant attaché, military, air, or naval, is a polite diplomatic cover for the local intelligence officer.

Browning listened in silence while Peterson outlined his requirements. They were two.

First, Peterson wanted to send an urgent signal to London in his own code. It could be sent over the normal wavelength, but it had to go out fast and no record of the transmission kept. Could do?

"No problem," said Browning. "It won't be the first time and doubtless it won't be the last."

"I'll want to send the signal personally, not use the duty operator."

Browning was surprised. Legation security, he said, was pretty tight. Peterson did not doubt it (though in this he was quite wrong), but still preferred to make the transmission himself.

"I might want to improvise as I go along."

Browning agreed, reluctantly, before asking what the second requirement was.

"An aircraft," said Peterson. "The sooner I'm in London, the better."

Browning glanced at his watch. It was nearly 6:30 P.M.

"We're expecting a BOAC Mosquito at Bromma around midnight. It'll be turning right around after refueling. I'm pretty certain it has another urgent cargo assigned to it, but if you can get the okay from London I'll see that it's yours. It'll mean traveling in the bomb bay."

"I've done it before."

"I'll get onto it then." Browning paused with his hand on the doorknob. "It must have been pretty rough over there."

Peterson looked at him innocently. "Over where?"

Browning grinned and went out.

Peterson thought about the signal he was to send. He had the cipher in his head, so encoding was no problem. What was, was how much he should tell London. It was improbable that the Germans had or could crack the cipher, but not impossible. Better play it safe, keep it brief. He would, after all, be delivering his report in person in a few hours.

Because to the receiving operator in the UK the signal comprised a meaningless jumble of letters, it was not realized until later that the last sentence was nonsense. When decoded initially, however, the signal read verbatim:

Information of inestimable value to ourselves and the Americans in my possession. Cannot emphasize too highly its import. Please confirm first

*BOAC Mossie mine and stand by for my arrival. In the event of an
emergency contact Kirsty [garbled] has full information.*

In the meantime, Unterscharführer Helmuth Falck had
not been idle.

After missing his quarry at Bromma, he decided to take
the advice offered and check the taxi rank. No one there
recalled a man answering Seidemann's description, but sooner
or later, Falck reasoned, the cab which had taken the fugitive
into Stockholm or wherever would return, either to drop off
an outgoing passenger or collect a fare from an incoming
flight. The cab would not be back, however, for at least an
hour, which gave him more than enough time to call his office
from one of the public booths, report his whereabouts and lack
of success, and see if there was a follow-up message from Prinz
Albrechtstrasse about this mysterious Seidemann.

When he emerged from the booth five minutes later, he
was considerably shaken. The latest intelligence relayed from
Frankfurt pointed to the fact that Seidemann was a British
agent in possession of information which, if passed on, could
be catastrophic for the Reich. Whatever the cost, he had to be
stopped. He should be eliminated in Stockholm. If that was
not possible the contingency plan for such emergencies should
be put into operation.

Falck did not need it spelled out. Berlin was putting his
head on the line. Failure would not be accepted. Nor was it
considered.

Flashing his security credentials, Falck was admitted to
the Lufthansa administration area of Bromma. He had at least
forty-five minutes before the cab driver could be expected to
return, and that was time enough.

Although nominally a civilian airline which flew unarmed aircraft, Lufthansa was known to be controlled from
Berlin. It was told what to fly, where to fly, what schedules to
keep, what cargoes to carry—much as BOAC's program was
governed by the needs of Winston Churchill's War Cabinet

and the requirements of the Ministry of Economic Warfare. With one major difference.

Certain members of Lufthansa were undercover intelligence personnel. It was their job to monitor BOAC's incoming and outgoing flights and, if an opportunity presented itself, radio the time of departure of a British aircraft—a civilian plane also, it should be noted—to Luftwaffe bases in Norway and Denmark. As the hangars of Lufthansa and BOAC were virtually next door to one another at Bromma, flying for the British airline was not to everybody's taste.

There was also another method of ensuring that BOAC planes did not reach England. It was risky and far from foolproof, but it had worked once and Falck intended using it again.

After briefing his agents, the SD Unterscharführer returned to the cab rank. He questioned each incoming driver, describing Seidemann and saying that he, Falck, was a friend who had unfortunately missed the earlier Lufthansa flight and had no idea where Seidemann was staying.

Ninety minutes and a dozen drivers later Falck had what he wanted, but not before a bundle of notes had changed hands.

Falck still had no idea exactly which apartment in the Garvargatan block Seidemann had visited first, but with his resources that wouldn't take long to establish. Whether it was a safe house or a girl friend, it could be dealt with later. In the meantime he would call his office, put a watch on the British Legation, and wait for Seidemann to turn up at Bromma. If he were any judge, there would be a BOAC aircraft appearing before the night was out.

Totally exhausted both mentally and physically, Peterson was in a deep sleep when Browning shook him with the news that it had turned midnight, the Mosquito was in and being refueled, and that permission had just arrived via normal channels for Peterson to have exclusive use of the aircraft.

"Permission hardly being the operative word," he added. "I've been told more or less directly that unless I see you safely on your way to the UK, my next appointment may well be in the Tower. You must be an extremely important fellow."

The two-seater Mosquito Mk Vi used by BOAC was almost as fast as the two main Luftwaffe front-line fighters, the Fw 190 and the Me 109, and had a greater range; it could complete the 800-mile journey between Bromma and Leuchars in Scotland in about three hours, compared to eight or nine for a DC-3 or Lodestar. But the fact remained that it was a two-seater and that both seats had to be occupied by crew members, the captain and radio officer. There was only one place for a passenger to travel: in the bomb bay. Lying there on a mattress, 30,000 feet above the Skagerrak with its flak ships, encased in a flying suit, Mae West, flying boots and parachute harness was not for the faint-hearted or claustrophobic. The passenger couldn't see where he was going or where he'd been. He had his own temperature control, communication with the pilot via an intercom, and an oxygen mask. Other than that, it was like being in a coffin.

They left the Legation in an unmarked car at 12:55 A.M., observed by one of Falck's men from the other side of Strandvägen. The German had no way of knowing who was in the flying suit, but he recognized Major Browning and knew his function. After following the car for a little while to confirm that it was heading west, toward Bromma, he drove to the nearest telephone and called Falck.

While Browning was using his influence to usher Peterson through Swedish emigration with the minimum of fuss and publicity, the captain and the R/O of BOAC Mosquito G-AGRD, on loan from the RAF for the duration, were sitting at a table in the general crew messing area. In front of them were two flasks of coffee and two packets of sandwiches. Peterson's flask and food were in a canvas hold-all at the R/O's feet. There was no need to advertise the fact that they were carrying a passenger.

Neither man was over twenty-five, and both looked tired, hardly surprising as they had landed just sixty-five minutes earlier after flying most of the way from Leuchars by instruments. They had expected to get a few hours' rest before making the return trip, but orders were orders.

A few tables away lounged several Lufthansa crews, talking, laughing among themselves. Before the war Lufthansa and BOAC personnel mixed readily, shared jokes and games of cards, indulged in friendly rivalry. But that was a long time ago. The two groups barely acknowledged each other now. In an hour's time the fellow countrymen of the Lufthansa fliers might be trying to kill the unarmed BOAC crew. It was easy to forget neither that nor the fact that Lufthansa was having a cushy war. The Germans' flights to the Swedish capital were not flown over enemy territory; there were no hostiles trying to shoot them down.

Although they were unaware of it, the crew of G-AGRD had more to worry about than the Luftwaffe this trip, and right on cue three of Falck's agents with the German airline went into their act. Mechanic's overalls covering his suit, Falck himself kept a weather eye on events from the far side of the mess.

Much later, not even the Lufthansa crew could describe with any certainty what happened or why. One moment the BOAC people were sitting quietly by themselves; the next they were involved in a brawl and a shouting match with two Germans wearing ground staff uniforms.

There was a scuffle, a table was knocked over, and the Mosquito's radio officer was floored.

It was all over as fast as it began, though while bystanders moved in to separate the quartet the third of Falck's men, taking advantage of the confusion, quickly swapped the two flasks of coffee, now rolling around the floor, for two others from a paper bag in his hand. The two original flasks disappeared into the bag, after which the German left the mess.

Browning learned of the fight as he was making sure Peterson was as comfortable as possible in the bomb bay. The Mosquito pilot shrugged it off. It was one of those things.

Browning wasn't so sure. The odd bout of fisticuffs was not unheard of between Lufthansa and BOAC, but that a scrap should take place on this night of all nights and with this particular crew left him uneasy. As did what he took to be the massive frame of Helmuth Falck driving away from the airport a little later. Just as the Germans knew Browning's real job with the British Legation, so too did Browning know who Falck truly represented.

Forty minutes out of Bromma the captain came on the intercom and asked Peterson how he was doing.

"I've curled up in better places."

The captain grunted sympathetically. Not for a gold clock would they catch him traveling like that.

"I'm sorry I can't let you drink your coffee or eat your sandwiches just yet, but I'm flying at twenty-eight thousand and you'd pass out in a minute without oxygen. Maybe later."

"Don't worry about it. Just keep us pointing in the right direction. What's it like up there where the rich people live, by the way?"

"That's what I wanted to talk to you about. We're above the clouds but so is the moon now. It's lighting us up like Piccadilly Circus before the war. The flak can't touch us at this altitude, but I wouldn't mind betting there's an Fw 190 or a Messerschmitt somewhere in the vicinity. There's a night-fighter base at Aalborg in Denmark and another at Lister in south Norway. There's also something at Kristiansand at the entrance to the Skagerrak we're not too happy about. So if you feel me throwing the plane around and I don't tell you what's happening for a few minutes, don't worry about it. It'll mean I've got my hands full, but in this we can outrun anything."

"You won't mind if I scream a little."

"Not a bit."

A further thirty minutes passed in relative silence. From time to time the R/O logged a routine weather report or other traffic from Leuchars, but not once did he himself transmit. That would have given the night-fighter controllers a fix, and they were still in Luftwaffe territory.

Occasionally, rubbing his jaw, he thought about the fight back at Bromma. It was weird, on reflection, totally uncalled for. If he hadn't known better . . .

The thought remained unformed as the flask behind his seat detonated, followed a moment later by the one behind the pilot's position. Both men died instantly, but such was the force of the explosion that the floor separating the cabin from the bomb bay was torn out and Peterson was also killed, head and chest ripped apart by the blast, even before the plane began breaking up.

Falck had timed the bombs to perfection. The Mosquito disintegrated twenty miles west of the Skagerrak, where the wreckage would fall into open sea. It was witnessed independently by two night-fighters of 10/Nachtjagdgeschwader 3 and an Fw 200 Condor long-range reconnaissance flight.

In due course the reports of these crews found their way back to Berlin and were compared with Falck's estimation of the situation. It didn't take long for Prinz Albrechtstrasse to pronounce itself satisfied that the plane seen going down in flames was the one carrying the fake Seidemann, and that he had perished without passing on to his paymasters what he had learned. The plan to turn the tide of the war in Germany's favor and gain ultimate victory for the Fatherland could go ahead on schedule.

One

Behind the blackout curtaining, the lights were blazing inside 21 Queen Anne's Gate, London, SW1, headquarters of MI6, otherwise known as the Secret Intelligence Service or SIS. The three men in the second-floor smoke-filled room had been up all night, but each of them knew it might be quite a few more hours before they were allowed the luxury of sleep.

At the head of the table sat the Minister of Economic Warfare, who doubled as chief of SOE, the Special Operations Executive. To his right was Charles Curzon, peacetime merchant banker and the Minister's second-in-command.

Further down the table old Etonian Stuart Menzies, director of MI6, contemplated his fingernails. Menzies was the "M" beloved of fiction writers, though in actuality all heads of SIS were known as "C" after Captain Mansfield Cumming, a former head of the service.

It was now approaching 5 A.M. on the morning of September 29, and there was no longer any doubt that Mosquito G-AGRD was down, the occupants certainly dead. Whether it was an accident or the result of enemy action would probably never be known. It was, in any case, immaterial. What mattered was that Eric Peterson's information had died with its possessor.

"We're achieving absolutely nothing by sitting here," said Menzies, carefully removing the skin from a cold cup of coffee and frowning with distaste. "The Mosquito's gone, Peterson's gone. Those are facts and they have to be faced. The only question remaining is What do we do next?"

"We've been trying to decide that for the past hour," the Minister reminded him gently. They were all tired, but something had to be resolved before any of them left the building. "Let's look again at what we have."

He picked up a decoded onionskin of Peterson's wireless signal.

"It's unfortunate that the word following Kirsty was so garbled as to be unintelligible and that Peterson didn't get back to us before he left Sweden, but I think we can safely assume he left something with a girl for reasons we can only guess at. Kirsty is a contraction of Kristine or Kristina. We don't know whether she was sharing Peterson's bed or just a trustworthy friend, but it's a starting point."

"It's nothing of the sort," said Menzies unhelpfully. "There's not one iota of evidence to suggest the garbled word was a surname. Kirsty could be the name of a club or restaurant. It helps us not one jot."

"It also doesn't make much sense," put in Curzon. "If what Peterson had to tell us was as earth-shattering as his signal leads us to believe, why risk involving an outsider at all? Why not simply write a brief report, seal it, and leave it in the Legation safe, to be opened in the event of his death?"

"I think you know the answer to that as well as I do," said Menzies. "God knows we've both dealt with enough agents over the last four years to realize that they are most peculiar people. They spend weeks, sometimes months, trusting no one except themselves, their own judgment. Most of them wouldn't even give their own mothers the correct time without considerable soul-searching. Then when they're safe they do one of two things—either get drunk or go straight to a girl. It might be irrational, but it's a fact. I've seen it hundreds of times."

Curzon nodded his agreement. Menzies had hit the nail square on the head. Peterson had been in Germany for six weeks, completely out of touch, his mission a roving brief in and around Frankfurt, a touch of sabotage if he could manage it, never knowing from one moment to the next if he was going to be picked up by the Gestapo. If he had a girl in Stockholm, it was only natural he would go to her. She would be his sheet anchor in a treacherous world. Irrational—as Menzies had said—but natural.

"Which seems to give weight to the theory that Kirsty is a girl, not a club or restaurant or anything else," he said.

But Menzies wouldn't buy it. "That's the likelihood, but it's not certain."

The Minister checked the mantelpiece clock. Dear God, he was due at a War Cabinet meeting in five hours, and at the rate they were going they'd still be debating the unfortunate Peterson when the war was over.

"Girl's name, restaurant, or club," he said, "it's something to work on, though I confess that even if the garbled word was a surname the sentence is still piffle. Assume her name was Jones. The sentence would then read, 'In the event of an emergency contact Kirsty Jones has full information.' I presume you confirmed with the receiving operator that only one word was lost due to static?" he asked Curzon.

"I did. He had a lot on his plate at the time, and as he didn't know the code he wasn't sure until I spoke to him that he'd actually missed a word. He's now convinced he did, however, but he swears it could be no more than one. Perhaps Peterson was in a hurry and omitted the word 'who.' It would make sense if it read, 'Contact Kirsty Jones *who* has full information.' "

"Well, we'll know more if and when we trace this mysterious Kirsty," said the Minister. He glanced at the onionskin

23

again. "Which leaves this puzzling reference to the Americans. Peterson did not signal the Allies or the Allied cause or the conduct of the war. He specifically mentions the Americans. Any ideas?"

Menzies shrugged. "None at all."

"Charles?"

Curzon hesitated. "I'd only be guessing."

"Guess away. It's better than nothing."

"Perhaps he wanted to tell us that the Germans are improving the defenses in the Frankfurt area. The US Eighth Air Force has been giving the place rather a pasting in the last few weeks. So has the RAF."

"Which hardly justifies the expression—what was it?— 'Cannot emphasize too highly its import,' " said Menzies. "I didn't know Peterson that well, but I would hardly have thought him the type to indulge in melodramatic hyperbole without good reason."

The Minister could see that they were getting nowhere, and there were equally pressing matters to hand, not the least of which would be explaining to Mr. Churchill why a Mosquito hitherto designated to ferry vitally needed ball bearings was used instead to bring an agent home, and was now lost. Like so much else in the day-to-day running of the war, this would have to be passed down to operational level.

"Then to sum it up," he said briskly, "we have to do something practical. If no one has any better ideas, I propose we send an experienced operative to Stockholm to try to trace this Kirsty woman—assuming it is a woman."

"The Legation could do that," said Menzies, reluctant to lose a man on what could be a wild-goose chase. "Major Browning could probably find out in half an hour who or what Kirsty is and save us valuable cargo space in another Mosquito."

The Minister vetoed the suggestion. "No, I don't like the idea of using Legation staff on this. It could turn out to be nothing—poor Peterson being paranoid—or it could be very big indeed. If the latter, we should have somebody on it full time from the outset."

He held up his hand to silence Menzies's protest. "Don't worry, I won't steal one of your people. Peterson was more our man than SIS's. We'll send an SOE operative."

That suited Menzies fine. If Special Operations wanted to chase their tails, that was their affair.

"What about bringing the Americans in on the ground floor?" suggested Curzon. "As they're already involved, albeit very obliquely, perhaps we could make it a combined operation."

"The OSS, do you mean?"

"Yes. If we find out what Peterson meant by his transatlantic reference we shall have to put them in the picture sooner or later. Bring them in now and it could save a lot of awkward explanations at some future date. You know how touchy they are about sharing intelligence. Besides,"—he smiled—"it'll help with the cost."

The Minister returned the smile. "Spoken like a banker. Any objections?" he asked Menzies.

"None that I can see. It's Curzon's show, anyway."

"Meaning, I suppose, that if anything goes wrong it'll be up to me to grovel in Downing Street."

Menzies had the grace to grin. "Something like that."

The Minister scooped up his papers. "Perhaps we're being too gloomy too soon," he mused. "You never know, the Mosquito could have turned back or made a forced landing somewhere. You will check again, won't you?"

"Of course," said Curzon, "but I'm rather afraid we've lost it."

At Leuchars in Fifeshire, Scotland, they were in no doubt that Mosquito G-AGRD would not be heard from again. To a man the standby crews and the ground staff were shocked into silence. They had lost aircraft before and no doubt they'd lose them again, but it still left them numb. One senior pilot was heard to complain bitterly that, if they were very lucky, the dead crew members might rate a couple of lines in tomorrow's papers. There were several murmurs of indignant agreement. Civilian pilots did not make headlines, although those who flew for BOAC took at least as many risks as combat fliers, and had for years.

It had not passed unnoticed by the wits of the day that British Overseas Airways Corporation, an amalgamation of Imperial Airways and British Airways, was born by Act of Parliament on April 1, 1940, April Fools' Day. To an outsider it seemed that the British Civil Aviation Authority's plan for the fledgling airline was a clear case of advanced lunacy. The proposal to continue flying established routes and of forging new ones when the Luftwaffe controlled most of Europe's skies left many people shaking their heads with disbelief.

The entire BOAC fleet was of course unarmed, and in the beginning mostly slow and cumbersome. Hudsons, Dakotas, Lodestars, Sunderlands, Catalinas, and Liberators were fair game for the fast day- and night-fighters of the Luftwaffe. But if the Mediterranean routes and the New York run were considered dangerous, the one between the UK and Sweden was regarded as suicidal.

Nicknamed by the crews the ball-bearing run because, while on the outward flight the aircraft carried mail, newspapers, and magazines, diplomats and government officials, the return-trip cargo was invariably ball and roller bearings, machine-tool steel, fine springs, and the like from the SKF works in Gothenburg. As almost every mechanical instrument of war requires anti-friction bearings of some description and as the British factories could turn out neither the quality nor the quantity, the Germans in general and the Luftwaffe in particular did everything in their power to prevent the aircraft getting through. Starve the Churchill government of bearings, and pretty soon Britain's war machine would grind to a standstill.

Although there were several routes into and out of Sweden, they all involved flying over enemy-occupied territory. The most direct—Leuchars to Bromma—took in the Skagerrak, that stretch of water separating south Norway from north Denmark which was flanked by some of the most powerful flak batteries in the world and at least half a dozen crack Luftwaffe fighter squadrons. Not even the introduction of the Mosquito early in 1943 made the trip a milk run, but at least this largely wooden aircraft, brainchild of the De Havilland Company, had great speed. Up to September 29, 1943, only two had been lost: G-AGRD, and G-AGGF, piloted by Captain L. A. Wilkins on August 17, 1943. The radio officer, N. H. Beaument, was also killed, and a confidential report, number C 454/CI, was unable to tell why the plane crashed into a hillside at 2,500 feet above Glen Esk.

That the Luftwaffe and German intelligence were taking a thoroughly unhealthy interest in the activities of Mosquitoes flying between Leuchars and Bromma was shown by a most secret minute sent to the Director of General Civil Aviation from Transport Command in May of that same year. In part it stated:

1. It is believed that German Night Fighter Units in Denmark have received special orders to make strenuous efforts to intercept and shoot down our courier aircraft on the Stockholm route.

2. The main danger area is that within 50 kilometres of The Skaw, and it is believed that a standing patrol is being maintained in this vicinity during the hours of darkness.

Captain Gilbert Rae, flying G-AGGC, could attest to that as, while carrying an unnamed passenger of great importance on July 24, 1943, his aircraft was attacked by two Fw 190s just west of The Skaw. By taking violent evasive action, Rae managed to outrun the German fighters, but his passenger blacked out and R/O Payne received cuts and bruises as a result of buffeting.

Rae received the OBE for his efforts and continued to fly

Mosquitoes. He was killed in August 1944, the accident report reading, inter alia: "There is insufficient evidence to show how this accident occurred."

At the time of his death Rae had completed 150 return trips to Sweden. He was twenty-six, a year older than the skipper of G-AGRD, whose reported death by the two night-fighters of 10/NJG 3, together with the deaths of the radio officer and Eric Peterson, had just brought a mighty sigh of relief in Berlin.

The offices of Department VI, Foreign Intelligence, of the RSHA, the Reich Main Security Office, were in a former Jewish old folks' home at Berkaerstrasse 32 in the Charlottenburg district of Berlin. Those present at the early-morning meeting were Reichsmarschall Hermann Göring, looking much the worse for wear after a night of too little sleep and too much brandy; Minister of Armaments Albert Speer; Gestapo chief SS Gruppenführer Heinrich Mueller; and SS Brigadeführer Walter Schellenberg, head of the Foreign Section, a small good-looking man in his thirties. The Abwehr, Military Intelligence, was not represented. Its director, Admiral Canaris, was gradually being eased out by the SS and would soon be arrested. Before the end of the war he was destined to be executed in Flossenbürg concentration camp.

Schellenberg was in the chair. Although the most junior member of the quartet, he commanded Unterscharführer Helmuth Falck in Stockholm.

"So," he was saying, "I think we can safely assume the fake Seidemann is dead and that he did not pass on to the British what he learned."

Göring was not so sure, and said so.

Impudently Schellenberg waved aside his objections. "Nevertheless, Herr Reichsmarschall, we must proceed on that assumption. There's no risk, as you are well aware. If the plan is not going to work, we shall know long before it's

28

necessary to commit ourselves irrevocably. That is one of the built-in safeguards."

"There's no such thing as a safeguard that's absolutely foolproof," snorted Göring. "And if we fail it's my neck, not yours."

Schellenberg and Mueller exchanged glances. It was well known that Göring's nerve had gone, that he was relying more and more on alcohol and drugs to keep going. The man who had boasted to the Führer that he would wipe the RAF off the map in a week and that not a bomb would fall on the Reich was a burnt-out shell. Both wondered why the Führer did not quietly retire him.

Speer said, "Intelligence work is not our sphere, Herr Reichsmarschall. We must trust those whose business it is."

"As we trusted Mueller's Gestapo, I suppose," Göring sneered. "Good God, a British agent lives openly in Frankfurt for I don't know how long and the Gestapo do nothing. That doesn't exactly fill me with confidence."

"We knew about Seidemann several weeks ago," said Mueller. "He was left at large in the hope he would lead us to his contact."

"And did he?"

"No," admitted Mueller.

"No," repeated Göring. "And not only that, but he calmly catches a plane for Sweden under your very noses." He turned to Speer. "And these are the people you are asking me to trust."

Schellenberg decided to use the big stick on the fat Reichsmarschall. Given half a chance, Göring would keep them here all day, raising objection after objection. It was not, in the last analysis, a question of trust at all. It was simply that Göring would do anything to avoid making a decision, any decision.

"I think you'll find, sir," he said deferentially, "that the Führer continues to give his unqualified support to the plan, has awarded it the highest priority. If you have any misgivings, may I suggest you present them to him?"

Göring shuddered at the thought. Since Stalingrad and El Alamein, the Führer's notorious rages had become more and more uncontrollable. It would take a braver man than the Reichsmarschall to face Hitler with nothing more than unsubstantiated fear as an argument.

"No, no," he said hastily. "You misunderstand me. If you are confident that the Allies are still in ignorance of our intentions, then we must, of course, proceed with the next step."

"Excellent," said Schellenberg.

"The next step being what?" asked Speer.

"To let the Allies know about our two guests."

"And when will you do that?"

"Soon," murmured Schellenberg, "but not too soon."

A little later in the day Charles Curzon met his American counterpart in the SOE's Operations HQ at 64 Baker Street.

Colonel Harry W. Mortimer of the OSS, Office of Strategic Services, was, like Curzon, a peacetime banker, giving the two men much in common from the outset. Which was just as well, as both were constantly in and out of each other's pockets, making sure there was no duplication of effort in occupied Europe or elsewhere. Mortimer was a short, wiry individual with a taste for black foul-smelling cigars. From time to time he presented a box to Curzon, who had never yet had the courage to light one up. His private vow was that he would smoke one the day the Hitler regime collapsed. Also present were two much younger men, both in civilian clothes: Majors Jack Fallon and Sam McKenna.

Earlier, Curzon had given considerable thought about who to send to Stockholm. Some sixth sense warned him that the mission would not end in the Swedish capital, and he had chosen Fallon from a short list of five for that officer's fluency in several languages, German and Swedish among them.

Without going into detail on the telephone, he had asked Mortimer also to bring along a linguist with operational experience, and he was not unhappy with the American's choice.

Though as broad across the shoulders and upper back as befitted someone who had once fought his way through to the semis of the 101st Airborne's heavyweight division, McKenna moved with the agility of a gymnast. Dark-complexioned and sporting a five o'clock shadow even this early in the day, he stood over six feet by a fraction. His shrewd eyes gave the impression they didn't miss a thing and also that they'd seen more than was good for any man who had, until a few years ago, believed that the human race could not possibly be as black as cynics painted it. He was in his middle to late twenties, and Curzon would find out later that he had spent the years from 1932 to 1937 at various educational establishments in Europe, his father, now dead, having held a roving brief from a New York bank that only he seemed to understand and a firm belief in the virtues of the Old World academy. Vacations were spent bumming around middle Europe and Scandinavia; and a natural ability for languages, inherited from his Swedish mother, had been honed to a point where no native-born German, Frenchman, or Swede could tell he was not one of their own. He also had a good working knowledge of several other European tongues.

Curzon came to the silent conclusion that he would be a useful man in a tight squeeze.

Not that Jack Fallon wasn't. Though a couple of inches shorter than McKenna and less heavily built, he had been "over the other side" more often than any other SOE operative in Baker Street, and had proved, from the beginning, to be a natural for special operations, possessing that rare combination of courage and quiet determination interlaced with a healthy respect for the talents of the opposition.

Before coming to Baker Street he had served in the infantry and later with the Long Range Desert Group, where he had earned a reputation for being a scrapper with a quick temper, which more than once had landed him in hot water before someone pulled his file, discovered he was fluent in a couple of languages, and wisely concluded he was the classic square peg.

First Stuart Menzies and later Curzon deduced that his irascibility was the result of frustration. He wasn't much of a team man. Alone or with one or two others was how he functioned best.

He was a square-jawed individual who grew his fair hair somewhat longer than King's Regulations permitted, and physically he could pass for a north German or Scandinavian. From what Curzon recalled of his service dossier, he was born in Yorkshire some thirty years ago, an only child of now-deceased parents. His prewar occupations were varied, which was one way of saying he had no roots. He had worked as a merchant seaman, mined for gold in South Africa, and dug roads as a manual laborer in Sweden and Germany, which was how he picked up his knowledge of those languages. He had broken horses in Tipperary and also served a short prison sentence for assault.

There was a footnote on the dossier to the effect that while in France in 1942 he had become deeply involved with a partisan by the name of Yvette Blanchard, who was later tortured and executed by the Gestapo while Fallon was elsewhere. By way of reprisal and quite alone, he kidnapped the commander of the firing squad and hanged him from a lamppost opposite his own headquarters during the hours of darkness.

Fallon's was the sort of curriculum vitae that would turn a postwar employer gray and probably get him no further than the outer office, but he was precisely what was needed in SOE. As McKenna was ideal material for the OSS.

Both men were essentially loners who knew what fear was, and both covered what they privately considered to be a weakness by a lot of wisecracking that neither truly felt.

After introductions were completed, Curzon informed

the other three what was known about Peterson's last hours and handed each of them a decoded copy of the Stockholm signal with the comment that the last sentence was not a transcribing error but a verbatim record of the transmission.

Mortimer read it through quickly and frowned. "Is this all? The way you sounded on the phone I thought you'd at least uncovered a plot to assassinate the President. You could have sent this across by dispatch rider."

"True," agreed Curzon, "but I thought you'd want to discuss it, be in on it from the start."

"Be in on what from the start?" Mortimer blew a huge cloud of smoke. "There's nothing here to be in on. One of your agents escapes from Germany, gets to Sweden, sends a message that doesn't make sense, and goes down in an aircraft. Okay, he says he has—had—information of vital importance to both our countries, but that could mean anything. Christ, I get stuff like this across my desk every day. If I paid attention to a tenth of it I'd need twice the number of operatives I have."

"Peterson was a good man," said Curzon quietly. "He wasn't given to making rash statements."

"He wasn't given to making any kind of a statement at all. I repeat, there's nothing here."

"There's a name. Does Major McKenna speak Swedish?"

McKenna started to say he did, that his mother was Swedish, but Mortimer cut across him.

"Now wait a minute. Hold it. If you've got some fancy idea about sending Major Fallon to Stockholm for a few days among the bright lights, that's your affair. But count Major McKenna out. I've got other plans for him."

Curzon shrugged. "Fair enough, but you're always complaining we never tell you enough. I thought this time I'd lay our cards on the table from the beginning. Certainly I'm sending Major Fallon to Stockholm and wherever his nose leads him after that. If you want us to go it alone, that's fine with me."

Mortimer shifted uncomfortably in his seat. Damn Curzon. It was quite true that the Baker Street Irregulars, as SOE were known to the other Allied intelligence services, sometimes played it a bit close to the chest, fought their own private war. It was equally true he'd had occasion to bitch about it in the past. Now Curzon was boxing him into a corner, no doubt for the usual tight-fisted Limey reason: money. It was an open secret that SOE had to fight the British Treasury for every penny, and a combined operation with the OSS always made it easier to twist the Treasury's arm. If he refused to cooperate, Curzon would feel perfectly justified in excluding the OSS from one or two future operations.

"You're trying to railroad me," he growled.

"I doubt if General Donovan would see it that way," said Curzon smoothly. William J. Donovan was head of the OSS and took his orders direct from President Roosevelt. "General Donovan might well think that any intelligence emanating from Frankfurt and the surrounding areas demanded US investigation."

Mortimer sat up and took notice. In his mind's eye he saw a map of central Germany and a target, so far known only to a handful of selected individuals, encircled in red ink.

"This is the first I've heard about Peterson being in Frankfurt."

Curzon was not slow to spot the change of attitude. "That was his brief and that, to the best of our knowledge, was where he went. Why, does it make a difference?"

"It could. I can't let you in on it until I've made a couple of calls, but it could make a big difference. Can I use a phone, scrambled and private?"

"Of course. Is it likely to take long?"

"Hard to say."

"Because if it is I suggest we let Major Fallon and Major McKenna go off and get acquainted. If they're going to work together we'd better see if they get along."

"I didn't say they were going to work together."

Curzon smiled disarmingly. "You didn't say they weren't, either."

Mortimer stubbed out his cigar. "Be back in an hour," he said to McKenna.

Outside it had started to rain and the temperature had dropped ten degrees during their short time in Curzon's office.

McKenna shivered. "Jesus Christ, why the Krauts ever wanted to invade England is beyond me. You wasted an awful lot of hardware and manpower during the Battle of Britain. You should have just sent Hitler a weather forecast. That would have trimmed his feathers. Come to London and see the changing of the seasons—all before lunch."

Fallon grinned. "We were keeping it as a secret weapon in case the going got really rough."

"Yeah, but you could have warned your allies. Me, I haven't been warm or dry a day since I got here."

"Which is how long?"

McKenna looked at him. "Is that a friendly question or am I being pumped?"

"A bit of both."

"Okay, then I'll tell you when we're behind a drink. Are the pubs open? I can't keep up with your licensing laws."

Fallon looked at his wristwatch. "They're closed."

"Doesn't matter. I know a club off Park Lane where they keep serving until the booze runs out, which it never does."

"That's a hell of a walk."

"Walk nothing. We'll get a cab."

"You'll be lucky."

"Watch this."

There wasn't a cab in sight when McKenna walked to the curb and held up a hand containing a ten-dollar bill, but a moment later two appeared as if by magic. They came close to causing a pile-up in their anxiety to reach the American first.

Inside the winner's cab McKenna said, "I haven't figured it out myself, either, but it never fails."

"It's a pretty expensive way of traveling—at ten dollars a ride."

McKenna looked horrified. "Christ, they don't get the ten. In gambling circles, which have been known to attract my attention before now, that sawbuck is known as the come-on. They get the regular fare and maybe a shilling extra if they're polite and don't try to gyp me."

Fallon took in the American's massive size. "Does that happen often?"

"Not very."

It seemed as if the establishment was run by Americans for Americans, mostly in uniform, but McKenna flashed a piece of plastic and had no trouble getting himself and Fallon past the enlisted man at the door.

To call it a club was an overstatement. It was no more than a couple of rooms, a few chairs and tables, and a bar occupying most of one wall. But there was no shortage of alcohol and apparently no rationing. Provided you could pay, you could drink as much as you liked.

There were quite a few women present too, again the majority in uniform. Only a sprinkling were Americans. The rest were from the three British women's services. Fallon counted at least a dozen assorted Wrens, Waacs, and Waafs. No wonder the poor Limeys couldn't get a look in with this kind of competition. Still, it was hard to blame the girls. It wasn't the easiest job in the world, pushing colored discs around a situations board, knowing the number of casualties even before the War Cabinet.

"Grab a table while I sort the drinks out," bellowed McKenna above the noise. "Whiskey do? It'll probably be rye or bourbon."

Fallon nodded. He had no trouble finding an empty table. Most of the others seemed to prefer drinking on their feet.

"Makes you wonder who the hell's fighting the war, doesn't it," said McKenna a minute or two later, putting down two brimming glasses of whiskey and a couple of beer chasers. "A well-aimed bomb now could wipe out at least a brace of Eighth Air Force generals and a couple of colonels on Eisenhower's staff. Cheers."

McKenna sank half his whiskey and followed it with a mouthful of beer.

"You've been here that long, anyway," said Fallon.

"How's that?"

"To say 'cheers.' "

"Oh yes, I was going to tell you about that, wasn't I? You sure you haven't been put up to this?"

"Quite sure. I'm just curious."

"Okay. Can we un-Mister and un-rank ourselves, by the way?"

It became Jack and Sam, and they shook hands for the second time in half an hour.

"I've been based here permanently for three months," offered McKenna, "some of which I've spent in France, some in Spain, and once in Yugoslavia with this guy Tito. Before that I was with the 101st Airborne—until somebody pulled my service sheet and discovered I'd spent a lot of time in Europe in the thirties. I've also been around one or two Pacific islands, but that's another story.

"Between quitting Europe and the Japs hitting Pearl, I found time to finish law school and get married. Both mistakes. I was never going to be the best lawyer the California bar had ever seen, and the lady in question couldn't figure out why I didn't want to join the DA's office and make a name for myself. The final stand-up fight we had could have won awards for invective, but eventually we walked away from each other, me watching my back the whole route. She was the kind who would turn and fire long before you'd covered ten paces apiece."

McKenna took another swig of beer. "Now it's your turn."

Fallon kept it short. Apart from the fact that his war occupied a few more months than McKenna's, their service careers were not that different.

"No wife?"

Fallon hesitated. "No wife."

"Wise man. It doesn't go with our line of work, though I think my own little bottled blond was a mite pissed off when the divorce came through in July. She'd got wind of the kind of outfit I'd joined and imagined herself wearing widow's weeds—and collecting the GI insurance if I cashed in. Ready for another?"

"My turn."

"Can't be done. Only United States citizens get to buy drinks here. House rule."

McKenna pushed his way to the bar. "Come on, buddy, shake it up."

The bartender was busy and it took a few minutes to get served. When McKenna turned away from the bar, he saw through the smoke that Fallon had somehow got involved in what appeared to be an argument with an Eighth Air Force captain and lieutenant, both worse the wear for drink.

McKenna decided to keep out. It would be interesting to see how Fallon handled it.

The SOE officer remained seated, apparently willing to accept the abuse in the interest of Anglo-American amity, until the captain reached out and grabbed a handful of his shirt. Then Fallon moved with bewildering speed. McKenna hardly saw what happened. One minute the captain and the lieutenant were standing up, the next they were in a crumpled heap on the floor.

McKenna abandoned his role as spectator when a couple

of other Eighth Air Force types began to take an interest. From what he had just witnessed, Fallon could probably take the place apart without breaking sweat, but that might mean the arrival of the MPs and lots of publicity.

Gripping Fallon by the arm, he ushered him into the street. "The winner and new champion. What the hell was that all about?"

"A minor disagreement about who was winning the war for whom. You weren't a hell of a lot of help, I might add."

"Jack, if I'm going somewhere with you—Stockholm, Berlin, or Tokyo—I'd like to know my back's safe if we get into a tight spot. I'd also like to give you a few lessons in sweet reason."

"I can't even spell it. Somebody pushes me, I push back. I've got a short fuse."

"Well, if you don't tell anybody, I won't. Hey, there's a cab."

Colonel Mortimer was on the scrambler phone for the best part of forty-five minutes. When he finally replaced the handset he was considerably shaken.

Curzon was waiting for him along the corridor. "Well?"

"I've had a word with a couple of people," said Mortimer, "and they're inclined to think your man Peterson stumbled onto something pretty big. Anyway, they don't want to take any chances."

"You're not telling me anything, Harry."

"Then try this for size. Around sixty air miles east of Frankfurt is Schweinfurt and the ball-bearing plants. Besides myself and one or two Eighth Air Force brass you're the only one to know that when we're good and ready, probably sometime within the next two weeks, the Eighth is paying the town a return visit, to flatten it for good."

Curzon remembered the Eighth Air Force's previous mission to Schweinfurt back in August, the appalling losses suffered. It was a priority target, one the Ministry of Economic Warfare kept insisting had to be leveled.

"Go on."

"That's all there is. Maybe what Peterson had to tell you had nothing to do with Schweinfurt, but then again maybe it did. He was in the right area."

"So?"

The intercom buzzed and a voice announced that Majors Fallon and McKenna were back.

"So?" repeated Curzon.

"So if Fallon's going to Stockholm, McKenna will go with him. But let's not say anything to either of them about Schweinfurt. We're only guessing, and I hope to God we're guessing wrong."

TWO

In mid-1943 the Bavarian township of Schweinfurt, located on the River Main, was home and workplace for some 60,000 souls. It was a pleasant little community at least eleven centuries old. It contained two breweries, those of H. Hagenmeyer and A. Hartmann, three banks, a hydro-electric generating station and a gas works, a customs office, law courts, two modern hospitals, seven schools, and a theater on Schillerplatz. There were four Protestant churches, three churches of the Roman Catholic persuasion, and a museum. There were military barracks in Franz Schubertstrasse and Neiderwerrnerstrasse, and the local headquarters of the Nazi Party and Gestapo was at Rückertstrasse 2, just across the road from the Town Hall. But Schweinfurt's main claims to fame were its engineering and metal works.

Allied intelligence had estimated that Schweinfurt produced almost 50 percent of all the bearings manufactured in Germany, in an area so concentrated that a daylight bombing raid should be a piece of cake. Target analysts predicted that even partial success would cause a massive breakdown in Nazi arms production, and on August 17, 1943, General Ira C. Eaker's Eighth Bomber Command set out to prove them right.

As this date was the first anniversary of American bomber operations from the United Kingdom, General Eaker decided to split his force and hit the Messerschmitt plant at Regensburg as well as Schweinfurt. This second air fleet under Colonel Curtis LeMay would, after bombing Regensburg, fly on to North Africa and land there, to prevent a bottleneck on the UK airfields when the planes returned. Casualties had been estimated at 7 to 8 percent, a figure considered tolerable.

The planners were way out.

Of the 230 aircraft that took off for Schweinfurt, only 194 came back. Thirty-six planes were completely destroyed and 122 of the surviving planes damaged, 27 so badly that it was doubtful if they would ever fly again. LeMay lost 24 aircraft out of 146. The loss for both missions was 16 percent, a frightening statistic. At that rate, five more raids would wipe out the Eighth Bomber Command.

Neither did the devastation inflicted upon Schweinfurt justify such losses. According to Eaker, he was "not satisfied with our bombing accuracy, though considerable damage seems to have been done to the ball-bearing plants." Nevertheless, they were back to almost full production within a matter of weeks, and that meant a return trip, all other things being equal.

Only Minister of Armaments Albert Speer knew the truth: that the August 17 attack had caused an immediate drop of 34 percent in ball-bearing production and that if it happened again, and later the RAF joined in to make it round-the-clock bombing, the war would be over in no time, the Reich on the losing end. Somehow a second raid had to be prevented.

Among those who had made August 17 such a fearful day for the B-17s were pilots of JG 11 (Jagdgeschwader, or single-engine fighter unit), flying Me 109s out of Jever, thirty miles west of Bremerhaven in northern Germany. Although he had taken part in several score air battles in the intervening weeks, that August afternoon was uppermost in the mind of the squadron's youthful Hauptmann as he crossed the airfield to his waiting plane, for only four of the eleven men from his Staffel who had flown that day were still alive. Until lunch, the count was five survivors, but Leutnant Hans Stepp, on a routine air test over the comparative safety of Wangerooge, had run into a squadron of Spitfires that appeared from nowhere. There wasn't enough left of young Stepp, age nineteen, to put in a handkerchief, though the usual ceremony would take place and an urn containing ashes from God knows what would be sent to his parents in Düsseldorf.

Hauptmann Otto Reinberger wondered how many families were fooled by the urns.

It really was becoming an awful business. No matter how many of the big American planes they put down, there were always more to take their place. And more crews. The same applied to RAF Bomber Command and the loss of the Lancasters and Stirlings and Halifaxes they suffered at the hands of the Luftwaffe night-fighter arm. Where on earth did the Allies get their replacements? The Luftwaffe couldn't manage it. The kids they were sending these days would have still been flying Arado 66 trainers in 1940, assuming they'd managed to complete Fliegereratzabteilung, recruit training depot. Now, with just a few hours in their logbooks and no idea how to attack the incredibly well defended B-17s, they hardly had time to make their bunks and stow their kit before a letter was being written to their wives or mothers, regretting their deaths.

And God knows what was going to happen when, as was being rumored, the Americans finally built the fighter that could escort the bombers all the way to the target and back, even deep into Germany. At the moment the P-47 Thunderbolts and the Spitfires were limited in range, but one day soon the Luftwaffe was going to have to tackle Allied fighters every inch of the way. It was a chilling prospect.

Aged twenty-six and a Berliner, Reinberger had worked before the war in a large publishing house and had not considered himself the outdoor type or particularly intrepid. Now, four years after joining the Luftwaffe, he had forty-three victories to his credit and wore the coveted Knight's Cross at his throat. He was a stickler for discipline, flying or otherwise, but as the Staffelkapitän it was up to him to set an example until the day came—as it must come soon—when he was promoted to the rank of major and given a Gruppe, three Staffels, of his own.

Which could well mean recommending as his successor the officer at present berating one of the black-overalled mechanics for some infraction of the rules, though God knows Oberleutnant Heinz Mahle would probably have every man on the base reading a chapter a day of *Mein Kampf* before a week was out.

Mahle was Reinberger's wingman, or Katchmarek, and probably the best flier in the Staffel after Reinberger himself. He resented being second man in the Rotte, or two-man flying team, frequently asserting that it was undignified for a pilot with his experience.

Reinberger was inclined to agree that it was a criminal waste of talent to keep him in a subordinate role, particularly as the Oberleutnant had achieved twenty-two kills when leading his own Rotte. But Mahle was headstrong. He needed the discipline of flying as wingman for a few weeks longer if he was ever to inherit the Staffel. Staffel commanders had responsibilities above and beyond personal glory-hunting.

He was perhaps a little young—twenty-three or twenty-four, as far as Reinberger could remember—to be considered for promotion to Staffelkapitän, but it was his devotion to the more unsavory aspects of Nazi philosophy which disturbed Reinberger most. It was not a criticism one could put in a fitness report, of course, not if one wanted to keep one's head, and doubtless it had no effect on the Oberleutnant's flying ability. But Reinberger had no real use for fanatics.

He was more the traditional fighter pilot's build, Ober-leutnant Mahle, a couple of inches shorter than Reinberger at five feet eight. In recent weeks he had attempted to grow a mustache similar to Adolf Galland's, General of Fighters, but it still didn't look right. The color was okay, as Mahle's hair was almost black, but it seemed to sprout in every direction. Reinberger made a mental note to ask him to shave it off if he couldn't cultivate it better. Really, it was like a well-used toothbrush.

"What was that all about?" he asked after Mahle had dismissed the thoroughly chastened mechanic.

"I caught the bloody man pissing up against my stabi-lizer," spluttered Mahle, hardly able to believe it. "Can you imagine that? Urinating against *my* stabilizer!"

The Oberleutnant's tone made it quite clear that it was perfectly acceptable to urinate against any part of any aircraft that did not belong to Heinz Mahle. In spite of himself, Reinberger found it hard to keep a straight face. "That's seri-ous," he managed.

"You're damned right it's serious. Discipline among the lower ranks is shot to hell on this airfield." He bit his tongue. "I'm sorry, that's not meant as a criticism of the Staffelka-pitän."

"I should hope not," retorted Reinberger, knowing full well that Mahle's ideal method of dealing with a disciplinary problem, real or imagined, would be to shoot the offender.

"Let's get airborne," he said. "There was no indication that the *Amis* are about to pay us a visit when I left the office, but they'll be over before the day's out."

Reinberger was not at all happy with the Daimler Benz 1,450-hp engine that powered his Me 109 Gustav, and he wanted to air-test it before the fighting started. His ground crew had stripped it several times without finding anything wrong, but every so often it tended to cut out completely. Replacements were hard to come by in a hurry, however, and 99 percent of the time the engine was perfect. Reinberger would have preferred 101 percent. Facing a wing of B-17s with a faulty motor was not his idea of entertainment.

They would not be looking for combat this afternoon, but that was not to say the RAF or the Americans would not provide them with some. For this reason each Messerschmitt's guns were fully loaded. It was also the reason Mahle was coming along.

"What's the drill?" asked the Oberleutnant.

"We'll climb to five thousand meters and try a few tight turns. Might as well get some practice ourselves while putting the engine through its paces. I'd like you to keep a little closer than you were yesterday. Or the day before, for that matter. You're tending to drift away, especially in a starboard roll."

Mahle puckered his brow in annoyance. You'd think he was a complete beginner the way Reinberger sometimes spoke to him. "I hadn't noticed," he said coldly.

"I know you hadn't, that's why I'm telling you. You wouldn't want to lose your Staffelkapitän now, would you?"

Not a bad idea at all, thought Mahle. Perhaps then he'd get the Staffel himself, though that could only be a matter of weeks anyway. "Hauptmann Mahle" had a nice ring to it.

If Mahle's promotion and the opportunity for greater glory could not come too soon for the Oberleutnant, there were others, the reprimanded mechanic apart, who muttered quiet prayers to whatever gods they believed in to please transfer the Staffelkapitän's wingman to another station, preferably on the Eastern Front. Among these were Oberleutnant Wolf Löhr and Leutnant Paul Weinrich, who watched the pair of 109s taxi and take off as though bound to each other by an invisible cord.

Löhr was the comedian of the Staffel and a hell-raiser whenever he got the opportunity, enjoying beer a great deal and women a lot more, though he was not much to look at. He fought a constant weight problem, and his fair hair was already thinning. He would be bald before his thirtieth birthday.

In combat he was a brave and fearless warrior, though what others put down to courage he called well-tried philosophy. When his number was up, that was it. There was not a damned thing he could do about it except fly as best he could, which was excellent. His personal tally of enemy aircraft destroyed stood at fourteen as of yesterday, when he had claimed a B-24, which was still to be confirmed. He had no doubt it would be. Life was like that for him.

For Weinrich, on the other hand, life was a constant battle against shyness and uncertainty about which he could do little except fight both weaknesses, doing so with a fierce determination he hardly knew he possessed.

At nineteen he was the baby of the Staffel, though that was his own description, self-mocking as usual. Certainly no one who had seen him fly a 109 thought of him as a baby, even if, with his pink cheeks and slender frame, he could pass for fifteen in a poor light. Neither did Löhr, whose wingman Weinrich was, consider him to be any less than an *Experte*. He had seen Weinrich make kills like the best and had also suffered when his young friend's aircraft had twice gone down in flames, watched for the parachute when he should have been watching his own now-unprotected back. It was Löhr's private opinion that Weinrich would end the war as one of its top-scoring aces, though naturally he said nothing of this. Weinrich would not have believed him in any case.

The 109s of Reinberger and Mahle executed a perfect tight turn at 5,000 meters. Löhr sang a few lines of the Horst Wessel song:

*"Die Fahne hoch, die Reihen fest geschlossen
SA marschiert mit ruhig festem Schritt."*

Translated it meant:

Up with the flag, close the ranks
The SA marches at a quiet, steady pace.

"He's not that bad," said Weinrich, knowing full well that Löhr's untuneful rendering was directed at Mahle.

"Not that bad! My dear Paul, if that mad bastard gets the Staffel when Reinberger's booted upstairs he'll have pictures of Himmler decorating the mess. Reinberger might leave a lot to be desired in the public relations department, but he's a flier first and foremost. I tell you frankly, if Mahle becomes Staffelkapitän I'll apply to join the Kriegsmarine."

"Still, he's a good pilot, Oberleutnant Mahle. See how he sticks close to Reinberger."

"He's probably wondering how he can shoot him down and claim it as an accident. There's only one thing worse than a dedicated Nazi and that's an *ambitious* dedicated Nazi. Mark my words, Mahle will be running the Luftwaffe before this war's over."

Three

Although BOAC pilots had brought the chore of flying from Leuchars to Bromma down to a fine art, it was still far from a milk run, and the airline did not run a scheduled service. Much depended upon the weather, intelligence reports of Luftwaffe activity in Norway and Denmark, and whether there was a priority cargo to be picked up at the other end, for a plane idle in a hangar was a wasted aircraft.

Because the fast Mosquitoes were at a premium and could only carry one bomb-bay passenger, it was originally suggested that Fallon and McKenna fly in a Dakota with other passengers, but this was vetoed when a secret memorandum from the BOAC station manager, Stockholm, found its way onto the Minister of Economic Warfare's desk. Part of it stated, "The new approved northern corridor, between $60°30'$ N and $62°20'$ N, is on the Swedish-Norwegian border." (The slower Dakotas had to take the long way around, not the more direct route over the Skagerrak, where they would be easy meat for the flak ships and the Luftwaffe.) A footnote added that the C-in-C of the Swedish Air Force had promised to mark certain military airfields in the vicinity of the corridor

49

for emergency use, but to please keep this very quiet, as his action was most unorthodox.

It was too risky and would take too long, the Minister concluded. The trouble with defining a corridor was that it quickly, by one means or another, came to the attention of every Luftwaffe commander in the area. If the Swedish Air Force C-in-C was being helpful to BOAC, it was only logical that the Germans would have their own contacts and supporters in the Air Ministry. No doubt BOAC would overcome the difficulties sooner or later, but it might cost aircraft and lives. For the moment it was safer for Fallon and McKenna to travel by Mosquito, even if it meant fighting the entire War Cabinet for use of the planes.

As it happened, no fight was necessary. Both Winston Churchill and President Roosevelt had seen the text of Peterson's signal and were anxious that the matter be investigated, the conundrum resolved, with the utmost expedition.

Fallon flew in G-AGEL, nicknamed *Gaggle of Geese* because of its code letters, and skippered by a twenty-eight-year-old veteran called James Masefield, known to the other crews as Dandy Jim because of the snappy way he dressed when in civvies. It was Masefield, as he tucked Fallon into the bomb bay, who told him he was flying in one of the finest aircraft ever built and that Göring was supposed to have remarked that he turned green with envy whenever he saw one, that De Havilland's had cobbled together a beautiful wooden plane that any damned piano factory could turn out.

Gaggle's radio officer, a dour Glaswegian by the name of Jock Munroe and an amateur pianist of some skill, remarked that he didn't know what Bechstein's would have to say about that.

McKenna went across in G-AGEM, captained by one of the oldest fliers on the route, thirty-six-year-old Bob Pitman. The R/O was a virtual novice, a youngster barely out of his teens. They generally gave the beginners to Pitman, a man always ready to help and advise and whose personal dossier described him as an outstanding individual possessing the highest qualities of bravery and leadership.

They were met at Bromma in the small hours of October 2 by Major Browning. Both men were carrying diplomatic passports, and formalities were minimal; but there was no earthly chance their arrival would go unreported. Browning estimated it would be about ten minutes before Helmuth Falck was given a full description of the Mosquito passengers, though it was nothing to worry about.

"You're not known in Stockholm. Even if he has a contact in Swedish immigration, he'll only learn you're new additions to the Legation staff."

Coming from blacked-out Britain, most visitors found the drive from the airport a short, sharp jolt. It was like changing planets or putting down Kafka and picking up something by the Brothers Grimm. The broad avenues leading to the city center were brilliantly illuminated, and public companies advertised their wares in flashing neon. There was not, of course, a single bombed building in sight.

In spite of the lateness of the hour as their car passed the Grand Hotel, Stockholm's largest and where most of the international press corps hung its hat, Fallon and McKenna saw liveried porters taking care of luggage. Browning told them that the hotel's showcases held some of the best displays of books, jewelry, and chocolates in the capital. There was a hell of a lot to be said for neutrality.

The assistant military attaché had fixed them up with accommodations in a two-bedroom apartment in Karlavägen, a tree-lined avenue not far from the Legation, in whose name the apartment was held. It had been screened for listening devices earlier in the day and found to be clean. To make sure it stayed that way, Browning had left a man there, who was now dismissed.

McKenna couldn't believe his eyes when he saw the

drinks table, which held three each of Gordon's gin, Johnnie Walker Black Label whisky, and a fine Amontillado he hadn't seen since 1939.

"Is that stuff for real?"

Browning nodded. "It is. Damned difficult to come by, I might add, especially the scotch. So take it easy. There won't be any more. When that lot's finished you'll be drinking wine—unless you fancy schnapps. The latest flavor the Swedes have come up with is tangerine, and I don't recommend it."

McKenna fixed drinks for all three while Fallon made a quick reconnaissance of the apartment. He was not expecting trouble; but establishing a line of escape long before it was needed had become force of habit. The apartment was on the third floor and overlooked what appeared to be a small park. A fire escape led down to street level.

"I presume I'm to be told why you're here," said Browning when they were all seated.

"How much do you know?" asked Fallon.

"Very little. I was warned by London to expect you and instructed to make myself useful, that's all."

Fallon could see the major's feathers were ruffled. "It's to do with Peterson, the signal he sent before he left."

"I rather gathered that. I knew about the Mosquito not making it, of course, though it's not common knowledge. I doubt if the BOAC ground staff at Bromma are aware of it yet, but I work pretty closely with the station manager and he got on to me as soon as he heard. He was pretty shaken, I can tell you. As a matter of fact . . ." Browning hesitated.

"Go on," prompted Fallon.

"Well, I was going to write a report about the incident, but as it all happened less than seventy-two hours ago I thought I'd sleep on it for a few days. There are enough rumors in this city without my adding to them."

Fallon nodded his approval. There was nothing more

frustrating and time-wasting in intelligence operations than unsubstantiated guesswork.

Quickly and without frills Browning told them of the fight that had taken place between the Lufthansa ground personnel and the skipper and R/O of G-AGRD, adding that he was fairly certain he'd seen Helmuth Falck leaving the airport a little later.

"It worried me at the time. It worries me even more now."

"You mentioned Falck before," said McKenna. "Who exactly is he?"

"Local SD doubling as something in Culture."

"Could he or one of his men have got at the Mosquito while the fight was going on?"

"Not a chance. BOAC's security is excellent."

"Then the fight was probably started to distract the crew's attention while something was slipped into their drinks or pockets," McKenna concluded. "Maybe a gas capsule or a pencil bomb. It's too much of a coincidence not to be sabotage."

"Which means Berlin knew Peterson was in Stockholm," said Fallon. "Christ, they must have moved fast. He was only here—what?—half a dozen hours?"

Browning nodded. "About that. Do you think they picked him up at the airport?"

"No. Otherwise they'd never have let him get to you. I think they were probably running a little late all round. By the time they knew he was on his way to Sweden, his plane had landed; by the time Berlin got through to Falck, Peterson had left the airport. And so on. Falck either guessed he'd head for the Legation and put a watch on it or he waited for the taxi to come back and quizzed the driver. I'm assuming he came by taxi, that you didn't meet him?"

"I didn't even know he was coming until he got here," confirmed Browning. He shook his head. "I'm slipping. I thought he was safe once the plane left."

"You weren't to know," Fallon said sympathetically. "I'd have thought the same myself."

"And we're still not one hundred percent sure they weren't picked off by a night-fighter," put in McKenna.

Browning was. "No, it was sabotage. You said yourself that any other conclusion would be too much of a fluke. We can't ignore the laws of probability."

McKenna got up and refilled the glasses. "Okay, let's examine what we've got. Peterson arrives here from Berlin and sends a flash signal to London. Berlin considers him so dangerous that they take all sorts of risks to sabotage his plane, risks that must have been considerable. The Swedes may be scared stiff of Hitler, but they're not going to take it lightly if the SD start making Bromma a battlefield. So where does all that leave us?"

"Did Peterson say anything to you?" Fallon asked Browning. "Did he leave anything with you for safekeeping?"

"Not a thing. I'd had dealings with him before, of course, so it didn't surprise me. He was always a secretive sort of chap. He just asked me if he could send a signal in his personal code and that no record of the transmission be kept. I agreed. It's not so unusual. What was in the signal, by the way? Am I allowed to know?"

They had discussed this in London, Fallon and McKenna, Curzon and Mortimer, and concluded that Browning would have to be briefed in full if he was to be of any help. His security clearance was, in any case, of the highest.

He whistled softly when he was shown a decoded copy of Peterson's wireless message.

"Ignore the last sentence," advised Fallon. "I know it's nonsense but that's how it came out at our end."

"It's not exactly nonsense. It at least solves a mystery for me."

"How so?"

"I've spoken to this Kirsty. At least I've spoken to a woman of that name, young by the sound of her. She telephoned the Legation this morning." He flicked his cuff and glanced at his watch. "Yesterday morning, I should say. She asked the switchboard for me and inquired about Peterson. I didn't tell her anything, naturally. I assumed she was some girl Peterson had got to know during one of his previous visits, but I couldn't tell her he was dead without revealing something of how it happened. Besides, I don't much care for getting personal calls from people I've never met or even heard of."

"Did you get her last name or where she lived?" asked Fallon.

"I'm afraid not. I asked for it, but she said it wasn't necessary for me to know. I told her to call back at ten o'clock this morning, because I knew you'd have arrived by then. She sounded a little nervous if I'm any judge."

"Shit," said McKenna. "Let's hope she's the persistent sort."

"Let's hope she's got something to tell us," said Fallon. "We're going to be wiping a lot of egg off our faces if Peterson's last sentence was a simple request to inform his girl friend if anything happened to him."

"It says she has full information," McKenna pointed out.

"It's also gibberish. It could also mean *give* her full information."

Browning confessed to being baffled. "Perhaps I'm missing something here, but why would Peterson involve a girl friend when he could just as easily have left a sealed envelope with me—to be opened in the event of his death?"

"We're not sure of the answer to that," admitted Fallon. "The best we've been able to come up with is that he was mentally exhausted after being under cover for so long and trusted no one except the girl. Unless he had reason to doubt your security, of course."

Fallon meant it as a joke, but the flicker of concern that crossed Browning's face made him think again. "You don't have a security problem, I hope."

Browning cleared his throat hesitantly. "It's possible, though I have no proof. There have been one or two inexplicable occurrences in the last week or two, however. A couple of Norwegian refugees I'd hidden away were suddenly pounced on by the Swedish police and interned. On another occasion one of my men swore he was followed to a secret rendezvous with a top-ranking Swedish naval officer when no one could have known about the meeting save a handful of people. Matters of that sort. Irritating but not crucial."

"When did all this start?" asked McKenna.

"Around the middle of last month."

"Then Peterson wasn't behaving cautiously because he suspected a leak. He was in Germany, out of touch, from the third week in August."

They left it at that. If it was anything more than happenstance, Browning would have to deal with it on his own. They had enough on their plate.

It was close on 3 A.M. before Browning left, saying he'd expect them at the Legation at nine sharp in case Kirsty telephoned early.

"We'll be lucky if she calls at all," muttered McKenna gloomily, draining his glass.

"How come?"

"It's only just occurred to me, but if the Krauts found out Peterson had gone to the Legation by quizzing the taxi driver who took him there, chances are they know about the girl too. Apart from the trip to Bromma, Peterson didn't leave the Legation after he arrived. He must have visited the girl on the way in. If this guy Falck is as dangerous as he sounds, he may think it safer to deep-six her."

"He'd already have done that if it was on the agenda."

"Maybe, maybe not."

"You're a pessimist, you know that?"

"It comes with the territory."

Fallon got to his feet. He was very tired and he knew

McKenna must be too. "Speculation won't get us anywhere. We'll just have to wait until tomorrow. I mean today. Either she calls or she doesn't, and that's all there is to it."

Kirsty Gottmar did phone at 10 A.M. on the dot.

The three men were in Browning's office when the call came through. Browning passed the receiver to Fallon and shared the extension with McKenna.

Fallon's Swedish was good, if rusty, but Browning had already told them the girl spoke excellent English.

"Eric Peterson told us you'd be calling," he said.

There was a few seconds' silence before the girl asked, "Where is Eric, please?"

"I'm afraid I can't tell you that over the telephone, but he asked us to meet you and give you a message."

Browning was right; she was very nervous. "What message?"

"It's a letter," lied Fallon, "and it's sealed. Eric said it was very important and that I was to see you got it without fail."

"Get her last name and address," mouthed McKenna.

"I'll send it to you if you like," added Fallon, "but the trouble is there's no surname or address on the envelope." He sensed her indecision. "Come along, Kirsty," he cajoled her. "Surely you can give us your surname and address."

"It's Kirsty Gottmar," she said finally.

"That's G-O-T-M-A-R?"

"Two *t*'s."

"And the address?"

There was a very long silence.

"Kirsty . . . ?" prompted Fallon.

"No, I don't think I should give you my address. That's not what Eric asked me to do."

"What did he ask you to do?"

"Just call this number and . . ."

There was what sounded suspiciously like a sob at the other end.

"Kirsty," said Fallon severely, "you appear to be in some sort of trouble, and I know Eric wouldn't want that. Neither would he forgive us if we didn't help or if we didn't deliver the envelope. If you don't want to give me your address, that's fine. But why don't we meet somewhere in an hour or two? You suggest a place."

It took a little more coaxing, but eventually the girl agreed. "Do you know the cathedral in the Old Town?"

"I'll find it."

"I'll meet you there—at midday."

"How will I recognize you?"

"I'll . . . I'll be wearing a red coat and a small red hat. I . . . I must go now."

Fallon hung up as the line went dead. "Nervous is the understatement of the year. That kid's scared stiff of something."

Browning was thumbing through the city telephone directory. "There are a number of Gottmars but only three K's. Do you want them checked out?"

It was McKenna who turned down the idea. "She might not have been phoning from home. Even if she was, if we go in like gangbusters she'll probably clam up for good. That's if she doesn't holler for the police. We're on foreign soil, don't forget, and I don't think anyone's going to thank us if the Swedish heavies start nosing around."

God forbid, thought Browning, imagining the subsequent interview with Sir Victor Mallet.

As telephone calls to and from the Legation were usually pretty light on a Saturday morning, the switchboard was generally manned by a single operator, in this case a woman in her late thirties. Although the holder of a British passport, she had lived in Stockholm for so long that she thought of it as home and got along with the Swedes as well as if not better than with her own people, who saw her, she was inclined to think, as a confirmed spinster with few interests outside the Legation. That she was popular among her colleagues was the result, she knew, of frequently volunteering for weekend duties, which everyone else loathed.

She considered some of the talk she heard around the Legation unfairly anti-Swedish and criticisms of the country's neutrality unjust. It was no crime, surely, not to want your cities occupied, your fine buildings bombed, your sons and fathers killed.

When approached at the end of August, therefore, by a handsome, understanding Swede of around her own age who said he represented a government department anxious to maintain Sweden's non-alignment, she was in no way bothered by conflicts of loyalty. If she heard anything that might involve a Swedish citizen, he asked her, would she be kind enough to pass it on? If Sweden was to remain neutral, she could hardly permit her nationals to engage in clandestine activities likely to offend one or another of the belligerents. He had a similar arrangement, he claimed, with a staff member of the German Legation.

She was only too pleased to help. In no respect could it be called treason. She would have reported an unauthorized approach by the Germans immediately. But this man was Swedish and remarkably kind. She had had dinner with him on several occasions. He cheered her up and had laughed good-naturedly when she had mistaken those Norwegian refugees for Swedes and caused, so she thought, a lot of unnecessary trouble. There was something in his attitude—she was sure it wasn't her imagination—which suggested his interest in her went deeper than pure business.

She had not taken yesterday's call from Kirsty Gottmar, but she had listened in carefully to this morning's when she realized that the woman asking for Major Browning was Swedish. And fifteen minutes after Fallon put down the phone she managed to get through to her friend, telling him what she had overheard. He thanked her, informed her he was greatly in her debt, and hinted that another dinner engagement was not unlikely in the near future.

She experienced a flutter of girlish excitement when he rang off.

It took the Swede, whose only connection with a government department was the fact that he had once served a prison sentence for non-payment of taxes, until eleven-fifteen to track down Helmuth Falck, after which the SD officer moved fast. Until now he had been willing to believe that Kirsty Gottmar was no more than the English agent's girl friend. Certainly there was nothing in her apartment to indicate otherwise, and neither had she acted suspiciously in the last couple of days, during which her every move had been watched.

But arranging a meeting with someone from the British Legation within hours of the two Mosquitoes landing seemed to indicate that there was more to her than met the eye. She would have to be dealt with.

It was a beautiful crisp autumn morning when Kirsty left her apartment in Garvargatan. The streets were a riot of color as the wind blowing off Lake Mälaren shook the leaves free from the trees and made a swirling kaleidoscope of reds, golds, and browns, a magnificent mad tarantella choreographed by some unseen dancing master. It would not be long before the snow came—a week, perhaps two—covering the city, making the Royal Palace in the distance seem for all the world like a giant wedding cake. It was a day to be shared with a lover— to take coffee together, a walk in the park, a ferry ride. It was a day to be shared with Eric, not one to be alone and fearful.

Not quite twenty-four years of age, Kirsty Gottmar was a tall pretty girl who knew how to make the best of herself. As far as she was concerned, her eyes were a trifle small and her mouth too sulky, but she knew her smile made up for those largely imaginary defects. It was the first thing Eric Peterson had noticed about her, for which she would be eternally grateful. Unconsciously, she had worn the red outfit because it was his favorite.

Falling in love with Eric all those months ago had come as a surprise; it was not part of the program. She had lost her parents in a motoring accident and been jilted by a boy friend she had known since her late teens all in the month of December 1942. Subsequently she had resolved not to get emotionally entangled with anyone again, but Eric had changed all that. Perhaps she saw in him someone even more vulnerable than herself; she wasn't sure. In any event, against her better judgment she had allowed herself to fall in love.

She did not know what his job was but suspected it to be highly dangerous. He laughed off her fears, saying he was no more than a civil servant whose greatest risk was sharpening pencils. She wasn't fooled. There was something about his eyes which told her he was frequently exposed to great peril, and on the rare occasions he spent the night with her his sleep was that of the damned. Civil servants—couriers or otherwise —rested more peacefully than that.

Then there was his sudden arrival at the apartment last Tuesday, his haggard appearance, his instructions to call Major Browning on Friday if she had not heard from him. She had not relished doing that. Swedish citizens were not encouraged to get in touch with the military representatives of foreign powers. There were regular admonitions in the newspapers and on the wireless that Swedes must do nothing to jeopardize their country's neutrality, yet it was common knowledge that Stockholm was full of spies. Perhaps that was it; perhaps Eric had something to do with espionage. She would ask him straight out when she next saw him. It wasn't fair she should be followed everywhere, have her apartment burgled without knowing why.

Eric would say she was fantasizing, of course. There wasn't a scrap of evidence to prove a burglary had taken place, but she knew, she absolutely *knew*, that someone had broken in during her absence, possibly more than once.

They were tiny clues but clues nevertheless: the hairbrush not where she had left it, some cans moved in the cupboard, the bedclothes disturbed.

Nothing was missing, that was the strange part, the reason she had not gone to the police. She had checked her jewelry and accounted for it all. She had hurried to the bread box in which she kept the housekeeping money and a thousand kronor for emergencies, but the notes were untouched. If she went to the police with such flimsy evidence they would tell her to go home and sleep it off, as they would if she told them she was being followed. But she was, she was sure of it. Without that certainty she would not have agreed to meet the men from the British Legation, but perhaps they could help her. Perhaps the letter from Eric would explain everything.

If only Ingrid were here, but Ingrid was spending the week in Gothenburg and would not be back until later this evening.

The red coat and hat made her easily identifiable even from a distance, and Falck and his men had no difficulty keeping her in sight. They were using the three-man tailing technique, which was virtually impossible to spot, even by a pro. One man walked ahead of Kirsty, one behind, and one shadowed her from the far side of the street. Every so often the one in front dropped back to look in a window, allowing Kirsty to overtake him, while the man behind made his way to the other side of the street. The third man crossed on the diagonal and took up the point position. Repeating the maneuver every couple of minutes, there was never a second when Kirsty was unobserved and very little chance she would detect her followers.

Falck knew how he was going to get rid of the girl and did not want to lose her. The method had not been used in the field before, at least not by him, but Prinz Albrechtstrasse had assured him that the experiments in Dachau and elsewhere had proved conclusive. He whistled softly as he walked, twirling his umbrella like any other respectable citizen out for a morning stroll.

Fallon and McKenna left the Legation early. It was a twenty-minute walk to the cathedral and they wanted to be on time.

Crossing Strömbron to the island which held the Old Town and the Royal Palace and which separated Lake Mälaren from the Baltic Sea, McKenna said, "Maybe we can get this whole thing cleared up in a couple of hours and be back in London tomorrow."

"You that anxious for another trip in a Mosquito?"

"Not especially, but Stockholm's another world. I've got the feeling I could get to like it if I stayed here too long."

Fallon saw where he was looking, at a trio of girls walking in the opposite direction, girls who would not have been out of place in a chorus line. Their hair was clean, their complexions fresh, their clothes well cared for. Some legends turned out to be disappointing myths, but it was true what everyone said about Swedish women. England with its careworn faces, rationing, and queues seemed a long way off.

They skirted the seaward side of the Royal Palace.

"Cathedral up ahead."

Coming from the opposite direction Kirsty had just crossed Vasabron when Falck decided to make his move. There were a lot of people around this Saturday morning, but in a couple of minutes she would have reached the cathedral and then it would be too late. He would have to take his chance now.

Signaling his intentions to the others, he increased his pace and was soon abreast of the girl, where he faked a stumble and collided with her, almost bringing her down. As he stretched out a hand to help her, she felt the tip of his umbrella scrape against her calf.

Nervous as she was she almost screamed, but a moment

later the big man was apologizing profusely in rough Swedish and she could see it was just an accident.

"I trust you are not hurt," he said.

"No . . . no," she stammered.

One of her stockings was laddered where the umbrella had caught her, but otherwise she was unharmed.

"I'm all right, really," she insisted as the man continued to beg her forgiveness for his clumsiness.

"If you're quite sure . . ."

"Honestly."

He tipped his hat. "Then I'll bid you good morning."

Kirsty hurried on, her heart pounding. Really, she would have to pull herself together. At the rate she was going she was heading for a breakdown. Or a regular pre-breakfast appointment with the bottle. This was Stockholm, center of what remained of the free world. Nothing bad could happen here.

Rounding a corner, she heaved a sigh of relief when she saw the back of the cathedral looming up ahead. But heavens, she felt faint, hardly able to focus. And what on earth was happening to her legs? It was an effort to walk in a straight line. God, how embarrassing. People were looking at her as if she were drunk, stepping out of the way. And her breathing. She could hardly breathe.

Suddenly she felt terribly cold. She saw a chestnut vendor on the other side of the road roasting his wares over an open brazier and moved toward him. She had to warm herself before she could take another step. She had to . . .

The chestnut vendor saw her coming and smiled, expecting a sale. Then he was shouting as she fell against the brazier, knocking it over, falling into the hot coals, her coat catching fire, her handbag, her hair . . .

From the front of the cathedral, Fallon and McKenna heard the commotion but paid it no attention. Then the clamor grew and they looked at one another uneasily. They heard someone say in Swedish, ". . . a young girl . . ."

"Let's take a look."

A crowd had gathered, but they pushed their way to the front. There was no doubt that the girl in the smoldering red coat and tiny red hat was Kirsty Gottmar, and there was equally no doubt she was dead. The 1,000-degree heat of the burning coals had made something of a mess of her face and arms, but she had once been pretty.

From the shadows Falck made a mental note of the time. Berlin had told him that the drug, a derivative of digitalis, took around 120 seconds to react in the bloodstream. Then the victim simply died, apparently from a heart attack.

He would have to radio Berlin that it worked and that a needle concealed in the ferrule of an umbrella was as good a method as any of administering the poison. He would also have to remind his masters that it was unwise, except in emergencies, to use the drug on young people without a record of heart ailments. An autopsy would doubtless prove nothing unless the pathologist knew what he was looking for, but there was always the chance some sharp-eyed doctor would see the pinprick on the corpse and ask questions.

Four

"We're stumped," said Fallon for the tenth time.

For two hours he, McKenna, and Browning had sat in their Karlavägen apartment punishing the whisky. Not one of the three men was in any doubt that Kirsty Gottmar had been murdered by the SD, though how it was accomplished defeated them.

It was a crushing blow, however, and Browning was also concerned that Falck was breaking with established pattern. "If he's been given orders to start his own private war over here, the city's going to be littered with stiffs within a month."

Fallon saw it differently. "It was a once-off killing. He'd know where she lived from the cab driver and he was probably watching her. When he got word that we'd flown in he put two and two together and decided to make his move. He may even have tapped her phone. It makes no difference."

"It makes a hell of a lot of difference," said McKenna. He was surprised at how deeply the sight of the dead girl had affected him. "Christ, we came over here because Peterson was killed and now his girl friend winds up dead too. Either there's a jinx on this whole business or the Germans have got this fucking town tied up."

"I take exception to that remark," said Browning quietly.

"You can take it to Dixie for all I care. The score is two to them and zero to us, and we're sitting here on our asses guzzling whisky."

"Have you got a better idea?" asked Fallon.

"You're damned right I've got a better idea. I say we bust into Kirsty's apartment and turn it upside down. It's not going to worry her now, and if there's anything there I'll find it. Failing that, we take a stroll over to the German Legation and play football with Falck's head."

"And where will that get us?"

"It'll make me feel a damned sight better, that's where it'll get us."

Fallon grinned across at Browning. "Now you see how they won the Colonies back. Any objections?"

"To the first suggestion or the second, or the one that tells Major McKenna the Germans have Stockholm tied up?"

McKenna had the grace to admit he had spoken out of turn.

"That's all right." Browning smiled. "I sometimes feel the same, but we're years behind the Nazis in the strong-arm stuff. Still, we're learning. As for breaking into Kirsty's apartment, we don't know exactly where she lived or whether the police are hanging around, but a couple of phone calls should sort that out. No, I've no objections, but you'd better count me out. If anything goes wrong the Minister would have an international incident on his hands and I'd be declared persona non grata. Besides, if you're caught you'll need a friend on the outside."

Leaving Browning to make his phone calls, Fallon and McKenna went out onto the small balcony which overlooked the park. Darkness fell early in Stockholm at this time of year, and already the streetlights were coming on.

"Damn me and my big mouth," swore McKenna. "That was what you British would call slightly below the belt, right?"

"Slightly. I know a little about him from Curzon. You can't tell now he's in civvies, but in uniform he wears the DSO and the MC, both of which he won for separate bits of lunatic bravery at Dunkirk and in North Africa. He's a professional front-line soldier, and I think he resents being stuck in this backwater, away from the action. But he's here because he speaks fluent Swedish and because someone's got to keep an eye on the Jerries—not to mention the Russians. This is strictly between you and me, but he's been over the border into Norway a score of times to bring out refugees and advise the underground. The career diplomats in the Legation don't much care for his cloak-and-dagger activities, and half the time he's fighting them as well as the Germans. He's tried to get back into the shooting war, but he's always turned down on the grounds that he's indispensable here. It's not the kind of job I'd care to do."

"Ouch," said McKenna.

"Forget it. I'm sure he has."

They were out on the balcony for half an hour and then a quarter of the way down the third bottle of scotch before the sound of the phone being replaced in the hallway told them Browning was finished.

"Thank God we've still got a couple of allies in Sweden," he said, pouring himself a drink.

"Kirsty Gottmar lives—lived—on Garvargatan, which is over on the west side of town." He referred to the piece of paper in his hand and gave them the street address and the number of the apartment. "It's on the second floor and the street door remains open until midnight. The concierge is generally around, and he's apparently a gossip, but he may be useful. I'll explain in a minute."

Browning took a long pull at his drink. "The police are

treating her death as natural causes, but there'll be an autopsy because she was so young. She seems to be without immediate next of kin and she shared the apartment with another girl, who hasn't been seen for a few days. The concierge reckons she's on holiday.

"The police have been over the apartment, but it was evidently just a routine check. They left without taking anything. The concierge is to call them if anyone turns up, but it seems they're merely trying to trace any surviving relatives. That's about it."

Fallon looked from McKenna to Browning in amazement. "I should think it is. How the hell did you wangle all that information?"

Browning shrugged modestly. "Part a police contact and part a journalist acquaintance on *Handels-och-Sjöfartstidning,* which is strictly speaking a Gothenburg shipping journal but which keeps a general reporter or two up here. The editor's Professor Torgny Segerstedt, who's a good friend of ours and an uncompromising enemy of the Nazis. He's got a bulldog called Winston, incidentally, who's trained to bite anyone speaking German."

"What did you mean about the concierge being useful?" asked McKenna.

"My journalist friend—I won't give you his name, if you don't mind—knows full well my function here at the Legation. I occasionally feed him exclusive information via the press attaché. It wasn't possible to ask him to phone the concierge and pump the man about Kirsty without arousing his curiosity, but I know him well and trust him. I merely said Kirsty had something in her apartment which belonged to us. He offered to help us get it back by keeping the concierge in conversation, ostensibly interviewing him about Kirsty's background. Unfortunately he can't leave the office before six, but he'll give me a call when he's ready to move. It's three-fifteen now. I'll be back at a quarter to six."

It was actually five-fifty when Browning returned. Fallon was drinking coffee and studying one of the evening newspapers and McKenna was in the shower.

At six-ten the telephone rang. Browning held a short conversation with the caller.

"He's leaving now. He'll be riding a green motorcycle, which he'll park outside the entrance to the building so you'll know he's arrived. He's got a date at eight o'clock, he says, so he hopes you won't take too long. Sound the horn when you're through."

Browning was smiling, but Fallon could not see the joke. "What's so funny?"

"He also said he hopes you know how to get into a locked apartment without a key. I told him I thought you'd manage."

McKenna emerged from the bathroom toweling his hair in time to hear the last remark. "You can bet on it. I've got gadgets that could crack the Bank of England."

"I shouldn't bother, old boy," said Browning lightly. "We moved the gold reserves back in 1940."

It was an ordinary spring lock and it took McKenna less than thirty seconds to manipulate the tumblers with his burglar tool. A minute later they had completed a quick reconnaissance of the entire apartment, which was identical in layout to their own in Karlavägen: two bedrooms, a sitting room, kitchen, and bathroom.

Both men carried pencil lights, but they chose to pull the curtains and use the main lights.

"What the hell are we supposed to be looking for?" asked McKenna.

Fallon wasn't sure. "We'll know it when we find it."

They worked as fast as they could, leaving each item they examined as they found it, but after an hour they concluded that whatever they were searching for wasn't here. It was just an ordinary apartment shared by two girls, the second as young as Kirsty, judging by the lingerie they found in the wardrobes and chests. They discovered Kirsty's jewelry and the kronor notes in the bread box, and a further cache of money behind a pipe in the bathroom. But short of tearing up the floorboards, that was it.

"We're missing something," said Fallon.

McKenna shot him a look of disgust. "Thanks for letting me know. I'd never have guessed it."

"No, I mean there has to be something under our noses we can't see."

"Perhaps she was carrying it, whatever the hell 'it' is."

"Let's hope not. The police aren't going to hand over her personal belongings to—"

"*Quiet!*" McKenna interrupted him, suddenly and urgently.

They heard it together, the unmistakable rattle of a key turning in the outside lock.

Conditioned as both men were to react instantaneously, Fallon doused the sitting-room lights in a flash and went into a crouch behind the sofa. McKenna flattened himself against the wall behind the door.

The hall lights went on and something heavy was lowered to the floor. A moment later the sitting-room door was pushed fully open.

McKenna sensed rather than saw the newcomer reaching for the light switch and launched himself across the room, his immediate objective to stifle any cry of alarm. His momentum threw both of them to the floor.

From his position behind the sofa Fallon had had a better opportunity to see the intruder silhouetted in the doorway. "You'd better let her up, Sam. Burglary's one thing, but they're going to draw the line at rape."

The main lights on, it took a few moments to persuade her they meant her no harm, but finally she nodded her agreement not to scream if McKenna took his hand from her mouth.

71

She scrambled to her feet blushing furiously, smoothing down her skirt where it had ridden above her thighs to reveal long, beautiful legs encased in dark stockings. McKenna had experienced a lot more than a gentle tremor of desire during the fifteen-odd seconds he had lain across her, and he was well aware the girl knew it. A court of law, he felt, would have forgiven him or at least understood his reaction, for she was quite lovely. Her green eyes were flashing with a combination of fear and anger and her red-gold hair, cut fashionably short, reminded him of some of the colors he had seen in the park. Like many Swedes, she was tall and slim, and he guessed her age correctly as mid-twenties. There could be little doubt that this was Kirsty's missing roommate.

"Who are you?" she stammered in Swedish. "What do you want and what have you done with Kirsty?"

"One question at a time," said Fallon. "Do you speak English?"

"Yes," she answered in that language. "Are you English?"

"I am. Attila the Hun here's an American. I'll get round to why we're here in a minute, but it might help if we knew who we were talking to."

She was starting to relax now, realizing they had no intention of hurting her.

"My name is Ingrid Lindahl and I share this apartment with Kirsty."

"Were— Are you close friends?"

"Not really. I only moved here from Gothenburg in July and found the apartment by answering a newspaper advertisement. Please," she repeated anxiously, "where is Kirsty?"

"Perhaps you'd like to handle that and make the introductions while I go and toot the horn of our friend downstairs," Fallon said to McKenna. "Keep it simple."

Fallon hung around on the far side of Garvargatan until the journalist left the block and roared away on his motorcycle. Newspapermen were newspapermen and he wanted to be sure that Browning's contact was not coming back to ferret out a story.

When he got back upstairs McKenna was alone.

"She's in the bathroom," said the American. "She took it pretty hard."

"How much did you tell her?"

"Just that Kirsty was found dead a few hours back and that we suspect the Germans had something to do with it. I asked her about Peterson. She knew Kirsty had an English boy friend, but she'd never met him. She had no living relatives, by the way—Kirsty, I mean."

"Better and better."

"Better and better how?"

"If what we're looking for isn't here, Kirsty must have been carrying it. But as I started to say a while back, the police aren't going to hand over her personal belongings to us, not without a lot of questions we can't answer. They'll give them to Miss Lindahl, however."

"They'll give what to Miss Lindahl?" queried Ingrid from the doorway.

Her eyes were red, but otherwise she was quite composed, ready to demand explanations. She only had their word for it that Kirsty was killed by the Germans, and they still hadn't told her why or what they were doing in the apartment.

Receiving McKenna's tacit nod of approval and acting as spokesman, Fallon felt they had to trust her. One thing in her favor was the fact that she hailed from Gothenburg, a city which had never wavered in its support for the Allied cause even when things had looked particularly black and the rest of Sweden, especially the capital, leaned toward the Nazis. Indeed, Stockholmers were inclined to sneer that when it rained in London the people of Gothenburg could be relied upon to put up their umbrellas in sympathy.

He told her as much as he dared: that prior to his death Peterson had worked for the British government and had left something with Kirsty, with or without her knowledge; that

73

the message or film or whatever was not in the apartment and must therefore be among Kirsty's personal effects; that they needed those effects badly.

"And you want me to go and get them?"

"Yes. As you were closest to her, the police will want to see you sooner or later to make a formal identification of the body. It won't be pleasant but it's something you'll be required to do. They'll doubtless also be happy to give you her belongings. All I'm asking you to do is bring them to us."

"And what if I refuse? How do I know you are who you claim to be? You could be English-speaking Germans."

McKenna was quick to seize on this. "Do you mean that if we were Germans you wouldn't help?"

"I . . . I suppose not."

"But if we're working for the Allies you will?"

"I didn't say that. I'm not sure what I should do. I have to think."

They were wasting time. Fallon decided to change tack, put some pressure on Ingrid Lindahl.

"Leave her, Sam." He faked a harshness into his voice. "We'll figure it out for ourselves, find another way. She's like the rest of her bloody countrymen—a fence-sitter. She doesn't want to know about the war that's going on in case it prejudices her precious neutrality. Leave her to her bright lights and chocolates. There'll come a day of reckoning."

Fallon started for the door. McKenna got the drift and followed.

"Wait a minute—please," called Ingrid.

"We've already waited enough minutes," snapped Fallon. "You're either going to help or you're not. If you are, fine, say so. If you're not, we'll try elsewhere."

"And if you're worried which side we're on," added McKenna, "we can give you a name at the British Legation who'll confirm we're the good guys."

"Make up your mind," said Fallon.

The green troubled eyes studied each of them in turn, looking for clues, trying to see if she could trust them, if they were who they claimed to be. She wasn't sure she liked the hard-voiced Englishman who was doing all the talking, but she felt an instinctive empathy with the one called McKenna.

"All right," she said finally, "I'll help."

The concierge would know which police number to ring, and they agreed it would be best if Ingrid went down to see him alone.

"Simply say you're just back from holiday and you're wondering if he's seen Kirsty," Fallon instructed her. "And when he tells you the bad news act upset, as though you're hearing it for the first time."

"It won't be an act," said Ingrid quietly.

"You were a bit hard on her," remarked McKenna when they were alone.

"Was I? Sorry. It's just that this business is tough enough without wheeling in amateurs."

"She's got a lot of guts. Most women would be lying on the couch with the smelling salts by now."

"I guess so." Fallon looked at McKenna curiously. "Are you taking over the role of her protector?"

"Maybe. Any objections?"

"Nary a one. She's not my type."

"Then I'm going to recommend you get your eyes tested. The last thing I need is a nearsighted sidekick. If someone who looks like that isn't your type, what the hell is?"

Fallon shrugged. "I'm not sure."

"High time you found out, buddy. This cockamamie war's not going to last forever. Someday you're going to be a civilian again and you'll need someone to bring you your pipe and polish your slippers."

"Leave it alone, Sam."

"Special Operations makes a fine mistress but a lousy wife."

"I said leave it."

McKenna backed off. Okay, so there was something in Fallon's past that still hurt. That wasn't so unusual. But he had got to like the Englishman over the last few days and he didn't want to see him put everything he had into an organization which would shuck him off like an old boot at the end of the day.

Ingrid was away ten minutes. When she came back she appeared to have been crying again. "Will one of you come with me?" she asked plaintively. "I'm not sure I can handle it alone."

McKenna volunteered with alacrity. "Where will you be?" he asked Fallon.

"At the apartment. Browning must be wondering what the hell's happened to us."

It was almost midnight before McKenna arrived back at Karlavägen looking as though he had gone a hard ten rounds with Joe Louis. Under one arm he carried a cardboard shoebox tied up with string.

"Where the hell have you been?" demanded Fallon. "We were beginning to think you'd been arrested."

"Now don't give me any flak," said McKenna wearily. "I've taken all I can stand from the cops for the last three hours. They've got a form for this and a form for that and a form to make sure you understood the first form. I thought Washington could win prizes for bureaucracy, but the Swedes are in a different league. Fix me a drink, one of you."

Browning was nearest.

"Where's Ingrid?" asked Fallon.

"I took her home and fed her half a bottle of brandy. And before you start carping, she needed it. Kirsty Gottmar wasn't a pretty sight. We didn't get the full impact from where we were standing, but she was pretty badly burnt. I tried to call you here about three-quarters of an hour ago, but the line was busy."

"That was me," said Browning. "I'm spending more time here than I am at my desk, and things are piling up."

McKenna tossed the cardboard box onto the table. "Well, that's it, the handbag or what's left of it and what was in her pockets. It wasn't only poor Kirsty that went into the coals. The bag did too."

Fallon cut the string with a pocketknife and tore off the lid. He groaned when he saw the state of the contents. The fabric of the handbag was nonexistent, and little that had been inside had survived the flames. All that remained of a couple of letters, some theater tickets, paper currency, and a handkerchief were fragments. There were some coins, a blackened lipstick holder, a twisted metal comb, and a compact whose edges were fused together. Fallon pried them apart with his knife and tossed the two halves onto the center of the table. The studs holding the mirror in place were already buckled from the heat of the brazier, and now they snapped, loosening the mirror. Each of the men had to look twice to make sure his imagination wasn't playing tricks, for behind the mirror was a folded piece of paper, charred to be sure but covered with writing.

McKenna was first to grasp the significance. "In the event of an emergency *compact* Kirsty Gottmar has full information!" he whooped. "Not contact, fucking *compact!* Maybe it was decoded wrong in London or maybe Peterson was tired or in a hurry and enciphered incorrectly. She probably didn't even know it was there!"

The message had been folded in quarters to fit behind the mirror, and parts were less burnt than others. When spread out across the table it read:

If anyth . . . happen . . . to me pleas . . . see tha . . . Kir . . . get anyt . . . du . . . Pay an . . . insuranc . . . I kno . . . wha . . . you bugg . . . ar . . . like . . . You get thi . . . in excha . . . for lookin . . . aft . . . Kirs . . . The Lunströ . . . in . . . furt . . . Alfre . . . and Nata . . . and you must . . .

Which was all that was decipherable. The remainder was carbonized ash. There was no chance it could be rebuilt in a laboratory. The compact had taken a buffeting—in the ambulance, the morgue, the police station—and the completely burnt portions were so much dust.

But the reason Peterson had left the note with Kirsty as opposed to Browning was now clear. Expecting his signal to be decoded accurately, he was merely trying to protect his girl, see that she got something out of his death.

Fallon was bitterly disappointed with what they had, that the major part of the message was testamentary. As for the rest, the umlaut over the *o* in "Lunströ . . ." seemed to indicate a surname, and "Alfre . . ." could only be Alfred. But it meant nothing to any of them.

"Better make an exact copy of this for all three of us to sign," he said. "The original won't take another handling."

"Then what?" asked McKenna.

"Then we go home. Can you arrange our flights?" he asked Browning.

"It might take a couple of days."

McKenna got to his feet. "Suits me fine. A quick shower and a change of clothing and—"

"Ingrid Lindahl?" interrupted Fallon. "I thought you said she was in a bad way."

"I did. Which means she'll probably welcome a little company. If we're only going to be here another two days I'd better get on the mound and start pitching."

"If you're going out," cautioned Browning, "keep clear of the Rainbow Restaurant in Stureplan. The owner's a Nazi sympathizer, and we suspect the Germans have got the place wired for sound."

"Thanks for the tip. I'd hate the Krauts to hear what I'm going to say."

Five hundred miles south of Stockholm the lights were still burning in the offices of Department VI of the RSHA, even though it was expected that the RAF would again be bombing Berlin that night.

Brigadeführer Walter Schellenberg had dined quietly with Gestapo chief Heinrich Mueller in the second-floor banqueting room, and the meal had now reached the cigars and brandy stage.

Dinner conversation had covered a wide range of subjects, not least of which was the subversive movement among high-ranking officers to overthrow the Führer, but now they got down to the main business of the evening. An intelligent man himself, Schellenberg had not much time for Mueller's intellectual capabilities, but the Gestapo boss was a first-rate if brutal policeman. In any case, he had to be in on the plan if only to act as additional counterweight to Göring's vacillations.

"So," said Mueller, luxuriating in the fine French brandy and the nine-inch Havana bought on the open market by the SS Purchasing Commission for senior SS officers, "the Führer was pleased."

"Delighted would be more accurate. You know how he enjoys anything slightly out of the ordinary. I think he's already half convinced that the original idea was his own."

"He has a lot on his mind," murmured Mueller, frowning at Schellenberg's words, which seemed to contain a tacit criticism of Adolf Hitler.

"Indeed he has," countered Schellenberg smoothly, "indeed he has. More brandy?"

Mueller pushed forward his glass. Schellenberg filled it almost to the brim, knowing Mueller's almost limitless capacity for alcohol.

"Anyway," he went on, "he has given us permission to go ahead."

"Was there ever any doubt?"

"None, but it's as well to be certain in these matters."

"How will you get word to the Allies?"

"By a circuitous route, I think, probably via Lisbon. It

should take around forty-eight hours to filter through to Queen Anne's Gate and Baker Street."

"Isn't that shaving it a bit close? That will make it October fourth or fifth. If they move before then, it will all have been for nothing."

"My information is that they're far from ready. Besides, give them too long and they might come up with all sorts of brilliant ideas. Put a little pressure on them in terms of time and they'll make mistakes."

"Let's hope so."

Schellenberg raised his glass and proposed a toast. "To a German victory that will make the Allies shudder."

Five

Because the weather suddenly took a turn for the better and BOAC were getting wary about flying in anything less than ten/tenths cloud unless the cargo was vital to the war effort, no aircraft could be made available to ferry Fallon and McKenna to the UK until the night of Monday, October 4, when the meteorological people promised a continuing ridge of low pressure over the Skagerrak and the North Sea. Though expecting it, Fallon was annoyed at the delay. McKenna, on the other hand, was delighted.

Arriving back at the Garvargatan apartment in the small hours, the American was surprised and delighted to find that Ingrid Lindahl greeted him warmly. She expressed no desire to go out on the town, but as neither of them could remember the last time they had eaten, she prepared a simple salad, which they washed down with a bottle of prewar Chablis, one of three she had brought with her from Gothenburg, a gift from her parents, who ran a restaurant. Later they drank coffee and brandy, and afterward it seemed the most natural thing in the world to head for her bed, where she proved to be uninhibitedly magnificent.

McKenna called Karlavägen early Sunday morning. On learning that their flight was not for another thirty-six hours, he promptly rejoined Ingrid between the covers.

Unable to get back to sleep after McKenna telephoned, Fallon showered, shaved, dressed, and went for a walk. Without conscious effort he found himself making for the Legation.

He hated enforced idleness, but he was also, he found to his annoyance, more than a little irritated at McKenna's intimacy with Ingrid Lindahl. It seemed irresponsible to be dallying with a woman when all over Europe people were being killed in their tens of thousands, but part of him accepted that he was being unreasonable. The fault lay in him, not McKenna, and the American's well-meant barb the previous evening about being wedded to the service was not that far from home. But since Yvette's murder, work had been a haven, and he knew he was not alone in finding refuge—albeit dangerous refuge—in Special Operations. He was, he supposed, just one more misfit among dozens of misfits. He'd heard Stuart Menzies once remark that most of the men and quite a few of the women in SIS and SOE would not last ten minutes in a line regiment, that they would be court-martialed for insubordination or even shot for some other infraction of the rules. There was a lot of truth in that.

Major Browning spent Sunday morning at the Legation. He had breakfasted by 7 A.M. and was at his desk forty-five minutes later, which was not at all his usual Sunday routine. But he was now firmly convinced he had a security leak on his hands and he wanted peace and quiet to consider the possibilities.

By nine-thirty he was sure he had the answer, unacceptable though it might seem at first sight. Short of a sophisticated listening device in the Legation—in his own office, for that matter, which was unthinkable—the only way Falck could have learned so quickly about the cathedral meeting with Kirsty Gottmar was via the Legation switchboard, more specifically from the woman on duty yesterday morning, Miss Evelyn Barling. No other solution fit the known facts.

That Evelyn Barling was an enemy agent stretched credulity to the maximum, but Browning was a firm believer in Conan Doyle's Sherlock Holmes. When the impossible has been eliminated, whatever remains, however improbable, must be the truth.

He knew he should report his suspicions to a higher authority, probably to the Minister himself, but at the moment it was all conjecture and he was loath to brand anyone a traitor without proof more substantial than unswerving faith in the dicta of a fictional detective. It was just possible— barely—that Falck had wiretapped Kirsty's phone, but that would not explain the Norwegian refugees.

He had checked the Sunday roster and confirmed that Miss Barling was on duty today. She seemed to do a lot of weekend work, which was odd in itself. He would have a serious talk with her when she came on at ten o'clock, though how he was going to tackle the problem for the moment escaped him.

He was debating likely avenues of approach when Fallon strolled in, and on the basis that two heads are better than one he told the SOE officer of his suspicions. It could no longer be considered a domestic internal matter, much though the career diplomats would like that. Miss Barling might well be on duty when the call came through confirming that the Mosquitoes for Fallon and McKenna had landed, which could put their lives at risk.

Fallon had a nose for action and he felt it twitching now. If Browning was right—and everything seemed to point in that direction—maybe they could turn it to their own advantage and kill, the *mot juste,* two birds with one stone.

The AMA needed little persuading, though if it ever came out it would mean the end of his career at the very least. Still, the thought of making the Nazis nervous, letting them know that even at this distance and in this city they were not safe, appealed to him. It was the next best thing to active service.

"Do we let McKenna in on it?"

"I think so," answered Fallon. "I can't see him wanting to miss it, not even for Ingrid Lindahl's charms. Besides, we're going to need her, but we'd better see if you're right about Miss Barling first."

To begin with, the spinster denied everything, but when Browning threatened to send her home for a more thorough interrogation by experts, she reluctantly confessed to passing occasional information to a man who worked for the Swedish government. She had committed no crime, however, she protested. The Swedes may not be our allies, but many of them were sympathetic to the Allied cause. And after all, she was involved in nothing more serious than reporting the actions of Swedish citizens to another Swede.

Browning demanded his name and let out an oath of despair when he heard it. "The man's on the German Legation's payroll!" he bellowed. "He's a bloody Nazi!"

Evelyn Barling turned chalk-white and burst into tears. How could she have known? He was always so courteous and charming.

He was so courteous and bloody charming, Browning informed her brutally, that as the result of the information passed to him yesterday a young Swedish girl was killed.

Evelyn Barling continued to sob piteously. She had no idea her friend was a Nazi. She would never do it again, given a second chance. What would happen to her now?

Browning gave her both barrels, sparing her nothing. She would be quietly removed from the Legation and flown back to the UK to be tried in camera. The best she could hope for was a few years in prison, the worst a morning appointment with the public hangman in Holloway Prison. If she cooperated, however, it might go easier for her.

She would, she said, do anything.

Leaving Browning to brief her, Fallon called Ingrid Lindahl's number from the switchboard telephone. McKenna was far from pleased at having his morning interrupted and at first flatly refused to persuade Ingrid to act as bait. Fallon asked him to let the girl decide. If it worked out as planned, Kirsty Gottmar would rest a little easier in her grave.

Twenty minutes later McKenna came through with the news that Ingrid was all for the idea. If anything happened to her, however, he would personally see that Fallon walked around in plaster for a year.

At five minutes to seven that same evening, at the southern end of Skeppsholmsbron, the bridge which connected the tiny island of Skeppsholmen to downtown Stockholm, Helmuth Falck waited in the open. A few yards away, out of sight, was one of the two men who had helped him tail Kirsty Gottmar the previous day.

Falck was thinking that perhaps he should do a little more to cultivate his Swedish friend with the contact in the British Legation. Up to now he hadn't bothered much. The man generally passed on low-grade intelligence which could otherwise be gleaned from a careful reading of the newspapers. But the information that had enabled him to nail the Swedish bitch before she could talk and now this, a clandestine meeting by her roommate with British security—perhaps the man's contact was going up in the world.

The SD Unterscharführer had not brought his umbrella. One young girl dying of a supposed heart attack would not be investigated too closely, but if her roommate went the same way all hell would break loose. He was untouchable, of course, even if by some million-to-one chance the police managed to prove anything. But Berlin had issued strict instructions that the drug was only to be used in an emergency, and this wasn't one. One lone girl should prove no trouble for two fully grown men, especially as she would have no reason to doubt his, Falck's, identity. She was not to know that the British officers had been delayed for half an hour. Now that *was* a useful piece of information to possess.

At three minutes past seven, with the bridge and the surrounding area otherwise deserted, he heard the clicking of high heels in the distance, heading in his direction across the bridge. He moved to where he could be seen. She appeared to hesitate before continuing toward him.

"Good evening," he said in Swedish when she reached him. "I understand you have something for me."

Falck's spoken Swedish was far from fluent, but his English was nonexistent. There was no way he could pass as a British intelligence officer if she wanted to converse in that language, and he held his breath. He would prefer to complete his business with the girl without violence.

Ingrid did not have to feign nervousness; she was scared stiff and didn't mind admitting it. If what Sam McKenna said was true, this was the man who had murdered Kirsty.

She nodded. "As I explained on the telephone, I found it in Kirsty's powder compact when I went to collect her things. It was written in English so I thought you should see it."

"You did well. Did you bring the whole compact?"

"Yes. It's badly marked where it fell into the coals, but I thought it best."

Falck held out a hand.

Ingrid hesitated. "There was mention of a reward."

"First I have to see what we're buying."

Ingrid fumbled in her handbag. Her fingers closed over the compact, but she left it where it was. Where on earth were McKenna and his associate?

She stalled for time. "Are you sure you're the man I spoke to at the British Legation? Do you have any proof?"

"Proof, girl? Don't be foolish. Just hand over the compact."

"Well, I'm not sure. Your voice sounds diff—"

Falck reached across and grabbed the handbag. Ingrid struggled to retain her grip on it.

86

"Give it to me and you won't get hurt," said Falck. "Klaus!" he called in German, "come and help me with this silly bitch."

As Klaus emerged from the shadows west of the bridge, Fallon and McKenna, who had been in position since six-thirty, charged out of the undergrowth from the east bellowing in German at the tops of their lungs.

Klaus was reaching inside his jacket when Fallon hit him with a shoulder charge that would have felled a bull rhino. The German went down like an empty sack. Fallon followed up with a vicious kick in the ribs, hard enough to force a scream of agony from Klaus but not do any permanent damage. They were going to need Klaus, if he behaved. They were not going to need Falck.

"What the bloody hell . . ." the Unterscharführer started to say before McKenna planted a huge fist in his face.

There was not that much difference in height between the two men, but Falck had spent too long in the fleshpots of Stockholm and was thirty pounds overweight, mostly around the middle, which was the next port of call for McKenna's right fist. The SD officer doubled up like a jackknife, his head coming down just in time to meet McKenna's knee coming up. There was a crunch of bone and cartilage as Falck's nose broke. A sob escaped his throat, part baffled rage, part fear. He had been around death often enough to recognize that his assailant had murder in mind.

Klaus was getting to his feet when Fallon hit him again, clubbing him two-fisted to the ground, where he lay stunned, hardly breathing.

Fallon clicked his fingers at Ingrid, gesturing her to throw across the compact and get the hell out of it, make for the bright lights on the far side of the bridge. It wasn't necessary for her to witness what happened next.

McKenna was in the process of breaking Falck's neck from behind, wrenching his head up and to the right and twisting. It was too easy a death for the bastard, but a man couldn't have everything.

The German's spinal column snapped with a crack like a rifle shot, and there was a sudden appalling stench as the sphincter muscle relaxed and he voided his bowels. Fallon took his legs and McKenna his shoulders, and they heaved him up and over the balustrade, into the bay.

Fallon tossed the compact at the unconscious Klaus. Let him think the attackers had dropped it in flight. Let him think what the hell he liked. It wouldn't fool the Germans for long. Neither would the handwritten note, charred but legible, behind the mirror, a note which said the Russians were planning a parachute drop of brigade strength on Berchtesgaden before the year's end. It wouldn't fool them, but it might give them a few uncomfortable weeks. In any case, the major object of the exercise had been achieved. Falck had murdered his last victim.

They flew out the following evening, October 4, the pair of Mosquitoes leaving Bromma shortly before midnight. McKenna had said his farewells to Ingrid earlier in the day, promising to be back before long. He meant it, too.

At 2 A.M. on the morning of October 5, while the aircraft were still over the North Sea, a coded cable was received at 64 Baker Street, datelined Lisbon. Deciphered it read:

HAVE INCONTROVERTIBLE EVIDENCE THAT ALFRED LUNSTRÖM AND HIS NIECE NATALIE LUNSTRÖM ARE BEING HELD BY THE GESTAPO IN SCHWEINFURT STOP APPEARS TO BE A PLOY TO PUT PRESSURE ON THE SWEDISH GOVERNMENT VIA FELIX LUNSTRÖM TO REVERSE DECISION REGARDING SALES OF BALL BEARINGS TO ALLIES STOP LUNSTRÖMS HAVE FREEDOM OF MOVEMENT BUT UNDER HEAVY GUARD WHENEVER THEY LEAVE THEIR QUARTERS COMMA A PRIVATE HOUSE NEAR VKF COMPOUND STOP UNDERSTAND FELIX LUN-

STRÖM BEING INFORMED SEPARATELY STOP GERMANS
APPARENTLY BELIEVE THAT PRESENCE OF LUNSTRÖMS
IN VICINITY OF BALL BEARING COMPLEX PRECLUDES
FURTHER ALLIED BOMBING AS THIS WOULD INEVITA-
BLY RESULT IN THEIR DEATHS STOP CAN IMAGINE
REACTION OF SWEDISH PUBLIC OPINION IF THIS
HAPPENED STOP LOCAL BRACKETS LISBON BRACKETS
TOP RANKING NAZIS QUITE OPEN IN THEIR INTERPRE-
TATION OF THIS MOVE STOP IF LUNSTRÖMS KILLED IN
ALLIED RAID SWEDES LIKELY TO REVERSE BALL BEAR-
INGS AGREEMENT STOP IF RAIDS DISCONTINUED
SCHWEINFURT CAN GEAR UP TO FULL PRODUCTION
ENDS

Six

Later in the war the Allies would get much tougher with the Swedes, the Americans in particular making threatening noises about dropping a few hundred tons of high explosive on Stockholm unless trade with the Germans ceased, but in 1943 it was not such an easy matter. The Swedes were still frightened that the Wehrmacht would turn its eyes northward, and any trade agreements tended to favor the Germans. It was thus considered something of a coup when two representatives of the British government, Ville Siberg and Bill Waring, flew to Stockholm in June 1943 and made a preemptive purchase of ball bearings. The trouble was, the bearings were not due off the production lines until mid-October, and the Germans calculated it would take very little to make the Swedes renege. All they needed was an excuse, and depriving Alfred and Natalie Lunström of their liberty gave them that.

Trade negotiations between the Allied and Swedish governments were generally conducted by hard-nosed businessmen; on the Swedish side by men such as the Wallenbergs, who largely owned the Swedish Enskilda Bank and, through it, the SKF ball-bearing company. But powerful as the Wallenbergs were, they paled into insignificance when compared to the Lunströms, who, by common consent, were reckoned to be one of the richest and most influential families in Europe, certainly the richest in Scandinavia, and who were getting wealthier by the minute, thanks to the unresolved disagreement between the Allies and Adolf Hitler. Governments and even monarchs listened when the brothers Felix and Alfred Lunström talked, and it was rumored they were already secretly financing various potential African heads of state in preparation for the day when British, French, and Belgian influence on that continent waned. Their empire was worldwide, their riches based upon banking, oil, mining, and industrial interests.

The Allied intelligence services had a roomful of dossiers on the family, because any individual or group of individuals who controlled much of the world's monetary transactions and raw materials had to be watched. But the dossiers were far from complete. While a great deal was known about Lunström holdings in British, American, and German companies, there was a paucity of information about the family's background. It was generally accepted that they were of Middle European extraction, possibly Bulgarian. They had first turned up in Sweden a couple of years before the outbreak of World War I, applied for and were granted Swedish citizenship, and adopted the name Lunström, so the legend went, for no better reason than it was the first one they came across in a street directory. No doubt their original names were somewhere in the Swedish archives, but they were largely of academic interest. There was nothing sinister in a Middle European adopting Swedish nationality, nothing sinister in their activities at all if making several fortunes from World War I and a dozen more from the present conflict could be excluded.

At sixty-one, Alfred Lunström was the senior by some seven years. Photographs showed him as a tall, cadaverous individual who favored dark-blue conservative suits cut in a style that might have been considered daring at Queen Victoria's diamond jubilee. With his shock of white hair and blue eyes he might have passed, if the onlooker was in a hurry, as a minor philosopher or a violinist playing with a provincial orchestra. It was only when the eyes were examined more closely that they were seen to hold all the warmth of a condemned cell.

He had never married and there was a strong rumor that he had been, as a younger man, a practicing homosexual, but that could have been his enemies talking. Basically Alfred Lunström was asexual. Only two things interested him: money and power. If there was a third, it was his niece Natalie, who had recently begun to accompany him everywhere, ostensibly as his assistant but in reality preparing for the day when she, the sole Lunström offspring, would be at the head of affairs. The dossier photograph showed Natalie to be a remarkably beautiful young woman. She was twenty-six and spoke half a dozen languages fluently. Her mother was dead, and a footnote added that she had killed herself in a fit of alcoholic depression.

Natalie's father, Felix Lunström, was fifty-four and reckoned, by people who had had dealings with both brothers, to be even colder and harder than Alfred. On the short side but heavily muscled, especially around the shoulders and upper arms, following a business schedule that would have killed most men, he still found time to work out two or three days a week, though there was always a stenographer on hand in order that he could dictate while exercising. Occasionally the stenographer would be required to perform functions of a strictly non-secretarial nature, for Felix was a womanizer of renown. It was his sexual proclivities that were supposed to have driven his wife to drink and eventual suicide, but the gossips who saw this as the reason Natalie was now spending more time with her uncle than with her father were quite wrong. Alfred was older and, assuming he had not bought the rights to immortality, would probably die first. It was therefore more important for Natalie to learn her uncle's contacts and methods of doing business before learning those of her father. They thought of such things in the Lunström family.

As far as their European interests were concerned, Felix generally looked after the cartel's affairs when dealing with the Allies, while Alfred dealt with Germany and German-occupied countries, though this was far from a hard and fast rule, their roles alternating as the occasion demanded. In either event, whether dealing privately or representing the Swedish government, the brothers took care to ensure that, whatever else happened, their empire continued to expand and prosper, war or no war. Like the Swedish nation as a whole, with one or two honorable exceptions, it could be said that the Lunströms had a foot in each camp, were playing both ends against the middle and doing it rather well. They tried not to offend governments, and governments tried not to offend them. At least that was the assumption until the bombshell cable from Lisbon, a piece of advanced Hitler lunacy in the opinion of Charles Curzon. One did not go around kidnapping and keeping under duress the head of one of Europe's leading families and his niece. It was one more sign that Hitler was mad.

The Minister of Economic Warfare was not so sure. The Germans might just pull it off, because there was not a chance on God's earth that Felix would allow anything to happen to his precious daughter. She was not just his flesh and blood; she was the sole heir to the Lunström multimillions. Besides, neither Felix nor Alfred had wholeheartedly subscribed to the Siberg-Waring agreement.

"It's a tricky, delicate situation," concluded the Minister. "One that will have to be handled with kid gloves."

He and Curzon were having an afternoon glass of sherry in the library of the former's apartment near the Houses of Parliament.

"You're surely not suggesting that even the Lunströms can force the Swedish government to renege on our deal or tell us how to run the war," protested Curzon.

"Don't be naive, Charles. To a large extent the Lunströms *are* the Swedish government, because their interests as traders coincide. As for running the war for us, that's precisely what they do every time we allow them to sell vital matériel to Hitler."

"I can't argue with that, but if we're going to be told which targets we can bomb by Hitler or the Swedes, we might as well chuck in the towel right now. If the Nazis get away with this one, there's no telling where it will end."

"I'm not saying they're going to get away with it, not for long anyway. They probably don't expect to. But if they can force the Swedes into reversing the Siberg-Waring contract or delay shipment, they've won a major bloodless victory. Alternatively, if they keep us away from Schweinfurt for a month or so, they have bought time of incalculable value."

"And made lifelong enemies of the Lunströms in particular and the Swedes in general."

"That doesn't sound like a banker talking, Charles. When it's all over and the Germans have got what they want, Hitler will apologize and say it was all a dreadful mistake. A few insignificant heads will roll, and then it will be business as usual. If a businessman only traded with companies or nations he liked and approved of, there wouldn't be too many contracts signed. There will be *none* signed with us if the Lunströms are killed by a British or American bomb."

"It's most unlikely an attack on Schweinfurt would single out the Lunströms, regardless of how close to the ball-bearing factories the Germans have them incarcerated. You've seen the statistics. The odds are greatly in favor of survival in an air raid."

"It's not an argument I would care to use on the East End Londoners, but in any case you're missing the point. They might survive the bombs but would they survive the Gestapo? One of Himmler's thugs would execute them immediately and make it look as though they'd died in the raid. The Germans would then turn to the Swedes and say, 'Look at the kind of people you're dealing with. We warned the British and the Americans, but they came anyway. Do you really want to help them win the war? Come into our camp.' "

Curzon stubbornly refused to accept this. "And we could equally argue that if the Nazis hadn't perpetrated this particular piece of ghastliness in the first instance, Alfred and Natalie Lunström would still be alive. Chances are the whole scheme would backfire on Berlin."

The Minister shook his head. "I'm afraid your understanding of practical psychology is a little wanting. Our bombers would have done the killing, that's all Felix Lunström would remember. After being told that his brother and daughter were in Schweinfurt, we still went ahead and bombed the town. In time he might see matters differently, but time is something we don't want Hitler to have.

"You know as well as I do that landings in France are contemplated for next summer, but it all very much depends upon the state of the Nazi war machine and the strength of the Luftwaffe, which could destroy the expeditionary force on the beaches unless it's seriously depleted. If Hitler buys himself a couple of months this year, they could make all the difference in the world between a landing next year or not until the middle of 1945. And if we leave it that long we may not only have to settle for something less than unconditional surrender, we may not even win the war.

"The public at large has heard Hitler go on and on about the wonder weapons he expects to have ready shortly, but thanks to our black propagandists in the PWE* they think it's whistling in the dark or the ravings of a madman. You and I know different. The intelligence reports about the German rocket tests and how far ahead of us they are in jet propulsion make terrifying reading. One or two squadrons of jet fighters would decimate our bombing fleets, and without bombers to reduce Germany's industry to rubble there won't be a landing

* Political Warfare Executive

95

next year or in 1945 or any year at all. The war will drag on and on. There's a lot more involved here than a few tons of ball bearings and the lives of a couple of Swedes. We can't allow Hitler any time whatsoever, and he knows it."

Curzon had never heard the Minister sound so gloomy. Surely it wasn't being suggested they allow the Swedes to back out of the agreement concluded by Siberg and Waring or, worse, lay off Schweinfurt as a target until the Germans very kindly allowed them back?

The Minister chuckled. "Quite right. That is *not* being suggested. I don't think Mr. Churchill would approve. We have to get our heads together and decide best how to handle this, but we can't make any hard and fast decisions until we've spoken to Felix Lunström, who's flying in this evening, incidentally. I offered to go to Stockholm, but he has business here to take care of anyway."

"Will I be needed?"

"That would be helpful. Be here at, say, eight o'clock. You might also keep those two men of yours on tap. What are their names—Fallon and McKenzie?"

"Fallon and *McKenna*," Curzon corrected him. "And McKenna's not one of ours. He's OSS, if you recall."

"Ah yes. Well, I'm sure you can arrange to have them both here by eight. It's possible they might be useful, having just returned from Sweden. You might tell them they did a good job, by the way, though I suppose it was all unnecessary in the long run. If we'd waited a few more days we'd have found out in any case that the Germans were holding the Lunströms. I assume that *was* what poor Peterson had to tell us?"

"I don't see that there can be any doubt about it, not in view of the charred fragments of paper found in the girl's powder compact."

"No, I expect not. How did Peterson's note get burnt, incidentally? Have I had a report?"

Curzon thought of what Fallon had written about the girl and the execution of the Nazi resident hatchet man.

"No, Minister. I don't think it's something you should know about."

"Ah, one of those, was it?"

"I'm afraid so."

The Minister turned his attention to a folder of documents on his desk, indicating the meeting was over.

Curzon got up to leave. "Until eight o'clock, then."

"Yes. In the interim you might like to have a word with Harry Mortimer. Check whether the Americans have anything planned for Schweinfurt in the next day or two. I know the RAF hasn't, but it will be useful to know the American position for when we see Lunström."

Curzon looked doubtful. "I think it's okay in the immediate future, but they're hardly likely to see it the way we do beyond that. If they're geared up to bomb a target they're going to bomb it, come what may. Unless, of course, you plan to take it to prime ministerial and presidential level."

"That's a little premature, but it would hardly be skillful politics if while we're talking to Lunström and attempting to work out our next move the US Eighth Air Force is plastering Schweinfurt. Have a word with Mortimer, there's a good fellow. Talking to Felix Lunström is going to be difficult enough without complicating matters still further."

"How much can I tell Mortimer about the Lisbon signal?"

"How much does he know?"

"Nothing from our end."

"Then you'd better tell him everything before he finds out from another source. God knows, we might need his assistance before we're finished with this business."

Curzon and Mortimer went for a walk in Hyde Park. Curzon talked, Mortimer listened. Explanations over, the OSS colonel said, "It looks like a hell of a mess and no mistake, but I'm not sure what I can do about it."

"You can tell me when the Eighth is going back to Schweinfurt."

"I don't know myself yet. Today's the sixth and it won't be this week if what I've heard up to now is accurate, but you can thank your weather for that. This damned early-morning fog is keeping the B-17s grounded more often than General Eaker likes."

"Try night flying."

"No thanks. We're not spending fifty thousand dollars a man to train pilots to have them miss this bloody little island of yours on the way home."

No offense was intended, and Curzon took none. He knew Harry Mortimer was very fond of Britain and the British, fog and all.

"Go on," he said.

"Go on what?"

"You said it wouldn't be Schweinfurt this week, but what about next?"

Mortimer gave him a lopsided grin. "Are you sure you wouldn't like to sit in on the target conferences? Christ, that's classified information."

"We're on the same side, in case you've forgotten. Besides, I'd only have to make a few noises in Whitehall and I could find out from General Eaker himself."

"You'll get me busted."

"I'll find you a job with my outfit. The date, please, Harry."

"What do I get in exchange?"

"I'll tell you the approximate date of D-Day."

Mortimer looked startled. "You know that?"

"Yes," Curzon lied.

"Well, Christ . . ." Mortimer thought for a moment. "I can't give it to you exactly because it's still flexible, but it's

98

penciled in for next Wednesday or Thursday, the thirteenth or fourteenth."

"That soon?"

"The days are getting shorter and it's a long hike. If we don't make it quick it'll be a tough one to handle until after Christmas, because God knows what you people have got lined up for us in the meteorology department. If we get thick fog in early autumn, it's my guess we'll have blizzards and maybe hurricanes come November. Besides, the Krauts are stepping up ball-bearing production again, according to our information. The sooner we discourage them, the better. Where does that leave you?"

"Where does that leave *us*," emphasized Curzon. "Whatever creek we're up, we're up it together."

They walked on in silence for a few minutes.

"There's no chance of postponing the raid, I suppose, give us a little breathing space?" asked Curzon, neatly sidestepping a youngster on an ancient bicycle.

"Not one, not without a direct order from the President, which I guess he'd be reluctant to give. The Krauts must know we've got our eye on Schweinfurt or they wouldn't have arranged this pantomime. If we don't go back it won't take them long to guess why. It'll take them till 1950 to stop laughing."

"My sentiments entirely."

"Why the hell don't the Swedes do something themselves?" demanded Mortimer a moment or two later. "Lean on the Germans and tell them that unless they stop fucking around with Swedish nationals they can kiss goodbye to anything that even looks like a ball bearing?"

"They're scared stiff of being invaded, that's why."

"Hitler wouldn't tie up a dozen divisions in Sweden. He hasn't got the manpower and it's not logical, not when he can get more or less what he wants with threats."

"Which wouldn't be the case if they told him to go to

hell. He'd be in there like a shot. Not because he wants to or can really afford the troops, but because he'd have no other option."

"Yeah, you're right."

As they neared Marble Arch, Curzon said, "Look, I've got to get back to my desk. I'm not sure how long this business with Lunström will go on for tonight or what if anything will be resolved, but can I see you afterwards, say in Baker Street?"

"Sure. Take as long as you like. The war's playing hell with my social life anyway."

The two men shook hands. Curzon was about to walk off when Mortimer called to him. "Hey, you didn't keep your end of the bargain. "When's the approximate date of D-Day?"

"Approximately—and you'll realize there are many factors to be considered—approximately sometime in 1944."

"Bastard," muttered Mortimer.

Seven

Fallon and McKenna arrived at the Minister of Economic Warfare's apartment just as the all-clear sirens were being sounded. The alert had proved to be a false alarm. The Luftwaffe were giving London a miss this night.

McKenna had never been anywhere near the apartment before, and this was Fallon's first visit also. Briefings usually took place in Queen Anne's Gate or Baker Street. This was very exalted territory for lowly majors.

Their passes handed across and identities verified, they were shown into an anteroom by a Royal Marines color sergeant and asked to wait. It was 8:15 P.M.

At eight-twenty they heard the doorbell ring, but the newcomer was ushered straight through to the Minister's study. They caught a brief glimpse of him as he passed the open door of the anteroom: a middle-aged man with iron-gray hair who looked, if his determined stride and pugnacious set of the jaw were any criteria, as if he was about to commit murder.

The Minister came around from behind his desk as Felix

Lunström was admitted. He extended his hand, which Lunström shook perfunctorily.

"You know Curzon, of course," said the Minister.

"Naturally," answered the Swede. "In happier times his banking interests and mine have frequently been competitors."

"With mine invariably coming off second best." Curzon smiled ruefully.

Lunström inclined his head in acknowledgment of the compliment. "Not altogether accurate, Mr. Curzon, but let us say I have had more luck on several occasions."

Lunström's English was impeccable, as were the clothes he wore. One would have thought, mused Curzon, he had just stepped from a fitting room in Savile Row and not flown in from Stockholm. Admittedly he had traveled by the neutral Swedish airline ABA along a well-defined corridor, but it was not unknown for the Luftwaffe to take potshots at Swedish planes and claim pilot error later.

The Minister pulled up a chair for the Swede and invited him to sit down. "May I first of all say," he opened diplomatically, "how much His Majesty's government deplores this latest German outrage."

Lunström gestured impatiently. "I would appreciate it if we waived the formalities. I do not have much time in London and none I can afford to waste."

"For the record—" began Curzon.

"For the record, Mr. Curzon, let us accept that the Germans are holding my brother and my daughter. That is a fact. We all know why they are being held. That is another fact. All that remains in the realm of conjecture is what is to be done."

"I take it you have independent verification that your brother and daughter are hostages?" queried the Minister.

"An unsigned handwritten message was delivered to my office in Stockholm to that effect. I immediately tried calling my brother at his Frankfurt hotel, but without success. A

German voice at the other end simply said that neither he nor Natalie was available. For the past two weeks I have spoken to them daily. That, together with our telephone conversation last night, is all the proof I need."

"I see." The Minister steepled his fingers and nodded for Curzon to take over.

The English banker plunged straight ahead. "Are we to take it, then, that your visit here is to tell us of your government's change of heart regarding the ball-bearing deliveries?"

"Nothing of the sort. To the best of my knowledge the Swedish government is unaware of what has transpired. For the present I prefer to keep it that way. Before I talk to them I wanted to talk to you, listen to your suggestions and arguments. But make no mistake, gentlemen; if I talk, they'll listen."

"Which seems to suggest you're willing to submit to blackmail with all its concomitant dangers," said Curzon. "If the Germans get away with this once, they'll try it again and again whenever an opportunity presents itself. I would have thought that, far from giving in to them, you'd be angry. Far from reconsidering the ball-bearing contract, I would have thought you'd be ready to cut off German supplies in their entirety."

"You're not being realistic, Mr. Curzon. Of course I'm angry and of course I do not willingly submit to blackmail, but what if I allowed the ball-bearing deliveries to proceed? The Gestapo would kill my only two living relatives. I am a skilled poker player in business, Mr. Curzon, and perhaps the Germans would not execute my brother and my daughter. *Perhaps.* I am not willing to use their lives as chips."

"Then you're not here to listen to our suggestions at all," said the Minister coldly. "You're here to tell us you will advise your government not to honor the Siberg-Waring agreement, which you could have done by telephone or cable."

"Not entirely." Lunström hesitated, and both Curzon

and the Minister could see that, despite an outward display of calm, the man was going through hell.

"Perhaps you'd be good enough to explain."

Lunström squared his shoulders. "I do not like being instrumental in dishonoring contracts, especially under circumstances such as these, but I will persuade my government to dishonor this one because of what is involved. I have a long memory, however, and there will come a time when I shall repay this barbarism in my own coin. That is as certain as the sun rising tomorrow. Nevertheless, you will realize that it is not only by allowing the sale of the ball bearings to proceed that I risk my daughter's life and that of my brother. Over that I have control. I do not have control over when and if the Allies carry out another bombing raid on Schweinfurt."

"Ah," breathed the Minister.

"In time, perhaps a month or two," Lunström hurried on, "I could bring pressure to bear on the Germans. There are many ways of doing this. I have the power to undermine the Reichsmark by using the various international facilities at my disposal, particularly as they relate to the exchange rate between the mark and the kronor. I could prepare a comprehensive survey of Germany's raw material needs and keep them short of essentials. As a last resort I could arrange a series of industrial disputes which would close many Swedish factories. But I can do none of this overnight, and if my brother and daughter are killed in an Allied bombing raid in the meantime, it will all be to no avail. I need time, gentlemen. I want you to give me that time. I want you to assure me that Schweinfurt will be left alone until, shall we say, the beginning of 1944. Give me that assurance and I will find a way to let you have as much matériel as you can pay for in the New Year."

Neither the Minister nor Curzon was 100 percent sure that Lunström could deliver what he promised, but the chances were he could. That he and his brother Alfred had not done so in the past was because they were waxing fat by playing off the Germans and the Allies against one another. Felix Lunström was only in the room now because he wanted help, though it had been a different matter in 1941.

Curzon's first reaction was to tell the man to go to hell, tell him that if he sat down to sup with the devil there was always a chance, as was now the case, he'd find himself on the menu. But he resisted the temptation. It was all academic anyway, but it would be interesting to see just how far Lunström would go.

"And if we agreed," he said, ignoring the Minister's look of alarm, "would that mean the present contract would still be reversed?"

"I'm afraid it must. The Germans want the same goods and it is impossible to double the output of our factories to satisfy you both. But in the long run you would benefit, you must surely see that."

The Minister sighed inaudibly. It was a piece of typical Swedish bargaining. For reasons of pure self-interest Lunström would give the Germans a consignment hitherto destined for British ordnance factories. By way of thanks for this treachery the British were expected to turn the other cheek.

"What you are asking is out of the question," he said. "Even if I could agree for His Majesty's government, which I cannot, President Roosevelt would never accept being dictated to by Hitler. To do as you suggest is precisely what the Nazis are gambling on. I am not suggesting for one moment that Schweinfurt is a priority target or any kind of future target at all, but it must be obvious to a blind man—as it is evidently obvious to Herr Hitler—that the Allies cannot allow the Schweinfurt factories to get into full production."

"You are condemning my brother and my daughter to death."

"Not us, Lunström. It's Hitler's finger on the trigger, not Mr. Churchill's."

"A most unhelpful comment. Is that your last word on the subject?"

"If I may, Minister . . . ?" Curzon was not willing to let it go at that. There would be fewer tanks and planes off the production lines without those ball bearings.

The Minister nodded wearily. "By all means."

"Perhaps the Swedish government should be informed of what has happened and given the option of putting diplomatic pressure on Berlin," suggested Curzon. "One or two members have friends in high places there. I mean no disrespect, naturally."

Not much you don't, you cunning old bastard, thought the Minister.

"It wouldn't work," growled Lunström. "The Germans are not . . ." He hesitated.

"Not like the British and the Americans?" queried Curzon sweetly. "I'm glad you appreciate that, Mr. Lunström, but they're not entirely impervious to threats of economic sanctions."

"I've already explained that I'm not willing to jeopardize the lives of my daughter and my brother by using them as poker chips."

"What you actually said was that you were unwilling to implement the contract under discussion because you feared for their lives."

Lunström frowned, puzzled. The Minister wasn't at all sure what Curzon was getting at either, but in matters requiring deviousness he was more than willing to let the former banker have his head.

"I don't understand," said the Swede.

"It's perfectly simple," explained Curzon. "What I suggested was the *threat* of sanctions, not the actuality. The Germans will expect some sort of reaction from your end. Indeed they will be very suspicious if none materializes. What I want you to do is persuade your Foreign Office to make belligerent noises at Berlin for a while. Let's say a week. I doubt very much if the lives of your brother and daughter will be endangered in that short space of time. They are the Nazis' trump card. They can only play it once. In the meantime, I ask you not to try to influence your government into canceling the contract with us. You do not have to allow us to transport the ball bearings physically to the United Kingdom once they are off the production lines—which I understand will be in the next few days—but neither should they go to the Germans."

The Swede shook his head. "I don't see where it gets us, how it helps."

"Perhaps not, Mr. Lunström, but can one week make that much difference? If after a week the situation remains as it is today, you must do as you think fit."

Lunström thought for a moment before nodding his acceptance of the conditions. "With one proviso. If the Germans increase the stakes during the coming week, make overt threats against my brother and daughter, I reserve the right to let them have the ball bearings, reverse my decision."

Christ, thought Curzon. Aloud he said, "Agreed."

After the Swede had gone, the Minister looked at Curzon curiously. "What the devil are you up to, Charles?"

"Let's have Fallon and McKenna in. With your permission, I'd like to explain this just once."

Fifteen minutes later Fallon and McKenna were in full possession of the facts. They now knew who the gray-haired man was and the significance of the charred note found in Kirsty Gottmar's compact. What they did not know was how it concerned them.

Curzon lit a cigarette. He had started the war as a non-smoker and was now on three packs a day.

"We seem to have reached an impasse," he said. "We need those ball bearings, and Felix Lunström can tilt the balance either way. I don't think I'm betraying any state secrets—though this information is not to be repeated outside this room—when I tell you that the US Eighth Air Force is scheduled for a return trip to Schweinfurt, probably on the thirteenth or fourteenth of this month. I do not expect Natalie and Alfred Lunström to survive that raid, and I don't think I need draw you a picture of Felix Lunström's probable reactions. So, the problem is the incarcerated Lunström duo. If they were not in German hands there would be no problem. I therefore propose, gentlemen, that we go in and fetch them out. More specifically, I propose that Fallon and McKenna do the fetching."

There was a stunned silence. Curzon beamed at the Minister and the two intelligence majors as though expecting applause.

McKenna said it for them all. "If you'll excuse the expression, I think Mr. Curzon is out of his fucking mind."

An hour later in Baker Street Colonel Harry Mortimer was saying much the same thing.

"You're out of your cotton-pickin' mind, Charles. All that tea drinking has softened your brain. I wouldn't give the scheme one chance in a hundred if the Lunströms were as free as birds and walking around unescorted, but they'll be guarded closer than a New Orleans pimp watches his girls, just in case they try something fancy themselves. You haven't got one chance in ten thousand. You're asking Fallon and McKenna to commit suicide."

Maybe, thought Curzon, but he had had the opportunity to sketch out a semi-detailed plan and he was nowhere near so pessimistic as Mortimer. Besides, he asked the American colonel, what alternatives did they have?

"Maybe none, but I'm not asking Sam McKenna to join the death-or-glory brigade. This sort of stuff went out with George Armstrong Custer and the Little Big Horn."

"Maybe Sam McKenna should have a say in that, Colonel," said McKenna from the other side of Curzon's office.

"Sam McKenna will do as he's damn well told," said Mortimer. "When you're a two-star general or the day comes the OSS is run by committee, maybe it'll be different. Until then, Major, you say sir and obey orders."

"Yes, sir," muttered McKenna, suitably chastened.

"Well, you're probably right," said Curzon cheerfully. "This should be an all-British show. The ball-bearing deal is with us, Peterson was our man, and Felix Lunström's present argument is with my Minister. I'm sure we can think of someone else to go in with Major Fallon."

Fallon fielded his cue. "Two or three names spring to mind, sir. There's Butler, Hedges, Green-Walters . . . There are also a couple of Canadians who are getting a mite fretful at being forced to cool their heels."

"*Canadians!*" bleated McKenna.

Mortimer knew when he was beaten. If he didn't, the expression of pure anguish on McKenna's face told him he'd probably have a revolution on his hands unless he agreed to at least listen.

"All right," he grumbled, "let's hear what you've got to say. But I warn you I'm in no way committed. If I don't like what I'm hearing I'm going to tell you in spades. Major McKenna can then complain to the White House, for all it will bother me."

Curzon had taken the trouble to call ahead and instruct the Baker Street duty officer to dig out street plans of Frankfurt and Schweinfurt, together with a large-scale map of central and southern Germany. These he now pinned to the cork-tiled wall. Out of the corner of his eye he saw the others look at one another, puzzled. Schweinfurt they understood, but Frankfurt was sixty miles away. Well, as Salome said to Herod, all would be revealed in time.

"Our information," he began, "is that the Lunströms are being held in a house near one of the VKF factories. As this intelligence came to us via the Gestapo, I think we can take it as gospel.

"As you can see, there are two plants down in this southwest corner of the town, designated VKF 1 and VKF 2. We believe VKF 2 manufactures the ball bearings for assembly and packing in VKF 1. My own guess would be that the Lunströms are incarcerated close to the latter. It's nearer the center of the town and more likely to get clobbered in an air raid, but it's really something that can only be ascertained on the ground."

"By asking the first Gestapo colonel they see, I suppose," chipped in Mortimer.

Curzon smiled tolerantly. "Something like that."

Mortimer shook his head. Maybe if he closed his eyes they would all go away.

"There are only two or three ways into Germany that I know of," Curzon continued. "Via one of the neutral capitals such as Stockholm or Lisbon, posing as neutral businessmen. Several things militate against that method of infiltration. In the first place, neither of you speaks Portuguese, so it would have to be Stockholm. Then again, after your last little visit there and the unauthorized disposal of Helmuth Falck, your faces may be in somebody's files—Swedish intelligence or the SD. Secondly, the Nazis are a bit cagey about issuing visas to foreign businessmen, for obvious reasons. Even those who obtain them are generally scrutinized pretty closely—too closely to be certain you wouldn't be picked up the moment you were on German territory. Our forgers are good, but I'd hate to put their work to the test in an operation we'll only get one crack at."

"Amen to that," murmured McKenna.

"Another method of getting in is via France overland. Both SOE and the OSS are experienced at dropping agents into France, and we're much more familiar with travel documents, identity papers, and suchlike. If we had all the time in the world at our disposal that's the method I would favor, but it could take several weeks to cross France into Germany and we don't have several weeks. The US Eighth Air Force is going to plaster Schweinfurt on the thirteenth or fourteenth, and we have to have the Lunströms out of there by then."

"I think I can give you an update on that," said Mortimer. "Not that it's going to help you much, but it's almost certainly the fourteenth."

"The fourteenth, then," said Curzon, making a note on a scratch pad. "Which gives us something over a week."

"On which date we'll all still be sitting here on our butts," growled Mortimer. "If they can't go in as foreign businessmen and they can't go via France, that's the end of the ball game. I might be a little rusty, but you seem to have run out of options."

"Not really. They fly in."

"Lufthansa, I presume." Mortimer chuckled at his own wit.

"No—the RAF."

"Jesus, let me out of this madhouse."

"Patience, Harry. We'll be here all night if you keep interrupting.

"The RAF will be bombing the center of Frankfurt three nights from tonight," continued Curzon, "the evening of October ninth and tenth. You'll go in with a Pathfinder wing, dressed as civilians, of course. Somewhere before the target area but not too far away, you'll go out of the hatch. I know you're still sixty miles from Schweinfurt, but it's the nearest we can get you."

"Why doesn't one plane go all the way?" asked Mc-Kenna. "Don't tell the RAF I said this, but it happens all the time that crews lose their bearings."

"I considered that, but it's too dangerous. If the Schweinfurt sirens go, the Nazis might take it into their heads to do something with the Lunströms. Even if they don't, they might move them and rethink the whole operation. It's too risky. Besides, we have an agent in Frankfurt, a woman. I'd rather not have used her—not even Peterson knew of her existence—but there it is. I'll give you the details in a moment."

Mortimer was starting to sit up and take interest. Curzon had obviously given this a great deal of thought, was not talking off the top of his head. If he was willing to risk one of his deep-cover agents, something no intelligence outfit did unless the chances of success were better than even, he must be confident it could be pulled off. This was no sacrifice mission. Mortimer had sat in on those before, as no doubt had Curzon. Missions in which—after blowing the bridge or the power station or delivering vitally needed arms—the agent was fully briefed on an escape route that did not exist. He was being condemned to death but not being told. But this wasn't one of those. By definition Natalie Lunström and her uncle had to get home in one piece or all bets were off.

But first things first. Getting Fallon and McKenna in would be hard enough. Apart from any trouble they might encounter on the ground, the Pathfinder aircraft had to deliver them to Frankfurt, avoiding flak and night-fighters en route. Assuming it could be done, they then had to make their way to Schweinfurt and somehow contact the Lunströms. Then— the big question—they had to get out. Yes, very definitely first things first.

"Okay," he said, "they're in. They've hit the ground, stowed their chutes, avoided the Wehrmacht. They've reached Schweinfurt, found the Lunströms, and managed to make off, with half the SS snapping at their heels. What next? Just how the hell do they get out of Germany?"

"By road to Switzerland, which is where my Frankfurt contact comes in." Curzon stabbed a forefinger at the wall map. "Look. Schweinfurt, Würzburg, Stuttgart, Lake Constance. Switzerland. It's around two hundred miles, give or take a few."

"And the lake is also the most patrolled stretch of waterway in Europe," objected Mortimer, continuing to play devil's advocate. "Both the Germans and the Swiss have fast launches cruising up and down it twenty-four hours a day. Because it's the obvious crossing point, it's the best-guarded. The Swiss toss you back across the border *whoever you are* if they catch you. The Germans feed you to the fish. There's no way in."

"Not without help."

"What sort of help?"

"Allen Dulles."

Dulles, the future head of the CIA, was President Roosevelt's personal representative and OSS resident in Switzerland. He had been known on more than one occasion to spirit people out of Germany under the noses of the Nazis.

"I'll see what I can do," said Mortimer.

"Make it fast, Harry. We've got less than three days and I want to wireless Frankfurt as soon as possible to expect visitors."

"I said I'd see what I can do, didn't I?" Mortimer scowled.

Curzon grinned at McKenna. "I think your boss is beginning to believe I'm not talking through my hat and he doesn't like it."

The OSS colonel snorted. "Let's say that fifteen minutes ago I thought you had one chance in ten thousand. Now it's one chance in ninety-nine hundred. Up to now I haven't heard anyone mention how our supermen here get to spring the Lunströms."

"That *is* going to be the toughest part of all," admitted Curzon, "but it's something that cannot be resolved here and now. I'll ask Frankfurt to help, at least try and establish where they're being held; but freeing them will very much depend on their routine and you won't know that until you're there." He shook his head as though suddenly realizing the magnitude of the task. "It may not be possible at all, of course. They might be surrounded by guards six deep."

"I doubt that, sir," said Fallon. "An old man and a girl wouldn't give much trouble, and the Germans will hardly be expecting a rescue party. It's a bit too—"

"How about lunatic?" suggested Mortimer.

"Perhaps you're right," mused Curzon. "It seems to work theoretically, but—"

"Shut up, Charles," interrupted Mortimer. "Don't try

and con an old con man. And don't start having second thoughts, or I might remember a few of my own. You say we've got three days?"

"Slightly less."

"Then we'd better get our act together. Grab yourself a pad and pen, Sam. You can be secretary and if you're good I'll let you sit on my knee."

Curzon smiled to himself.

Over the next three hours, far into the early morning of Thursday, October 7, they thrashed out the details. Mortimer suggested they parachute into Germany wearing RAF uniforms, just in case they had the misfortune to be picked up on landing, their civilian clothes and papers in hold-alls. Neither Fallon nor McKenna liked the idea. It was too negative, implying immediate failure. Certainly if worst came to worst, a uniform would be a passport to a POW camp, while civvies meant a firing squad; but on the whole they preferred to take their chances.

Mortimer was also worried that they were to fly in a Pathfinder Lancaster, which by definition would be in the vanguard of the raid. Pathfinder fatalities were much higher than in the rest of Bomber Command. But Curzon pointed out that there would be a hell of a lot of activity on the ground once the main force came over, increasing the chances of two parachutes being seen.

Their Frankfurt contact was a thirty-year-old German woman by the name of Magda Lessing. She lived in Wolfgangstrasse, east of Grüneburg Park and a block north of the Heinemannsches Musik-Institut. She had a direct radio link with the SOE's communications center at Bletchley Park, but in case of accident they would be provided with an emergency frequency for contacting Bern, Switzerland. If Allen Dulles agreed to help, Bern was where Curzon and Mortimer would be from the middle of next week, to meet the Lunströms coming across. Curzon hoped to persuade Felix Lunström, closer to the time, to allow the much-needed ball bearings to be loaded aboard BOAC aircraft at Bromma, ready for a fast take-off if the operation proved successful. But he would obviously want to talk to his brother and daughter first, and a further radio link would be set up with the British Legation in Stockholm.

The question of cover stories and documentation provided the basis for argument. Fallon and McKenna were no strangers to occupied France and the Low Countries, but this would be their first mission into Germany itself, where any citizen was likely to be stopped at any time by the Kriminalpolizei or the Gestapo and asked to prove his identity. Outside the Reich, forged laborer's papers usually did the trick. In Germany it would be different, particularly for men of obvious military age. Not that the documents themselves would be any problem. SOE's forgers had copies of practically everything and were adept at producing counterfeits capable of passing a cursory examination.

Curzon suggested providing them with discharge slips and disability books, showing them to have been invalided out of the Wehrmacht, but Fallon wasn't keen. It would mean feigning a limp or some such and that was the kind of thing a man could easily forget under pressure.

Mortimer came up with the idea of exemption papers, proving they were engaged in essential war work, but that too was turned down on the grounds that workmen could not wander around freely when they should be in their factories.

It was McKenna who finally offered a possible solution. The mission was an incalculable risk anyway, so why not go the whole hog and pose as Gestapo?

"Give us something that says we're on a special undercover operation from another city, say Hamburg. They're not likely to question one of their own too closely and we might find the cover useful for getting at the Lunströms."

Mortimer was not so sure, but Fallon was enthusiastic. "We might as well do it in style. Besides, if the RAF's going to give Frankfurt a shellacking on the ninth there won't be too many people checking papers for a few days."

Curzon was inclined to agree. The choice of Hamburg as a base was also excellent, as the July raids, code-named Operation Gomorrah, had by all accounts made quite a bonfire of that city's records. From tomorrow morning until they boarded the Lancaster on Saturday night, Fallon and McKenna could study all the SOE's files on the Gestapo for background, as well as brushing up on their spoken German.

At 3 A.M. the meeting broke up. Mortimer had urgent business elsewhere so wouldn't be seeing them again before they left, but in accordance with tradition he neither shook hands nor wished them luck. That was reputed to alert the devil.

"Just make sure you're a hell of a long way from Schweinfurt on the fourteenth" was his parting comment. "If you're not you'll find yourself looking up at the Eighth Air Force, and they've been getting a lot of practice lately."

Eight

On Friday afternoon, October 8, the skipper of one of the crews which had been "getting a lot of practice lately," twenty-four-year-old Captain Joe Calhoun, was beginning to wonder if they weren't perhaps overdoing it. He wouldn't find out until much later, but of the 399 Eighth Air Force bombers which had left their English bases to attack Bremen and Vegesack, thirty would never reach home and twenty-six would receive major structural damage. Superficially at least, Calhoun's ship, a B-17 nicknamed *Heartless Hazel,* was one of these twenty-six.

He hadn't troubled to leave his seat since turning for England, but reports coming back from the left-waist gunner O'Malley and Schaeffer in the tail turret had already told him that there was a hole you could damn near drive a jeep through in the port side of the fuselage just aft of the main spar. A barrage of uncannily accurate flak had got them just after they started their bomb run, and it was a mystery how that son of a bitch O'Malley hadn't been blown to bits, why *Hazel* was in one friggin' piece, for that matter. A letter of commendation to the Boeing Company in Seattle was first on the list when they got back. *If* they got back, because those bastard Fw 190s and Me 109s from the fighter base at Jever were still buzzing around like hornets.

"Come on, you bastard," he urged the huge aircraft. "Don't quit on me now."

He was unaware he had spoken out loud, though in the co-pilot's seat twenty-two-year-old Hank Quincey could well understand his skipper's anxiety. This was Calhoun's twenty-fourth mission; one more and he would have completed his tour. Quincey didn't look that far ahead. He was only on his tenth.

Like most of the other bombers flying today, *Heartless Hazel* was an "F" mark of the Boeing Company's most famous aircraft, the B-17 Flying Fortress, and was part of the 91st Heavy Bombardment Group stationed at Bassingbourn in Cambridgeshire.

Defensive armaments varied from war zone to war zone and sometimes plane to plane, but *Heartless Hazel* was equipped with eleven .50-caliber Browning machine guns: two each in the tail position and the upper and ball turrets, one in each waist aperture, the radio room upper hatch, and either side of the nose. The crew numbered ten: pilot and co-pilot, navigator and bombardier, flight engineer and radio operator, the latter four individuals all doubling as gunners as and when the occasion demanded. Aft of the radio operator's cubicle were the left-waist and right-waist gunners, and the tail-end charlie. The loneliest spot in the aircraft was generally accepted as being the ball turret, where the gunner sat in a kind of bubble slung underneath the plane and thus had first look at anything the flak batteries were tossing up.

The Eighth Air Force crews came from every state in the union and from towns large and small in every state. They were farm boys, slick city boys, boys barely out of school; they were mechanics and lawyers and factory workers and some who had never done a stroke in their lives; they were football players, hockey players, baseball players; and they were mostly in their early twenties, a few in their late teens.

To a man, they wanted to get home to Oregon or Georgia or Alabama or wherever, to wives, sweethearts, or parents; but those flying today would gladly accept the one-street village of Bassingbourn, lousy weather and warm English beer notwithstanding. During the last few months they had developed a fondness for Bassingbourn, its inhabitants, and its one tiny pub, the Hoops, that many of them were too shy to talk about. Ten miles away, Cambridge might offer more in the way of entertainment, especially in the Bull, but Bassingbourn was home. And the crew of *Heartless Hazel* were relying upon Joe Calhoun's skills and the structural strength of the B-17 to get them there. Unless the Luftwaffe had other ideas.

In the right-waist gun position Max Shapiro yelled over the intercom that he had four 109s coming at him from three o'clock high, and he simultaneously opened fire. It was impossible to tell, naturally, but he had the feeling that this same quartet had tried their luck with *Hazel* just a couple of minutes ago. Maybe they'd seen that fucking big hole in front of O'Malley and were thinking that *Hazel* was about to become a straggler, which generally speaking was a death warrant. Well, in no way was *Hazel* about to drop out of the box, if he was any judge of planes and Calhoun's flying ability, and he hoped to Christ he was. Because Shapiro shouldn't have been flying the Bremen mission at all. He was skipper of his own plane and on his shoulders wore the paired silver bars of a captain. Captains did not get assigned to midships gun positions, not unless they'd fouled up somewhere or were crazy.

Shapiro hadn't fouled up but he was beginning to doubt his sanity. His own aircraft had taken a pasting three days earlier and his ground crew reckoned it would be another four or five days at least before she was airworthy once more. So when Bremen was announced as the target and Ted Edwards, *Hazel*'s regular right-waist gunner, had cried off with a bad stomach, what had good ol' Max Shapiro, the marvel of Kansas City, Kansas, done? Why, he'd gone up to his old buddy Joe Calhoun and volunteered—volunfuckinteered—to take Ted's place, get another mission on his score card while he felt lucky.

Dumb bastard!

Shapiro saw the sudden winking lights that were the 109s' cannon and machine guns and he flinched involuntarily while continuing to fire. He didn't hit anything, but neither, as far as he could tell, was *Hazel* hit. And almost as soon as he had called that there were fighters in his sights, they were gone, skimming the upper fuselage, half-rolling out of the killing zone.

Behind Shapiro nineteen-year-old Mike O'Malley let go a burst without success. Jesus Christ, his eye was off today, but it made a guy shake having an officer standing behind him, a full-blown captain at that. Probably the reason he'd missed that Messerschmitt two minutes ago.

In the nose, Lieutenant Ken Cornelius, *Hazel*'s navigator, was calculating on a pad how long it would be before they could expect to meet up with the Spitfires and the P-47s. The fighters were unable to escort the bombers to the target and back, but they sure as hell were always waiting at the limit of their range. "Little Friends," they were known as, and there were few more welcome sights to returning Eighth Air Force bomber crews.

Five minutes, he reckoned, and showed his note to the bombardier, who was wrestling with a jammed ammo belt and cursing at the top of his voice.

It was three generations since the first of the Concannons had left County Cork and settled in New York City, but you wouldn't know it listening to one of the youngest of the clan, Lieutenant Billy Concannon, who was going to be twenty years of age in December. If the fucking gun (may the Holy Mother forgive me) didn't keep on jamming, he thought viciously, giving the breech a thump with a gloved fist the size of a dinner plate. It did the trick, and a second later Concannon was giving a war whoop as chunks of metal tore off a Messerschmitt making a head-on attack. It rolled to port, twisting and jinking to escape the deadly stream of fire, but guns from the Fortress on *Hazel's* starboard hammered it with crossfire, and soon a plume of white smoke billowed from the engine cowling.

The Messerschmitt pilot turned his machine over on its back, released the cockpit cover and his restraining harness. *Hazel's* crew saw a black-clad figure fall from the doomed fighter, and a few moments later a yellow parachute open.

"I'm claiming that bastard!" Concannon called over the intercom, knowing he'd be given half at best. The gunners in the adjacent Fortress would claim the other half.

Hazel's controls were still responding and the bomber was keeping up with the returning stream, but elsewhere other B-17s were not going to make it.

From his gun platform in the mid-upper section of the fuselage, the flight engineer, Sergeant Bob Baker, a tall Texan who was the best pitcher in the 91st, had a clear view of the carnage. Even as he confirmed to Calhoun that Concannon's 109 was burning as it fell, a tremendous whoosh at five o'clock high signaled the end of a B-17. One minute the Fortress was there, the next it wasn't. There wasn't even a sign of bits of metal or even—Christ help us—bodies raining down. There was just nothing.

From his own gun position just aft of Baker's, Jimmy Ryan, the radio operator, witnessed the same phenomenon. Youngest of *Hazel's* crew by a couple of months, he was an amateur boxer of some renown and there was talk of him turning pro when the war was over. He doubted he would. If he got out of this mess alive he would have done enough fighting to last him a couple of lifetimes.

In the tail turret Sergeant Donald S. Schaeffer got in a couple of bursts at a pair of marauding Fw 190s, but they veered off and went for an easier mark. Which was just as well for their little Kraut kids and dumpling-eating Kraut wives, was the unspoken opinion of Sergeant Schaeffer, who was acknowledged to be the best air gunner aboard *Hazel*. His ability to calculate deflection angles and distances was considered uncanny, until one day he let slip that his pa had started taking him on hunting trips when he was five and had given him his first rifle when he was ten, precisely half a lifetime ago. Shortly afterward someone picked up a magazine, and there was Donald S. Schaeffer, only son of Louis Schaeffer of Schaeffer Industries. When asked how, with that kind of clout, he had still managed to get drafted, Donald S. Schaeffer answered that one day when the war was over he'd be expected to marry a girl picked out for him by his parents, sire a bunch of Schaeffer kids, and settle down behind a Schaeffer desk for the rest of his Schaeffer life, making more Schaeffer millions. This was the only excitement he was ever likely to see.

From the loneliest berth in the ship, Sergeant George Bushman, who was also *Hazel*'s smallest crew member, swiveled the ball turret to track a solitary 109 but held his fire when he realized it was out of range and unlikely to attack from below in any case. A few months ago the fighters used to come swarming up through the groups, cannon hammering as they came. But it had proved too costly for the Luftwaffe. The Eighth Air Force bomber streams flew in considerable depth and the fighters were getting raked by the defenders every inch of the way. Now the attacks were generally from abeam or frontal.

The change of strategy had made life a little easier for the belly gunners, but it was still a crew position nobody wanted, and a small guy was always pleased when an even smaller guy joined the ship, for by tradition the ball turret went to the man who could squeeze easiest into its narrow confines.

Bushman didn't mind it too much. Sure the flak scared the shit out of you over the target, but if your number was written on a shell, it would be all over quick. A man wouldn't know too much about it.

At the controls Calhoun called through to Cornelius. "How long before we can expect to meet up with the P-47s, Ken?"

"Couple of minutes. How's she handling?"

"Just fine, though I reckon we're going to be grounded for a week while they plug that hole."

"Well, that's a terrible shame, so it is," Concannon piped in. "And me waitin' to deliver all those lovely fuckin' bombs —may the Holy Virgin forgive my mouth—onto the Fatherland."

Calhoun grinned behind his oxygen mask. "You'll get plenty of other chances, Billy."

Which was more than could be said for some other poor bastards. It was hard to keep anything more than a rough tally of what was happening to the B-17s around you when you were in the middle of a dogfight, but Calhoun had counted six going down and there were doubtless plenty of others he hadn't seen. Two more in the forward low group—the 322nd, he thought it was, but he couldn't be sure—seemed to be in trouble, but the Fortresses around the damaged plane had closed ranks and no one was falling behind. Still, there were planes all over the sky and it wasn't finished yet.

"Now hear this," he said to the whole crew. "The Luftwaffe know as well as we do that the P-47s will be alongside shortly, so they'll throw everything they've got at us in the next sixty seconds. Keep your eyes peeled. The Eighth has lost more than one plane by the crew goofing off."

But there were to be no more losses that day. Hardly had Calhoun finished speaking when a dozen single-engine fighters appeared as if from nowhere, making a lightning lateral traverse from port to starboard. Even at the speed they were moving, it was possible to pick out the red, white, and blue roundels of the RAF. A moment later a score or more P-47s bounced down from above. The Little Friends were here.

Someone—it sounded like Max Shapiro—shouted,

"Look at the bastards go!" And from the upper turret Bob Baker confirmed that the Luftwaffe were heading for home.

Hazel echoed with a few cheers, and it took a couple of seconds for Calhoun to get the crew's attention. "Okay, you bastards, let's have a little less noise." But he could well understand their jubilation. They were alive and they would not have to face the angry fighters and the fearsome flak for a few more days.

Hauptmann Otto Reinberger and his wingman Heinz Mahle were among the last to land at Jever after the tangle with the B-17s. As the Staffelkapitän taxied his 109 up to the dispersal pad he made a swift count of the assembled aircraft. He appeared to be two short, but he could not tell whose machines they were from the distance. Not that their absence necessarily meant they were lost; they could have got into fuel or other trouble and landed at another airfield. Even if the planes were gone, the pilots might still be alive.

Reinberger clambered down from the cockpit and beckoned across to his chief mechanic, a grizzled Oberfeldwebel who had been with aircraft since their baptism in combat on the Western Front in the First War.

"There's still something wrong with that engine," he complained. "I had a cut-out in a power dive and it didn't cut back until I leveled off."

"I've put in for a replacement, Herr Hauptmann, but it could take a fortnight. I've also stripped it, as you know, without finding the source of the trouble."

"Strip it again, Meindl. If you lose your Staffelkapitän you know who takes over." He jerked a thumb at Mahle, who was gesturing with two flattened hands, showing his own ground crew how he had made a kill. Reinberger had witnessed the B-17 going down in flames and made a mental note to again remind Mahle that it was his job to watch his Staffelkapitän's back.

Oberfeldwebel Meindl grunted. "I'll have the men work all night on it. How was the hunting?" he added.

"Good. I'll be claiming one bomber as definite. I saw lumps fly off another, but I lost it after that. It will have to go in the log as possible but doubtful."

"If only the others were as conscientious, Herr Hauptmann."

Reinberger knew what he was getting at. The Luftwaffe was tightening up its procedure for verifying kills, but there were still many fliers who swore that anything they shot at went down. The rate some of them logged scores, there shouldn't be an Allied aircraft left in the sky. It was worrying for the High Command, who were at pains to point out that it didn't help the war effort one jot to make inaccurate claims. If they couldn't gauge how many aircraft the enemy were losing, it was impossible to compare the relative strengths of the opposing air forces.

Reinberger accepted gratefully from Meindl a far from clean rag and wiped the oil and dirt from his forehead. "Who's unaccounted for?" he asked, indicating the two empty parking slots.

"Leutnants Süssmann and Weinrich. Süssmann's almost certainly dead. They're not sure about Weinrich."

"Christ." Reinberger handed the oily rag back and walked across to where Oberleutnant Wolf Löhr, number one in the two-man Rotte whose other member was Weinrich, was sitting downcast on the port wheel of his 109. The Staffel comedian was a long way from laughing now.

"What happened, Löhr?"

The Oberleutnant began to get to his feet, but Reinberger waved him down.

"We were making a head-on attack on one of the leading B-17s. I got a couple of bursts in and peeled off. The nose gunner got Paul."

"Parachute?"

"I can't be sure. He was in formation one second, gone the next. I think I picked out his aircraft going down, but there were a dozen or more parachutes in the air and I had to watch my back."

"Well, we'll just have to wait and see. Try not to worry about it, Weinrich is a good flier and lucky with it."

Löhr looked up at his Staffelkapitän. "Was it a successful day? Everywhere I looked there was a bomber in flames or in trouble."

"It seemed to be good hunting, but we'll know more after debriefing. You'd better get along there while it's all still fresh in your mind. How did you do, by the way?"

"Three B-17s. Paul will confirm— Paul might be able to confirm them."

"*Three!* My God, Löhr, that's magnificent!"

"*Danke,* Herr Hauptmann, but three out of three or four hundred isn't much, is it? There are just too many of them. We don't seem to make any impression, no matter how many we get."

Löhr levered himself to his feet and trudged off flatfooted in the direction of the debriefing hut. Reinberger was about to make a quick check on the remainder of the Staffel's kills when Mahle collared him.

"I trust you will be in a position to confirm my kill, Herr Hauptmann," he said formally.

Reinberger said he would, "Though I'd still prefer it if we came back with my tally as three and yours nil. That way I'd know you were more concerned about my tail than increasing your personal score."

"The *Ami* practically flew into my guns," protested Mahle. "Not to have shot him down would have been criminal."

Reinberger nodded. Mahle was right, of course, and there was no point in making an issue of it.

"We lost Leutnants Süssmann and Weinrich. Süssman is probably dead. We're not sure about Weinrich."

"Süssman and Weinrich?" Mahle was frowning and Reinberger knew without any shadow of doubt that his wing-man was having difficulty placing their faces. Christ, how could he possibly recommend promotion to Staffelkapitän for such a man, regardless of how good a flier he was.

In spite of being last into the debriefing hut, Reinberger was among the first out. He stood quietly by the entrance smoking a cigarette.

Before he had taken more than a couple of puffs he saw a vehicle heading in his direction from the main gates. It was growing dark now but he recognized it as an ambulance. They were bringing home the dead meat.

But it wasn't that at all. Next to the driver, the second man in the cab was wearing a flying suit. As the ambulance came to a halt, Reinberger made out the pink cheeks of Paul Weinrich, who was grinning from ear to ear and appeared to be in one piece.

The Leutnant tumbled out of the cab and tossed Rein-berger a clumsy salute, something between a wave and a curtsy. Although he was delighted to see the youngster, the Staffelkapitän took a couple of deep breaths to bring his emotions under control. It wouldn't do for an officer in his position to act like a student at end of term.

"Where the devil do you think you've been, Weinrich?" he demanded. "And where the hell's the aircraft we sent you out in?" he was unable to resist adding.

Weinrich took the question quite seriously. "Well, sir, I got into a spot of trouble with a Flying Fortress, but I managed to flip over and bail out before my machine went into spiral. Christ, I must have missed a couple of other B-17s by centimeters as I was falling, but I took good care to drop clear of the stream before opening my chute. Anyway, I landed in this field about ten kilometers away, and as luck would have it this ambulance was passing—"

"Hold it, *hold it*." Reinberger held up his hand to cut off the Leutnant's babblings. "Save it for the report."

127

"Yes, sir. Of course, Herr Hauptmann." Weinrich hesitated. "Er, did Löhr get back all right?"

"Why don't you ask him yourself?"

Löhr was just leaving the debriefing hut. He yelped with delight when he saw Weinrich, jumped on his wingman and pummeled him so hard that both men fell to the earth.

"You bastard!" he bellowed. "What the hell do you mean by bailing out and leaving me to look after myself? What kind of *Katchmarek* do you think you are anyway?"

Laughing, Weinrich scrambled to his feet and hauled Löhr up. "Were you worried about me?"

Löhr's expression was one of incredulity. "Me? Was I worried about you? Was I hell! I said to myself that if ever there was a crafty one for getting out of where it was hottest, that one was Paul Weinrich. Why the hell should I have been worried? Come on, let's get your debriefing over and done with and see if we can't perhaps persuade the mess waiter to open the bar."

Reinberger watched them go. Now, they were the real Germany, not bastards like Mahle.

A few hundred miles southeast in Schweinfurt, a fair-haired woman in her late twenties or early thirties was thinking much the same thing, that the real Germany was not the arrogant, swaggering SS swine outside the law courts in Rüfferstrasse; the real Germany was men like Hugo, killed like so many others by those criminal madmen in Berlin. But one day soon it would all be different. The gangsters would be gone, tried in their own courts and condemned, and in their place would stand honorable men and women. And if it took an Allied victory to bring about that state of affairs—well, so be it.

There was no doubt about it, people who knew her were apt to repeat, that Magda Lessing had let herself go since her husband was killed on the Russian Front in the autumn of '41. Such a tragedy. They remembered her as a very lovely high-spirited girl, always ready with a quip for the depressed or help and advice for those who had lost sons in France. Now she was considerably underweight, wore little makeup, and dressed in severe clothes more befitting a woman twice her age.

It would have surprised those same people to learn that Frau Lessing was not and never had been in the least distressed by her husband's death, that she had not loved him since that evening in 1938 when he came home drunk, blood on his shiny black uniform, boasting how he had kicked the shit out of a bunch of Jews and Communists and that the SS were going to show the world just how it should be run. Crystal Night, they'd called it, when throughout Germany Jewish businesses were destroyed and Jews and other enemies of the Nazis beaten up and lynched.

A week later she had surprised Hugo Engmann by at last agreeing to become his mistress, and a month after that she was working for British intelligence.

From the first day they met, Hugo had made no bones about the fact that he hated the Nazis, though as a lecturer at the Johann Wolfgang von Goethe University in Frankfurt he paid lip service to their doctrines and was a member of the Party. It was, he confessed to her after they became lovers, the only way he could keep his job and be of some use to the anti-Nazis both inside and outside Germany, and he suggested she follow his lead. If war came, the opposition inside the Reich would be wiped out overnight, and only from the outside could help be expected. It was not treason, because Hitler was not Germany; he was not even German.

She agreed to go along with his suggestion with an alacrity which astonished her, for she did not consider herself to be a political animal or especially brave. But she joined the Party and attended the meetings. Her husband was delighted. It would undoubtedly aid his career.

Shortly before Christmas that year Hugo introduced her to an Englishman who was ostensibly in Frankfurt on business.

129

So he was, but it was a business far removed from that on his calling card.

In no time flat he made it quite clear that he wanted her to act as an undercover agent. (British intelligence attempted to recruit a number of women as opposed to men in this period, fearing, as turned out to be the case, that all able-bodied men would soon be called up.) She would be provided with a small, powerful transceiver and asked to wait. When war came—there was no "if" with this man—she would be obliged to tune in to a given frequency at the same time each night and listen, just listen. Except for one five-second trans-mission once a month to show her control she was still alive and operational, she was not to use the radio at any other time unless asked. Her code name would be Canaan, and did she accept?

She did.

Charles Curzon, who was her Frankfurt visitor, used her very rarely. She was too valuable to risk on routine stuff such as the results of Allied bombing raids in and around Frankfurt. He was confident she would pay her way sooner or later.

Hugo Engmann suffered from a chest complaint and was not called up during general mobilization. For reasons of per-sonal security he and Magda also kept their affair a secret and met less and less often as the war progressed. At the time of his arrest two years earlier there was nothing to connect the pair.

She never found out what the charges were. He simply disappeared from the university and was never seen again. His rooms were cleared out and another tenant installed. It was as though he had never existed, and she couldn't make too many inquiries for fear of attracting attention to herself. It was just coincidence that the telegram informing her of her husband's death arrived within days of Hugo's abduction, and it was for Hugo she wept, perhaps even for Germany. There was now even more reason for the Nazis to be overthrown and she wished to God London would use her more often, but only twice since 1941 had she been asked for information.

When the call came last evening, therefore, she almost missed it and her instructions. But London was accustomed to dealing with underactive agents and repeated it. She was to travel to Schweinfurt at the first available opportunity and reconnoiter the area around both VKF complexes. She was looking for a young Swedish girl and a much older white-haired Swedish man. She would probably recognize them as foreigners because they would be much better dressed than the average German. They would also almost certainly be under guard. If she did not see the Swedes, she was to look for any private house or apartment building in the vicinity of the factories that seemed to be guarded for no reason.

She was to take no action other than establish the Swedes' whereabouts. That achieved, she was to return to Frankfurt. She was, in any case, to be back at her own apartment by the evening of the ninth, when she should expect visitors in the small hours. They would identify themselves with the words "Exodus three, verse eight." She looked it up. ". . . unto a land flowing with milk and honey; unto the place of the Canaanites."

Curzon thought of adding that Fallon and McKenna would be arriving during or after a bombing raid, but that would be a terrible breach of security. Magda Lessing was an intelligent and brave woman; she'd be okay.

She was also fortunate—or rather it was foreseen years ago that she would be—in that her Frankfurt job with the Ernährungsamt, or Food Office, and her membership in the Nazi Party gave her certain privileges, priority gasoline coupons, and the use of an official car, which were unavailable to ordinary citizens.

Thus it was the easiest thing in the world to persuade her boss that she needed to go to Schweinfurt to investigate a report that Malzfabrik Schweinfurt AG, the malt factory in

Hauptbahnhofstrasse, was buying black market barley at inflationary prices to the detriment of other malt factories around. Schweinfurt had a small sub Food Office of its own, but it was suspected that some of the employees were in on the racket, falsifying records.

She had no real confidence in her ability to spot the Swedes from London's sketchy description (though she understood their need to keep the transmission as short as possible), and it was therefore with astonishment verging on incredulity that she saw a well-dressed couple who just had to be the pair she was looking for leaving an apartment building in Landwehrstrasse, quite close to the German Red Cross offices, within sixty minutes of arriving in Schweinfurt. The man had a thatch of white hair, the ages and sexes were right, their clothes were very emphatically of foreign manufacture and expensive, and Landwehrstrasse was only a few hundred meters from the VKF assembly plant in Schultesstrasse. If further confirmation were needed that she'd struck gold at the first time of asking, the couple were being escorted toward a waiting staff car by four men in plain clothes who just had to be Gestapo. Neither the girl nor the old man looked very happy.

Still, she had to be sure.

Quickly crossing Landwehrstrasse, head down as though deep in thought and in a hurry, Magda contrived to collide with the girl, causing her to stumble. She was, Magda noticed, very beautiful, with fine aristocratic features.

"I'm sorry," she stammered. "I just wasn't looking where I was going."

Her expression one of annoyance, Natalie Lunström said it didn't matter, but she said it first in Swedish, only correcting herself and repeating it in German a moment later. Then she and the older man were bundled into the staff car, which sped away.

Magda Lessing did not understand Swedish, but she knew a foreign language when she heard one.

After making a mental note that the number of the apartment building was Landwehrstrasse 18, to cover herself she paid a visit to the malt factory and made herself thoroughly unpleasant for an hour. She would have stayed longer, but after a while she became aware that she was under scrutiny by a small middle-aged man dressed similarly to the quartet she had seen escorting the Swedes. Unmistakably he was a Gestapo officer. She was doing nothing wrong, but she thought it better not to push her luck. Warning the manager that her inquiries were far from complete, she left Malzfabrik.

Her next stop was an apartment in Horst Wesselstrasse, which the Ernährungsamt kept for visiting employees. After opening the windows to let some air into the place, she sat down and made a few notes about the Swedes, describing each of them. She had no idea why the information was required or when it would be needed, but she preferred not to trust her memory.

By 10 P.M. she was back in Frankfurt, where to complete her day she called in at the National Socialist Headquarters in Sachsenhausen to see if there were any odd jobs that needed doing.

At 10 P.M. GMT in Baker Street, Curzon received a call on the scrambler phone from Mortimer confirming that Dulles was willing to help with a border crossing from Germany to Switzerland. The details of the escape hatch would be on Curzon's desk first thing in the morning, but neither man could have known that Fallon and McKenna were not destined to use it.

Nine

Neither Fallon nor McKenna had ever jumped from 21,000 feet before, but that was the designated height for the RAF Lancasters due to give Frankfurt a shellacking in the small hours of October 10.

Each man wore a thick flying suit over his civilian clothes, oversized boots covering walking shoes, and heavy gauntlets. Each was equipped with a portable oxygen mask and bottle. Both carried flashlights, German cigarettes, matches and currency, and a good supply of amphetamines, in this case Benzedrine. If things got rough, sleep might be hard to come by.

At 0125 word came back via the intercom from the aircraft's skipper, Wing Commander Bradford. The jump master told them to get ready. They were a score or so miles west of Frankfurt and it was time to go.

McKenna went first, launching himself into the night like a cork from a bottle. Fallon followed a split second later, forcing himself to count slowly to twenty before pulling the ripcord in order to fall clear of the bomber stream.

Long before he hit the ground the distant horizon was lit up by the first of the bombs falling, the probing beams from the searchlight batteries, the flashes from the flak guns. But below it was pitch-black.

He sensed rather than saw the earth rushing up to meet him and at the last moment, more by luck than good judgment, yanked at the rigging lines to sideslip away from a clump of trees. A fraction of a second later he was down and slapping at the quick-release catch to get out of the chute.

As far as he could tell he had landed in open country, as per program. At least there was soil beneath his feet, not concrete, and now that he had a better perspective he could see no houses. Neither, for that matter, could he see McKenna.

But first things first.

He struggled out of the flying suit, gauntlets and flying boots, and buried them, together with the chute and oxygen equipment, as best he could in the grove of trees. They would be found before long inevitably, but one of the advantages of coming in with a bombing fleet was that the Germans would assume the gear belonged to a flier.

The task complete, he risked the flashlight, pointing the beam southwest. As McKenna had bailed out with no more than a couple of seconds' lead, he shouldn't be far off.

Nor was he. An answering flash came from an adjacent field perhaps two hundred yards away. Fallon walked toward it, tensed in case the signaler was someone else.

But it was McKenna all right. The American had already stashed his parachute gear and was sitting on a log rubbing his shins. It was nothing serious. He'd simply grazed himself on landing.

"Will you look at that."

Ten or twelve miles away, Frankfurt was taking a fearful pounding as wave after wave of Lancasters homed in on the Pathfinders' markers.

But it was far from a one-sided affair. Every now and again there were faint, sudden explosions in the sky, explosions that were not flak shells but aircraft dying.

"Poor bastards."

Fallon nodded somberly, though there was another side to the coin. The 93 to 95 percent who made it would be back in the mess swilling beer before he and McKenna were anywhere near Frankfurt.

"Did you see which way the road was?"

"Over there. I only missed it by fifty feet. What about the lights?"

"We'd better ditch them. And as paid-up members of the Gestapo, we'd better start talking German."

Just as Berlin was said to know exactly what went on at 64 Baker Street and even that off-duty SOE officers spent most lunchtimes in the Wallace Head pub, Blandford Street, London W1, so Charles Curzon knew a great deal about the Gestapo and its place in the command structure of the SS, under whose banner it marched. This knowledge he had spent two days passing on to Fallon and McKenna, drumming it in until their heads spun, reminding them, when they complained that it was impossible to absorb so much in such a short time, that the fragment of information they failed to take in could be the fragment that cost them their lives.

They were to stick to their story, if it came to a confrontation, of being on a special mission from Hamburg, the importance of which could not be revealed. Their identity documents and other papers were printed on German presses and were virtually foolproof. Their clothing down to their underwear was of German manufacture. All that could let them down was a stroke of exceptionally bad luck.

But there was no danger of that this night. The citizens of Frankfurt and environs had other things on their collective mind.

The last of the bombers had gone by 2:30 A.M., and to begin with it seemed as if the road they were on was a conduit for every fire engine, ambulance, police vehicle, and Wehrmacht truck in the Reich, which kept them diving into hedgerows until they rationalized that such actions were more likely to attract attention than the opposite. There would undoubtedly be patrols out looking for downed fliers, ready to pounce on anyone behaving suspiciously. It was better to remain out in the open, and it soon became apparent that no one in the vehicles was in the least interested in a couple of civilians, though the closer they got to Frankfurt the more crowded the road became. Whether the others—and there were soon several hundred—were city residents caught away from their homes during the raid or whether they were men and women from outlying townships coming in to see what they could do to help, there was no way of telling. If the latter, it was surely a wasted journey, for from five or six miles out the city was an awe-inspiring sight, a wall of flame and smoke that licked the heavens.

The same thought occurred to them both: bombs could not discriminate between friend and foe. Magda Lessing could well be burnt to a frazzle.

At 4:30 A.M., when they were tired and footsore, Rebstock Airfield loomed up ahead, the forest of the same name blazing fiercely where a few dozen incendiaries had fallen short of the target.

They had committed a street map of Frankfurt to memory and knew they must soon be crossing Max Immelmannstrasse. Wolfgangstrasse, where Magda Lessing lived, lay a mile and a half further on, somewhere among the flames and the rubble, the choking dust and falling masonry.

It was shortly after this that they came across the RAF flight sergeant being strung up from a lamppost by half a hundred men and women, mostly civilians, who had fashioned a crude gallows.

The airman was quite young, about nineteen. He was

crying and through his sobs shouting something about being a legitimate prisoner of war. But the mob was baying for blood and would have none of it. This was one of the terror fliers who had just wreaked such havoc on their city, and he was going to pay the ultimate penalty. He might have had the luck to parachute clear of his bomber, but his luck stopped here.

McKenna sensed that Fallon was in the mood for heroics and held on to him tightly by the arm. "Don't be a damned fool."

In any case, it was too late. Even as they watched, the rope tightened on the airman's neck, to the jeers and cheers of the crowd.

They pressed on.

Some of the streets were no longer recognizable as streets, and access to others was being forbidden by uniformed troops, SS as well as Wehrmacht.

At the intersection of Bismarckallee and Königsstrasse, where the Deutsche Kleider-Werke AG was ablaze and would not be producing any clothing for a while, they were turned back. A little later, again trying to cross the north-south-running Königsstrasse at the Bockenheimer Warte junction, they were stopped by a patrol. The SS Unterscharführer in command warned them curtly that it was unsafe to proceed. It was believed a bomb with a delayed action fuse had landed somewhere in the vicinity and everyone was being asked to use a different route until the engineers and the bomb-disposal people declared the area clean. Where, he asked, were they heading.

"Wolfgangstrasse," answered Fallon without hesitation.

The Unterscharführer looked them up and down, obviously curious. In spite of their long hike from the drop zone, they knew they looked healthier and better fed than the average German, but it turned out there was more to it than that.

"I have cousins on Wolfgangstrasse," said the SS sergeant. "What number are you looking for?"

Fallon invented one on the spur of the moment, unwilling to incriminate Magda Lessing and hoping to Christ it wasn't where the Unterscharführer's damned cousins lived.

The German checked his clipboard. "That's east of Grüneburg Park. First reports say that that area missed the worst of it."

"I'm pleased to hear it."

"You have relatives there?"

McKenna took over. "No, business."

"Business at five o'clock in the morning with half the city on fire?" The Unterscharführer's eyes widened with disbelief. He was a thick-set man in his middle thirties and had risen to the rank of sergeant more due to his prowess with a truncheon than any deductive ability. But there was something here that didn't quite add up. "What sort of business?"

"Government business," answered McKenna. "Private and urgent government business."

The Unterscharführer hesitated, uncertain of his next move. The big man's voice was authoritative, but there was something about both men's appearance, perhaps their accents . . .

"You're not from these parts, are you?"

Fallon exchanged a quick glance with McKenna. While being briefed on the RSHA infrastructure they had conversed in German with Curzon and a German refugee, who'd assured them their accents were perfect. If the Unterscharführer was merely being officious, that was one thing. If he was genuinely suspicious, that was another. It was time to go on the attack, play up to the hilt their roles as middle-ranking Gestapo officers.

"Are you trying to say something, Sergeant?" demanded Fallon. "Because if you are, kindly say it and get it over with. As my partner has just told you, we have urgent business in Wolfgangstrasse and you're keeping us from attending to it."

"I merely suggested you didn't come from these parts."

"You're damned right we don't," snapped McKenna. "You could fit what's left of this rathole of a city into a small corner of Hamburg and the sooner we're back there the better we'll like it."

"You're from Hamburg?"

"Well done, Sergeant," said Fallon sarcastically. "You can see what we're up against now, can't you?" he added to McKenna.

McKenna fielded his cue deftly. "That I can, but it'll all be different in a few days. Transfer most of these bastards to the Russian Front, that'll be one of my recommendations."

The Unterscharführer didn't like the sound of that at all and Fallon kept him off balance by producing his papers from an inside pocket. This was as good an opportunity as any to test the standard of the forgeries.

He thrust them at the German. "Here, Sergeant, perhaps these are what you want to see. Take them, man, take them. Maybe they'll convince you we're not fifth columnists dropped in by the *Tommis.*"

McKenna sucked in a deep breath. Christ, that was an overdose of bravado. But he followed Fallon's lead and produced his own papers.

The Unterscharführer was reluctant to accept either set until they were slapped into his hands. He was in over his head here, he realized that now. No one antagonized the SS unless . . .

One glance at the Gestapo identity papers was enough to convince him he had made a big mistake. But it was the phony rank assumed by both Fallon and McKenna that shook him: Sturmbannführer. Christ, he'd been cross-examining a couple of field officers.

He stiffened to attention and handed back the documents. "I'm sorry, Herr Sturmbannführer," he managed, addressing Fallon, "but you must understand—"

Fallon waved him to silence. "*I* must understand nothing," he raged. "*You* must understand that the Gestapo does not tolerate obstructionists. Your name?"

The Unterscharführer gave it.

"Then you may expect to be transferred to the Russian Front as soon as I can get the papers processed, you and this shuffling bunch of incompetents with you."

The six-strong patrol, who had taken a lively interest in the argument up to now, backed off as a man at this second mention of the Russian Front.

"Now before you make matters worse and I decide to advocate a more severe form of punishment," Fallon went on, "perhaps you will direct us to Wolfgangstrasse via a route that does not involve us being held up by more idiots or unexploded bombs."

The Unterscharführer almost fell over himself in his anxiety to comply. "Of course, Herr Sturmbannführer. You go north for a couple of hundred meters until you come to the trolley depot, where you turn right onto Sophienstrasse. Follow that until you pass Palmengarten, and Wolfgangstrasse is less than a kilometer ahead. The number you want—"

"Thank you," interrupted Fallon, "but I think we can find it without any further assistance from the likes of you. Dismissed!"

The SS NCO's arm shot out like a ramrod in the Nazi salute. "Heil Hitler!"

Fallon turned his back without responding.

Out of earshot, McKenna said, "Jesus Christ, Jack, what was all that about fifth columnists being dropped in? You didn't have to put ideas into his goddamn head."

"That sort of bastard hasn't got room for more than one and he'll be more worried about his transfer east than anything else for the next month. It proves the documents hold up under scrutiny anyway."

"Maybe, but let's not risk it again unless we have to, huh? Come on, let's move out."

As the Unterscharführer had stated, most of the buildings east of the Grüneburg Park were untouched. The main damage from the bombing raid seemed to be in the west and south of the city, around the railway station.

Magda Lessing's address was a ground-floor front apartment, and it was a few minutes before 6 A.M. when they knocked on her door. She was awake and dressed and more than a little worried at the non-appearance of her expected visitors.

To her suspicious inquiry from behind the closed door, Fallon gave the recognition signal: Exodus three, verse eight. It might sound melodramatic in London, but it was the sort of thing that saved lives over here.

She hustled them inside and shot the bolts. In German she said, "London might have let me know you were arriving with half the RAF."

Ten

The apartment had seen better days, but then so had many buildings in the Third Reich—and England too, for that matter. It boasted two bedrooms, a small sitting room, a bathroom, and a kitchen, but for the moment there was nothing coming out of the taps and no gas to cook on. With heavy irony Magda told them they must blame the Royal Air Force for the inconvenience. She did, however, produce a kettleful of water left over from the previous day and a tiny kerosene stove, and insisted upon preparing them breakfast while they talked.

It was a frugal enough affair. Ersatz coffee made from a mixture of chicory and acorns, a little sugar, some powdered milk. The solid food consisted of thick slices of black bread spread thinly with something that tasted like kippers. There was no butter.

In spite of being ravenous, Fallon and McKenna felt guilty about consuming the woman's meager supplies. God knows, she looked as though she herself hardly ate, though there was no doubt that at one time she had been pretty.

Sensing their discomfort, she told them not to worry.

"Tomorrow's Monday, the start of the new rationing period. There'll be plenty in the cupboard tomorrow night, perhaps even a little butter for Party members."

McKenna was surprised. "You're one?"

"Of course. It's excellent cover and grants me privileges that make working for London easier. It also keeps away the curious—my neighbors, that is. As you may be aware, members of the Party are not exactly popular these days, not since the tide turned against us."

"You still think of it like that?" asked Fallon. "Them— meaning the Allies—and us?"

"I am a German first and foremost," said Magda with simple dignity. "I don't like what the Allied bombers are doing to our beautiful cities and I am frightened of what will happen when the invasion comes, as it must one day. But more than anything, I fear the Nazis. They would rather see Germany in ruins than capitulate, and we are told that Mr. Churchill and President Roosevelt will accept nothing less than unconditional surrender. While the Nazis are in power, that is. But if there were a coup—if Hitler and Himmler and Goebbels and the others were removed from office and arraigned—I think perhaps the Allies might be willing to bargain, talk to a more reasonable government. That is why I work for London."

The meal at an end, Fallon thanked Magda and unthinkingly reached into his jacket pocket and brought out a pack of cigarettes. Magda's eyes sparkled when she saw them. "My God, tobacco! I haven't seen a cigarette for a month."

"Take them," said Fallon. He had several more packs in his raincoat.

"Do you mean it?"

"Of course. But remember to keep them out of sight, or someone might wonder where they came from."

"I'll tell them I have a rich lover." She smiled, and for a moment they saw the woman she had once been.

Pushing his coffee cup to one side, McKenna told Magda it was important they get to Schweinfurt as soon as possible and asked her if she had had any luck in tracing the Lunströms' whereabouts. She astonished them by saying she had and quickly described the events of the previous Friday.

"Naturally," she said, "I've no certain proof they're the pair London asked me to look out for, but the ages and the descriptions fit, they were heavily guarded, and the girl at least wasn't German."

"It has to be them," said McKenna.

"How were they guarded?" asked Fallon.

"By four men in plain clothes, almost certainly Gestapo. Counting the driver of the car, five men in all."

"How did they appear?"

"I'm sorry, I don't understand."

"Were they manacled or handcuffed or anything like that?"

"No. They seemed far from happy, but that's about all."

"Five guards," muttered McKenna. "Christ."

Magda was curious. "Am I permitted to know who these people are and what you plan to do with them?"

Fallon thought about it. They were going to need a lot of Magda's help so she was entitled to be told some of it. About half.

"It's safer all round if you don't know the whole story, but I can tell you that the Swedes are important to us, the Allies, perhaps even to the Germany you'd like to see exist. We're here to take them to England. How doesn't matter, except that when we've separated them from the Gestapo we'll need a car. Can you manage that?"

"It will take some explaining, but yes, I can manage a car." She looked at each of them in turn and shook her head. "But I don't think I've made myself entirely clear. You won't be able to get anywhere near them. Even talking to them would, I think, be a problem. Freeing them is impossible."

Fallon grinned cheerfully. "Nothing's impossible, but we won't find the answer sitting here. How soon can you get us to Schweinfurt?"

Magda thought for a moment. "Wednesday, perhaps Thursday."

That wouldn't do at all, protested Fallon, without telling her that come Thursday Schweinfurt was going to be a smoking ruin.

Magda interrupted him. "You don't understand how things are here in Germany. As a result of the raid it's going to take the heavy labor squads several days to clear the roads, and private or non-priority travel is forbidden, to avoid creating bottlenecks. Apart from that, I have a job to do. I can't just disappear without giving at least forty-eight hours' notice. On top of that, the Party hierarchy here in Frankfurt would think it very odd if I wanted to leave while there is still so much to be done. Much more than the ordinary citizen, Party members are expected to help out after an air raid—set up temporary shelters for the homeless, roll bandages, distribute soup and blankets. I should be doing that now and I would have been were it not for your arrival. But I must leave soon, otherwise someone might come to investigate, see I'm still in one piece. I'll try to get away by Wednesday, but that's the best I can do."

Fallon looked at McKenna in despair. They could try for Schweinfurt by themselves, of course, but if what Magda was saying was true they wouldn't get farther than the city limits, if that far. But Wednesday—Christ, that was cutting it close. Less than twenty-four hours to free the Lunströms from the clutches of the Gestapo and get the hell out of Schweinfurt. But if that was how it had to be . . .

"Try for Tuesday at the outside," he urged. "You have no idea how vital this is."

"I'll try, but I'm rather afraid it will have to be Wednesday and even that might be difficult."

She would tell her supervisor at the Ernährungsamt that

she was far from satisfied with last Friday's inquiries at Malz-fabrik, that she needed a couple of days in Schweinfurt to sort the whole affair out once and for all, especially insofar as it concerned government employees in the sub-office. He would kick up a fuss, of course, protest he couldn't spare her, but she knew she could handle him, hint she might still be willing to take that week's leave with him at some quiet hotel in Bavaria. She would drive the two Allied agents to Schweinfurt herself. They could all stay at the Horst Wesselstrasse apartment until the business was done.

She explained her scheme to Fallon and McKenna.

"What about the car?" asked the American. "We'll be needing transport for afterward."

"Will you be needing me?"

McKenna hesitated. They couldn't leave her behind with Schweinfurt about to be bombed to a cinder, but if they took her car she would be stuck. Much depended upon how long, if at all, it took them to free the Lunströms.

"That's hard to say."

"I understand. If you don't need me I can always report the car stolen after a few hours."

Magda got up from the table and pulled a corner of the blackout blinds. The clock said it should be getting light outside, but the palls of smoke and dust rising above the south and west of the city made it as black as midnight. The worst of the fires, however, now seemed to be under control.

"I must go," she told them, "but don't open the door to anyone, no matter how hard they knock or who they claim to be. There's only one spare bedroom but there are two beds in it. If you're awake before I return, please feel free to help yourself to food. There's also an extra saucepan of water in the kitchen. Do you have razors?"

They did, and toothbrushes, which was all they carried in the way of toilet articles. Curzon had given the thumbs-down to the idea of a small suitcase each, containing changes of linen and so on. A man with a suitcase was always likely to be stopped and questioned, especially after a bombing raid when looting was rife.

When McKenna pointed out that as they purported to be visitors from Hamburg luggage was almost essential, Curzon reminded him gently that the Hamburg artifice was only going to work on a superficial level. If they were taken and interrogated in depth nothing was going to help them, suitcase or no suitcase. They would, however, be issued handguns, a Walther pistol apiece and a single clip of ammunition. McKenna said thanks very much.

After Magda had gone, the American made a quick reconnaissance of the other rooms, including the German woman's bedroom. He rummaged through the coats and dresses in the wardrobe and handkerchiefs and underwear in the chiffonier. Most of the stuff was pretty old, but it was all clean.

Tucked away at the bottom of the laundry basket, covered with a couple of blankets, he was horrified to find the wireless transceiver, but he reasoned that in such a tiny apartment no hiding place was really safe. Magda's best cover was her membership in the Party and her work at the Food Office.

In the sitting room Fallon had opened the blackout blinds, something Magda had overlooked. Leaving them drawn during the hours of daylight would only attract attention.

"Anything?" he asked when McKenna returned.

"Apart from the fact that a kid of six would find the radio in thirty seconds flat with his eyes shut, no. There hasn't been a man in her bedroom for years, either, or I'm from Cleveland."

"Who were you expecting—Mata Hari?"

"Just someone a little different, I guess. This is the first time I've been up real close to a genuine anti-Nazi German willing to risk her neck by working for us, and I can't figure out what makes her tick. She seems—I dunno—so ordinary."

"That's the last word I'd use to describe her."

"Okay, point taken. But you know what I mean."

"You've got a romantic idea about undercover work, Sam. If she was persona grata in Berlin and spent her days drinking champagne and hopping in and out of bed with Nazi brass, that would be okay. But living out here in the sticks, working for the Food Ministry, that doesn't fit the picture. Right?"

McKenna grinned. "I guess I've seen too many movies."

Fallon agreed. "Anyway," he added, "ordinary or extraordinary, she's all we've got. We've got to trust her and her judgment."

"Maybe we should take a crack at getting to Schweinfurt ourselves."

"How? Hire a car?"

"Walk if need be. If she can't get us there until Wednesday and the Gestapo have got the Lunströms in a box, we'll be going to Switzerland by ourselves come Thursday. If there were fifty of us and we had maybe a week or two to work on the problem, that would be different. As it is, we're going to be in a hurry and that leads to mistakes. We go charging in like gangbusters waving a couple of lousy pistols and we end up shaking hands with a firing squad."

Fallon stretched wearily. "Sam, Sam, we never did have a week and we haven't got a fifty-strong back-up either. There are just the two of us. We know where the Lunströms are and that's a bonus we didn't have yesterday."

"They might move them around."

"Why should they? They won't be expecting trouble. Anyway, we can either pull it off in a day or we can't pull it off at all."

"When the hell did you become a philosopher?"

Fallon thought briefly of Yvette Blanchard. "A long time ago. If you can't have what you want you have to make the best of what you've got."

"Thank you, Ella Wheeler Wilcox."

Fallon chuckled. "Piss off and get some sleep."

Young Bruno Scheer, aged sixteen, had accumulated quite a few bits and pieces of Allied aircraft since 1940, and was tempted, when finding Fallon's flying suit, boots, gauntlets, and oxygen equipment, unearthed by one of his father's bullocks maddened during the air raid, to keep them for himself. But the penalties were too severe if he were ever found out, and he reluctantly told his parents of the cache. Parachute silk fetched a fortune on the black market, but Herr Scheer, a loyal member of the Party, had no hesitation in reporting the discovery to the head of the Frankfurt SD (Internal), Obersturmbannführer Eugen Meyer, early that Sunday morning, October 10.

A fastidious officer with a deserved reputation not only for brutality toward Allied airmen but for painstaking diligence, Meyer referred to his preliminary list of captured aircrew and was puzzled to see that not one had been picked up anywhere near Scheer's farm. Further, there were no reports of a bomber down in that area or anywhere close. Superficially that didn't mean much. The damned *Tommis* (and the daylight-raiding *Amis*) would and could fly on for fifty or sixty kilometers after their aircraft had received a mortal blow. And it was just conceivable—assuming that the bomber had crashed elsewhere—that only one man had succeeded in bailing out. Conceivable but unlikely.

He concluded that a thorough investigation was warranted and ordered a blanket search within a radius of two kilometers from the copse. His hunch paid off when he learned just before midday that a second set of flying gear had turned up.

Which meant two *Tommis* on the run. Or did it?

He was about to summon his adjutant and order the man to supervise personally a comprehensive search, using Waffen SS troops on this occasion and not those Wehrmacht idiots, when he remembered a recent directive from Brigadeführer Schellenberg.

Unearthing the file, he scanned it quickly. Well, perhaps that was the answer. Even if it wasn't, it could do no harm to let Berlin know immediately, let them decide. If it was a wild-goose chase he'd lost nothing. If the reverse, there might well be a commendation or a promotion in it for him.

He asked the switchboard to connect him with Schellenberg's Berkaerstrasse HQ as a matter of priority and was told, when through, that for the present all the Brigadeführer's calls were being rerouted to Prinz Albrechtstrasse, though the SD chief was at this moment in conference with the Führer. Would Meyer care to leave a message? Meyer would, and he was later to reflect that had it not been for a fugitive steer and an acquisitive youth the whole business might have turned out differently.

In Berlin, of course, they knew all about the Frankfurt raid long before midday and had assessed the damage down to almost the last brick. But only an estimated 200 to 250 bombers had hit this secondary target, and of far greater concern to those who attended the morning conference in the Reich Chancellery was the pounding the Ruhr had taken from the main force of 450 to 500 bombers. First reports suggested that the production capabilities of Essen, Dortmund, and Düsseldorf would be down by 25 percent. A senior member of Speer's staff was heard to remark that it would be better if Frankfurt were raided every night than the coal and steel complexes of Germany's industrial heart attacked. Eminently logical though this comment was, he was immediately rounded upon by Hitler and subjected to a severe dressing down. Wasn't the man aware that any—*any*—bombing raid on any—*any*—German city was not to be tolerated? Anyone thinking otherwise was stepping perilously close to treason and had better watch out for his head. Victories against the RAF and the US Eighth Air Force were just around the corner and whoever thought otherwise was a defeatist.

The main business of the morning over, Hitler closed the

conference and dismissed everyone save Göring, Speer, and the sinister Martin Bormann, and called in Mueller and Schellenberg.

Those officers who hung around the anteroom eating the sandwiches and drinking the heavy Munich beer which were always on hand timed the meeting with the two SS men at fifty minutes and heard, on more than one occasion, the Führer's voice raised in anger. Apparently the old guard were starting to quarrel among themselves and the Swedish Minister to Berlin's name was mentioned often.

When Schellenberg and Mueller emerged at a few minutes after one o'clock their expressions were grim. But if anyone could have seen them fifteen minutes later in Mueller's Prinz Albrechtstrasse office, they would have noticed a complete change of attitude.

Mueller reread the message from Meyer and said, "Well, do we tell him?"

"No, we can't be sure. The Führer likes only good news. This is no news at all."

"To you, perhaps not. To me, it says everything."

"Would you feel the same if the whole idea were yours and not mine?"

Mueller admitted he would not.

"I'm glad to hear it," commented Schellenberg. "We're close now, very close, but we must not run before our horse to market."

"So we do nothing?"

"There's nothing to be done."

Later that evening Magda Lessing returned to Wolfgangstrasse with the news that she had spoken to her chief at the Ernährungsamt and received his reluctant permission to revisit Schweinfurt. She could not, however, leave before Wednesday morning without arousing suspicion. She was very sorry, but there it was.

Fallon and McKenna consulted briefly and concluded that

London would have to be told. Curzon had expressly forbidden breaking radio silence except in an emergency, but he and Colonel Mortimer would be sitting in Bern worrying themselves sick for no reason unless they knew Thursday to be the earliest possible date for the border crossing.

Routed via the SOE's communications center at Bletchley Park, the signal arrived on Curzon's desk at 9:35 P.M., where the former banker had just finished reading a report from Wing Commander Bradford, whose Lancaster had returned safely. The signal was six words long: UNABLE TO REACH DESTINATION BEFORE WEDNESDAY.

That was too damned close for comfort, thought Curzon, and he immediately contacted Harry Mortimer. Was there, he asked, any chance of the Schweinfurt mission being put back? There was none. Subject to favorable weather conditions, the ball-bearing factories were due to be leveled on the fourteenth.

Eleven

Taking Reichsstrasse 26 east of Lohr-am-Main was not only the most direct route, Magda explained, but would bring them into Schweinfurt via the southwest suburbs and along Ernst Sachsstrasse, which housed one of the VKF ball-bearing factories. She said it mischievously and was obviously guessing, but in her own mind she had evidently made a connection —erroneous except in the most oblique way—between the Swedish-owned VKF works and the fact that Natalie and Alfred Lunström were Swedes. Fallon and McKenna ignored the bait but agreed that the most direct route suited them fine. After being forced to cool their heels for seventy-two hours, the sooner they reached Schweinfurt the better.

They had experienced no problems in getting out of Frankfurt, still smoldering in places, and neither did they expect any en route. The Food Ministry Opel was tanked up to the gunwales with gasoline and there were three spare jerrycans in the trunk. Magda also had a signed *laissez-passer* from her supervisor stating that she was on vital war work and entitled to gas on demand. He had balked a little at issuing this, but Magda argued it would make things easier if she had to travel around collecting evidence from barley growers. The promise of a few days in Bavaria had settled the issue.

It was an absolutely glorious mid-autumn morning with scarcely a cloud in the sky, and they made good time until held up by a roadblock outside Arnstein. A Wehrmacht patrol was looking for downed fliers from Saturday's raid, and the young Gefreiter in command was prepared to be awkward until McKenna bullied him into letting them jump the queue waiting to be searched, cursing him in gutter German and threatening him with a charge of sabotaging the war effort.

A few kilometers short of Schweinfurt they passed a small airfield on the left-hand side of Reichsstrasse 26. On the tarmac near a group of dispersal huts were parked three Ju 52 transports, Iron Annies as they were known in the Luftwaffe. A barbed-wire fence surrounded the field, but it didn't seem big enough to hold a bomber or fighter squadron and there were certainly no other aircraft of size to be seen, no other aircraft at all except for what Fallon recognized as a brace of Fieseler Storch reconnaissance planes and an Arado 66 trainer. He asked Magda if she knew what went on here.

"I believe they're doing some kind of experiments with airborne long-range radio. Voice, that is. You probably know that voice transmissions have a limited range and a working knowledge of Morse requires an intensive period of training."

Fallon did. A thorough grounding in Morse and an elementary wireless course were mandatory in the SOE and the OSS, though the knowledge was rarely used in the field.

"I think the idea is," went on Magda, "to extend the voice range so that anyone in an aircraft can transmit and receive without special schooling."

"Surely such experiments would be top secret," said Fallon curiously. "How come you know about them?"

"They're no secret in the Ernährungsamt. The victualing requirements for the base come through the office, giving the number of personnel, their function, and so on."

Thank God for German efficiency, thought Fallon. "Have you told London?"

"No. Don't you know I'm not allowed to transmit? Is it important?"

Fallon considered it damned important. If the Luftwaffe ever got into the position of being able to send voice signals over huge distances, a skilled wireless operator schooled in Morse would not be a crew requirement in a bomber. That sort of intelligence was always at a premium in the Ministry of Economic Warfare, because it meant more bombers in the sky or more guns on the same number of bombers. Weight that was not taken up by a wireless operator could be used for defensive armaments. The airfield would probably be worth a raid by a couple of squadrons of fast-flying Mosquitoes.

Five minutes later they were in Ernst Sachsstrasse, passing the VKF 2 works opposite the main railroad station. There was considerable evidence of bomb damage from the August raid, but nowhere near as much as one would have expected after a clobbering by 230 B-17s. Some rebuilding was in progress and, judging by the general air of activity in the vicinity, the plant was back to somewhere near full production.

For another twenty-seven or -eight hours, thought McKenna with grim satisfaction. Come tomorrow, my fine workers for the greater glory of the Third Reich, you'll be sitting in shit a block deep.

The route to the Ernährungsamt's apartment in Horst Wesselstrasse took them via Landwehrstrasse. Magda pointed out number 18 as they passed. The building was a big old structure on four floors, but there were no guards to be seen. Neither was there any sign of Natalie and Alfred Lunström, but this did not mean they were not inside. A thorough reconnaissance would have to be made later.

Swinging right-handed into the north-south thoroughfare that was Hermann Göringstrasse, they were slowed by a crowd some fifty strong outside St. Kilian's Church. It was spilling out into the road and totally of civilian makeup, and at first they thought it was a wedding, rare though anything other than civil ceremonies were in Germany. But when Magda was finally forced down from a snail's pace to full stop, it became apparent that the mob was in anything but a celebratory mood.

The object of their anger was flat against the heavy church doors, behind a cassocked clergyman who was remonstrating with the mob: a young man dressed in RAF blue.

It didn't take a million guesses to sketch in the scenario. The flier—doubtless one of those the Arnstein patrol was looking for—had bailed out and sought sanctuary in the church until he could be taken to a POW camp. Somehow he had been discovered and now the mob wanted vengeance for the US Eighth Air Force raid of two months ago.

The priest was doing his level best to defuse the situation, but the crowd were in no mood to listen to sermons on brotherly love and the Geneva Convention. They were ready for a neck-stretching party.

"He's a goner," said McKenna grimly. "Put your foot down, Magda. Let's get the hell out of here before we do something stupid."

Fallon told her to hold it and pull in to the curb. "Now," he said sharply when she hesitated.

He remembered the other kid in Frankfurt during the small hours of Sunday, how they had just walked on. Lunströms or no fucking Lunströms, he wasn't about to stand by and witness another flier lynched.

"What's on your mind?" asked McKenna casually. "Is this where the Seventh Cavalry ride in? That's supposed to happen in the last reel."

"I've rewritten the script. Besides, it's the last reel for that poor bastard unless we do something more than sit on our hands."

McKenna didn't hesitate. "Okay, how do we handle it?"

"Not we, me. One of us should stay with the car, ready to get out fast in case they won't cooperate."

"Okay, you stay."

"Not bloody likely. He's RAF, more my responsibility than yours."

McKenna sighed. "Jack, it's high time you realized that this war wasn't put on for your exclusive entertainment. Now cut the chatter and tell me what you've got in mind."

Fallon grinned. "We go up and take him. If anyone gives us an argument we flash our papers. We'd better make it fast, though. There might be some genuine troops or Gestapo on the scene in a minute."

"Lead on, Macduff. Keep the engine running, Fräulein."

The priest was of the Roman Catholic persuasion, and the RAF flier, a fair-haired twenty-four- or twenty-five-year-old sporting a fine ginger mustache and a four-day beard, wore the rank tabs of a flight lieutenant. The priest seemed relieved at the appearance of two men in plain clothes claiming to be Gestapo, though it was highly likely that if Fallon and McKenna had worn space helmets and announced they were from Mars, the clergyman would have been happy to see them. The flight lieutenant didn't appear to understand a word of German or the significance of the newcomers, but the mob sensed they were about to lose their victim and bellowed and screamed that they would handle the *Tommi* in their own way.

Fallon addressed the nearest group. "You're right to want to string him up. I can't blame you for that. But he's worth more to us alive than dead. Dead he's just a lump of meat; alive he might have something to tell us."

While Fallon was talking, McKenna took hold of the flight lieutenant by the arm and walked him unhurriedly to the waiting Opel. The mob jostled both of them and a few spat at the RAF officer, but it lacked leadership. And when Fallon jumped into the back seat and snapped at Magda to take off, only a handful bothered to hurl stones at the disappearing car.

The entire performance had taken less than two minutes.

Fallon slipped out of his raincoat. He was nearer the flight lieutenant's size than McKenna.

"Here," he said in his native tongue, "wear this over your uniform."

The RAF officer's jaw dropped a foot. "You're *English?*" he said incredulously.

"I am. The jolly green giant next to you comes from the other side of the pond. Now put the damned raincoat on before someone sees that uniform and smells a rat."

The flight lieutenant's name was Bob Travis and he had a thousand questions to ask. Fallon said he'd answer a few of them when they got to their destination, which they reached five minutes later.

The Ernährungsamt's apartment was a large three-bedroom affair on the third floor of a building overlooking a girls' high school. The larder was empty apart from some ersatz coffee and powdered milk, but the water and gas supplies were working and Magda got on with preparing hot drinks.

"You'll find a razor in one of those pockets," Fallon said to Travis. "Go to the bathroom and give yourself a shave. Take off the mustache too. There's not a lot we can do about the uniform right now, but you'll look a lot less conspicuous without the hairy lip."

"What are we going to do with him?" asked McKenna, when he and Fallon were alone.

"What the hell can we do except take him with us when we leave? It's a big enough car. One more passenger isn't going to make that much difference."

They discussed it for ten minutes, debated the pros and cons.

"Maybe he'd prefer to give himself up," said McKenna finally. "To the Luftwaffe police, I mean, not the mobs or the Gestapo. It will mean a POW camp, but he might prefer that to the alternative. If we're caught we're for the chop, capital C. Anyone with us will probably get the same treatment."

"Let's ask him, shall we?"

"Ask him what?" said Travis, coming back into the room. Now that he was clean-shaven Fallon could see they had overestimated his age by a couple of years. He could be no more than twenty-two. Fallon couldn't remember what it was like to be twenty-two.

"Ask him what?" repeated Travis.

"Major McKenna here thinks you might want to surrender to the Germans—to the Luftwaffe police, that is."

"Why should he think I'd want to do that? I'm not anxious to see the inside of a Jerry POW camp."

"There are worse fates if you're taken in our company."

Travis did not need it spelled out. An American and an Englishman in plain clothes deep inside Germany were not on holiday.

"I'll take my chances—if you'll have me along."

"It could be very dangerous."

"And piloting a bomber isn't?"

"Yes," said Fallon, "tell us about that. I assume you were on the Frankfurt raid, but you're a hell of a long way from there."

Travis explained that he was—had been—the skipper of a Lancaster in the third wave. Immediately after bombing the target they'd had an encounter with a night-fighter—a Ju 88 he thought it was, but he couldn't be sure. They didn't even get a good look at it. It had crept underneath the Lancaster and raked it from end to end with *schräge Musik*—slanting music—the Luftwaffe term for upward-firing guns.

The navigator and flight engineer were killed instantly and most of the instrument panel shot to hell in front of his eyes. How he'd escaped unscathed was a miracle.

"I didn't know which way was which, but I took a guess at what I thought was west and missed it by one hundred and eighty degrees." He shrugged apologetically. "You have to remember there was a lot going on.

"We'd lost the port outer as well, and the Ju 88 was still prowling around, obviously not going to quit until he destroyed us. So I did the only thing I could. I put the nose down and headed for what I thought was home."

To cut a long story short, he concluded, the nightfighter's next pass took out the port inner and he gave the order to abandon ship. He thought the bombardier and two of the air gunners made it, but he hadn't seen them since. Not surprising, really, as he had to keep the plane steady while everyone else bailed out. It must have covered ten or fifteen miles before it was his turn.

"Anyway, when I hit the deck I hadn't a clue where I was. I hid for a day and a night in a barn, then I started walking. But it was slow business as I could only travel during the hours of darkness. I had some idea about making for Switzerland, but with the Wehrmacht all over the countryside you can't always take the route you want. Still, you could have knocked me down with a feather when I arrived in Schweinfurt last night. This was one town I wasn't expecting to see this trip.

"I hid in the church because my watch was broken and I wasn't sure how long to daylight. I started off in the organ loft and ended up in the confessional. It might have been okay if only the priest had found me. I couldn't understand a word he was saying, but he seemed a decent enough sort. Not so one of his acolytes, who took one look at the uniform and made off to raise the lynch mob. I think the priest was trying to get me to a Wehrmacht barracks when they turned up. You know the rest."

Magda returned with the coffee as Travis finished his story. Watching the flight lieutenant lap at his cup greedily, she said something in rapid German.

"She wants to know when you last ate," Fallon said.

"Not properly since Saturday night—apart from some raw turnips and a bar of chocolate."

Fallon translated.

"We're going to need some provisions in any case," Magda said. "And I'd also better keep the car's tanks full. I took the liberty of appropriating food coupons from the office."

"Wasn't that risky?"

"Perhaps. But I can—what do you say—cook the books when I get back."

There was the question of getting in and out of the apartment for Fallon and McKenna, for time was very short and they had none to waste. As it was highly likely Magda would be doing most of the to-ing and fro-ing, it seemed logical that she should hang on to the only key. Travis wasn't going anywhere dressed as he was and speaking no German, but he had to know who was on the other side of the door before opening it. They settled on a Morse V—the opening di-di-di-dah chords to Beethoven's Fifth—which introduced the BBC's German language service each day. There was no danger, Magda assured them. In spite of laws proscribing such treason, most Germans listened to the BBC whenever they could and it was something of an in-joke to rap on a neighbor's door with a V. If Travis didn't hear it, he was to stay put and keep quiet.

Magda was first to leave, to avoid all three of them marching into the street as though on parade. When she got up after finishing her coffee, she seemed faintly amused that Travis immediately sprang to his feet also. She said something to McKenna before she went out.

"What was that all about?" asked Travis.

"She said it's been a long time since anyone bothered to stand up when she left a room and that it's nice to meet a gentleman, even if he is English. I don't think she rates Fallon and me."

"Am I allowed to ask who she is?"

"You're allowed, but you don't get an answer. Let's just say she's a charming German lady who appreciates good manners. If you're ever unfortunate enough to be picked up at a later date, you never met her. Understood?"

"Understood."

"And to forestall the other obvious question you have in mind," Fallon added, "neither are you permitted to ask what we're doing here or when you'll be getting out. We have a job to do. When it's done, we'll go. Not before."

Travis nodded somberly. "That sounds fair enough. I don't want to ask for any special favors. If it wasn't for you I'd probably be dead by now. I didn't thank you for getting me away from that mob, incidentally, but I do so now. I can well understand it would have been easier to drive on."

"You owe us one," said McKenna.

He had meant it as a flippant remark but Travis took him seriously. "Anything I can do."

"For the moment just keep your head down. Lock the door and keep it locked until you're sure we're on the other side. I'll leave you some cigarettes and if you get bored you can ogle the schoolgirls across the street. But for God's sake don't let anyone see you."

"You can bank on it."

Twelve

In spite of its strategic importance, Schweinfurt was a relatively small town whose commercial district occupied a square mile north of the River Main and east of the railway station. In the center of this was the Rathaus, the Town Hall, in Markt, just a few fast goose steps from the Nazi Party HQ and the principal Gestapo offices in Rückertstrasse.

Fallon and McKenna opted to split up, reasoning they could cover twice as much ground that way. McKenna would investigate the lay of the land around Landwehrstrasse 18, while Fallon would scout from the Rathaus down to the river and back again. It was important to familiarize himself with the town center, establish the location of one-way streets or streets closed due to bomb or other damage. If they managed to get the Lunströms free of the Gestapo and did not take Magda with them, they would feel mighty bloody sick running the Opel up a cul-de-sac.

It was two o'clock when they left Horst Wesselstrasse, and the afternoon was not living up to the morning's promise. It was still warm, but the sky was now overcast and there was the smell of rain in the air.

They had studied a large-scale map of the town back in London, together with what SOE called "program notes"—information gleaned from aerial photographs, agents, captured Luftwaffe fliers who came from the vicinity, and prewar Baedeker guides. There was something called the Rückert Monument opposite the Rathaus and a restaurant nearby. They would meet there in a couple of hours and compare notes.

Thirty minutes earlier the head of the Schweinfurt Gestapo, Hauptsturmführer Walter Knobel, had received a telephone call from Eugen Meyer in Frankfurt which kept him occupied for a quarter of an hour, part of it spent in argument. After he replaced the receiver he sat deep in thought for a long time, occasionally scratching his near-bald head with the stub of a pencil.

It was said of Knobel that he was the perfect secret policeman because he looked so ineffectual—middle-aged, on the short side, developing something of a belly due to an overfondness for beer. He was a cartoonist's dream of the henpecked husband and it was easy to imagine him being bullied by an overbearing wife and teased by his children. But this was an inaccurate picture. He was married, true, but he had not seen his wife, who lived in Berlin and with whom he got along famously, since late spring. Neither did he have any children. And beneath that shining dome was a keen mind.

If someone had described him as cruel he would have protested. He was a policeman in the Reich and the Reich was at war. It was well known that acts were committed in wartime that would not be tolerated or even contemplated when countries were at peace. If captured, Allied fliers and other enemies of the state were given short shrift at his hands; that was because this war was total. Blame it, not him.

Finally tossing away the pencil stub, he buzzed for his assistant, Unterscharführer Willi Heinnemann. Heinnemann was twenty-four, big and brawny and a little slow, but a good worker and a devout Party member. He also knew how to take orders, did Willi.

"Herr Hauptsturmführer?"

"Who's watching our guests, Willi?"

"Burgsdorf and Grauert. Is anything the matter?"

"I've just had a long conversation with Obersturm-bannführer Meyer in Frankfurt. Apparently Berlin is becoming concerned that we are treating our charges too harshly."

"That's nonsense, Herr Hauptsturmführer. They have everything they want."

"Except their freedom, Willi, which is evidently upsetting the Swedish government."

"Are we worried what the Swedish government thinks?"

"Our worries have nothing to do with it, Willi. When all this is over Berlin doesn't want our guests complaining to Stockholm that we were less than civil."

"When all this is over?" Heinnemann frowned, confused. "I'm afraid I don't understand. I thought we were keeping them as hostages to prevent the Allies bombing the ball-bearing factories."

"So we are, Willi, so we are. But from what I can gather there's more to it than that and their captivity is not to be for the duration. Sooner or later, perhaps in a couple of months, they will be freed and returned to Sweden. They are important people, Willi. Berlin does not want them going home with tales of how badly they were treated."

Knobel could see that Heinnemann was not following a word of this. To the Unterscharführer hostages were hostages, to be held until no longer needed. Setting them free in a couple of months would mean the big American Flying Fortresses again bombing Schweinfurt.

Patiently Knobel tried to explain. "You do understand that the Reich needs Swedish raw materials, do you not? That without them the Führer cannot prosecute the war to a successful conclusion?"

"Of course."

"And that the Lunströms are a powerful family in Sweden and elsewhere, very close to the Swedish government?"

"I've been told as much, Herr Hauptsturmführer."

"Then perhaps you can understand also that while the Swedes might accept our present actions as the natural consequence to their refusal to give us more matériel, they would be less than happy if the Lunströms return home and spread malicious lies about our keeping them constantly under lock and key. It might even go badly with you and me personally."

"But it wouldn't be true, Herr Hauptsturmführer," protested Heinnemann. "They are allowed out for exercise several times a day. They have a radio and they are given newspapers. The apartment is well stocked with food and liquor. They live better than we do."

"But they are not permitted to move around as we are."

Heinnemann shook his head in bewilderment.

"Never mind, Willi," said Knobel. "You'll see what I mean. Go and get the car. We'll pay our guests a visit."

It was a short five-minute drive from Gestapo HQ to Landwehrstrasse 18, and at the wheel of the unmarked staff car Heinnemann sincerely hoped that whatever Knobel had in mind as a result of his conversation with Frankfurt, it would not involve extra duties. They were severely undermanned as it was, the total Gestapo complement being six operational officers, himself and Knobel included. In view of Schweinfurt's size this would normally be enough, because there were always the regular police and the military to call on in an emergency. But since the Lunströms' arrival it was twelve-hour, two-man shifts—Burgsdorf and Grauert, Schumacher and Pickert. As the officer commanding, Knobel always made sure he got a good night's sleep and, as senior NCO, Heinnemann only filled in when one of the others was indisposed. But if Knobel planned to give the Lunströms greater freedom of movement, it could well mean more work all around. Which did not appeal to Heinnemann at all.

As long ago as 1940 the Gestapo had requisitioned the

whole of Landwehrstrasse 18, the original plan being to use the apartments—one to each floor—as accommodations for visiting dignitaries who did not wish to take their girl friends to hotels. But when it became apparent that no VIP in his right mind would want to spend much time so close to such an obvious target as the ball-bearing factories, the idea fell fallow. Even the presence of the Red Cross offices nearby did nothing to allay their fears that what might start out as an orgy could well end in a funeral. Gradually the due process of bureaucracy took over and now the first three apartments were used as a storage space for the overflow from Rückertstrasse. The fourth would have gone the same way except that Knobel, with characteristic insight, foresaw that it could be useful as an additional interrogation center, especially for German nationals who were suspected of subversion or treachery. He could then truthfully say to any callers at Rückertstrasse that the object of their inquiries was certainly not there.

Heinnemann parked the car and led the way upstairs to the top floor. Knobel brought up the rear, puffing like a grampus. There was an elevator, but it hadn't worked since the American raid in August. It was jammed right outside the Lunströms' door, and a handwritten note on the grille said it must be considered unsafe until examined by engineers.

So much for the famed German quality of getting things done, thought Knobel wryly.

Burgsdorf answered Heinnemann's knock and raised his eyebrows in surprise when he saw who the visitors were.

"Herr Hauptsturmführer," he said politely. "Is anything the matter?"

Knobel recalled Willi Heinnemann asking him exactly the same question twenty minutes ago. There must be something in his manner that caused his underlings to suspect the worst when he appeared.

"Matter, Burgsdorf? Am I so infrequent a caller that my presence causes alarm?"

"Of course not. It's just that—"

"It's just that you and Grauert were about to crack a bottle and play a hand of bridge with the Lunströms and I am interfering."

"Certainly not. Grauert and I—"

"It was a joke, Burgsdorf, for the love of God," snapped Knobel. "I am well aware that bridge is beyond your intellectual capabilities and that you consider wine a drink fit only for subject races such as the French and the Italians."

He brushed past Burgsdorf, who looked questioningly at Heinnemann. What the hell was eating the old man?

Knobel stood in the middle of the large sitting room. Heinnemann was certainly right in saying that the Lunströms lived better than the Gestapo, far better. The elevator might be out of order, but the rest of the building—at least this apartment—could have come from an Emil Jannings or a Hans Albers film. There were paintings on the wall, thick carpets underfoot, and the drinks table was groaning under the weight of alcohol. The furniture, pilfered from a source he had long forgotten, was quality, and this was only one of eight rooms. Beyond the sitting room was a drawing room and a dining room, three bedrooms, a bathroom and a kitchen. Berlin was making a mountain out of a molehill—or rather the Swedish government was. No one except the most important Party or SS official lived like this any longer.

He banished the thought as it occurred, considering it disloyal if not treason. Those with the highest office deserved the highest rewards. Anyone who thought otherwise was a communist.

"Where are they?" he asked Burgsdorf.

"In the drawing room, Herr Hauptsturmführer."

Knobel waited, but it was useless. They were recruiting the dregs nowadays. Heinnemann wasn't much, but he was a damned sight better than the others.

"Would you like me to fetch them myself?" he asked sarcastically.

The penny dropped. Inclining his head and mumbling

an apology, Burgsdorf went through to the drawing room and reappeared a moment later with Natalie and Alfred Lunström in tow. Behind them, Grauert stood in the open doorway.

At Knobel's side, Heinnemann sucked in a deep breath and whistled softly. There was nothing like Natalie Lunström in Germany, not to his knowledge. Perhaps Grauert, Burgsdorf, and the others were not so stupid doing shift work, not with bonuses like this.

No stranger to the workings of human nature, Knobel sensed his assistant's surge of barely controlled lust and was compelled to agree that Heinnemann was showing taste for the first time in his life. She looked not unlike a young Greta Garbo.

She was extremely tall, far taller than Knobel himself, and slim as a whip. Her hair was ash-blond and cut to shoulder length, where it swung freely whenever she tossed her head, as she was doing now. She had the nose and profile of an aristocrat, a woman born to give orders; and judging by the iridescent fire in her gray-green eyes, she had given many a man the runaround. She was wearing a beautifully tailored lightweight tweed suit, and around her throat was a double strand of pearls that must have cost as much as a front-line fighter. Knobel knew from her dossier that she was twenty-six and unmarried.

"Good afternoon, Fräulein Lunström, Herr Lunström," he said jovially. "I trust you are well?"

Alfred Lunström glared down at Knobel over the top of his half-moon spectacles, eyes as hard as flint. He was a tall, wiry man; thin-faced, cadaverous. Like an undertaker, thought the Gestapo captain, who privately rated the Swede as one of the toughest characters he had ever met, which in the Third Reich was saying something. He might be in his sixties and that shock of white hair could fool the unobservant into thinking he was ready for the old folks' home, but he was about as frail as a panzer division.

Lunström spoke perfect German, as did his niece. "What

kind of fool question is that, Knobel?" he asked. "How the devil can we be well when you keep us locked up here for twenty-three hours out of every twenty-four? A man of my age needs more than a quick trot around the block to keep him fit. Be careful, I might just drop dead on you, and if that happens it wouldn't be a day before you joined me."

Knobel refused to be baited. "You look perfectly healthy to me, Herr Lunström, though I agree the present arrangements are imperfect. Perhaps we might consider an alternative."

"The only alternative we wish to consider," put in Natalie," is an airplane to Stockholm. In that event, if Hitler is extremely lucky—and I mean *extremely*—the Swedish government might agree that this whole miserable affair was an unfortunate mistake and continue trading with Germany as before, providing my uncle and my father don't ask them to do otherwise."

"You overestimate Sweden's bargaining powers, Fräulein."

"And you underestimate my family's importance."

"No, I don't," said Knobel slowly. "I certainly don't." He beckoned Burgsdorf and Grauert to one side. "Take a couple of hours off," he told them. "If we're not here when you return, wait by the telephone."

The two Gestapo men were surprised at this reprieve from a dreary duty, but they were not about to look a gift horse in the mouth. They left the apartment before the Hauptsturmführer could change his mind.

Knobel turned to Heinnemann. "See about some coffee, Willi. The real stuff. I'm sure you'll find some in the kitchen."

To get there Heinnemann had to pass within a few feet of Natalie. As he did so he caught a whiff of expensive perfume, a strong, heady smell that made him weak with excitement. Christ, what he wouldn't give for a night with her. An hour. It would be like dipping it in honey, and all the more sweet because it was obvious she scarcely knew he existed.

171

Well, given a chance, he'd teach the aristocratic bitch a few tricks she'd never forget.

"Now, perhaps we can sit down and discuss your complaints," said Knobel lightly. "I'm not as young as I was and those stairs have made my legs ache. Please," he added.

Natalie glanced at her uncle, who shrugged his shoulders and sat on the sofa. After a moment's indecision Natalie joined him. Knobel chose an armchair opposite.

"You will appreciate," he said, "that it gives the Reich government no pleasure to keep you here under these circumstances, but that we are living in hard and difficult times. However, I am empowered to grant any small requests that will make your hopefully brief stay less onerous."

"You can begin by answering the question we've asked every day since your thugs arrested us in Frankfurt." Natalie's eyes flashed angrily. "Why are we being held at all? We are citizens of a neutral country on legitimate business in Germany, and all we've heard so far is that our papers are not in order and some nonsense about a suspicion of espionage. Which is a downright lie, as you well know."

"Natalie," said her uncle gently, "we've been over this a dozen times ourselves. Berlin wants something from your father—or perhaps wants him to use his influence in Stockholm. They'll hold on to us until they get what they want. That's correct, isn't it, Knobel?"

"I don't know the details, Herr Lunström," answered Knobel truthfully. "My function is merely that of guardian—"

"Jailer," interrupted Natalie.

"Untrue, Fräulein. I can assure you that if you were in one of our prisons you would find life far less agreeable. But I digress. Arguing over definitions will get us nowhere. I am here to see what I can do to make your life easier. If you want for nothing I am wasting my time." Knobel started to get to his feet.

"Wait," said Lunström. "Perhaps there are one or two

things." He turned to his niece. "My dear, would you be good enough to help—what's his name?—young Heinnemann with the coffee while I have a word in private with Knobel?"

Natalie looked doubtful and Knobel understood the reason for her hesitation. "You have nothing to fear from Heinnemann, Fräulein. If he says or does anything to offend you, he will answer for it with his head."

"Please, my dear," said Lunström.

Natalie nodded and went out.

"That was one of the things I wanted to talk to you about, one area where you can help," said Lunström. "My niece is a beautiful woman. It disturbs her that two of your men are always in the apartment, watching her every move. She can hardly go to the bathroom without making a public announcement of her intentions, which is embarrassing to put it at its mildest."

"And your suggestion, Herr Lunström?"

"That your men stand guard outside—either outside the front door or at street level. That's the only way out apart from climbing across the rooftops, which is hardly practical for an old man and a young girl, even if we had anywhere to go once out of the building."

Knobel considered the request. It was well within his brief. "I think that could be arranged," he said.

"I would deem it a favor."

"Then it's done. Is there anything else?"

"The matter of fresh air and exercise I mentioned earlier. We need to get out of the apartment more often. We have adequate stocks of food here, of course, but Fräulein Lunström has to do all the cooking and a break from that would do her the world of good. May I therefore suggest we be permitted to lunch or dine out more regularly—or, if that's impossible, perhaps take tea in the open? I assure you that any small courtesy will not be forgotten."

That too was within the guidelines suggested by Obersturmbannführer Meyer.

"Why not?" said Knobel expansively. "In fact, we shall do it immediately after finishing coffee—before it rains. There's an excellent terraced restaurant across the square from the Rathaus. Would that suffice? You understand that we shall have to be with you at all times—or at least within earshot?"

"Of course."

"Then that's settled," said Knobel, feeling pleased with the way things had turned out. Powerful or not, people were all pretty much the same when in captivity. Even if he was accustomed to caviar and truffles, give a starving man a piece of dry bread and he licked your hand.

Lunström smiled his gratitude.

McKenna reached Landwehrstrasse 18 at two-thirty, five minutes too late to see Knobel and Heinnemann arrive. But there was something about the car parked outside the entrance to the building which intrigued him. It flew no pennant, nor was it in any other way identifiable as an official vehicle, but he was familiar with the transport the Gestapo used in France and the Low Countries and would have wagered a year's pay that whoever had driven up in the unmarked car was now calling on the Lunströms.

Taking up a position on the far side of the street, he was rewarded almost immediately by the appearance of Burgsdorf and Grauert, who were laughing at some private joke. If those two weren't Gestapo he'd apply for a commission in the Wehrmacht.

After pausing to light cigarettes, they walked south along Landwehrstrasse in the direction of the river. He gave them twenty minutes to make sure they were not just stretching their legs, then crossed the road to the entrance to number 18.

The street doors were hinged back and there was no sign of life inside. Looking up, he saw that while the windows on the first three floors were shuttered, those on the top floor were not.

Shit, he thought, nothing ventured, nothing gained, and he went inside, ready with a story about looking for a fictitious Herr Schmidt if confronted. He could hardly use his phony Gestapo papers here.

The elevator was out of order, but twisting his neck and peering up the shaft, he thought he could see the cage on the fourth floor. That made things tricky, leaving the stairs the only way up and down.

Taking them two at a time, he found himself on the first floor, outside the front door of an apartment designated A. There was a slot for a nameplate below the knocker, but it was empty. A hasty reconnaissance of the corridor revealed that this was the only apartment on the floor, and he guessed correctly that the layout was identical on the other levels.

He took a deep breath and rapped on the door. It was no more than a tap, but to McKenna it sounded like the drums heralding Armageddon.

No one answered. He tried again and waited. Still there was no sign of life. He would have staked money that the first three floors were uninhabited, but conjecture was one thing, proof another.

From his pocket he brought out the same tool he had used to gain access to Kirsty Gottmar's Stockholm apartment and inserted it in the lock. It was going to be just too damned bad if a pajama-clad night worker was on his way to see who the caller was.

Thirty seconds later he was inside. As soon as his eyes became accustomed to the darkness he saw that no one had lived here for months, probably years. They were using the place as a storeroom.

Pulse racing and fully aware he was taking an appalling risk that could blow the entire operation, he made the same discovery in the second- and third-floor apartments. He was tempted to look through some of the filing cabinets, but he had asked the gods for too much already, and demanding more would incur their wrath.

He was halfway up the stairs between the third and fourth floors when some sixth sense screamed a warning. The sound of a door opening followed by voices stopped him in mid-stride. For a fraction of a second he froze, caught in a no man's land of indecision. Then his brain snapped into gear and he ran down to the third-floor apartment, reaching for his burglar tool as he did so. If he tried to gain the street he could run into the other pair coming back.

At first the lock refused to budge. Beads of sweat broke out across his forehead. The people above were descending the stairs, still talking in German.

Concentrate, you bastard, he urged, and a moment later the door clicked open.

But there was no time to re-engage the lock, not without being heard. All he could do was push the door as close to the jamb as possible and hope for the best.

He edged along the wall, flattening himself against it. Outside the footsteps came to a halt and a voice asked, "What the hell's that door doing open, Heinnemann?"

"I don't know, Herr Hauptsturmführer."

"Well, shut it, man, shut it. And make sure it stays shut."

McKenna's nerve ends were shrieking. He tensed, prepared to fight his way out. But the lock clicked into place and the footsteps receded.

It took him a few seconds to get his breathing under control. Dear Christ, that was too close for comfort.

Crossing to the shuttered windows, he peered through the slats. His angle of vision was restricted, but he could just make out the group getting into the staff car: a small middle-aged man, a much taller and younger one, and two people who had to be Natalie and Alfred Lunström.

His next move was obvious. Having got this far without

being discovered, he had to take a look inside the fourth-floor apartment. Unless they were garrisoning the entire Schweinfurt Gestapo up there, chances were it was now empty and he might never get another opportunity as heaven-sent as this.

Two minutes later he was helping himself to a large slug of brandy, drinking straight from the bottle and making sure he replaced it exactly where he found it.

The Nazis were certainly not making the Lunströms suffer, he concluded after inspecting each of the rooms. There was enough liquor on the table to throw a fair-sized party, the bed linen was clean, and there were items in the pantry he hadn't seen since before the war, many of them British and American brands. There were jars of honey, jam, marmalade; tins of ox tongue, calves' liver, several varieties of fish. The bread was fresh and so was the milk. The Lunströms could hardly live much better than this in Stockholm. Except of course in Stockholm they could choose their own company.

He examined the windows. Only in one of the bedrooms were there bars and they were very old, presumably put there to prevent some previous occupant's small child from killing itself. The reason the others were unbarred soon became apparent. There was no way in or out via any of them, not unless you were a cat or could find some other method of leaping twenty feet to the adjacent building, and someone had taken the precaution of dismantling the fire escape a dozen feet from the ground.

He realized he was allowing his mind to wander, considering problems that were better left until later. He had accomplished in a few short minutes more than he would ever have dreamed possible half an hour ago, but now it was time to leave.

On the way out he saw the note propped up against the telephone cradle. It was addressed to somebody named Grauert, instructing him to call Hauptsturmführer Knobel at the Rückert Restaurant as soon as he returned.

Thirteen

Fallon in the meantime had combed the town center with the diligence and attention to detail of a municipal surveyor planning a by-pass. By 3:45 P.M. he reckoned he knew every side street in the rectangle bordered by the museum and public baths in the north and the Bayerische Staatsbank and hydro-electric generating station overlooking the river.

As far as he could see, there were no major obstructions blocking a quick getaway, but he would hate to have to throw a car around these narrow thoroughfares with the Gestapo or the military on his heels. Which might in any case, he thought ruefully, be anticipating events unwisely.

As 4 P.M. approached, he made his way toward the tree-lined square which contained the Rückert Monument, a popular gathering place judging by the number of people sitting on the public benches and on the terrace of the open-air restaurant. As was the custom since the Nazis came to power, the restaurant was bedecked with blood-red flags each sporting a black swastika in the middle of a white circle. There must have been two dozen of them, most not much smaller than the gigantic banner flying from the Rathaus itself. Fallon thought cynically that if the Allies could corner the market in cotton, the Third Reich would collapse overnight.

McKenna was already there, waiting by the monument, and even from a distance Fallon could see the expression of grim satisfaction on his face.

"Don't tell me," said the SOE major, sotto voce. "While you were waiting you entered the local lottery and picked up first prize."

"Better than that." The American grinned. "I don't want to point, but do you see the terrace of the restaurant over there?"

Fallon said he did.

"Okay, start from the left and work your way along. At the fifth table there's a group of four, three men and a woman. Got them?"

"Yes?"

"Time to hang on to your hat, old buddy, because the guy with the snowy hair is Alfred Lunström and the woman is none other than his niece Natalie. The big bruiser's called Heinnemann, and I've got good reason to believe that the little fat Kraut is a Gestapo captain by the name of Knobel." McKenna waited for a reaction.

Fallon looked him up and down. "I see you've been wasting your time again."

Keeping a weather eye on the terrace, they promenaded around the square while McKenna explained his movements since two o'clock.

"And when I saw the note from our friend the Hauptsturmführer," he concluded, "I put two and two together, figured that even if there was more than one Rückert Restaurant in town chances were they'd be having their tea party close to Gestapo HQ, and came straight here. I'll tell you something, though. There were a couple of minutes a while back that I thought were going to be my last."

It was a magnificent individual achievement to have accomplished so much in such a short time, and Fallon said so.

McKenna gave a self-mocking bow. "Just trying to make up for getting into the war late."

They took another turn around the square. The Lunströms and the Gestapo looked set to stay until it got dark. They weren't saying much to each other, but, that aside, they were acting like any other group of people enjoying a relaxing afternoon.

Fallon remarked how cozy it all seemed to be. "Perhaps cozy's the wrong word. I admit they don't look like bosom pals, but I guess I was expecting them to be surrounded by a dozen armed stormtroopers."

McKenna confessed that this had troubled him to begin with. "Then I remembered that Curzon asked Felix Lunström to make a few belligerent noises via the Swedish Foreign Office. It appears it worked and someone in Berlin has decided to soft-pedal security. Which could be in our favor."

Fallon agreed. "If Landwehrstrasse 18 is likely to be as hard to crack as you say, our best bet's right here and now. But we can't just walk up and ask them to come for a stroll round the block."

"Knobel and the other guy wouldn't be too much trouble to take out," suggested McKenna. "Fake a fight. While I keep them occupied, you could be long gone with the Lunströms."

Fallon shook his head doubtfully. In the first place there were a lot of uniforms around, and Magda and the Opel were not. "And in the second place," he said, "there might be more of them than just—what did you call them?—Knobel and Heinnemann. The Gestapo are great believers in insurance. But the biggest drawback is the fact that the Lunströms don't know we're here. If we try to drag them off by force they'll wonder what the hell's going on and maybe kick up a fuss. If I have to sit down and explain who we are, we'll all end up being given the rubber-truncheon treatment."

McKenna snapped his fingers. "The note I told you about was an instruction to someone named Grauert to phone Knobel here, so what's wrong with anticipating him? One of us finds a booth and puts in the call. That'll at least get Knobel off the terrace long enough to maybe slip a message to the Lunströms, let them know someone's around."

"And the big guy? They're not going to oblige us by both leaving."

"Christ, do you want sugar on it?"

Fallon was about to retort that he didn't want sulphuric acid on it either, when McKenna nudged him. "Hold it. I think they're moving."

But it was only Knobel and Heinnemann who were getting to their feet, apparently in response to some request made by a uniformed waitress. It didn't take long to figure out that Grauert had pre-empted their proposed fake phone call by making the legitimate one himself.

Knobel disappeared inside the restaurant while Heinnemann stood by the door, near enough to hear if his chief wanted him but also in a position to keep an eye on the Lunströms.

Long before McKenna urged him to hurry, Fallon was already at work with a pencil and a scrap of paper.

"Friends at hand," he scribbled. "Get rid of your guards by midnight."

It sounded melodramatic, but that couldn't be helped. Neither could he risk a word-of-mouth message, which might be misinterpreted or interrupted before he could finish.

He showed McKenna what he had written.

"We're going to try for the apartment?"

"I don't see we have a choice. We can't take them here, and Christ knows if they'll be allowed out again today. It has to be the apartment and it has to be tonight. Keep the big fellow occupied."

"Leave him to me."

Moving quickly, they crossed the square, McKenna slightly ahead. He bounded up the steps to the terrace as though anxious to answer a call of nature, barging into Heinnemann with such force that the German was carried back through the door of the restaurant and almost fell.

"Sorry," said McKenna, his hands outstretched in apology. "I wasn't looking where I was going."

"You should be more careful," spluttered Heinnemann indignantly. "This isn't a bear garden."

"I said I was sorry." McKenna put an edge on his voice. "If you'd find a seat instead of blocking the doorway you wouldn't get hurt."

Heinnemann's eyes flickered with alarm when he realized he could no longer see the terrace.

"It's you who'll get hurt, my friend, unless you get out of the way."

"Now wait a minute."

Heinnemann tried to brush past, but McKenna, apparently by accident, moved the same way—and then back again as the German changed direction. They engaged in a sort of crab dance. It was a scene that was enacted fifty times a day on busy streets and it occupied only ten seconds. But they were more than enough.

The moment Heinnemann stumbled back through the doorway, Fallon had made for the Lunströms' table, the scribbled note crushed in his hand. Alfred was facing the square, but Natalie could see him coming.

When he was level with the table he faked bumping into it, muttered his regrets, and thrust the note into Natalie's hand, saying quickly in Swedish, "Hide it and read it later."

And then he was gone, continuing on down the far steps and into the square, but not before he had registered a pair of wide, startled eyes looking up at him fearfully. He was staggered by the woman's beauty. The dossier photograph did her no justice at all.

Behind him Heinnemann had regained the terrace and McKenna was complaining loudly to anyone who cared to listen as he left the restaurant that if *that* was the caliber of

182

clientele the Rückert was letting through its doors nowadays, in future he would be taking his business elsewhere.

By the time Knobel finished his phone conversation with Grauert, the note was safely tucked away in Natalie's purse, Alfred Lunström was wondering if his ears had deceived him, and Fallon and McKenna were on their way back to Horst Wesselstrasse.

It wasn't much of a plan, Fallon was thinking a couple of hours later. In truth, it was no plan at all, but it was the best they were going to come up with. They had chewed over the problem from every angle, but there was nothing to do but go in via the ground-floor entrance and straight up the stairs, bluffing their way through if they could, fighting if necessary. The alternative suggestion proposed by McKenna—that of somehow getting across from the roof of the adjacent apartment building and in one of the unbarred windows—begged too many questions. In the first place the Lunströms might not have managed to get rid of their guards, whose brief could be—this was an unknown factor—to remain with their charges *inside* the apartment at all times. If that was the case, they were wasting energy by not taking the most direct route. In the second place, making the leap across twenty or so feet from one building to another in pitch darkness was an unacceptable risk. They might find a ladder or planks or some other method of bridging the gap on the roof of the adjacent building, but that was asking a lot of fate.

Fallon was also concerned about the total number of guards, though McKenna was inclined to believe there were never more than two.

"Remember, I saw two leave earlier and there were no others in the apartment when I broke in."

Two, in any case, would be the logical number to look after an old man and a girl. Any more would be overkill.

"But the damned nuisance of it," he added, "is that we don't know where they are and won't until we're on top of them. If they're inside the apartment we don't have to pussy-foot around on the stairs. If they're outside, once they're dealt with we don't have to worry about anyone waving guns in our faces when we knock on the door."

"And if there are more than two?" queried Fallon.

"Why don't you take a look?" asked Flight Lieutenant Travis.

They had almost forgotten he was sitting there listening to every word. Magda was in one of the bedrooms catching up on some sleep, and Fallon and McKenna had conducted their entire discussion in English.

"How do you suggest we do that?" asked Fallon.

"By using the fire escape. I heard Major McKenna say there was a fire escape that goes up the outside of the building."

"I also said that some security-conscious bastard had thoughtfully removed the bottom dozen feet, maybe more."

"That doesn't matter. What sort is it, a ladder or steps?"

"Iron steps."

"Next to the wall?"

"Of course. That's the point of a fire escape, isn't it? It wouldn't be a whole hell of a lot of use if it was away from the wall."

"Hm. A ladder's easier because of the wide spaces between the rungs, but steps shouldn't be that difficult. It's just a question of being a bit more accurate with your aim."

McKenna looked at Fallon. "Am I missing something here or is he genuinely talking gibberish?"

"You're not missing anything. Spell it out, Travis," said Fallon. "They might enjoy guessing games in the RAF, but we're simple folk who like the *i*'s dotted and the *t*'s crossed."

Travis grinned self-consciously. "It's something I remember from boarding school. Our fire escapes used to finish some distance from the ground also, the theory being that it was easy to drop the last eight or ten feet but it prevented intruders getting in. Actually, they were less concerned about intruders—who the devil wants to break into a school?—than boys trying to sneak back into the dormitories long after lights out. But they weren't very bright. We simply got hold of a length of rope and made a grappling iron, using anything as a weight and muffling the sound by wrapping it in old rags. Then we slung the 'iron' over the lower rungs of the ladder and walked up the wall onto the fire escape proper. I haven't seen any ropes around here, but it would be the easiest thing in the world to knot a few sheets together. You can use what you like as a weight."

McKenna shook his head sorrowfully. "You know, he's just made me feel my age. Now why the hell didn't we think of that?"

"Comes of not having a privileged education," answered Fallon. "Which room leads out to the fire escape?"

It was the sitting room. McKenna drew a rough sketch to show Fallon the layout, how the sitting-room windows overlooked a narrow alley.

"Then that's our way in and maybe out too," said Fallon. "Thanks, Travis."

The young flight lieutenant smiled his appreciation. "Think nothing of it. Just look upon it as my entrance fee."

That was something else they had to discuss. If all went well, they could be leaving Landwehrstrasse 18 in one hell of a big hurry. Magda would be needed with the car somewhere in the vicinity, but allowing Travis to remain with her was asking for trouble. If she was spotted and questioned by a patrol, she should be able to bluff it out, being a German citizen on legitimate business in Schweinfurt. But Travis was dressed in RAF uniform and did not speak the language. They could overcome the first disadvantage by continuing to let him wear Fallon's raincoat, but there was nothing they could do about the second. If he opened his mouth, that was it, and they could not jeopardize the entire mission for the sake of one junior officer. He would have to stay in Horst Wesselstrasse. They would try to come back for him later.

Travis took it all philosophically. "Don't worry about it. I'm better off than I was this morning, at any rate. If worst comes to worst, I'll try to make it on my own."

Fallon checked his wristwatch. It was seven-thirty, time for them all to get some rest. It could be a long night.

At seven-forty in the Rückertstrasse Gestapo HQ, Knobel received the answer to the call he had placed earlier. Willi Heinnemann was in the next room reading the day's edition of the *Völkischer Beobachter* when Knobel appeared in the doorway.

"What time did you arrange for the shifts to change, Willi?"

"Ten o'clock, Herr Hauptsturmführer. I told Schumacher and Pickert to go straight there and Grauert and Burgsdorf to call it a night when they were relieved. Was that in order?" he asked anxiously.

"Perfectly. Do Schumacher and Pickert understand they are not to trouble the Lunströms with their presence, that they are to keep watch from the ground-floor main entrance?"

"Yes, sir. They grumbled a bit, but I soon shut them up. I also took the precaution of asking the exchange to disconnect the telephone and leave it disconnected."

"Well done, Willi. I should have thought of that myself. Our guests may be very important people, but we can't have them phoning Stockholm, can we?"

Heinnemann had a girl to see tonight and wanted to get away early.

"I'm afraid you'll have to cancel it," Knobel told him. "We're expecting visitors. Well, one visitor."

"Tonight, sir?"

"Tonight, Willi."

"May I know who and why, Herr Hauptsturmführer?"

"Soon, Willi, soon. When I know more. But I can tell you one thing. This business is deeper—much, much deeper —than we thought."

At 11:45 P.M. Fallon and McKenna with Magda Lessing at the wheel left Horst Wesselstrasse in the Opel. Because of the severe shortage of gasoline in Germany, civilian vehicles were not encouraged to travel at night, and all three occupants of the car were edgy until Magda finally parked it in Ludwigstrasse, opposite the Fensterwerk–Eisenbau Hermann Vogel, makers of steel window frames. From there it was a two-minute walk to Landwehrstrasse 18.

After she killed the lights Fallon gave Magda her final instructions. "I don't know how long it's going to take us to get in there or what we'll meet on the way, but if we're not back in a couple of hours we've run into trouble and won't be returning. In that event forget Travis—he knows the score—and go like a bat out of hell back to Frankfurt and wireless London we didn't make it. That's most important. Make whatever excuse you like to your boss at the Food Office, but it's vital London know before morning that the Lunströms are still in Schweinfurt."

Not that Curzon would be able to do much, he thought, but at least he'd be in the picture. As for himself and Sam McKenna—well, they'd be beyond making decisions.

They'd torn three bedsheets into strips and plaited them, fashioned a makeshift rope fifty feet long which McKenna was now wearing coiled around his body under his raincoat. They had tested its strength, played tug-o'-war with it, and it had held. For a weight they were using a marble doorstop wrapped in a pillowcase to deaden the noise. This Fallon was carrying.

"Let's make it once around the block to see what we can see," suggested the American.

It was a sensible decision and one that paid off, for as they passed the entrance to Landwehrstrasse 18 they caught sight of a couple of cigarette ends glowing in the darkness beyond. They had no way of knowing that these belonged to Pickert and Schumacher, both cursing whatever idiot had decreed that henceforth watches would be stood in the open.

"That's looking hopeful," muttered Fallon as they swung left-handed into Theresienstrasse. "If the buggers are guarding the main door, chances are there's no one in with the Lunströms."

McKenna led the way down the alley which would bring them out underneath the fire escape.

"We'll soon know," he said. "I just hope to Christ I've judged the distance from the ground correctly."

He had, with a few feet to spare.

After freeing himself from the sheets and tying on the weight, it took him a couple of abortive attempts to get the range. But at the fourth try the doorstop sailed through the gap between the first and second steps and down to where Fallon was ready to catch it.

Grasping both ends of the now double-strength sheets, McKenna clambered up the wall. Fallon quickly followed him. They pulled the sheets up behind them and stashed the bundle beneath the window ledge of the first-floor apartment.

At the top of the fire escape the sitting room's blackout curtains were open a crack, leaving enough of a gap for them to be able to see into the room. Natalie Lunström was curled up on a sofa. She appeared tense and ill at ease, as well she might, thought Fallon. Her uncle was standing over her, drinking from a cup. There was no one else in sight.

Fallon felt a surge of wild exultation. The Swedes had somehow got rid of the guards. It was going to be all right.

"Here goes," he murmured, and rapped on the window.

The effect on the Lunströms was electrifying. Natalie sat bolt upright as though stung, clasping her hand to her mouth, and her uncle came close to dropping the coffee cup. But he recovered his composure quickly, came across to the window, and opened it.

Sixty seconds later Fallon had explained who he and McKenna were and their purpose in Schweinfurt. Natalie was silent and appeared stunned by it all, but her uncle had a dozen questions he wanted to ask.

They were speaking in English and McKenna had to cut the old man short. "You'll forgive me, sir, but we haven't got time to go into all that now. We'll explain as we go."

Alfred Lunström appeared to be in no hurry. "Go where —Major McKenna, is it?" McKenna nodded. "Go where, Major McKenna? You're in the middle of Germany. I admit you've been extremely resourceful up to now, but it's stretching the imagination to its limits to think you can get us all away."

Natalie started to say something, but her uncle silenced her with an imperious wave of his hand.

Fallon couldn't believe what he was hearing and fought back an angry retort. Christ, they'd risked their necks to get this far, and here was this stupid old fart starting a debate.

He swallowed hard. "You don't understand, sir. Whether we succeed in getting out of Germany is immaterial for the moment, but we have to get you away from Schweinfurt before the US Eighth Air Force pays a return visit to the ball-bearing factories, which I assure you will be very soon."

Lunström frowned. "Ridiculous, Major Fallon. My German captors have informed me that the Allies know where my niece and I are being held. They would not risk killing us in a bombing raid. You have your facts wrong."

Fallon was staggered. This was not at all the reaction he had expected and he felt like taking the scrawny old man by the neck and wringing it. He controlled his temper with difficulty.

"You have my word," he said, gritting his teeth, "that my information is accurate. I have it on the highest authority that the Americans will be here tomorrow afternoon. In a little over a dozen hours this area of Schweinfurt will be a wasteland."

That seemed to have shaken the old bastard, he thought, watching Lunström's expression change.

"You're sure of this?"

"Absolutely."

The Swede's smile was reminiscent of a tiger upwind of the watering hole while the smaller animals were feeding.

"Thank you, Major Fallon," he said.

There was the sound of a doorknob turning. Fallon and McKenna whipped around in time to see three figures emerge from the drawing room. Two of them they recognized—Knobel and Heinnemann—the latter holding an MP 40 Schmeisser machine pistol. The third was Eugen Meyer, who was dressed in the full uniform of a lieutenant colonel in the SS with its SD cuff patch.

It was he who spoke, in heavily accented English. "Yes, Major Fallon, thank you very much. Reichsmarschall Göring will be able to make good use of that information."

Fourteen

Thirty seconds passed in horrified silence before Fallon and McKenna fully realized they had walked into a carefully laid trap, that far from being held in Schweinfurt against their will, the Lunströms were part of the plot, and that a senior SS officer wearing security markings had just been told the date, almost the hour, that the US Eighth Air Force would be carrying out a bombing raid against the ball-bearing factories. It was a revelation that could mean the total destruction of every plane and man in the fleet, because if the Eighth were in one place they could not be in another, and the Luftwaffe could withdraw fighters from other sectors with impunity.

Fallon looked slowly from Alfred to Natalie Lunström, whose beauty suddenly seemed cold and distant, and wondered in passing if Felix Lunström was also involved.

"You bastards," he said softly to no one in particular.

Though equally stunned, McKenna had a fast recovery rate and was not about to let it go at that. He could see only one weapon, Heinnemann's Schmeisser, and reasoning that he would never get a better chance than right now launched himself at the Gestapo Unterscharführer.

But Knobel was more than half prepared for such heroics and stuck out a foot. McKenna tripped over it and Heinnemann finalized the argument by rapping the American behind the ear with the MP 40's butt. Remembering his confrontation with McKenna earlier in the day, he was about to finish the job when Meyer interfered.

"Enough! They have much to tell us before they face a firing squad."

Fallon helped McKenna to his feet. "Take it easy, Sam. You're not going to do the cause a lot of good as a corpse."

Meyer ordered them searched, and both men were relieved of their pistols and phony documents. Knobel scrutinized the latter items carefully and was amused to see that the Allied agents were traveling as Gestapo officers. But the forgeries were good, very good indeed.

"Take them and lock them in one of the bedrooms," he instructed Heinnemann, *"but be careful.* If they as much as blink without your permission, shoot them."

"There'll be no shooting," said Meyer sharply. "I thought I just made it clear I do not want them harmed until after a full interrogation."

Meyer outranked Knobel considerably, but the Gestapo captain was far too old and wily a hand to be intimidated on his own territory, especially as he could justifiably complain that this entire operation had been conducted between Berlin and Frankfurt without his knowledge. Even now he scarcely knew more than he had a dozen hours ago. Mueller and Schellenberg might be working in close harmony for the moment, but in a week or two it would be back to the old infighting.

"Shoot them in the legs, Willi," he said quietly, "but do as you're told and shoot them if they cause trouble."

Meyer clicked his tongue in annoyance but let it pass. He nodded to Heinnemann, and the Unterscharführer marched Fallon and McKenna off at gunpoint, the American leaning on Fallon for support.

Meyer beamed at the Lunströms. "Congratulations. You both played your parts magnificently."

"Don't include me in that," said Natalie icily. "Until a few hours ago I had no idea I was playing a part at all."

"So you said earlier," Meyer acknowledged.

"And until a few minutes ago," Natalie added, "I had no idea what that part entailed."

Meyer's eyes narrowed.

"My niece is young," put in Alfred Lunström hastily. "She has yet to learn that war—like business—involves sacrifices. There are no rewards for those who come second."

"You're planning to murder hundreds of airmen," Natalie accused.

"Those same airmen," countered Meyer, "were—are—planning to murder, as you call it, hundreds of civilians here in Schweinfurt tomorrow. You yourself would have been included in that number."

Natalie disagreed. "No, I would not. Neither would my uncle. The Allies sent those two men to ensure we were not here." She turned on her heel and walked across to the window. With a sudden angry movement she closed the curtains, comprehending now why they had been left partly open in spite of the blackout regulations.

There was a moment's uneasy silence, broken by Knobel. "All this is irrelevant, Herr Obersturmbannführer, and we are wasting precious minutes. Berlin should be told at once what has occurred here."

Meyer nodded his agreement, his eyes flicking from Lunström to his niece. His information was that both parties were willing accomplices, but it now seemed the girl was far from that.

"Get them for me, will you."

Knobel picked up the telephone and frowned when he realized the line was dead. Then he recalled how Heinnemann had asked the exchange to disconnect the number and snapped his fingers in annoyance.

"No matter," said Meyer. "We'll make the call from Rückertstrasse."

"What about us?" asked Alfred Lunström. "This business has already occupied enough of my time. The sooner I am back in Sweden, the better."

Meyer said he would have to consult Berlin. "But as I understand it," he added, "you are to be flown to Stockholm in a couple of days, compliments of Lufthansa and with the regrets of Berlin for the inconvenience."

Lunström confirmed that that was his understanding also. "And then we can forget it. If I decide not to make an issue of it, no one else will either."

Meyer lowered his voice to a whisper. "What about your niece?"

"Leave her to me. She'll see matters differently once I've spoken to her."

"I can assure Berlin of that? It could have unfortunate consequences all around if she decides not to remain silent. It's better if the Americans never find out how their entire Eighth Air Force was destroyed."

"You can tell Berlin not to worry. You might also tell them that I would deem it a favor *not* to be in Schweinfurt tomorrow."

Meyer smiled thinly. As a rule he didn't much care for Swedes, but this cynical old man was an exception. He followed Knobel to the door. "Expect us to be away about an hour, perhaps two," he said to Lunström. "If you want to retire, do so by all means. I doubt very much if you'll be moved before morning." He put on his cap, clicked his heels formally, and followed Knobel out.

When they were alone, Lunström studied Natalie's back for a while before asking if she would like a drink.

She turned from the window. "Yes. Yes, I think I'd like a very large brandy to put me in the mood for your explanations. I presume I am to be told why I've been used as an unwitting pawn in whatever devious game you're playing."

The drinks poured, Lunström patted the sofa. "Come and sit beside me."

"I prefer to stand."

"As you please."

Lunström shook his head sorrowfully. "You disappoint me, you know, but I suppose I expected this attitude or I would have told you what was happening from the first. However, a daughter of Felix Lunström shouldn't react like a hysterical schoolgirl. It was all very necessary, believe me. There's a war on. People get killed in wars."

He could see he was not impressing her and tried a different tack.

"You were given an expensive education, taught to ride, fly, shoot, ski—on profits partly made from the manufacture and selling of arms and war matériel. Those same profits have given you property on five continents and a personal apartment in many of the world's major capitals. You have an airplane of your own, a boat, and I've lost count of the number of cars you've owned or still own. You're a director of many of our companies all over the world, a substantial shareholder in others the family does not control. Your entire upbringing has been geared to taking over the empire when your father and I are no longer here. You are now and will continue to be one of the richest women on the planet, solely because of decisions your father and I take daily—decisions that might not receive high marks among humanitarians but which make governments listen when the name Lunström is mentioned. You have not learned the most basic lesson of all, my dear: the world is and always has been a battlefield. It will never change, because human nature is acquisitive. Understand that and you will understand everything."

Natalie stifled the urge to smash the brandy glass in her uncle's face. What he was saying was true. She was not a fool.

She could read a balance sheet as well as anyone and knew that someone had to suffer in order for the Lunström family to hang on to what it had won. But there had to be limits. Surely a line had to be drawn somewhere.

"I accept what you're saying," she said calmly. "I can even justify it by arguing that if we—one of our companies —does not supply armaments or oil, others will. I can even go part of the way with your criticism of the human race, but you forget the rule of law, as the Nazis have forgotten it. Human beings may be all you say they are, but man invented law to protect the species from its own frailties. Without law we're nothing, there's no future, no hope. And under international law Sweden is a neutral country, free to trade with any nation but ally itself to none. What you have participated in here is the act of a belligerent—and one on the side of the Nazis, at that."

Lunström was faintly amused. "I see. You mean if the situation were reversed, if the plot had been concocted with the Allies and a Luftwaffe air fleet was to be wiped out over London, that would be acceptable?"

"The Allied do not kill women and children in gas chambers."

"Propaganda," snorted Lunström, "and none of our concern."

"Then what is our concern, Uncle Alfred?"

Natalie suddenly realized he had not answered her original question: What was this, this plot, all about and how did he figure in it? He had spouted financial philosophy and talked about the human condition, but she was still completely in the dark regarding his present motives.

"To protect our interests in Germany and in German-occupied territories," he said simply. "In return for my help I have been promised by the highest authority in the Reich that every piece of property, plant, and machinery we own or have an interest in but which is sequestered under wartime regula-

196

tions will be given back and the damage made good by the German government."

"By the highest authority, do you mean Hitler?"

"Yes. I have had several private talks with the Führer and Reichsminister Speer, and they have given me unqualified assurances."

Natalie could not believe her ears. "But this is madness!" she protested. "You're presupposing Germany will win, which is not only by no means certain but extremely doubtful."

"And if the American Eighth Air Force is destroyed?"

Natalie was appalled by her uncle's cynicism, but pressed on. "It will only delay Germany's inevitable defeat."

"Perhaps, but a more likely outcome will be a clamor for a peace agreement from the citizens of the United States. Even if that does not happen and the war continues, I will have done my part, Felix his."

"My father?"

"Certainly. While I look after the family's interests in the Axis countries, he does the same with the Allies. Whatever happens—providing it's kept secret—one side or the other will rebuild our factories, doubtless by enforcing reparations on the losers."

A horrifying thought occurred to Natalie. "Is my father part of all this, this plot to destroy the Americans?"

"Of course not. Haven't I just explained that his sphere of interest is with the Allies? I have no doubt that at this moment he is worried sick because something might have happened to you."

"And that doesn't trouble you?"

"Naturally it does. I am not an inhumane man, Natalie, no matter what you might think. But sometimes unilateral decisions have to be made for the good of everyone. Felix will understand when I explain it to him."

Natalie sank into an armchair, utterly confused. It was all too incredible for words yet it was merely an extension of

197

something she had witnessed most of her adult life—the principle of divide and rule. She had sat in on board meetings and voted her holding where decisions were taken to ruin this competitor or make a deal with that one. It had all seemed like a glorious game, because the defeated were never seen. They were just names on a piece of paper. A stroke of a pen, a stock issue, and they were wiped out. No one actually got killed, and if she were totally honest with herself the decision to annihilate the American bombers was the logical next step. They were just something else to be shuffled around the global board, more pawns.

She looked at her uncle over the rim of her glass. It would be comforting to call him mad, drunk with power and corrupted by it, but that was an oversimplification. He was as sane as any man she had ever met, but so too was Reichsminister Speer, and he also was a willing instrument in Hitler's hands. He too was a Nazi.

With a start she realized what she was thinking, that her uncle was deceiving her by saying his actions were just for the family good. He *believed* in Hitler as much as any Party hack.

"Of course I do," said Lunström loftily, genuinely surprised that her statement should come out as an accusation. "Why do you think it's mostly I who negotiates with Berlin while your father handles London and Washington? They trust me, that's why. And before you accuse me also of having a secret desire to wear jackboots, let me qualify what I have just said by adding that I have no real political beliefs, only an unswerving conviction that any totalitarian right-wing regime stabilizes a nation and is good for the economy. The democracies are corrupt and decadent and must one day fall to the communists if they are allowed to continue as they are. It will not happen for fifty years, possibly a hundred, certainly not until long after I am dead. But happen it will unless something is done to prevent it. That I won't be here to witness it doesn't matter. My responsibility is to the Lunström empire, which is a corporation in perpetuity. Hitler will help keep it that way. That's why I support him. I hope you can understand that."

Natalie understood nothing more than whatever excuses he made for himself, her uncle was as much a Nazi as the people who ran Germany and staffed the camps. He could put any label he liked upon his beliefs, but it all came down to the same thing: anyone who thought as he did, who considered the sacrifice of three or four thousand American fliers to be no more than a business gambit, was from the same mold as Hitler, Himmler, Goebbels, and the others.

He had to be stopped, the useless slaughter prevented. The only question was How?

Hauptsturmführer Knobel was seething by the time they arrived at Rückertstrasse. It was only just sinking in that he had been made to look a complete fool in the eyes of the Swedes, at least as far as the old man was concerned. Meyer refused to answer any questions during the short drive from Landwehrstrasse—a sensible enough precaution with Pickert and Schumacher listening to every word from the front seats —but while they were waiting to be connected to Berlin Knobel tackled the SD colonel once again.

"I think I'm entitled to know," he said irritably. "After all, there was I, politely trying to do my best for the Lunströms when all the time the man was playing the same game as the rest of you. He must have been laughing up his sleeve when I agreed to withdraw the guards and take him and his niece for some fresh air."

"We had to give the Allied agents a chance to make contact," said Meyer. "When we found the parachutes and flying suits near Frankfurt and accounted for every airman who had bailed out in the vicinity, we suspected they were close. We had to let them get at the Lunströms without making it too obvious."

"I appreciate that now," grumbled Knobel. "What I still

can't understand is why I wasn't apprised of the whole thing from the beginning. Schweinfurt is my territory."

"Security. The fewer who knew, the better our chances of success. While you considered the Lunströms to be genuine hostages you were unlikely to betray us with a slip of the tongue."

Knobel spluttered with indignation. "Betray you! Just who the hell do you and Berlin think you're dealing with, some kid, some beginner? If I'd been let in on Berlin's thoughts from the start, I might have been able to offer practical suggestions. You'd have looked pretty stupid, wouldn't you, if they'd tried to spirit the Lunströms away this afternoon instead of passing that note? Or if they hadn't got here until Friday? That would have left Schweinfurt in ruins and somebody's head on the chopping block."

"Not mine." Meyer lit a cigarette, stuck it in a long ebony holder, and waited for Knobel to calm down. He had too much respect for the little policeman's ability to wish to antagonize him unnecessarily. Besides, it could still turn out to be a long war and he would have to work with him again. "I'm not being secretive or obstructive when I tell you that I know very little more than you," he said, blowing a near-perfect smoke ring. "I don't know, for example, whether Alfred Lunström is in this willingly or whether he was coerced because we have something on file against him. Berlin does not consult me on such matters.

"I only know what I've been told and what I have been able to deduce by reading between the lines—that Schellenberg and Mueller dreamed up a scheme which will tomorrow destroy the US Eighth Air Force and set the Allies' program of large-scale daylight bombing back by a year. By which time, of course, we shall have the secret weapons the Führer has promised us. Mueller and Schellenberg reasoned that by holding such important people as the Lunströms in Schweinfurt and letting the Allies know we had them, pressure would be brought to bear. They would have two options. One: leave

Schweinfurt alone, which would suit us admirably. Two: attempt a rescue before the town was next bombed.

"Since the August raid was a relative failure, no one doubted the Americans would be back. We didn't know when, but if that could be established the Luftwaffe would be ready and waiting. There'd be none of the usual guesswork regarding the target, no one really knowing it until the damned B-17s are overhead. There'd be no need to hold hundreds of fighters at readiness elsewhere, to take care of a minor diversionary raid. The agents sent in to rescue the old man and the girl would have to know the real date or they would be working in the dark and might be too late."

The telephone in Knobel's office rang. Meyer picked up the receiver, but it was only the operator informing him of a slight delay in calls to Berlin.

Meyer replaced the handset. "A brilliant scheme, eh? A magnificent concept marvelously executed."

"Perhaps."

"Perhaps?"

More to throw a hundred volts of doubt through Meyer and shake those arrogant bastards in Berlin than for any other reason, Knobel adopted the role of devil's advocate. He suggested that if Mueller and Schellenberg were capable of Machiavellian strategy, so too were the Allies.

"What if Lunström is working for or with American and British intelligence? Or if that seems unreasonable, what if the Allies, suspecting a trick, sat down and found a way to turn the whole business to their own advantage—by giving their agents false information, say? *They* believe Schweinfurt is the target for tomorrow—later today, I should say—but what if it isn't? What if it's elsewhere? The entire Luftwaffe fighter arm will be formed up on a flight path between England and Schweinfurt while the Eighth Air Force bombs Berlin or Hamburg."

Knobel started to enjoy himself. "Or consider this, that the target *is* Schweinfurt, but not until Friday. I need hardly tell you that if the pilots are geared up for a good day's killing later today and nothing happens, they will be at a psychologically low ebb on Friday."

Meyer was startled by the suggestion but considered it a possibility. Brought up in a world of intrigue where nothing was ever as it seemed, he had to admit that whatever Brigadeführer Schellenberg could come up with the Allies could counter. They would not even have to know they were being plotted against. All they would need to assume was that their agents stood no chance of liberating the Lunströms and feed them false information. Then, when they were captured, they would be able to pass on no more than they knew, even under torture.

He would have to put the supposition to Prinz Albrechtstrasse. If anything did go wrong they would be looking for scapegoats.

The phone rang again. This time it was Berlin on the line and Meyer stiffened to attention before speaking.

Ten minutes later Schellenberg told Meyer to stay by the phone until he called back. He smiled with grim satisfaction at Mueller, who was listening on the extension. "So," he said, "we have them."

"Let's hope so. What do you make of that business about it being an Allied counterplot?"

"No more than Meyer getting nervous. We'll soon know, anyway, when we get the two agents up here. If I can get an aircraft off the ground within half an hour they'll be in Berlin before dawn. A session with some of your people in the cellars will soon tell us whether or not we're being double-crossed."

"Göring should be informed right away. He'll have a thousand preparations to make and you know how he vacillates." Mueller's mouth became a sneer. "Besides, it would be a pleasure to talk to the Reichsmarschall while he can still understand what we're saying."

Schellenberg agreed. "We must also tell the Führer," he

added. "I think this time we can give him what he's looking for. Has there been an air-raid warning tonight?"

"Not for Berlin."

"Good. Then he won't alter his schedule. God, how the man works. No wonder half his field commanders are burnt out."

"Some of them will be more than burnt out before this business is over," murmured Mueller.

Schellenberg fumbled through his briefcase until he found the document he was looking for, a list of Hitler's appointments for the small hours.

"We're in luck. Speer's due in. We can kill two birds with one stone. But first Göring. You're right, it would be nice to catch our fat airman before he passes out."

Reichsmarschall Göring was having a late dinner with two of his senior commanders, Generaloberst Günther Korten, newly promoted Luftwaffe Chief of Staff, and Generaloberst Hans-Jürgen Stumpff, commander of Luftflotte 5, when the call came through. Like his master, he wasn't sleeping too well these days; and if he couldn't, neither could anyone else. But he was far from drunk.

He listened patiently to what Schellenberg had to say, asked several pertinent questions, and replaced the receiver.

He looked unseeingly at the telephone for fully five minutes, his thoughts on Generaloberst Hans Jeschonnek, who had committed suicide in August, right after the first American raid on Schweinfurt. It seemed a bad omen.

When asked point-blank why the Generaloberst had killed himself, Jeschonnek's adjutant, Major Werner Leuchtenberg, answered, "Because the general wished to shine a light on the terrible shortcomings of the Luftwaffe leadership."

He had almost court-martialed Leuchtenberg for that remark. Certainly the Luftwaffe had not done all that was required of it, but which branch of the armed forces had? Was he, the only holder of a Reichsmarschall's baton in Germany, to be blamed for the irresolution of others?

It was easy for the intriguers of the world, the Muellers and the Schellenbergs, to say, "Here is what the Allies will do. Stop them." They did not have to answer to the Führer if it all went wrong—if, for example, the Eighth Air Force did not turn up in strength over Schweinfurt. They would retreat into the woodwork like the vermin they were.

Perhaps it was fortuitous that Stumpff and Korten were dining with him tonight. He would discuss the whole problem with them even if it meant no sleep for anyone. To the best of his recollection he had 1,100 front-line day-fighters at his disposal, three or four to each B-17 in the biggest bombing fleet the *Amis* could put up. If Schellenberg's intelligence was accurate, the Luftwaffe could inflict the most massive defeat they had ever suffered on those philistines from the so-called New World.

If Schellenberg was right.

In Rückertstrasse, Meyer and Knobel were sipping coffee laced with brandy. The Schweinfurt days were still quite warm, but the temperature dropped rapidly once the sun went down. Knobel could not resist the dig that if Meyer had had the courtesy to be a little more forthcoming in advance, Heinnemann would not have ordered the phone disconnected and they could now be sitting in the comparative luxury of Landwehrstrasse 18 waiting for Schellenberg to call back, give them fresh orders, tell them what time the Berlin plane was due. What was more, they could have spent the intervening hours conducting a preliminary interrogation of the Allied agents.

"They'll keep," growled Meyer. "They're not going anywhere."

Which was the same conclusion Fallon and McKenna had come to. Heinnemann had locked them in the one room that had bars on the window and taken the additional precaution of remaining on the far side of the door, unwilling to risk getting jumped in spite of the Schmeisser. He had also wielded the gun butt with considerable force, as it was twenty minutes before McKenna came around properly and felt fit enough to talk. He had a lump the size of a small egg behind his right ear, but the skin was unbroken and there were no signs of concussion. Still, it was almost twenty-five minutes past midnight before he and Fallon got down to the serious business of discussing their plight.

"No wonder it was so goddamn easy to get at the bastards," said McKenna bitterly. "We walked straight into it."

"Which I suppose is what Peterson was trying to tell us all along," Fallon hazarded. "We'll never know for certain, of course, but it seems reasonable to assume he saw the Lunströms in Frankfurt looking a bit more pally with the Gestapo than would have been the case if they were genuinely under arrest. He may even have got close enough to find out for sure, overhear one or two conversations; otherwise the SD would have had no reason to suspect and murder him. He'd spent some time in Sweden, so he'd doubtless know the Lunströms by sight and reputation."

"I'll kill the bastards if I get anywhere near them," vowed McKenna. "I swear to Christ I'll wring both their necks and to hell with whether the Krauts shoot me or not."

"It's more likely to be not," advised Fallon. "You were out cold at the time, but that SD colonel said something about interrogating us before we get the chop. That's on the bright side, anyway. It gives us some breathing space."

"Maybe we could convince them the raid's not scheduled for tomorrow after all," suggested McKenna hopefully.

"Would you believe it?"

"No." The American looked at the window. "Have you tried the bars?"

Fallon nodded. "Solid as rock. It would take us a week to get one loose."

"So what the hell do we do?"

"Did they leave you anything we could use? I've been through my own pockets."

McKenna searched his. They had taken his burglar tool, matches. "Nothing."

"Then we've got to get that bastard with the Schmeisser in here somehow."

Fallon walked over to the door and hammered on it. "Open up. We've got something we want to discuss with you."

Heinnemann laughed and shouted something they did not catch.

"You're wasting your time," said McKenna.

"Maybe, but if we don't get out of here and get a message to Curzon, there's going to be the biggest bloody massacre in the history of air warfare come this afternoon."

Fifteen

If Fallon and McKenna were in a mood of black despair because they knew precisely what was happening, in his Baker Street HQ Charles Curzon felt much the same way because he did not. Since receiving Fallon's wireless signal stating that the earliest possible date for reaching Schweinfurt was Wednesday, he had spent many of his waking hours on the telephone to Felix Lunström, trying to persuade the Swedish industrialist not to block the export of the Siberg-Waring ball bearings, now off the production lines; to allow them instead to be loaded aboard BOAC aircraft ready for shipment to the UK, where they were desperately needed, or many ordnance factories would be in dire straits before the week was out.

On Tuesday afternoon, October 12, Lunström had agreed —with a stringent proviso. He knew nothing of the rescue operation but suspected Curzon had something up his sleeve. The ball bearings could be loaded, but the aircraft would not be allowed to move until he had an absolute assurance that his elder brother and daughter were safe. If that were not forthcoming within the next couple of days, then, in accordance with their verbal agreement made in London the previous week, the Germans could have the entire stock.

Curzon cajoled and wheedled, but try as he might he could not get the Swede to budge on the issue, and the former banker's normally placid disposition was not helped by the fact that the Minister of Economic Warfare, under pressure from the War Cabinet, was never off his back.

No less disgruntled were BOAC, who resented having their entire operational fleet of Mosquitoes tied up at Bromma. But Curzon insisted upon it, threatening to call in Winston Churchill himself unless the airline stopped squawking. He could, however, understand their frustration. They had lost their aircraft without being told why, and that was not the customary modus operandi. Usually they were consulted on all matters involving civilian planes, even those of the utmost secrecy, and they did not know why they were being treated as office boys on this occasion.

There had to be limits, BOAC insisted. One could not keep eight Mosquitoes in the Bromma hangars indefinitely.

There *were* limits, Curzon advised them. Come the afternoon of October 14, the Mosquitoes would have left one way or the other, loaded or empty.

As anxious as Curzon was Harry Mortimer. Word had filtered through from the White House that it was not in long-term US interests to have powerful enemies in Stockholm, which would certainly be the case if anything happened to Alfred and Natalie Lunström, regardless of how they died. There was talk in high places that one day in the near future President Roosevelt would be asking Sweden to see the light, perhaps even declare herself a belligerent in the Allied cause, and there was no doubt that if some of the Swedish airfields were modified to take B-17s and B-24s, the bases would be of inestimable value in carrying the war deeper into the Reich. What was more, the P-47 and Spitfire fighter escorts, whose range was limited flying from England, would be able to protect the bombers all the way to Berlin.

But Mortimer's major concern was a personal one. Sam McKenna was his man, and he wanted him safely home.

As the clock ticked up to 0045 on the morning of October 14, the OSS colonel lit up his third cigar of the evening, an action which made Curzon groan with open despair.

"Do you have to smoke those, Harry?" he grumbled. "My office already smells like a third-rate brothel."

Mortimer grinned good-naturedly. "You're one up on me there. I've never been in a third-rate brothel."

"I'm serious. Every suit I've worn for the past two weeks stinks of the wretched things."

"I thought you liked them. What about the boxes I've given you?"

Curzon was saved by the telephone ringing. He snatched at it, but it was only the duty officer asking if he and Colonel Mortimer would like some coffee. "No," he snapped. "And kindly keep this line clear." He slammed down the phone.

They were waiting, he and Mortimer, for word from Eighth Bomber Command HQ telling them whether Mission 115, Schweinfurt, was definitely on. The weather since Monday had been dreadful, the thick early-morning fog lasting well into the afternoon and grounding bombers destined for other targets. But a decision on 115 was expected at any time. When it came they could go to Switzerland. There was an aircraft standing by to take them there, but there was no point in going if the mission was scrubbed. In that event, at least there was no danger of the Lunströms being killed by the US Air Force, and it would be necessary to rethink the whole business in London. If the B-17s flew, however, Curzon wanted to be in Bern. As he had told the Minister: "We have to assume Fallon, McKenna, and the Lunströms are going to make it across the border, and when they do I want to be on a direct radio link to Stockholm immediately, putting Alfred Lunström on the microphone if I can, because you can bet your life Felix will know about the raid within hours of it happening, and God knows what he'll do then."

"What the hell's keeping them?" he muttered.

"Have you taken a look outside recently?" asked Mortimer.

"Bad?"

"You couldn't see the other side of Baker Street twenty minutes ago."

"What's the latest area report?"

"For London more of the same, but it's not London we have to worry about. It's all those airfields out in East Anglia and the conditions over Europe. They'll go if they can, there's no doubt about it. The brass are sick and tired of hanging around and it's not doing much for crew morale either. They'll go if it lifts only a fraction."

Curzon hoped so. In spite of the predicament he faced with Felix Lunström, every day that passed gave German industry greater production capacity. He knew the statistics as well as he knew the veins in his arm. Not counting the engines or the guns, the airframe alone for a Ju 88 called for 1,056 anti-friction bearings. An 88mm flak gun used 50; a 200cm searchlight needed 90. Knock out Schweinfurt and the Germans would soon find they were 50 percent defenseless. The raid must go on.

The Eighth Air Force crews were not the only ones suffering from lowered morale. Stuck in Bromma now for almost twenty-four hours, the skippers and the R/Os of the Mosquitoes were fed to the teeth with the place. Stockholm was fine as a city, a splendid, brightly illuminated break from the austerity of blacked-out Britain. But they were not allowed into Stockholm; they were restricted to the airport, asked to keep the office informed of their whereabouts, told nothing more than the fact that they might be required to take off at a few minutes' notice. When they asked the station manager what was going on and why, as they were already cargoed-up and fueled-up, they could not leave at once, all they received by way of reply was a mystified shake of the head. They slept where they could, read magazines, played cards, and occasionally quarreled among themselves.

They were aware that something big was afoot, because not even the older hands could recall the hangars bulging with Mosquitoes. But what that something was they had no idea.

Dandy Jim Masefield, skipper of the *Gaggle of Geese,* said it for them all: "Anyone would think we were in the bloody RAF."

He was to remember those words before a dozen hours passed.

Another Briton burning the midnight oil in the Swedish capital was Major Browning, the assistant military attaché. He had a little more information than the BOAC crews, but not much. Soon, very soon, London had informed him, the radio room could be getting a signal from Bern, Switzerland. When that happened he was to call the number on his desk and get Felix Lunström to the Legation immediately. There would be no trouble with the Minister; Downing Street had seen to that.

At his headquarters in a former girls' school near High Wycombe, Buckinghamshire, now code-named Pinetree, Brigadier General F. L. Anderson, CO of the US Eighth Bomber Command, read over his briefing message for the crews, which would be given to them if Mission 115 got the green light. It was now just after 1 A.M. and a real pea-souper of a night outside, but tomorrow's forecast looked promising.

The message stated:

To all leaders and combat crews. This air operation today is the most important air operation yet conducted in this war. The target must be destroyed. It is of vital importance to the enemy. Your friends and comrades who have been lost and who will be lost today are depending on you. Their sacrifices must not be in vain. Good luck, good shooting, and good bombing.

Anderson wondered if it said enough, or indeed too much. It might not be good psychology to remind men that they would not all be coming back. On the other hand, they were experienced fliers who knew the score. Trying to fool them with honeyed words would only earn their contempt.

He chose to leave the message as it stood and called across an aide. Two things remained to be done. The first was to tell his chief, Major General Ira C. Eaker, overall commander of the US Eighth Air Force, that 115 was on as far as he was concerned; the second, to call that OSS colonel at the London number and tell him the same.

Curzon handed the phone to Mortimer, who listened briefly before replacing the receiver.

"It's on," he said. "Let's go to Switzerland."

Sixteen

Alfred Lunström was deep in thought, hardly aware that his niece was still in the sitting room. Which suited Natalie fine.

For the past ten minutes she had racked her brain desperately for some way to help the Englishman Fallon and the American McKenna, but the odds against her were overwhelming. She was one woman against an armed German and a time limit. Meyer and Knobel had said they would be away an hour, perhaps two, and that was fifty-five minutes ago. If she was to move it would have to be quick.

There was one thing she could do, a slight chance, but the thought of it made her shiver. It appeared, however, to be the only solution. She got to her feet.

Lunström looked up. "Are you going to bed, my dear?"

"Just to lie down, not to sleep. This has all been too much for me to absorb. I'm not thinking clearly."

"I'm delighted to hear you say so. Mull it over, by all means. I'm sure you'll conclude that empires such as ours are not made or kept without unpleasant decisions being taken."

"Are you staying up?"

"I think it would be wise. I'd like to hear what Meyer has to say when he returns. I trust German efficiency, but not that much. I want to make sure they're getting us out before . . ." He hesitated. "Well . . . getting us out soon."

Natalie said good night. If Lunström was aware of not receiving the customary kiss on the forehead, he made no comment.

She closed the sitting-room door carefully behind her and walked swiftly and purposefully through the drawing room. Beyond that was the corridor which led to the bedrooms. Hers was the furthermost, wedged between the bathroom and her uncle's bedroom. The one containing the two Allied agents was at the other end of the passage, next to the kitchen. Heinnemann was sprawled on a chair outside it, the Schmeisser across his lap. He was cleaning his nails with a matchstick and looked up as Natalie approached.

She gave him one of her most dazzling smiles. "Still the faithful watchdog, Unterscharführer? Don't you ever relax?"

Heinnemann sprang to his feet as though being addressed by Reichsführer Himmler himself. This was the first time the stuck-up bitch had done more than nod to him. "Not when there's a job to be done, Fräulein," he said importantly.

"It's nice to know we're in such safe hands."

"You needn't worry on that score. They won't be going anywhere until we're ready to deal with them."

"Deal with them?"

"Put them somewhere where they can't do you or your uncle any harm."

"We're both very grateful, Unterscharführer. These past couple of weeks haven't been very pleasant, as you may well imagine."

"I can understand that, Fräulein Lunström."

Natalie ran her fingers up and down his lapel. "For lots of reasons," she said meaningfully. "Do you know what I'm saying?"

Heinnemann was beginning to sweat. The girl's face was a mere six inches from his own. He could smell her perfume, the cleanness of her hair, the warmth of her body.

"I . . . I'm not sure, Fräulein." To his horror he felt his trousers bulging, an enormous erection growing.

"I'm sure you do."

Tensing herself, Natalie moved her hand downward and brushed it softly against the Gestapo sergeant's groin. Heinnemann let out an involuntary moan. "Fräulein . . ."

"Natalie . . . please. Call me Natalie."

Leaving her hand where it was, flicking her fingers against Heinnemann's stiffness, she put her other arm around his neck. "This is what I mean, Unterscharführer," she whispered. "It's so long since I was with a young man."

Heinnemann reached down and put his hand up Natalie's skirt. He felt her shudder and misunderstood disgust for desire.

"Not here," she murmured. "My room."

Heinnemann was practically out of his mind, but part of it still remembered the task he was charged with. But what could go wrong? The door was locked from the outside and he had the key in his jacket pocket. He wouldn't be away that long. He didn't want to make love to this smooth, satiny Swedish bitch. He wanted just to fuck her, plant his seed in her, feel her writhe, make her suffer.

He felt her hand working faster on him and heard her say, "Please. In my room. Now."

Fallon was crouched with his ear to the door.

"What the hell is it?" asked McKenna. "Somebody coming for us?"

"I dunno. I don't think so. Just somebody talking. Heinnemann and the Swedish girl, I think."

"Can you hear what they're saying?"

"No. Hold it. No, they're going away."

Schellenberg called back at 1:15 A.M. Meyer said, "*Jawohl, Herr Brigadeführer,*" several times before hanging up.

"The plane will be here around 0330 hours," he told Knobel. "We're to have Majors Fallon and McKenna at the airfield by then."

"The experimental one?"

"Is there another?"

There was, but it was further out.

"Are they sending an escort or do they want us to provide one?" asked Knobel.

"Anxious to get out of Schweinfurt?" Meyer smirked. "Can't say I blame you, but you're going to be disappointed. Berlin is sending its own people."

"What about warning the flak batteries?"

"Berlin will take care of all that."

"And the Lunströms?"

"They're to travel with me to Frankfurt by road."

"I think I might join you. There are several things in Frankfurt I've been meaning to do for some weeks."

Meyer grunted. "I can imagine. Well, we'll see. In the meantime, let's get back to Landwehrstrasse and pass on the good tidings to the Swedes."

Heinnemann closed the bedroom door behind them and leaned the Schmeisser against the jamb. Natalie thought she was going to be physically sick when he unbuttoned his fly and made her take his penis in her hand, while his own huge paws were caressing her thighs, trying to part them. He buried his head in the nape of her neck, slobbering like an animal, muttering the most frightful obscenities intermingled with declarations of love. He was virtually out of control now and she knew she had to be quick or she would find herself being raped where she stood.

"On the bed," she breathed. "Not here."

They backed toward it, walking like two tired dancers at the end of a marathon competition. She tried to let go of him, but he growled his displeasure and forced her to retain her hold.

They fell back across the bed, Heinnemann's bulk massively on top of her but exactly where she'd planned, her head near the bedside table and the heavy glass ashtray.

He pulled her skirt roughly above her waist and looked down with glazed, half-seeing eyes.

"A moment," she protested as he reached for her, but he insisted he could not wait, that it had to be now, that he was crazy with love for her beautiful body.

She felt for the ashtray, gripping it firmly. He was tearing at her underclothes, frenzied with desire to be inside her, and was within inches of succeeding when she brought the ashtray crashing down on the back of his skull.

He tried to raise himself up, his mind unable to accept what was happening. Natalie hit him again . . . and again . . . hatred for him and his filth adding power to her blows.

Finally he slumped forward, still, his head pouring blood, his breathing dangerously shallow.

She pushed him away and struggled to her feet, wasting precious moments straightening her clothing and recovering her composure, listening all the while for any sign that her uncle had heard the commotion and was coming to investigate. But he was separated from her by three closed doors and had evidently heard nothing.

She steeled herself to touch Heinnemann, go through his pockets until she found the key to the third bedroom. Then snatching up the Schmeisser, she flung open the door and ran along the corridor.

Crouched ready to spring as soon as they heard the sound of the key in the lock, Fallon and McKenna remained rooted to the spot when Natalie appeared.

She held out the Schmeisser. "We haven't much time," she said urgently. "Meyer and Knobel will be back at any moment."

Fallon, who was nearest, took the machine pistol, looking bemusedly from McKenna to Natalie. Her hair was mussed, her face flushed, but she was still the loveliest woman he had seen in years.

McKenna found his voice first. "What the hell's going on and why are you suddenly siding with the good guys?"

Natalie explained as fast as she could that until a short while ago she had no idea her uncle was involved in a plot or what that plot was, how he was now alone in the sitting room, Meyer and Knobel having gone to Rückertstrasse, and how she had knocked Heinnemann unconscious, perhaps even killed him. McKenna asked if the Meyer in question was the man Curzon had warned them about, the head of the Frankfurt SD. Natalie confirmed he was.

"Show us where you left Heinnemann," said Fallon.

She led them along the passage to where the Gestapo sergeant was lying in a widening pool of his own blood. The renewed sight of him brought back the past few minutes. Putting her hand to her mouth, she rushed into the bathroom, where a moment later she could be heard vomiting.

They examined the German, felt his pulse, saw the disarray of his clothes, his position on the bed. There was no doubt in their minds how she had got hold of the Schmeisser, nor that her change of attitude was genuine. It had taken a whole barrelful of guts to do what she had done. Heinnemann's skull was caved in. She must have hit him several fearsome blows. Without medical attention he wouldn't last the night. Certainly he was no longer a threat.

McKenna relieved him of his Walther, which was still in the shoulder holster. Now they were both armed and things were looking up.

Natalie emerged from the bathroom pale and drawn.

Fallon and McKenna joined her in the corridor, shutting the bedroom door behind them.

"You say your uncle's alone through there?" asked McKenna.

"He was when I left him."

"Then I suggest we get him and get the hell out of here."

"He won't go with you."

McKenna was in no mood to consider Alfred Lunström's views in the matter. They had traveled a long way to get Natalie and her uncle and that was what they were going to do.

"He'll have no choice, not when I stick this in his face." He brandished the Walther.

Fallon hesitated, his mind racing. "We can't leave yet. You say Meyer and Knobel are due back soon?" he asked Natalie.

"Yes. Any time."

"Then we have to wait."

"Are you crazy?" demanded McKenna. "Are you out of your mind?"

"Far from it. If they arrive back to find us gone they'll know we're getting out by car and throw up roadblocks for fifty miles around. We can't take that sort of gamble. We have to wait for them and dispose of them. Then we've got all night."

"And if they get waylaid and don't turn up till morning? The B-17s will be taking off nine, ten o'clock. We've got to let them know the mission's blown before they're airborne. A B-17's not a motorcar. You can't get three or four hundred of them to do a U-turn in midair."

"I've considered that," said Fallon. "If Meyer and Knobel are late and we can't make the Swiss border, we'll head back for Frankfurt and radio from there."

They were sure to be back was Natalie's opinion. "They only went to Rückertstrasse to phone Berlin for instructions because the line here is disconnected."

McKenna thought about it. They were his people, his fellow countrymen, flying the B-17s, and he didn't care for toying with their unsuspecting lives. But what Fallon was suggesting made sense. If Meyer and Knobel returned within ten minutes of their own departure, it was doubtful if they'd clear the city limits before being recaptured.

"Okay," he grunted reluctantly. "Okay. But let's put that bastard Lunström on ice before he decides to come through here and use the bathroom. Sorry," he said to Natalie.

She attempted a weak smile and almost made it. "That's all right. I've been thinking of him as something of a bastard myself for the past hour."

The Swede's thin face was a picture of disbelief when Fallon and McKenna preceded Natalie into the sitting room, but it didn't take a moment to fathom what had happened. "You damned little fool," he cursed his niece. "You don't know what you've done."

He stood up. At his full height he was almost as tall as McKenna. "But it will all be to no avail. You can't escape, not in time to be of any use. I just hope I can persuade the Gestapo—before they order the firing squad—that you, my dear, were temporarily deranged."

McKenna pushed Lunström in the chest—hard, forcing him to sit down again. "If anyone's deranged, old son, it's you. And if there's any shooting to be done, you can take my word for it that you'll be first in Valhalla."

There was nothing to do now but wait.

From the apartment's entrance, a small hallway for coats and umbrellas led to the nearer of the sitting-room doors, which Fallon left open, ordering Lunström to sit quite still and remain in full view. If he made any sign whatsoever to the Germans it would be his last act on this earth. McKenna, who was flat against the wall, would see to that.

Natalie was told to stand by one of the big armchairs where she could be seen, ready to duck behind it if there was any shooting. With any luck, there wouldn't be, but that was far from a money-back guarantee. Natalie smiled, saying she understood, and Fallon reminded himself that they still hadn't thanked her for putting Heinnemann out of action. That was the first item on the agenda when the current business was over. The second was to get to know her better.

Satisfied he had covered all the angles, he took up his own position in the hallway behind the door, which he left ajar for the moment. If things went according to plan the Germans would be caught in the crossfire the second they came in. They might not think much of McKenna's pistol, but they sure as hell wouldn't argue with a Schmeisser at close quarters.

Five minutes passed before there was the sound of a car drawing up outside. A moment later a couple of doors slammed and he heard voices and footsteps on the stairs. There seemed to be more than two of them, and he remembered the brace of guards at the ground-floor entrance.

He slipped the latch quietly. "There are four of them," he called softly to McKenna.

There were—Meyer and Knobel, Pickert and Schumacher. Trouble the furthest thing from their collective mind, they came through the front door like sheep heading for the abattoir. Schumacher was last. As he half-turned to snap the lock, he came face to face with Fallon. His complexion turned the color of week-old snow.

"Guten Abend," said Fallon.

When McKenna stepped into view, Meyer let out an oath of enraged disbelief and for an instant it seemed as if he and Pickert at least would make a fight of it. But discretion and the combined firepower of Carl Walther Waffenfabrik AG and Erfurter Maschinenfabrik had the last word. Without another sound all four men trooped meekly into the sitting room, where McKenna started to disarm them, beginning with Meyer.

That should have been it, game, set, and match; and so it would had Magda Lessing not chosen that precise moment to put in an appearance.

Schumacher had not engaged the lock and neither had Fallon, and Magda found the door open. Seeing what was taking place in the sitting room and concluding that her earlier fears were groundless, it was with something approaching relief that she said breathlessly, "I thought you were in trouble."

All eyes turned toward her. In the fraction of a second it took to absorb who the newcomer was, Knobel acted. With that same sense of self-preservation and total lack of concern for anyone else's fate that had kept him alive for fifty-odd years, he pushed Pickert in the back. The German collided with Fallon and grappled with him.

Knowing this to be the only chance he'd get, Knobel raced for the door as fast as his short legs would carry him, dragging a pistol from his pocket as he ran. He threw Magda to one side, let loose a shot over his shoulder, and sprinted down the stairs, slamming the front door behind him.

Although it would not be true to say that Fallon and McKenna had forgotten all about Magda, because of the events of the last couple of hours she had not occupied much of their thoughts. But they had been in hers.

Waiting in the Opel around the corner in Ludwigstrasse, she had counted the minutes, referring to her wristwatch practically every other one. They had said they might be away two hours, but at the beginning she had confidently expected it to be a lot less. She was not too concerned when twelve-thirty came and went without any sign of them, and only slightly more so at one. But as the time approached one-thirty she started to worry. Something must have gone wrong. It shouldn't have taken them this long to persuade the Lunströms that their immediate future lay elsewhere.

She recalled Fallon telling her that if they were not back when the two hours were up she was to return to Frankfurt and radio London. But she couldn't just leave without knowing what had happened. They might turn up the very minute she left and they would be stranded without transport.

So she disobeyed Fallon, locked the car, and walked slowly toward Landwehrstrasse 18, keeping in the shadows on the far side of the street. At this hour they were virtually empty except for the occasional Wehrmacht truck or fire patrol, and therefore the black official-looking automobile which turned into Landwehrstrasse attracted her immediate attention. Some sixth sense told her that the occupants were connected with the Lunströms, and she was not at all surprised when the car pulled up outside number 18 and four men got out.

Perhaps not surprised but certainly plunged into the depths of despair when she observed that three of the men were wearing the sort of plain clothes that were almost a badge of office for the Gestapo, while the fourth was in the full uniform of an SS Obersturmbannführer.

It was dark, she was thirty meters away, but the SS colonel was carrying his cap and she thought she recognized him. It took her a moment to place his face before she realized she had seen him, always in uniform, at Party meetings in Frankfurt, where he had occasionally lectured the faithful. His name was Meyer and his department was SD (Internal).

Her heart pounded with fear. If the Frankfurt SS were here it meant Fallon and McKenna were surely in grave trouble—if not now then in a few more minutes, for the four men were entering the building.

Logic beseeched her to leave at once, make for Frankfurt, but years ago logic had also told her it was foolhardy to risk her life working for the British. She hadn't listened then and she didn't listen now. She might be able to help.

They had left no guard at the entrance, and she knew

from listening to conversations between Fallon and McKenna, watching them prepare the makeshift grappling iron, that the Lunströms were being held on the top floor.

The decision taken, she crossed the street quickly, went into the building, and walked silently up the stairs. The door to the apartment was ajar and she could hear voices. Peering through the crack and into the sitting room beyond, she observed that Fallon and McKenna, far from being in custody, had the situation under control. Meyer and the Gestapo officers had their hands raised above their heads and McKenna was in the process of disarming them.

With a sigh of relief that was audible she pushed open the door to its fullest extent and went inside.

"I thought you were in trouble," she said.

It was then that all hell broke loose.

Magda found herself hurled to the floor as Knobel raced past, and she winced involuntarily when the shot rang out. While Fallon wrestled with Pickert for possession of the Schmeisser, Schumacher tried to follow Knobel's example and method of egress, fumbling for his pistol as he made for the door.

McKenna had no alternative but to shoot him. In spite of the alarm bells in his brain ringing out a warning that any more shots would bring people running, McKenna had no hesitation in pumping two 7.65mm Parabellum bullets into Schumacher's back, killing him instantly.

The American swung around in the same movement, dropping automatically into a firing crouch and stopping Meyer in his tracks. The only German so far disarmed, a split second earlier Meyer had considered sticking in his two cents' worth and had taken a couple of paces toward McKenna. Now he thought better of it and flung his hands in the air. "Don't shoot."

Alfred Lunström had hit the floor at the sound of the first shot but was unhurt. Natalie, her face white, was half hidden behind the armchair.

Even as McKenna was torn between wanting to assist Fallon and getting after Knobel, Fallon threw Pickert from him and pointed the machine pistol at his chest, yelling at him to stand still. But Pickert was either more stupid or made of sterner stuff than the others, for he came charging in again, face contorted, bellowing like a man possessed of devils.

Fallon squeezed the trigger, feeling the Schmeisser buck and rear in his hands. Half a magazine of 9mm shells ripped great holes in Pickert's torso, the impact flinging the German upward and backward like a rag doll discarded by a truculent child.

Huge gouts of blood surged from his wounds, spattering Natalie, who let out a scream of terror. But her cries went ignored as Fallon and McKenna sprinted for the stairs.

Knobel was old and slow and unfit, but he had twenty or thirty seconds' start, and that was enough. They had only got as far as the third-floor landing before they heard the sound of a car starting up, the clash of gears, the high-pitched whine of an engine being overrevved. Knobel had got away and there was no doubt what his next move would be. In a few more minutes the building would be surrounded by police and troops.

Back in the apartment, they came to a rapid decision. There was no question, not now, not immediately, of making for the Swiss border or Frankfurt or of even getting out of Schweinfurt. Knobel would have every exit road blocked before they could cover ten kilometers. It would have to be Horst Wesselstrasse, there to take stock.

It was a cruel choice to be faced with. If they left at once they might just make Switzerland before the B-17s were airborne. If they waited for a few hours until the first heat was off, they could still get to Frankfurt in time to signal London. If they were caught in either act they were dead and no use to anyone.

"What about him?" McKenna jerked a thumb at Meyer.

Fallon hesitated. The man was an SS colonel of infamous

repute and would indisputably have had them tortured and shot if the positions were reversed. Fallon could kill him in cold blood if necessary, but he might be useful. He would have a knowledge of the area and of SS procedure. He would know what his men would do next and, with perhaps a little physical persuasion, could be made to tell what he knew.

"Bring him with us."

With more time he might have decided otherwise, but seconds were precious, minutes at a premium.

Alfred Lunström was disinclined to move until McKenna jabbed him in the stomach with his pistol barrel and herded him toward the door.

Bringing up the rear, Magda Lessing was abject in her contrition, repeating over and over again her despair.

Urging Meyer ahead of him at gunpoint, Fallon told her brutally to shut up and concentrate on thinking of the quickest route out of the area. She had disobeyed orders, true, but she had acted from the purest of motives. Nevertheless, he thought as they gained the empty street, the fat was certainly in the fire now.

Seventeen

Travis was dozing in a chair, fully dressed, when noise entered his dream. He was again flying that last raid on Frankfurt and the flak was coming up thick and fast, some of the shells bursting so close that bits of shrapnel rattled against the fuselage. There was darkness to his right and he banked the Lancaster that way; anything was better than staying where the searchlights could find you, especially that big brute that was edging closer and closer, bloody near blinding him. His flight engineer, Dusty Miller, was saying something, shouting it, but he couldn't understand a word. Jesus, he was sleepy.

Dusty punched him on the shoulder. *Wake up, Travis, wake up.*

Travis tried to edge away from the punches. Why was Dusty doing that?

With a start he opened his eyes to find Fallon standing over him, shaking him. He blinked in astonishment and struggled to focus. Where on earth had all these people come from—the girl, the tall man with the white hair, the— Dear God, the man in the SS uniform. "What the hell's going on? Are we under arrest?"

"Take it easy," said Fallon. "We've got him, not the other way around. Are you awake?"

"Yes, but—"

"Not yet, Travis, not now. It'll all be explained later, but for the moment you've got a job to do."

McKenna had coralled Meyer and Alfred Lunström on the far side of the room. They were going to stay right out in the open where they could be seen.

Fallon handed Travis the machine pistol. "Do you know how one of these works?"

"I've fired a Sten on the range."

"Then you can use this. And I do mean use it. There's a lot at stake and either the SS colonel or Lunström might get heroic ideas. Doubtful but possible. If they do, shoot them. Never mind the noise. A little more trouble isn't going to hurt us one way or the other."

Travis was curious. "The civilian's Lunström?"

"Right."

"But I thought he was one of the people you'd come here to take out."

Fallon sighed. "So did we, Travis, so did we. Just shoot him if he moves."

"Where will you and McKenna be?"

"Sitting right here, putting our heads together to see if we can figure some way out of this mess. Magda, you'd better come in on this."

"Can I do anything?" asked Natalie.

"We could all use something hot to drink and maybe a sandwich. The kitchen's through there."

Fallon watched her go. Sitting beside him, McKenna said, "Yes, sir, that is one very beautiful young woman."

Fallon feigned indifference. "I suppose so. I hadn't really noticed."

"If I didn't know him better," said McKenna, winking at Magda, "he'd almost have me believing that."

The German woman managed a smile. Because everything had happened so fast, she hadn't yet had an opportunity to tell anyone she recognized Meyer from Frankfurt. It was doubtful if he would remember her; she'd simply been a member of an audience. She also thought she'd seen the Gestapo officer who'd escaped somewhere before, but she put that down to imagination and didn't mention it.

"Doesn't matter a whole hell of a lot," said Fallon when she explained. "Whatever we decide to do with Meyer, you're a bit too involved to leave sitting over a radio. When we go, you come too."

"To England?"

"To England, Switzerland—to wherever we can manage. You've done your job. Curzon will go along with that. As they say in the POW camps, for you the war is over."

"It may also be over for us," drawled McKenna, "and maybe a bit more than the war. It's a nice idea to take Magda with us and one I go along with, but I haven't heard anyone suggest how any of us gets out, not in time to save three thousand American fliers from getting the chop, that is."

"Well," said Fallon, "that's what we're here for."

They tossed a few suggestions back and forth, but in the end concluded they were working in the dark. Until they knew precisely what was happening at street level—how thoroughly the Gestapo and the military were hunting them—they couldn't make a decision on their next move. Someone would have to go and take a look.

"It has to be me," said Magda, brushing aside the inevitable objections. "I'm the only one with valid papers."

Regrettably that was a fact. Knobel had taken the phony Gestapo identity documents back in Landwehrstrasse and they were either still on him or in his office safe. They were well enough armed, with handguns belonging to Heinnemann, Pickert, and Meyer—they seemed to have somehow overlooked Schumacher's—as well as the Schmeisser, but they couldn't hope to shoot their way out of trouble.

"Don't take any chances and go on foot," McKenna advised her. "Don't go too far either. We know they'll have roadblocks up further out; that doesn't have to be verified. Just get a general impression of what's going on in the immediate area, because you can bet your life it's the same elsewhere."

She was back in fifteen minutes. "The whole north end of town is crawling with troops," she reported. "There are patrols everywhere, mostly mobile. It's quite easy for one person to avoid them, but it would be impossible for all of us —especially with those two along." She nodded in the direction of Lunström and Meyer. "Perhaps they won't keep it up all night," she added hopefully.

"Oh, they'll do that all right," said McKenna grimly. "And most of tomorrow too. They might not know where we are, but they know they've got us boxed in. And while we're boxed in we won't be sending any signals to London."

Berlin had come to the same conclusion.

Walter Schellenberg practically threw a fit when Knobel came on the telephone with details of the disaster. Not an hour ago he and Mueller had had a private audience with the Führer, who was openly delighted with the success of the stratagem. If the information was accurate the Luftwaffe could destroy every American bomber capable of flying. Now he would have to go back and inform Hitler that there was a hitch.

Calming down, he asked Knobel what steps he had taken to ensure that the Allied agents and the Lunströms could not get out of Schweinfurt. Knobel said he had, on his own authority, alerted the military even before calling Prinz Albrechtstrasse. Foot and mobile patrols were scouring the streets, and all the roads—major and minor—out of Schweinfurt were blocked or in the process of being blocked.

"How do you know they did not get out before the roadblocks were set up?" demanded Schellenberg.

"I don't, Herr Brigadeführer," answered Knobel respectfully, "but I also took the precaution of alerting garrison commanders as far south as Würzburg and as far west as Frankfurt. Roadblocks will be set up in those areas, all vehicles stopped and searched. Even if they are out of Schweinfurt—which I doubt—they will not get far. They have no papers, Herr Brigadeführer."

"Make sure the patrols in the Würzburg vicinity are especially vigilant," ordered Schellenberg. "If they're going anywhere it will be in that direction, toward Switzerland." He had a thought. "Of course, they may not have to get out physically at all, not if they have a radio on hand."

Knobel considered that unlikely, and said so. "Why would they bother? Until a few hours ago they had no idea a plot existed. Their function was simply to rescue the Lunströms."

"They would still have to escape from Germany," Schellenberg reminded him.

"Naturally, but I believe it is as the Brigadeführer suggested. They were hoping to travel south and cross the border into Switzerland. Their route would have been arranged well in advance. They would have no need to radio ahead."

Schellenberg was inclined to agree, but he was still worried. What had looked like the basis for a cast-iron success a short time ago was now in jeopardy. Damn those incompetent fools!

"Stay by the phone or leave word where you can be found," he instructed. "I'll get back to you."

Schellenberg chose to postpone telling Hitler that something had gone wrong. There was a good chance the whole matter would be resolved before daybreak and he would have incurred the Führer's displeasure for no reason. But Mueller would have to be kept in the picture and so too would Göring.

He could not raise the Gestapo chief, but Göring came on the line immediately, being still in conference with Stumpff and Korten.

In spite of Schellenberg's soothing reassurances, the

Reichsmarschall was alarmed. "A little while ago," he said pompously, "you were telling me you had incontrovertible evidence that the US Eighth Air Force would bomb Schweinfurt tomorrow—today, I should say—and that the agents who unwittingly divulged this information were in custody. Now you tell me they've escaped, yet you *still* expect me to commit every fighter in the Reich to the defense of the ball-bearing factories."

Schellenberg counted slowly up to ten. "Not defend Schweinfurt, Herr Reichsmarschall, but attack and destroy the American bombing fleet."

"The distinction is not lost upon me, Schellenberg, but the fact remains that your intelligence source is no longer in captivity. The agents could have communicated with the Allies. Have you considered that? Men with sufficient ingenuity to have got as far as Schweinfurt and contacted the Lunströms *and* escaped with them from the combined forces of the Gestapo and the SD are men to be reckoned with. Would I had a dozen such individuals."

Schellenberg used the same argument on Göring as Knobel had used on him. The agents would have no need for a radio; they had no idea they were walking into a trap.

"And if you're wrong, Schellenberg?" Göring did not wait for an answer. "If somehow the Allies have received word that we are waiting for them on either side of their course to Schweinfurt and decide to attack elsewhere? What will happen then? No, don't interrupt me. *I'll* tell *you* what will happen. We shall have deployed upwards of a thousand fighters in south Germany with nothing, *nothing whatsoever,* in the north. Far from being a major victory for the Luftwaffe and the Reich, it could turn out to be a disaster. And who would the Führer blame, Schellenberg?"

Schellenberg could see full well which way the conversation was leading. Göring was wavering. He had been no more than a lukewarm supporter of the stratagem from the beginning, mistrusting, as he did, any operation which involved the clandestine, the playing of chess at the highest level. He preferred a straightforward fight where the enemy could be seen and counted and defeated by greater numbers. Nothing would please the fat baboon more than evading a decision and justifying his inaction by saying he could not risk having a thousand planes in one place while there was the remotest possibility the B-17s would be in another. Worse, the Führer would be compelled to agree with him—and all because those bastards in Schweinfurt had allowed themselves to be tricked.

It wasn't in Schellenberg's nature to plead, but he did so now. The plan was his, his alone, the original conception worked out through many a long and sleepless night. Mueller (and for that matter the Führer) might think they were equal partners, but it was he, from his position as head of RSHA VI, who had so finely divined Alfred Lunström's true political leanings, his greed; it was he who had contacted the Swede, persuaded first Speer and then Hitler that it was all worthwhile, that, properly handled, Lunström could prove to be a good and valuable friend to Nazi Germany. And for what? To see everything evaporate, disappear like straw in the wind because an inadequate air force commander no longer had the balls to do the job?

Not if he could help it.

When—not if, *when*—the US Eighth turned up over Schweinfurt in a dozen hours while the bulk of Göring's fighters were elsewhere, it would be no use saying, I told you so. The chance, the marvelous once-in-a-lifetime opportunity, would have gone and would never recur.

So Schellenberg pleaded, used all his considerable powers of oratory on the Reichsmarschall. The agents did not have a wireless or access to one. They were trapped in Schweinfurt. The Reichsmarschall *must* commit his fighters.

There was such a long silence when Schellenberg finished speaking that he thought Göring had broken the connection. But he hadn't.

"You are a persuasive advocate, Schellenberg," he said

finally, "and I am not entirely convinced you are guilty of wishful thinking. But I have a greater responsibility than the success or failure of one operation, a single reckless cast of the die. I will go this far and no further. I am at present in consultation with Generals Stumpff and Korten. Between us we are attempting to decide how best to deploy the forces at my disposal. We shall continue to do that, giving you the benefit of the doubt. But if there is the slightest sign later today that Schweinfurt is not the primary target, that we have either been duped from the beginning or that the *Amis* have received word of our trap and are going elsewhere or splitting their forces, I shall not hesitate to withdraw the fighters from the northern and eastern airfields. Is that understood?"

"It is, Herr Reichsmarschall."

"Good. And one other thing, Schellenberg: I and I alone will be the final arbiter of the Americans' intentions."

The line went dead.

It was, thought Schellenberg, as much as he could hope for under the circumstances, though in spite of the fine words —"I have a greater responsibility than the success or failure of one operation"—no doubt for the record, he was still sure the Reichsmarschall was a reluctant and faint-hearted ally who would seize upon any excuse to leave the northern fighters where they were. Only one thing would make him change his mind, and that was the recapture and thorough interrogation of the Allied agents.

Hauptsturmführer Knobel, who was as much to blame for the shambles as the missing Meyer, would have to work a little harder if he wanted to retain his rank—and his head.

Knobel was far from happy when he finished speaking to Schellenberg. He had pointed out that Meyer had had local command of the operation, not Walter Knobel. Meyer had allowed himself to be taken or killed by the Englishman and the American, not Walter Knobel, who had shown enough presence of mind to make a run for it. What was more, Walter

Knobel had, in fifteen short minutes, sounded the alert, contacted the military, thrown up roadblocks, and returned to Landwehrstrasse 18 to count the dead and make sure the premises had indeed been vacated. Walter Knobel had done a good job, which was a damned sight more than could be said for a lot of others.

But such sentiments cut no ice with Berlin; he knew that. Schellenberg wanted only results. If they were not forthcoming, not even his own chief, Mueller, would be able to protect him. Mueller was in this as much as Schellenberg and he too would be looking for a whipping boy.

It was useless, also, to point out that with Heinnemann in the hospital and probably dying, and Pickert and Schumacher already dead, the effective strength of the Schweinfurt Gestapo was now reduced to three: himself, Grauert, and Burgsdorf, who were now waiting for orders in the outer office.

But what to tell them? Go out and comb the streets? That was already being done. Search every house in town? An impossible task, though it was reasonable to assume that if the fugitives had not already left Schweinfurt—doubtful—they were holed up somewhere. But where? And had they simply forced the lock of a shop or house or apartment, or had the funk-hole been arranged well in advance? If so, by whom? Traitors were not uncommon among the subject peoples of the occupied territories but almost unheard of in the Reich. Yet, it was not inconceivable.

He thought again of the woman he had knocked to the floor in his haste to leave Landwehrstrasse 18. Although he had caught only the briefest glimpse of her face, something about it was familiar. She had spoken in German and she *was* German, he was sure of it, but she wasn't from Schweinfurt. He would stake his life on that. He smiled sardonically to himself. He might just have to.

According to Meyer, the Allied agents had landed by parachute the night of the Frankfurt raid. But why Frankfurt when, in a matter of minutes, the pilot of the aircraft could have flown them twenty or thirty miles closer to their destination without greater danger to the Lancaster than it was already undergoing? He was no flier, but he knew that thirty miles was nothing to a Lancaster, which had a cruising speed of 180 mph. Ten to fifteen minutes would have brought the bomber over Schweinfurt. Why, then, the outskirts of Frankfurt?

It could be—it wasn't certain, but it was far from unreasonable conjecture—that Frankfurt was chosen because London had a deep-cover contact there; the German woman, who would furnish the agents with a place to hide, food, information—until it was time to do something about the Lunströms.

Was he making the facts fit the theory? He thought not. He was not an infrequent visitor to Frankfurt. It was possible he had seen the woman there.

Knobel took pride in a first-class memory for faces and the ability, even months later, to recall the exact time and place of a meeting. It therefore followed that he had never actually met the woman, that he had merely seen her in passing but that something had drawn his attention to her. Could she be a shop assistant where he had made a purchase? Unlikely. He was a creature of habit and knew all the assistants who served him regularly. Some kind of public servant then? A factory worker? A nurse, a clerk, a teacher?

No, he had already decided she was not from Schweinfurt and he had not been out of town for three weeks. He was sure the encounter was more recent than that.

He reviewed every place he had visited in the course of his duties for the last ten days. St. Josef's Hospital, there to pay his respects to an old comrade who was dying. The public baths in Rüfferstrasse to investigate a report that one of the attendants was voicing anti-Party slogans. The law courts? A possibility, but why should someone from Frankfurt—assuming his theory was correct—be in the Schweinfurt courts when unnecessary travel was discouraged? The forestry office, the paint works in Bellevue, the Hotel Krone, Friedrich Pflaum's garage in Schultesstrasse, the malt factory in Hauptbahnhof-strasse, Robert Zeuner's radio—

He stopped. Friedrich Pflaum's garage? No. But . . . the malt factory! That was where he had seen the woman. The damned malt factory! A few days ago. A week, was it? While he was investigating an anonymous tip-off—false as it turned out—that the factory was holding on to key personnel, men and boys who should long ago have been in the Wehrmacht. The woman was in one of the offices creating hell about . . . about . . . He could not recall the nature of her complaint, but the factory manager was obviously in awe of her authority.

His yells brought Grauert and Burgsdorf racing in from the adjoining room.

It was around 0315 hours that orders finally came down from Brigadier General Anderson's Pinetree HQ that Mission 115, the bombing of Schweinfurt, was on, subject to favorable weather conditions. The forecast looked good, and commanders were to proceed on the basis that the Eighth would fly today.

Teleprinters chattered out the news to bases at Alconbury, Bassingbourn, Grafton Underwood, Polebrook, Thurleigh, Hardwick, Great Ashfield, Knettisham, Thrope Abbots, Molesworth—names that had meant nothing to the B-17 crews eighteen months earlier, that could, even now, be identified only on large-scale maps, quaint English villages and towns that belonged to another more distant, gentler era.

Between 0330 and 0430 each of the squadrons' operations officers made the rounds of the Nissen huts which housed the crews and roused those who were to fly on the mission, though the target was still a closely guarded secret known only to a few senior ranks.

The men called struggled from their bunks, cursed, coughed, lit cigarettes and cheap cigars, scratched, yawned, hunted for gear, and wished the devil and all his bad luck on those fliers who were to remain behind.

As always, it was bitterly cold and damp, as bad inside the barracks as out. There was never enough heat, never enough coal to go around. The men loathed the English climate as much as they feared any German fighter pilot.

Outside, the fog was as thick as hominy grits, and more than one crew thought of heading straight back for the sack. There would be no briefing. It would all be called off in a couple of hours. Others felt the opposite: All else being equal, Anderson would have them airborne before noon.

As each man stumbled through the mud—always the wretched mud—to the ablutions, he could not see the huge grassy airfields, each a couple of miles long and bisected by runways of concrete and macadam. Nor could he see the massive hangars and the dispersal areas where the great planes sat brooding, waiting for life. But once in a while he could hear the sound of those men whose task it was to prepare the B-17s for flight: the mechanics, engineers, the armorers loading the high explosives and the incendiaries. And those with experience knew that today was race day.

There were heroes, actual and potential, aplenty in the Eighth, but few foolish enough not to admit they were scared. Back home the politicians and the newspapers depicted each crew as clean-cut, smiling, intrepid airmen who knew no fear, who were twice as good as any Kraut. The fliers knew better and were not ashamed to admit it.

A few months earlier a US aircraft company had sponsored a magazine advertisement showing a B-17 gunner peering over the sights of his machine gun and pouring a stream of lead into a Focke-Wulf 190. The caption read: "Who's afraid of the big bad Wulf?" A squadron commander had torn out the page and pinned it to the bulletin board with a scroll

238

of paper for signatures. Every man in the unit signed his name beneath the words "WE ARE."

And so they were, but few men invented stomach pains or other fake ailments, not even when word went around that briefing was to be in ninety minutes, at 0700.

Eighteen

At five minutes to six McKenna returned from a second, longer reconnaissance of the streets. He had taken a risk by going out, but he needed to see for himself if Magda had exaggerated. She hadn't. Perhaps the troops were not so alert as a few hours ago, but the patrols were still there, motorized and foot. It was, in any case, too late now to make for Switzerland, though Frankfurt remained on if they left within the hour.

He suggested as much to Fallon, that one of them and Magda take a shot at it. More than that probably wouldn't make it, but two might just get through.

Fallon felt compelled to play devil's advocate. "By walking all the way? Come off it, Sam. By driving there in the Opel? You'll be inside a cell with your balls in a meat grinder before daybreak, which will make matters worse than they are now."

"How come?"

"If you're taken by the Gestapo they'll soon find out we were unable to contact London. If they didn't break you they'd break Magda. As it stands, they can't be certain whether we're in or out, whether we got through the net. It might make them reconsider their plans."

"And if it doesn't?"

"Chucking away your life and Magda's isn't going to help anyone."

"Neither is sitting here." McKenna knew Fallon was talking sense, but the inactivity was driving him mad. "We've got to do something, for Chrissake. We can't just hang around waiting for the fucking bombs to drop."

Fallon nodded. "You're right on that score, of course, which is something we continue to overlook. Even if the Luftwaffe puts up every fighter it has available, some of the B-17s are bound to get through, which'll leave us in the middle of a bombing raid. But without documents . . ." He hesitated. "Now wait a minute . . ."

McKenna looked up sharply at the change of tone. "You've thought of something?"

"Maybe. Let me think . . ."

Fallon struggled to marshal his thoughts. Like McKenna, he hadn't slept for twenty-four hours, and the Benzedrine tablets helped only marginally.

"We can't get through the roadblocks because the patrol commanders will have our descriptions, right? Even if we kept our heads down, we have no valid travel or identity papers, right?"

"Right."

"Okay, but who does have papers? Who among this merry band of pilgrims does have the authority to go more or less where they please?"

McKenna glanced around. Magda was asleep in one of the bedrooms and Natalie was in the kitchen preparing yet another pot of ersatz coffee to help keep them awake. Alfred Lunström was curled up on a sofa, dead to the world, and Meyer was sitting on the floor, back to the wall, eyes closed. A few feet away Flight Lieutenant Travis kept a weary eye on both of them.

"Magda, of course," he said, "and probably Lunström and Natalie, though their names are doubtless on a wanted list."

"What about Meyer?"

"Well, Meyer, naturally, but I don't see how that helps. He's about your build but he doesn't look like either of us, and SS credentials contain a photograph of the legitimate bearer."

"I wasn't thinking of borrowing them. I was thinking of persuading him to lead us through the roadblocks in person. I doubt if anyone would question the authority of an SS security colonel in full uniform."

"Agreed, but it might take more than a little arm-twisting. Lack of sleep's fried your brain, Jack. Meyer's no fool. He knows we're not going to shoot him in cold blood. All he has to do is wait. He'll have figured out for himself that sooner or later we'll make a break for it."

"Leaving him here, right? We'd tie him up and knock him on the head and let him sweat it out until someone finds him."

"Something like that."

'Then let's tell him we're pulling out in the next fifteen minutes, before it gets good and light, because we want to be long gone when the bombs start dropping. He'll go for it. He has to, because it makes a damned sight more sense to take our chances on the road than it does to hang around here waiting for an air raid. But here's the twist: he's not coming with us. We're going to bind him and gag him, truss him up like a turkey. Then he can count the hours until the sirens go. I don't know about you, but it would scare the hell out of me to be stuck up here while the B-17s leveled the place. His alternative is to help us. There'll be a gun in his ribs all the way. If he puts a foot wrong, tries to raise the alarm at a roadblock, he's dead. He's also dead if he doesn't get us through. We might not shoot him while he's sitting against that wall, but outside it's every man for himself and a different matter entirely."

"It might work," said McKenna cautiously.

"It'd damn well better," retorted Fallon, "because I'm fresh out of ideas. Why don't you put it to him anyway. Take him into one of the unoccupied bedrooms and maybe lean on him a little."

"It'll be a pleasure."

Meyer was unwilling to go with McKenna at first, but the American was taller and heavier and in a hurry. Ignoring Meyer's protests, he dragged him to his feet by the collar and frog-marched him out of the room. The door closed behind them as Natalie came in from the kitchen with a tray of hot coffee.

Awakened by the disturbance, Alfred Lunström refused curtly, but Travis took a cup, smiling gratefully.

Natalie came over to Fallon and sat beside him. As she handed him the cup the heavy gold bracelet she wore on her left wrist caught the edge of the tray. The fastening snapped and it fell to the floor.

Fallon picked it up. It must have weighed four to six ounces and the initials NL were subtly interwoven in the design. "Clasp's broken," he said. He put it on the sofa between them. Natalie left it there.

"What's happening with Meyer?" she asked.

"Sam's going to put a little pressure on him, try to persuade him to get us out of here."

"How?"

Fallon explained. "But if it doesn't work," he added, "we're going to have to decide pretty damned fast what happens to you and your uncle."

"I don't understand."

"We're wanted, but you're not—at least not in the same way. I know you killed or seriously injured Heinnemann, but there's more at stake than the death of one Gestapo sergeant.

If you went down to Rückertstrasse and gave yourselves up, I'm sure Knobel wouldn't harm you. Neither would Berlin. I don't like the idea of letting your uncle go, because he's caused us enough trouble with maybe more in the offing, and I'm getting fond of the notion of taking him back to England with us—assuming we can get out. On the other hand, he carries a lot more clout than you."

"No," said Natalie firmly.

"No what?"

"No, I'm not going anywhere, either with my uncle or alone. I prefer to take my chances with you and Sam McKenna."

"That's out. You don't know what you're saying. If Meyer won't play ball we're stuck here until after the raid at the very least, and enough aircraft will arrive over the MPI to make that prospect unpleasant."

"MPI?"

"Mean Point of Impact, the middle of the target. Even if only a few dozen planes get through, there are going to be a lot of buildings flattened and brisk business in the undertaking profession."

"I still refuse to go. Apart from my uncle coming with me—which I don't believe I want either—how do you think I'd feel knowing I'd left you and Sam McKenna and Frau Lessing and the RAF boy to face whatever's coming while I was flown or driven to safety. The answer's no, and in case you haven't noticed I'm a very determined woman."

Fallon took in the pugnacious set of her jaw, the sparkle of battle in her eyes, and concluded the discussion was closed.

Although not a man to indulge in fanciful thinking, if some secret genie from a lamp had offered to grant him one wish there and then he would have asked that he and Natalie Lunström could have met under different circumstances; circumstances where time was their ally, not the enemy. She was everything a man could want—beautiful, warm, courageous, tough in the best possible way. And rich, of course. Aye, there was the rub. The genie would have to be asked for a further boon because their worlds were poles apart. He picked up the bracelet, symbol of the gulf that separated them.

She seemed to divine his mood, because he felt her hand touch his. "Thank you," she said.

"For what?"

"For not trying to talk me out of staying. I'm an added responsibility, I realize that."

"We wouldn't be here at all if it wasn't for you."

He gave her the bracelet. She examined it for a moment, the broken clasp, before passing it back.

"Keep it until we're out of this," she said impulsively, "until we're in London or Stockholm. It's one of my favorites, but I'll feel happier knowing you have it."

He put it in his pocket, wondering, in view of the conditions, if it would ever be returned. Still, they were safe enough for the time being.

Or so he thought.

Forty-five minutes earlier Knobel had succeeded in tracing the manager of the malt factory, rousing him from the bed of his mistress in Deutschhöferstrasse. The man was far from being pleased at being disturbed in such a cozy nest and was prepared to give the telephone caller a piece of his mind until he realized he was talking to the Gestapo. After that he was cooperation personified.

Yes, he remembered the woman who had called at the factory a few days ago and if the Hauptsturmführer would kindly give him a moment to collect his thoughts he would try to recall her name. It was Listing or Lansing or . . . No, it was Frau Lessing from the Ernährungsamt in Frankfurt, some nonsense about buying black-market barley, which the Hauptsturmführer should understand was a malicious lie.

The Hauptsturmführer made a mental note to look into the matter at some future date and hung up after ascertaining that the manager had no idea where Frau Lessing would stay while in Schweinfurt. Probably the Hotel Krone or Ross, no? Those were the two biggest.

But never a man to miss anything, however unlikely it might seem on the surface, Knobel had already checked the Krone and the Ross as well as the Bayerischer Hof and the Post Bahnhof and several smaller ones. With negative results.

Getting hold of the head of the Ernährungsamt in Frankfurt was proving difficult. His name was Weitkus and he was apparently a reserve fire-watcher with twice-weekly duties. The Frankfurt Gestapo were inquiring into what beat he was on and would call Knobel back as soon as he was located.

Knobel told them to hurry. "I am not exaggerating when I tell you that the future of the Reich may depend upon the speed with which you act."

But Frankfurt had heard that sort of talk before and classified the request as routine. They would turn up Weitkus as quick as they could, but they were not going to break their backs doing it, not at this hour of the morning.

When McKenna ushered Meyer back into the sitting room the expression on his face was one of triumph, while that on the security colonel's was of a man who had looked deep into the innermost workings of his soul and discovered he was mortal. The manner in which he was carrying his left arm suggested McKenna had been far from gentle in eliciting co-operation, though no one had heard anything because of the handkerchief gag. The American made quite clear to Travis that this was to remain in place.

Travis ordered Meyer to take up his former position, on the floor, back to the wall.

"Well?" demanded Fallon.

McKenna glanced at Natalie.

"I'll go away if you wish," said the girl.

Fallon told her to stay. "You might as well hear this from the beginning, assuming there's something to hear and that grin on Major McKenna's face isn't the result of overdoing the amphetamines. We're going somewhere, I presume?"

"That we are, Doctor Livingstone, that we are. In spades. We're also going quicker, more directly, and a whole hell of a lot safer than either of us thought a few minutes ago."

"His mother was frightened by John Barrymore," Fallon explained to Natalie. "He's being dramatic and keeping us in suspense because he knows there's no hurry. When you're quite ready, Sam."

McKenna took a mouthful of coffee from a cup on the tray and grimaced. "Jesus Christ, it tastes like paint remover. I thought nothing could be worse than this stuff hot, but you should try it cold."

"Sam," Fallon prompted him.

"Okay, I'm getting there." He put down the cup. "It took a little doing, but when Meyer got the message we weren't kidding about leaving him behind, he chose to get on the team. I had to jump on his arm a bit, but, Christ, it's an imperfect world.

"In the first place it was the Obersturmbannführer himself who gave me the idea. To get the conversation going and show him I meant business, I asked him what his plans for us were if the positions had been reversed. He said they were going to take us to Berlin for an in-depth interrogation so that Schellenberg, who seems to be running the show, could be sure we weren't pulling a fast one, that the US Eighth Air Force was genuinely on its way. Schellenberg was sending a plane, which was due in at three-thirty. And that's when it hit me."

"I'll refrain from making the obvious comment. Kindly get to the point."

"It's staring you in the face. A plane—a nice big juicy fat plane all the way from Berlin just for us."

Fallon snorted with disbelief. "You're not expecting the two of us to hijack Schellenberg's plane, I hope. In the first place it's probably done an about-turn by now, now that we've had the bad manners to escape. Secondly, even if it hasn't there'll be an escort aboard. And lastly, the pilot might choose not to cooperate."

"Christ, you're real jumpers to conclusions, you Limeys. I didn't say anything about hijacking the Berlin plane. I said that's what gave me the idea. But we take one of the others, *one of the Ju 52s we saw coming in.* Remember? The old Iron Annies. You asked Magda what they were and she told you."

Fallon began to see daylight.

"What do we need most of all right this red-hot minute?" McKenna went on. "We need a quick way out and a means of contacting Curzon and Mortimer in Switzerland. Okay, now we have both. Remember what Magda said about the 52s? They're experimental jobs for voice transmissions over long distances. We grab one and get the hell out of here."

"And who the blazes is supposed to fly the damned thing?" asked Fallon, but McKenna saw from the direction he was looking that he'd answered his own question almost before it was out.

The American grinned happily. "That's it—Travis. We have our own pilot right here on tap. We use Meyer to get us through the roadblocks, onto the airfield and into the plane. If you're right about Schellenberg's aircraft doing an about-turn when we went missing—and that seems a pretty good bet—we tell anyone who gives us flak that the Lunströms are wanted in Berlin p.d.q. Depending upon what time we get airborne, we might not need the radio at all. We just head south and dump the bloody thing down—in Lake Geneva if necessary."

"And Meyer's agreed to all this?"

"Meyer doesn't know the half of it yet, but he'll agree all right. He knows it's either that or a front-row seat at the fireworks show."

"We'd better check that Travis can fly a 52."

Travis, of course, said he'd never handled one, but that

one aircraft was pretty much like another once you knew where all the knobs were. If it meant quitting Schweinfurt he'd get the 52 airborne, no question of that.

Fallon told Natalie to wake Magda. It was almost six-thirty-five, time for them all to clean up before leaving, shave and wash. Getting onto the airfield and aboard the Iron Annie was going to present enough problems without them turning up looking like a bunch of refugees from the soup kitchens.

He pondered what to do about Alfred Lunström. Once in the Opel, Meyer would behave because the alternative was a bullet in the ribs, and the same would have to go for the Swede: mouth closed and no trouble or it was the end of the road.

Wordlessly, Lunström nodded his acceptance of the conditions, and Fallon was satisfied he would not try to raise the alarm. He had no way of knowing that the Swede was biding his time. Lunström too now thought it a sensible idea to get out of Schweinfurt and he had an ace up his sleeve no one knew about. But the moment to play it was not yet at hand.

At 0654 hours the telephone rang in Knobel's office. It was the Frankfurt Gestapo to say they had Paul Weitkus.

"Put him on," snapped Knobel.

Weitkus was terrified he had broken some law and it took Knobel a valuable minute to calm him down. Not for the first time did the Hauptsturmführer reflect that the Gestapo's reputation was frequently counterproductive; a man couldn't think clearly when he was scared stiff.

There was nothing to worry about, he assured Weitkus, just a few routine questions to answer. Now, did he have an employee by the name of Frau Lessing?

Yes, Magda Lessing did work for the Ernährungsamt.

And where was Frau Lessing at the moment?

She was in Schweinfurt, but surely the Hauptsturmführer knew that, as he was calling from there. Had something happened to her?

Nothing had happened to her. What was she doing in Schweinfurt?

She was checking on suspected black-market barley dealings at Malzfabrik.

How long had she been here?

Since yesterday. What was this all about?

It would be explained later. Where did Frau Lessing stay while in Schweinfurt?

The Ernährungsamt had an apartment there for staff with overnight business. It saved on hotel bills and petrol. Of course, Weitkus understood that it was not strictly legal, what with the housing shortage due to the bombing—

"I'm not in the least interested in that," barked Knobel. "Just give me the address."

"Horst Wesselstrasse number forty, apartment C," answered Weitkus, and was left talking to nobody as Knobel slammed down the phone and yelled for Grauert to get the car.

Knobel, Grauert, and Burgsdorf arrived at Horst Wesselstrasse 40, apartment C, at 0703, eight minutes after Fallon, McKenna, and the others had vacated the premises. But it could have been eight hours as far as the Gestapo captain was concerned. He'd missed them.

At the various Eighth Bomber Command airfields the briefing for Mission 115 began soon after 0700. At Bassingbourn in Cambridgeshire, home of the 91st Heavy Bombardment Group, a groan went up from the assembled crews when the cover was removed from the target map and the destination announced as Schweinfurt. One of the loudest cries of disgust came from Captain Joe Calhoun, skipper of *Heartless Hazel*. "Christ, and this is my last mission."

In the sudden hush that followed he threw an embarrassed glance at his co-pilot, Hank Quincey, and wished he had not used those precise words.

The briefing at Bassingbourn was identical to that being given to the other groups. First the crews listened and made notes as the flak officer, with the aid of reconnaissance photographs, showed them the areas of heaviest anti-aircraft concentration in Belgium and Germany and advised that the stream was routed well clear of most of them. Over Schweinfurt itself flak was expected to be light. Few crews believed this. In August it had been thick enough to walk on.

Then came the bombing leader with details of the bombloads the B-17s were to carry. He was followed by the group navigation officer with a breakdown of the route. There would be a separate, more comprehensive briefing for all navigators later.

Finally the intelligence officer stood up and drew a small circle on the target chart to indicate the MPI. For the 91st this would be the VKF 1 works, part of which was only a few hundred meters from Landwehrstrasse. The IO also informed them that the IP (the Initial Point where the group was committed to the target) was twenty miles southwest of the town. It was possible, he added, that the Luftwaffe could muster 300 fighters along the route.

Allied fighters, the IO went on, P-47s and Spitfires, would escort the bombing fleet as far as Aachen—the limit of their range—and cover the retreat.

The crews were reminded not to talk about the target when they left the room in case the mission was scrubbed, and not to wear squadron insignia on the raid. If shot down and taken prisoner they were to reveal only name, rank, and serial number.

Outside, most of the crews reckoned a scrubbing was very definitely in the cards. The fog was as thick as ever.

Joe Calhoun hoped they would go. In spite of his earlier comment and all-too-clear memories of the August raid, he wanted to get this twenty-fifth mission over and done with. It was like waiting for the other shoe to drop. It would have been pleasant to have had a milk run to go out on, but, he reminded himself, there were no easy ones at this stage in the war.

Perhaps surprisingly, the majority of the crews were also anxious for Mission 115 to be given the green light. Now that they were briefed and knew the target, they were keyed up, the adrenaline flowing furiously. All in all it was better to get it over with. A scrubbed mission did not count toward a tour, and the same dangers would be there tomorrow.

Among the few who did not want to make the raid under any circumstances was Sergeant Ted Edwards, *Hazel*'s right-waist gunner. He had missed the October 8 mission to Bremen by claiming stomach cramps, and as soon as the briefing was over he reported to the MO with the same complaint again. He was lucky that the medical officer was a sympathetic individual who well understood fear, and Ted was grounded—as much for the safety of the remainder of *Hazel*'s crew as for any other reason. A waist gunner who was paralyzed with fright was a liability. The MO made a marginal note on the medical report recommending that Edwards be given a thorough psychological check-up with a view to reclassifying him as unfit for flying duties.

Captain Max Shapiro, who had flown in Edwards' place on October 8 and whose own Fortress was still not considered airworthy, quickly heard of the defection and again offered his services to Calhoun.

(He wasn't the only one trying to bum a ride that day. Over at Polebrook, base of the 351st Bomb Group, the film actor Clark Gable, in actuality a ground officer but one who had taken the trouble to qualify as an air gunner and who was a popular man in the outfit, was trying the same tactic. He was turned down by every skipper he approached. Not one wanted to be responsible to history for not bringing back the star of *Gone With the Wind* in one piece.)

Shapiro expressed some surprise that *Hazel*, after the pasting she had taken over Bremen, was also not grounded.

"There wasn't much structural damage, just the skin."
Calhoun gave a lopsided grin. "Or maybe I've got a better
maintenance team than you."

"It's not that at all," chipped in the bombardier, Irish-
man Billy Concannon. "It's just that they're keeping his own
plane on the deck to stop it getting holed. He can't expect
anything else if he keeps bringing it back shot to fuck, may
the Holy Virgin wash my mouth out with carbolic."

"Never mind the wisecracks," Shapiro growled. "Do I
get a ride or not?"

"You're a glutton for punishment, Max." Calhoun shook
his head in mock amazement, though he fully understood that
Shapiro, now on the twenty-one or twenty-two mark, wanted
to notch up the full score-and-five while he felt lucky. "Why
don't you sit this one out? Maybe Hitler will throw his hand
in tomorrow."

"Yeah, and then it'll be the fucking Japs. Am I in or
not?"

"Waal, I dunno. How did he do last time, O'Malley?"
Calhoun asked the left-waist gunner.

Nineteen-year-old Mike O'Malley grinned. "Not bad,
Skip, for a beginner."

Although realizing he was being joshed, Shapiro turned
away in disgust. "Well, fuck you."

Calhoun called him back. "If you promise not to waste
too many bullets on those nasty Krauts. Remember they cost
three dollars apiece."

"And if you promise not to swear just because you're
being shot at," put in Concannon.

"And if we go at all," added Hank Quincey.

"Oh, we're going, all right," said Shapiro.

Hazel's navigator, Lieutenant Ken Cornelius, continued
to doubt it. So did flight engineer Bob Baker and radio operator Jimmy Ryan. Tail gunner Don Schaeffer, only son of
multimillionaire Louis Schaeffer, was convinced it was on, and
ball-turret gunner George Bushman agreed with him.

It took a while, but eventually Bushman, Shapiro, and Schaeffer were proved right.

Shortly after 9 A.M. a weather reconnaissance Mosquito flying high over Germany flashed back to Pinetree the magic words: "The Continent is clear."

For the most part it was, but not on the outskirts of Schweinfurt, not at this hour, a fact that was causing considerable anxiety among Fallon, McKenna, and the others.

Nineteen

Perhaps it was because there were other vehicles on the roads now and the task of questioning the occupants of each as well as keeping the traffic flowing was beyond the capabilities of most roadblock commanders, or perhaps the all-night vigil had dampened their enthusiasm, but the Opel was rarely held up for more than a few seconds; and after a while it had all become too ridiculously easy. Meyer's credentials and his imposing uniformed presence up front saw them past patrol after patrol, through roadblock after roadblock, while McKenna's Walther in the small of his back ensured the SS colonel's continued cooperation. More often than not, when a sharp-eyed NCO spotted the Obersturmbannführer's silhouette behind the windshield, they were waved straight through. No one seemed to think it the least odd that a female civilian was driving the Opel or that the passengers in the back averted their faces when the car was forced down to a crawl, and they were beyond the town limits and on Reichsstrasse 26, heading southwest, by 8 A.M., by which time it was light. Or would have been were it not for the fog, part natural, part industrial pollution from Schweinfurt's factory chimneys.

Approaching the airfield's main gates, Travis advised caution. The administration buildings and the runways were also shrouded in low-lying mist, which was thick enough here to reduce visibility to a few yards. Doubtless it would clear in an hour or so, but for the moment no aircraft would be permitted to take off. The RAF officer suggested they wait outside the wire, well away from the gates, until the fog showed signs of lifting.

Fallon and McKenna were reluctantly compelled to agree. Remaining pulled off the road outside the wire might be dangerous, but it was less so than hanging around the airfield itself, where they would be under the constant scrutiny of Luftwaffe personnel. Even more threatening was the possibility that someone would have the wit to call Berlin and verify whether this oddball group really did have permission to take one of the precious experimental 52s. Ideally, using Meyer as a lever, they wanted to bully or bluff their way onto the airfield and aboard a plane before anyone got too curious.

But by nine-fifteen visibility had improved only marginally—just enough to see the outlines of three Ju 52s in the middle distance—and Fallon was beginning to worry. He was no meteorologist, but he knew the fog would lift when the heat of the sun was sufficient to burn it off. That could happen in one hour or three, but there was the rub: In three hours the B-17s would be on their way.

He handed the Schmeisser to Travis with instructions to use it if Meyer stepped out of line, and beckoned McKenna from the car. "We've got to get out of here, Sam."

"You took the words right out of my mouth. Any suggestions?"

"Yes. First things being first, we've got to get aboard one of those 52s."

"Muscle our way on?"

"We'll have to be a bit more subtle than that. We'd look a mite foolish if we succeeded and found the plane we were on wasn't fueled up. Secondly, Travis doesn't know the runways or the length of the field, and piling up before we can unstick isn't my idea of an exit ticket. Thirdly, we need greater visibility, which precludes trusting to luck, blasting our way aboard, and sitting tight until this bloody fog lifts. They'd either blow us to pieces or block the runways, and that's it. Good night, Vienna."

"So?"

"So we forget the strong-arm stuff and bluff our way through. Maybe the airfield commandant won't bother to check with Berlin, but if he does I think I've come up with the answer. We're not only bringing the Lunströms but one of the Allied agents for interrogation as well. You."

"Me?"

"Sure. The other one—me—got away."

McKenna was lost and admitted it. "You told me a couple of hours ago that Meyer's been talking to Schellenberg," Fallon said. "Fine. He can talk to him again. If the commandant won't play ball and give us an aircraft, we get Schellenberg to use the big stick on him."

"Now hold on, buddy," protested McKenna. "I know we're in a jam, but I hope you're not suggesting we let Meyer and Schellenberg have a cozy little chat. Gun in his back or no, the Obersturmbannführer might just take it into his head to blow the whistle."

"It won't be Meyer." Fallon managed a smile at McKenna's expression of bewilderment. "It'll be me in Meyer's uniform."

McKenna held his head in mock despair. "You're going to talk to *Schellenberg?*"

"If it comes to it, why not? I know as much about this operation as Meyer, probably a hell of a lot more. Enough to fool Schellenberg, certainly. If there's any inconsistency in the sound of our voices, Schellenberg will put it down to a poor connection. Meyer and I are close enough in size for his uniform to fit me, and I'm not going to be taking any crap from the guards or anyone else about papers. I'm going to be moving fast. No one will question my authenticity once I ask to speak to Berlin."

"It's lunacy," said McKenna finally, "but I admit it's one of the last shots we've got. There's a snag, though. What if the genuine Berlin aircraft and escort is still over there?"

"I can only see the outline of three 52s, the same number we saw coming in. It could be parked in a hangar or further out, hidden by the fog, but we agreed a while back it's probably done a U-turn. They can't be so well off for aircraft that they can afford to have one sitting idly on the tarmac on the off chance we'll be picked up. Anyway, I'll cross that bridge when I come to it. We'll give the fog another half-hour to see if it lifts any, then we'll move. Once we're through the gates, you and the others remain in the car. Short of presenting him with a detailed flight plan, I'll get whatever information Travis needs from whoever's in charge."

Meyer protested volubly when he was ordered to strip to his underwear and exchange his clothes for Fallon's, but McKenna reminded him that his usefulness was virtually at an end—which his life certainly would be if he persisted in being obstructive.

The uniform fitted Fallon as well as could be expected, though the breeches were a little loose around the waist and the boots pinched. But those were the least of his worries.

At nine-fifty a combination of the rising sun and a light breeze started to brush away the mist. Another thirty minutes and Travis reckoned flying would be possible. He was not in the least disturbed that he was not to be furnished with a detailed weather report. He would have visibility and that was meat and drink to a flier. He would also have some help. Natalie had proffered the information that she was an experienced pilot of light aircraft, though she had never handled anything as big as a 52. Still, she understood the fundamentals of flying and would be an invaluable help with the throttles and flaps on take-off.

Fallon adjusted Meyer's peaked cap to the correct angle. "Okay," he said, "let's go."

The first of the Eighth Bomber Command's aircraft were airborne shortly after 10 A.M. The weathermen had predicted that the cloud would top out at 2,000 feet, but it was 6,500 before the lead planes were above it, an unforeseen circumstance that delayed assembly and compelled the vanguard squadrons to circle, firing signal flares in an attempt to attract stragglers. Much later it would be established that assembly took two hours.

To begin with, the air fleet comprised a total of 377 bombers, almost 3,800 men. Of these, 163 B-17s belonged to the First Air Division, 154 to the Third, and 60 B-24s to the smaller Second. But of this latter group only twenty-four managed to find one another over the rendezvous. Rather than send such a pitifully small force against a target as well defended as Schweinfurt, Brigadier General Anderson ordered them on a diversionary raid to the Frisian Islands.

Heartless Hazel took off at 10:17 A.M. At the controls, Calhoun and Quincey peered anxiously through the Plexiglas canopy as the huge bomber swam upward. All pilots hated cloud and feared a midair collision as much as they feared the Luftwaffe and flak. It only needed the plane up front to lose a little power, and that was goodbye to twenty men.

Co-pilot Quincey counted off the altitude: 4,000, 5,000, 5,500. Christ, was there no end to the soup? So much for the frigging meteorologists.

Although he had confessed it to no one save Calhoun, Quincey had had a bad dream about this mission a couple of days earlier, when he absolutely *knew* that *Hazel*'s next target would be Schweinfurt and that she would be singled out to take the brunt of the enemy attack.

Calhoun had tried to reassure him, saying that *Hazel* was just one of a crowd, no more important or less than any other plane.

But in this he was quite wrong.

The brace of Luftwaffe sentries on guard at the entrance to the airfield wanted to know precisely who the newcomers were, chapter and verse, until Fallon leapt from the Opel and started screaming at them, demanding to be taken to the CO instantly or heads would roll. One glance at the SS runes on Fallon's collar and the sinister SD diamond on his left sleeve decided the guards in favor of discretion. One of them hopped on the running board to give directions and three minutes later Fallon was explaining his problem to the middle-aged commandant, a Major Busch. He wore Luftwaffe engineer flashes but no pilot's wings, and Fallon judged correctly that he was a desk man whose job was to keep the base running smoothly and oversee the radio experiments. He seemed flustered at the presence of a high-ranking SS officer on the base and not in the least inclined to ask for identity documents.

Feigning annoyance when informed that the plane originally dispatched by Schellenberg had been turned round in mid-flight, Fallon kept his explanations short and sweet. He and his party had to get to Berlin urgently. Germany's future depended upon it. He did not need a pilot—there was one in his group—but he did need one of the 52s parked out on the tarmac, and runway clearance.

"There are no runways in use, Herr Obersturmbannführer. As you will see for yourself, for the present we are weathered in."

"The fog is beginning to lift. Within half an hour visibility will be excellent. I have my pilot's assurance on that."

"May I talk to this pilot of yours?"

"You may not. His presence in Schweinfurt together with that of the others in my party is somewhat delicate. For that reason I cannot allow any of them to leave the vehicle. This is security business, not Luftwaffe."

"Then I'm rather afraid the Luftwaffe cannot help you. Without authority you can hardly expect me to place one of our experimental airplanes in the hands of someone I do not know, to be flown by someone I have never met."

Fallon did not have to ask himself twice what a genuine SS colonel would do under the circumstances. He unfastened his gun holster and took out the Luger—Meyer's Luger—which he pointed at Busch's head.

"I have no time to argue with you, Major. I have already explained that the business we are on is vital to Germany's future, but you apparently refuse to take my word for it. I must therefore ask you to call Berlin at once and allow me to speak to Brigadeführer Schellenberg. He will give you the necessary authority, which comes to him directly from the Führer. Do it now."

Busch paled with anger at being threatened in his own office. A full report would be made and a day of reckoning would come, but that was in the future. For the moment his choices were limited. The Obersturmbannführer looked the sort to shoot first and worry later.

It took fifteen minutes to track Schellenberg down at his own headquarters in Berkaerstrasse, where he was catching up on some much-needed sleep, and for every second that passed Fallon sweated blood.

Finally he saw Busch, though seated, stiffen to attention. Schellenberg might be SS and no friend of the Luftwaffe, but he was a very senior officer indeed.

Wordlessly he handed the receiver to Fallon, who took a deep breath before saying, "Herr Brigadeführer? Meyer."

At the other end of the line Schellenberg was suddenly wide awake. "*Meyer?* I thought you were dead. Where the hell are you? More to the point, where the hell have you been?"

"It would take too long to explain, Herr Brigadeführer.

Suffice it to say that I'm still in Schweinfurt and that I have the Lunströms and one of the Allied agents. What I need now is an airplane to take us to Berlin, but all that's available are some Ju 52s full of experimental radio equipment which this fool here refuses to let me have."

"Let me talk to him."

The conversation between Schellenberg and Busch was short and mostly one-sided. Fallon could hear Schellenberg shouting from where he stood. The Luftwaffe Major, jaw clenched, said, "Of course, Herr Brigadeführer," twice before handing back the phone.

"You'll get your aircraft now, Meyer," said Schellenberg, "but it will take you two hours to get here and there are some things I must know before then. Luftwaffe monitoring stations have picked up radio signals from England indicating that a massive bombing fleet is becoming airborne. Can I take it that the target is still Schweinfurt, that the Allied agents did not manage to contact London?"

It was too good an opportunity to miss. Fallon fabricated as he went along. "No, Herr Brigadeführer. I said a moment ago I had recaptured one of the agents. The other eluded us. We have to assume he's been in touch with London."

"But how the devil could he? Are you trying to tell me there's a clandestine transmitter somewhere in Schweinfurt?"

"I have no idea."

"*No idea?* That doesn't sound like you, Meyer. What does Knobel have to say on the subject?"

Fallon realized he was going on too long. He had his aircraft and he had sown a few seeds of doubt; that was enough. Any second now Schellenberg might ask a question he could not answer.

"I have to leave, Herr Brigadeführer. If I'm to be in Berlin—"

"*Damn being in Berlin!*" screamed Schellenberg down the phone. "You will—"

But Fallon had hung up.

"You heard the Brigadeführer's orders," he said coldly to Busch.

He had still not holstered the Luger. Busch eyed it distastefully while telling Fallon he could have the 52 on the left-hand dispersal pan. The Luftwaffe Major had heard the words "Allied agent" and "London" and knew he was out of his depth. But one thing puzzled him. The Obersturmbannführer had told Schellenberg that the 52s were full of experimental *radio equipment,* whereas all he, Busch, had said was that they were experimental aircraft. The long-range voice testing gear was supposed to be a secret. Still, it was reputed that the SD knew everything, and the sooner this representative of that unsavory service was out of his office the better he would like it.

"Fuel?" demanded Fallon.

"Three-quarters. It was due to fly some medium-range trials later in the day. It's more than enough to get you to Berlin. Your pilot should use runway two-nine. The tower will—"

"The tower will do nothing," said Fallon, envisaging the reaction if Travis's plummy English voice acknowledged take-off instructions. "Your permission will suffice. Is there a radio aboard?" he added, not wanting to be fobbed off with a plane from which the wireless had been removed for maintenance.

Busch confirmed there was. It was very valuable, and the Luftwaffe would like it back in one piece.

"It will come to no harm," said Fallon, wondering if there was any way the Swiss would hand over the entire plane to the Allies. He put the Luger away and clicked his heels. "Heil Hitler."

Busch stood on the veranda and watched the Opel drive across the left-hand pan. He saw six, seven figures—some of them evidently female—leave the car and begin boarding the 52 before the ringing of the telephone summoned him back to his desk. It was the base operator informing him that Berlin was again on the line, Brigadeführer Schellenberg.

263

Busch instructed the operator to tell Berlin he could not be found and asked that a call be put in to the regional headquarters of the Oberkommando der Luftwaffe in Munich. He wanted to talk to one of his own senior officers before having any further truck with the SS.

When he returned to the veranda the 52 was already at the head of runway two-nine, which ran slightly north of west, the direction of the prevailing wind. The fog was almost non-existent now and he could feel the heat of the sun. It was going to be a lovely autumn day.

More because of concern at what this unknown pilot was going to do with one of his precious aircraft than idle curiosity, he waited until the plane took off. For someone in a hurry, the pilot seemed to spend a long time at the end of the runway; and he gave the three 830-hp BMW engines more gun than was strictly necessary before beginning to roll, but that could be because he was unfamiliar with the type. Nevertheless he could fly well enough. Even though he used virtually the whole length of two-nine, he managed to unstick without much of a wobble.

Then something odd happened.

The 52 was making a series of upward right-hand spirals to gain altitude in the prescribed manner, but when it was at approximately 1,500 meters it leveled out and headed due south. Instead of plotting a course northeast for Berlin, the pilot was flying in the opposite direction.

Fascinated and bewildered, Busch continued to keep the plane under surveillance until it was a mere speck in the distance, even going back to the office for his field glasses. Fifteen minutes passed. There was no doubt about it. The 52 was going the wrong way.

But when he thought he'd lost it, when even the powerful Zeiss lenses could no longer pick it up, it changed course again. At first he thought it was his imagination or a different aircraft, but he soon realized it was the same one. Still at the height of 1,500 meters, it was now flying the opposite of its

264

original southerly course, though even this would not take it to Berlin. It was too far west of north for that, traveling straight up the backbone of Germany—toward Hannover, Hamburg . . . Denmark?

It passed overhead at 11:40 A.M., half an hour to the minute since take-off.

Now horribly aware that something was seriously amiss, he ran back to his office and snatched up the phone, yelling at the operator to connect him to the radio control room.

Part of the experimental equipment aboard each 52 enabled them to be tracked from the ground over huge distances, up to 1,000 kilometers, whenever they transmitted. Busch ordered the control room to do just that and keep him informed of the fugitive's progress if it transmitted, which he was told it hadn't up to now. He had unequivocal orders from Schellenberg to give Meyer the plane, and no one could deny it, but it was his head the Luftwaffe High Command would want if—God forbid—something happened to the aircraft.

What the hell could they be up to?

He had no way of knowing that fifteen minutes earlier Alfred Lunström had thrown a wrench in the works.

At 3,000 feet and still climbing, Travis was starting to enjoy himself. Flying a three-engine plane was a completely new experience, and it took him a while to get the hang of synchronizing the port and starboard motors with the one in the center. He had no idea of the capacity of the fuel tanks; but relating size to performance, he guessed that, full, they would give him a range of 800 to 900 miles. Three-quarters full, therefore, would easily get them to Switzerland, whose borders were less than a couple of hundred miles away.

Sitting on Travis's right in this specially converted model and communicating with him via headphones and a face mike, Natalie was an invaluable help. She had the light-aircraft pilot's natural understanding of engine pitch. Under his guidance she could safely be left to watch the instruments, freeing him to get this unfamiliar plane up to a reasonable altitude. Not too high—that would be a waste of fuel—5,000 feet (or 1,500 meters as the cockpit dials here measured it) should be about right.

He hadn't had a chance to open up all three engines in level flight yet, but he estimated she would cruise in the region of 140 mph. God willing, they'd be sitting down to lunch in Bern, though Fallon had warned him they could expect trouble from Luftwaffe fighter patrols the closer they got to the frontier. German markings or not, the Luftwaffe were going to be mighty curious at one of their 52s overflying neutral territory, regardless of whether or not Schellenberg successfully identified the occupants and ordered pursuit. It was going to be a case of nose down and hope for the best, because the plane had no guns with which to defend itself.

Designed primarily as a transport aircraft for paratroops, the Iron Annie, workhorse of the Luftwaffe, normally carried a crew of four: pilot, co-pilot/navigator, and two gunners to man one 13mm MG 151 machine gun and a pair of 7.9mm MG 15s. In this case the guns had been removed. The plane wasn't going anywhere near a battle, not with all that secret equipment on board, the workings of which Fallon and McKenna were attempting to unravel as the 52 strained for altitude.

The radio room occupied the entire length of the aircraft aft of midships, a compartment all of its own and separated from the main body of the plane by a door in the bulkhead. This was hooked back at present but was lockable from the outside, presumably to prevent thieves or the curious getting too close when the plane was unguarded.

Fallon and McKenna each had a rudimentary knowledge of radio, but neither had seen anything like this outside a major transmitting station. They were faced with banks of dials and switches on both sides of the fuselage, though fortunately all were labeled with words or symbols to denote function. To keep the balance of the plane in trim, the massive power pack which fed the system was outside the compartment, forward over the main spar, where Meyer and Lunström were being watched by Magda armed with the Schmeisser.

She had the usual instructions: Shoot to kill if either made a false move. She hoped she could do it.

Alfred Lunström was convinced she could not—not instantly, without hesitation—and it was upon that conviction he intended making his play. For he had no intention of going to Switzerland—to be interrogated and humiliated by the Allies, perhaps even interned for the duration. If he could help his German friends by preventing Fallon and McKenna warning the Eighth Air Force of the impending trap, so much the better. But the main objective was to get this plane to fly him to a place of safety. North, not south, would put him over non-hostile territory, because north was either Germany, occupied Denmark . . . or Sweden. There was an airfield at Malmö, and the distance between there and Schweinfurt was around 400 air miles. He had no idea how much fuel was in the Ju 52's tanks, but every mile they flew south was a mile too far. He would have to act fast. At least he had the means to effect a takeover of the plane.

During the pandemonium in Landwehrstrasse 18 a dozen hours earlier, when Fallon and McKenna were briefly on the landing pursuing Knobel, he had picked up Schumacher's pistol. He had dropped to the floor at the sound of the first shot, and Schumacher fell beside him after being killed by McKenna. So much was going on that no one had seen him pocket the weapon, not even Meyer—*especially* not Meyer, who would doubtless have insisted they use it right away, earning them both the same fate as Schumacher. His only thought to begin with was to keep it hidden and wait for his moment, which had now arrived.

A meticulous man in all things, he went over in his mind the number of weapons he had seen on display since Landwehrstrasse. Still dressed in Meyer's uniform, Fallon had the

Obersturmbannführer's Luger in the hip holster. McKenna had the Walther pistols belonging to Pickert and Heinnemann, and the woman Lessing was holding the Schmeisser. He himself had Schumacher's Walther nestling snugly in an inside pocket, where no one had bothered to look, because what could one old man do?

He studied the disposition of the enemy. Fallon and McKenna were occupied with the wireless equipment and by the looks of things had mastered at least part of the secrets of transmission, for there were half a dozen red lights glowing. Travis and Natalie were forward at the controls and no danger, and Meyer, who must be considered at least a temporary adversary because he would try, if the takeover attempt was successful, to set the aircraft down on German soil, was slumped against the fuselage, asleep or exhausted. That left Frau Lessing.

The first intimation Magda had that something was wrong with the Swede was when he lurched suddenly to one side, almost falling off the wooden packing case on which he was sitting.

"What's the matter?" she called in German above the roar of the engines.

"My heart," answered Lunström in the same language. "Pain here. I need a pill."

"Where are they?"

"Inside pocket."

Magda threw a glance over her shoulder. Inside the radio compartment, visible through the open door but with their backs turned, Fallon and McKenna had heard nothing. She didn't trust Lunström and wanted to ask if it was all right to let him get his pills, but they had other things on their mind. Still, he couldn't harm her, one old man, not if she kept her distance. If it was a trick to snatch the Schmeisser it wasn't going to work. He could get his own pills.

She nodded her permission. Lunström struggled to his feet, bracing himself against the fuselage. He reached into an

268

inside pocket and Magda found herself staring down the barrel of a pistol.

If it's possible to be shocked into immobility, that was her condition for a full ten seconds. Two would have been enough, for in that time Lunström was at her side, relieving her of the Schmeisser.

Still she made no move. Her brain sounded the tocsin, urged her to make a noise, scream, but her voice refused to obey the commands. Even more incredible no one else appeared to have noticed what had happened. Meyer's eyes remained closed. Fallon and McKenna continued playing with dials and switches. They did not look up until Lunström, unhooking the door from its restraining catch, slammed it shut and locked it.

Reacting the faster, McKenna was about to hurl himself against the bulkhead when Fallon pushed him to one side. Just in time, as for good measure Lunström fired several shots through the woodwork. They hit nothing vital, man or material, but that was small comfort, because a moment later the dials went dark as the Swede immobilized the power unit.

Ordering Meyer, now very much awake, to remain where he was, Lunström urged Magda forward at gunpoint. Natalie might give him an argument, but Travis would change course when he realized that the alternative was the Lessing woman's life.

At 11:26 A.M. Fallon felt the aircraft bank to starboard and begin a slow turn through 180 degrees. From the observation window McKenna confirmed that they were now heading in the opposite direction.

Forty minutes later the leading B-17s on Mission 115 crossed the English coastline south of Felixstowe, but by this time, battling a head wind which had reduced its speed to 120 mph, the Ju 52 was fifty miles north of Schweinfurt, plunging deeper into Germany.

Twenty

At 12:20 P.M. the underground control bunker of the German Twelfth Air Corps at Zeist in the Netherlands reported direct by land line to Göring in Berlin the approximate size and direction of the Eighth Air Force armada. Its findings were confirmed by units of Fernaufklärungsstaffel (Long Range Reconnaissance) and Küstenfliegergruppe (Coastal Patrol). Admittedly the fleet was still largely in British air space and there were certainly other important targets en route, but all the signs pointed to an objective somewhere in the Frankfurt-Schweinfurt vicinity.

Göring was not yet convinced that he and the entire Luftwaffe High Command were not about to become the victims of a gigantic bluff. It could still be a fatal command decision to deploy every fighter he had down south. The Americans had pulled such tricks before. There was nothing to prevent the air fleet making a sharp left turn and heading for Berlin. And then where would he be, with his fighters being forced to land and refuel at the precise moment the bombs started falling? The Berliners would have his ass. They had never forgiven him for boasting in 1940 that not a single bomb would drop on the capital.

In the special operations room set up on the second floor of the Reich Chancellery, he backed his argument by citing the wing of B-24s now making for the Frisian Islands. Exact numbers were hard to come by as yet, but reports emanating from Wangerooge Island and units of JG 11 at Jever suggested between twenty-four and thirty-six aircraft. What were they doing up there if the day's target was Schweinfurt. And what about the Allied agents? They were still at liberty, were they not?

On the far side of the operations room, near the shaded window which overlooked Wilhelmstrasse, Walter Schellenberg was beside himself with rage at Göring's lack of resolution. It was all going to be for nothing—the planning, the months of scheming. With the exception of Mueller, whose florid complexion seemed to indicate an early-morning session with the brandy, he hadn't a friend or ally in the room. They were mostly Luftwaffe, Göring's people, and they would go along with any decision the Reichsmarschall made. The Führer wouldn't interfere either. He was elsewhere, considering other urgent problems. He would only wish to be told the result, not how it was arrived at.

The Brigadeführer swore silently. After failing to raise Major Busch, he had put out an urgent message for Knobel, instructing the Schweinfurt district military commander to track down the Gestapo captain at all costs. Knobel was on the phone within minutes and ordered to the airfield to establish precisely just what the hell was going on. He had reported back a quarter of an hour ago, and Schellenberg now knew that the man he had spoken to earlier was not Meyer but, from the description, one of the Allied agents in Meyer's uniform. He had also learned that the agents, the Lunströms, and several others, with possibly Meyer among them, were now aloft in a Ju 52 which was flying an eccentric course. A 52 which *he* had given permission for them to take and which contained radio equipment powerful enough to contact London. Christ, how could anything go so wrong!

But it had not transmitted yet. It had not so much as put out a peep. If they could find it and shoot it down before it did, maybe Göring would be convinced that the Americans could not conceivably know they were flying into a trap. Even if the message was sent, it was surely impossible to turn 300-odd bombers in midair and direct them elsewhere.

But the clue was the 52, and the problem was where the devil to look.

At 12:21 P.M. and at an altitude of 5,000 feet the 52 was just west of Eisenach in the province of Thuringia, birthplace of J. S. Bach and sixty air miles north of Schweinfurt.

After getting over the shock of Lunström being in control of the aircraft and being ordered to set course for Malmö in southern Sweden, Travis had tried to bluff by saying that not only did he have insufficient fuel for such a trip, but without proper charts and flying only by dead reckoning and from memory, he doubted he could find Sweden, let alone Malmö. But that hadn't worked. With a cynical smile Lunström merely told him to get as close as he could, adding that he was sure Travis would do his best. If the aircraft was forced to land before Sweden, he would find himself in Germany or occupied Denmark.

Equally stunned by the rapid turn of events, and in spite of his threats against Magda Lessing, Natalie was prepared to do battle with her uncle, but he retreated aft before she could give him an argument. When she began to unstrap with the intention of following, Travis placed a restraining hand on her arm. Having heard the shots but not knowing if they had hit anyone, whether Fallon and McKenna were wounded or worse, he was now nominally in command of the escape party and he wanted time to think. Besides, he was a flier, Lunström was not. There were many things a flier could do—subtle changes of direction, for example—which would not be noticed by the average layman.

Apart from avoiding an unpleasant and potentially hazardous scene with his quick-tempered niece, Lunström had a more pressing reason for returning amidships once he was satisfied Travis had altered course: the need to keep both eyes and the Schmeisser on the radio-compartment door. He too had no way of knowing if he had hit Fallon or McKenna, but if he hadn't they remained dangerous adversaries who would not quit easily, and he was only one. He could not trust Meyer with Schumacher's pistol, for the SS colonel was quick to make quite clear what he considered to be the best policy.

"Force the pilot to land at the nearest Luftwaffe airfield before we're shot down. It will not take them long to realize they've been fooled or the significance of the hijacked plane being equipped with long-range wireless. Neither will they ask us twice. When the fighters catch up, their orders will be to destroy us."

Lunström disagreed. This was just one more Ju 52 among the many others that must be airborne today over Germany, and no one had any real idea in which direction they were heading. The Luftwaffe couldn't afford to send up pursuit fighters, not today of all days. They were going to need every one they could muster elsewhere.

The 52 might be equipped with long-range wireless, but no one was going to be receiving any signals, not with the power unit on his side of the locked door.

At 12:23 P.M. in the radio room of the US Legation in Bern, Charles Curzon and Harry Mortimer were rapidly coming to the same conclusion. Neither was the sort to admit defeat while there was still hope, but the very nature of their wartime jobs made them realists. One way or another, they should have heard from Fallon and McKenna by now if they'd got out of Schweinfurt with the Lunströms in tow. If they hadn't, if all or any of them were alive but still in the town,

273

then God help them. The B-17s had already crossed the English coastline, and zero hour for the first wave over the target was 1430.

The duty officer in the radio room, a major from Boston, kept looking across at them irritably, wondering how much longer his highly trained operators would be tied up, for Dulles had given them four radios on the front burner.

The first was tuned to the emergency frequency, and a second was in voice contact with Dulles's people on Lake Constance. A third transceiver had an open priority frequency to the British Legation in Stockholm, where Major Browning in person was keeping a listening watch. Felix Lunström was but a telephone call away and could be at the Legation within minutes. Browning wasn't at all sure what would happen next, but he knew the Mosquitoes could be airborne in less than half an hour once permission for take-off was granted. The ball bearings were needed in the UK so urgently that the Ministry of Economic Warfare was willing to risk a daylight run, which the crews and BOAC had agreed to make, rather than have the planes sitting on the tarmac at Bromma until it got dark.

(What Browning didn't know was that German trade officials in Stockholm were doing their utmost to get the cargoes unloaded, and another dozen hours might see them successful, regardless of what happened to Alfred and Natalie Lunström.)

A fourth wireless operator was in touch with the SOE's communications center at Bletchley Park, just in case Fallon and McKenna used normal channels.

Allen Dulles was not taking part in the operation at grass-roots level; but the great man's Boston surrogate was once heard to complain loudly that, between them, Curzon and Mortimer had commandeered enough manpower and air space to launch the Second Front. Mortimer rounded on him with a mouthful of invective, telling him to shut up or his next posting, starting five minutes hence, would be mess officer in the Aleutians.

As 1224 hours approached and the airwaves remained silent, Curzon had a damned good mind to tell Stockholm the Lunströms were safe and fake it from there. But a moment's reflection convinced him otherwise. Felix Lunström might accept his word that Alfred and Natalie were free and in good hands, but if he lied to gain a short-term advantage and they were later found dead in the rubble of Schweinfurt, that was the end of his credibility. The war would not be over today. He might have to deal for many years with Sweden and the Swedes.

He was more than willing to lie in the Anglo-American cause, but not if the lie could be detected and prove counterproductive.

"What do you think?" he asked Mortimer. "Another hour?"

"Another six if need be. They could be out of Schweinfurt. They could be trying to get past the German border patrols right now."

"Do you believe that?"

"I don't know what to believe."

Fallon and McKenna had not been idle in the hour since Lunström trapped them in the radio compartment. Guessing correctly that once the Swede had forced Travis to change course he would take up a position on the other side of the locked door, ready to shoot them if they tried to break out, they concluded there was not much they could do for the present. Which was not the same as doing nothing.

Before Lunström disconnected the power supply they had begun to make some headway in their understanding of the complicated equipment. Some but not much. While also figuring out the best way to retake the aircraft, therefore, they would pass the time fathoming the rest of its secrets. True they lacked voltage to carry out a practical test, but they had all the dials and switches in front of them and it was simply a matter of examining each to determine its function. Once that was achieved and the transmitter tuned to the correct wavelength, they could think about breaking out. It was not the slightest use getting involved in a shootout with Lunström and possibly Meyer if they were unable to broadcast. They might be wounded in the attempted breakout, which would make it difficult to think clearly. Ideally, they wanted everything set up in such a manner that the only thing necessary would be to reconnect the power unit.

They had worked quickly and feverishly, but it still took time. After half an hour they thought they were getting somewhere, and it was then they discovered they could communicate with the flight deck directly and independently of the main power source. At least that's what the symbols on the switch and the hand mike seemed to indicate.

It took them a moment to work out why there should be two separate systems. It was McKenna who came up with the solution. "Presumably, whoever's back here has to be able to talk to the pilot, give him instructions regarding altitude and direction without allowing him to overhear the main conversations, ship-to-ship or ship-to-ground. If you're a three-star general trying to direct an air battle with another three-star general in plain language—which I presume is what this expensive toy is all about—you won't want the crew having a front-row seat at the strategy conference."

Fallon agreed that that was probably the answer. "Let's give it a spin," he suggested.

"What if Lunström's up in the flight deck?"

"He won't be. He'll be right outside that door."

"Meyer?"

"I don't think Meyer's an equal partner in this enterprise. If he was, we wouldn't still be in the air."

"Makes sense. Okay, give it a try."

Fallon donned the headphones. "Let's hope the signal's a light and not a buzzer."

"It won't matter a whole hill of beans. No one's going to hear anything above this racket."

There was no flashing light, buzzer, bell, or anything else on the flight deck. The same link which enabled Travis and Natalie to talk to each other above the noise of the engines was wired to the radio compartment intercom. All Fallon had to do was depress the transmit button.

Travis was so startled and relieved to hear Fallon's voice crackling in the headphones that for a moment he thought Lunström had lost control of the plane.

It took Fallon a second or two to calm him down. "Can you hear me clearly?"

"Yes."

"And Natalie?"

Natalie nodded. "Yes."

"Okay. Presumably Lunström's elsewhere?"

Travis glanced over his shoulder. "Watching the radio room like a hawk, Schmeisser and all."

"And Meyer?"

"Sitting down, back to the fuselage on the starboard side. Next to Frau Lessing. Lunström's in charge."

Fallon told Natalie to keep an eye on her uncle and asked Travis where they were going.

"Malmö. Actually I had this crazy idea of making for the UK and I've been trying to edge northwest, but at this time of day the sun's directly astern on a true northern heading and the old man keeps checking through the observation windows. If I change course the sun will pop up over the port wing."

"Then don't change course," advised Fallon. "I want to keep Lunström away from the controls so that I can talk to you freely, but he'll be up there every thirty seconds if he thinks you're trying to trick him. For the moment I prefer him where he is—until McKenna and I have figured out which switch does what back here. I don't know how long that'll take us, but when we're ready I'll come through to you again. We'll figure out something then."

It had taken them a further twenty minutes before they

were satisfied they could operate the radio, that each switch and dial was in the correct position. All that remained now was to reconnect the power supply.

The lock on the door was a far from flimsy affair, but it would shatter under the impact of a couple of bullets. The door itself opened outward. The problem was Lunström and the Schmeisser. They would have to put him off balance.

"Let's get Travis to toss the plane around a little," suggested McKenna. "While Lunström's on his back, we bust out."

"Fair enough, but I'd better do the busting and you handle the lock. You're bigger than I am, and we're going to be a bit cramped for space out there."

Fallon called up Travis. The pilot answered immediately. "We're about to make a move," he heard Fallon say. "What's Lunström's exact position?"

"About ten feet from the door and slightly port of center. He's keeping well away from Meyer and sitting on a packing case."

"Fine. When I go off the air give us a count of five seconds, then sideslip to starboard. Make it as violent as you like. We'll be ready for you. Straighten up as soon as you can. Got that?"

"Got it. Good luck."

Travis counted slowly under his breath. One . . . two . . . three . . .

McKenna stood to one side of the door, pistol pointed at the lock, bracing himself against the bulkhead.

Fallon crouched on the floor, lowering his center of gravity, feeling for a handhold.

Travis wondered about the strength of the airframe, just how much punishment a Ju 52 could take if he began using it as a Spitfire.

Four . . .

Natalie, who remembered doing this sort of thing for

fun, kept her eyes firmly fixed on an invisible dot on the horizon, knowing that this was the fastest way to reorientate herself.

On five, Travis heaved the control column hard over and stamped on the right rudder. Where a moment earlier the Iron Annie had been floating along as majestically as a swan on a summer river, now it took on the aerodynamic proportions of a ten-ton boulder, yawing wildly and losing 300 feet in a matter of seconds.

For the first of these seconds gravity was reduced to a minimum. Meyer and Magda Lessing found themselves being catapulted forward and upward before being slammed back against the fuselage with sickening force. To begin with, Lunström was thrown the other way, the Schmeisser flying from his grasp, but then he too careened forward, crashing into Magda and knocking her cold.

Travis was right to be concerned about the effects the buffeting would have on the airframe, for the midships port hatch aft of the main spar was wrenched open under the strain and flapped against the inside of the fuselage like a bird's broken wing.

The instant Travis straightened up, McKenna shot away the lock and stood aside as Fallon charged through. Luger in his right hand, he burst open the door with his shoulder.

Lunström was sprawled in a heap and moaning, and Magda was quite unconscious, blood pouring from a head injury. But Meyer was still in one piece and the leveling-up maneuver had tossed him in the opposite direction, up-side of the open hatch, where some baleful deity had seen to it that the Schmeisser was within inches of his fumbling hand.

Fallon was steadying himself for a shot when Travis looked back to make sure the tail assembly hadn't fallen off. Reacting with a speed that scared him when he realized Fallon could have gone too, he threw the control column hard to port. Meyer had nothing to hold on to. He teetered momen-

279

tarily in the hatch, began to scream with terror, and then he was gone. It might not be a Luftwaffe airfield but at least it was German soil.

When Fallon picked himself up, McKenna heard him complain: "Those were my bloody clothes he was wearing."

At 12:25 P.M. in the radio room of the US Legation, the operator supervising the wireless tuned to the emergency frequency stiffened in his seat. "I'm getting something, but it's not . . ."

Curzon and Mortimer raced over to him. "You're getting something but it's not what?"

"You told me to expect a message in Morse. Well, there's something on this wavelength but . . ."

He flicked a switch and rotated the volume control. Suddenly Fallon's voice was filling the room.

At precisely the same moment in the tracking room of the Schweinfurt experimental airfield, a panel in front of the German operator lit up.

"The 52's transmitting, sir," he called across to Major Busch and Hauptsturmführer Knobel.

They were at his side instantly.

"Can we listen in?" demanded the Gestapo captain. "Can we hear what's being said?"

Busch shook his head. "Not without knowing the frequency they're sending on, and that could take an hour."

"Then what the hell is the use of the damned equipment?" said Knobel angrily.

"It's use," answered Busch calmly, "is that we can trace the approximate whereabouts of the airplane—if they transmit for long enough."

At first Curzon and Mortimer thought Fallon had gone insane or was transmitting under duress. That he should be in a hijacked Junkers 52 some 5,000 feet over central Germany was hard enough to swallow, but what he was saying about Alfred Lunström and the fate awaiting the Eighth Air Force was too fantastic to even contemplate. But gradually it dawned on them that Fallon was neither mad nor a captive, that over 300 B-17s were heading for oblivion. And there was nothing they could do about it. Turning them around, calling off the raid at this stage, as Fallon was suggesting, was out of the question. It was impossible to change the direction of a huge slab of bombers in midair, off the cuff.

"Then you must get some of them to make a feint attack elsewhere." Via the loudspeakers Fallon's voice boomed around the radio room. Security was shot to hell. Everyone was listening—the other operators, cipher clerks, stenographers, the major from Boston. "Do you read me?" Fallon demanded. "You must make a feint elsewhere—north, Bremen or Hamburg or anywhere away from Schweinfurt—any number you can spare. *Do you understand?* The Luftwaffe know they're coming. Impossible or not, you have to try it, convince the Germans we got through to you, that the Schweinfurt mission was called off."

Curzon picked up the microphone. They had to have a minute to think. "Can you hold?"

"Where the hell d'you think we're going?"

"They're north of here," the German operator said. "Way north."

"Can you pinpoint the spot?" asked Busch.

"It will take a little while longer. As you are aware, Herr Major, it's all a question of measuring the strength of their signals, the length of time the beam takes—"

"Forget the goddamn explanations," swore Knobel. "Just hurry it up."

Mortimer was standing next to the radio that was in contact with Bletchley Park, waiting to be put through to Brigadier General Anderson at his Pinetree headquarters. He was empowered to invoke Roosevelt's name in emergencies, and he intended doing so now.

Curzon was a few feet away, muttering something about Mosquitoes.

"Damn the Mosquitoes and damn the ball bearings," snarled Mortimer unreasonably. "The Eighth Air Force is making its own ball-bearing run right now, and it could be the last it ever makes. There's more at stake here than a few lousy Mosquitoes."

"I was thinking of using them as a decoy," said Curzon mildly. "Whatever Pinetree comes up with, we're going to need more than a few B-17s turning left to fool the Luftwaffe."

"I'm hoping for more than a few."

"Nevertheless, the Germans won't buy it. They'll see it for what it is, a desperate bluff."

"And you're suggesting making a dummy run with eight unarmed Mosquitoes and civilian pilots. They'll be crucified."

"Not necessarily. The pilots are not exactly inexperienced at running the gauntlet, you know, and I think you'll agree it takes as much skill to evade an enemy fighter in an unarmed aircraft as it does in one with the capability of hitting back. The crews have been told they'll be flying by day. It will just be a question of rerouting them somewhat."

"What about Felix Lunström?"

"To hell with him. He shouldn't have a brother who's a Nazi. Besides, my agreement was simply to tell him if Alfred and Natalie Lunström got out of Schweinfurt and were in safe hands. I can truthfully answer yes on both counts."

"You're a devious man, Charles."

"Thank you. I take that as a compliment. Do you want to hear more?"

"Spell it out," said Mortimer.

While waiting for Curzon to come back on the air, Fallon and McKenna took stock. Magda was still unconscious and looked like remaining that way for some time, but the bleeding had stopped and they had made her as comfortable as they could, covering her with a raincoat. Alfred Lunström's left shoulder was broken and his face the color of ash, but no one was much concerned about his pain and he was unlikely to cause them any more trouble. Meyer, of course, was back in the Fatherland, and the hatch door lashed in place with rope. Everyone else was unscathed.

Only six minutes had elapsed since they broke out of the radio compartment, but already Travis had plotted a new course by dead reckoning. No one was much interested in going to Sweden, where Alfred Lunström might manage to pull a few strings, and doing a U-turn and making for their original destination of Switzerland didn't appeal either. Apart from the fact that they might be showing up on someone's radar screen by this time—someone who might decide to investigate an aircraft flying such an eccentric course—Switzerland would mean overflying Schweinfurt, right across the bows of the Eighth Bomber Command (if Curzon couldn't turn the fleet) and half the Luftwaffe. Besides, Travis confessed, on dead reckoning alone from their present position—just south of Nordhausen if he were any judge—he couldn't guarantee to get them within a hundred miles of Bern or Geneva, and fuel considerations prohibited nosing around looking for landmarks. But England, now, that was a different kettle of fish. Even though RAF Bomber Command flew exclusively by night, he knew this part of Germany from map exercises, and with a bit of luck he could make one of the East Anglian airfields. As the Duke of Wellington might have said, it would be a damned close-run thing, but what did everybody think?

Everybody thought it was a good idea.

Fallon was a little concerned because Travis wanted Natalie to remain up front, but the flight lieutenant pointed out that if anything happened to him she was the only one who stood any chance of flying the plane and landing it safely.

Curzon came back on the radio at 12:36 P.M. with the

news that they were working on the question of trying to turn the B-17s. He sounded as if he were fifty yards away, not 300 miles.

"But you can forget that side of it and concentrate on getting out of German air space."

Fallon said they were doing so. "The pilot—who's due a VC incidentally—regrets he can't give you an exact course, but we'd all be obliged if you'd warn anyone who might be interested not to shoot down a Ju 52 without double-checking."

"I'll see to it," said Curzon. "If your radio equipment is all it seems to be," he added drily, "our people at Farnborough will be very interested."

"Thanks a million. How do we get in touch with you if we run into trouble?"

"Colonel Mortimer and I will be here until it's all over, but I wouldn't try too hard to contact us unless it's vital." Curzon's voice was suddenly avuncular, concerned. "If the Jerries can build a radio like that, you can take money they've got ways of tracking the mother ship."

"It had crossed my mind."

"Good. Keep it there. Good luck."

"Got him!" said the German operator in Schweinfurt. "Got the bastard! Coordinates . . . let me see." He consulted a map. "He's near Nordhausen, heading west-northwest."

"There's a fighter base nearby," advised Busch.

It was tempting, but Knobel wanted to talk to Schellenberg before making any such move. The 52 had transmitted. Presumably that meant that someone, somewhere knew a trap was being laid over Schweinfurt. There was nothing to be gained by chasing after the Iron Annie, not when every fighter might shortly be required elsewhere.

"I'll talk to Berlin first."

Twenty-one

"You are not gonna believe this."

It was 1252 hours when Jimmy Ryan, *Hazel*'s wireless operator, came through on the intercom, his voice incredulous. The B-17 was at 24,000 feet over the North Sea, one of a group of aircraft toward the rear of the bombing fleet. So far there was no sign of enemy fighters, but they were probably waiting until the P-47s and the Spitfires went home.

"Not gonna believe what, Jimmy?" asked Max Shapiro. "Roosevelt's running for Pope?"

"The war's over?"

"Somebody just bailed out?"

"Give him a break, fellas," said Joe Calhoun. "Not going to believe what, Jimmy?"

"We're being given a different target."

There was a shocked silence.

"Get lost, Jimmy," said Billy Concannon. "Not even as a joke."

"You got that applejack up there again, Jimmy?"

"I'm serious. We're being sent to Bremen. Thirty-six planes."

Calhoun looked across at Hank Quincey in the co-pilot's seat. Jimmy Ryan wasn't kidding.

"It's a Kraut trick," said Quincey.

"Are you in voice contact with Pinetree?" asked Calhoun.

"No, Morse. And I heard Lieutenant Quincey. It's no trick, not unless the Krauts know today's code letters."

To guard against German wireless operators creating havoc by issuing false orders, every message to and from Pinetree was preceded by a four-letter code, which was only given to the crews at briefing and was changed for every mission.

"Let's have it all, Jimmy."

"Well, the message is not directly to us, you understand. It's to Colonel Butler, but it concerns us. It lists the serial numbers of— Let me count. . . . Oh Christ, I don't know, about forty or fifty Forts and it tells Colonel Butler to collect thirty-six of them and make for Bremen, targets of opportunity. We're on the list. It— Hold on. Colonel Butler's radio man is asking for verification."

"I should damn well think he is," said Ken Cornelius, *Hazel*'s navigator. "What the hell's going on, Joe?"

"Search me. Keep us in the picture, Jimmy."

"Right."

"Do you want me to start figuring a new course?" asked Cornelius.

"No. Yes. This is probably no more than a foul-up back at Pinetree, but we'd better be ready for anything they throw. What's going on, Jimmy?"

"Hold it. Let me take this down. There's some kind of row in progress—if you can believe a row in Morse. Colonel Butler is telling Pinetree no deal. He's going to Schweinfurt. He"—Ryan chuckled—"he's just told them that if they want to treat a bunch of B-17s like dodgems, go hire a fairground. Jeeze, that's the first time I've heard *that* word in Morse. Looks kinda funny when you write it down."

Calhoun could imagine the language being used. He

knew Frank Butler quite well and had even flown in his plane—*Dallas Dragon*—a couple of times. He was one of the youngest bird colonels in the US Air Force, and one of the toughest. His crew swore he chewed a six-inch nail to the target and back, and that when he eventually spat it out the end was like a squashed cigar.

"Jimmy?"

"You'll be getting it all yourself in a minute. Pinetree's just told Colonel Butler to contact every plane on the list via ship-to-ship and get his tail over to Bremen with thirty-six of them. Failing that . . ." They heard Ryan whistle. "Jesus Christ, it's an ultimatum. He either goes to Bremen or he goes to the stockade."

Aboard *Dallas Dragon,* Frank Butler went white with anger when his radio man translated the last sentence into plain language and he heard that it was authorized by General Eaker, overall commander of the US Eighth Air Force, himself. But he knew Eaker was not prone to issuing high-handed statements unless there was no time or room for argument. Something must be seriously wrong.

"Bring that list down here," he ordered his wireless operator. "Let's see how many of these bastards are actually in our vicinity."

Back at Pinetree, Brigadier General Anderson, on an open telephone link to Eaker's Widewing Headquarters, hoped to God they were not making a mistake. It was a hell of a risk to take, sending just thirty-six aircraft on a separate raid, especially on the unconfirmed say-so of a spook colonel in Switzerland. But Mortimer had cited Presidential authority, and there was no arguing with that.

Eight hundred miles northeast of the B-17 stream, the crews of the eight BOAC Mosquitoes at Bromma listened in stunned silence to the briefing by the station manager, who had just finished talking by phone to Major Browning at the Legation.

They could not be told all of it, the station manager informed them, because there was a lot he did not know himself. But it was on the highest authority that they were being asked to fly the following route: from Bromma to Gothenburg in Swedish air space, then directly over Denmark to East Anglia. The precise location of the UK airfield would be given to them when they were airborne, because for the moment time was of the essence.

There was no flight plan being filed with the Swedish Air Ministry, so there was a possibility they would be buzzed by Swedish fighters. That was considered unlikely, however, as Gothenburg was a mere two hundred miles away; they should be out over the Kattegat before the Swedes knew what was happening.

Denmark was a different matter. They would be overflying some nasty Luftwaffe fighter bases. Worse still, the object of the exercise was to be seen, not take advantage of one of the Mosquito's natural assets, its ability to function at high altitude. They were to fly low, almost hedge-hop. Unless conditions dictated otherwise, 500 feet was the suggested maximum.

That was it. If they took off immediately they should be crossing the Kattegat by 1330.

Jim Masefield, skipper of *Gaggle of Geese,* acted as spokesman for the crews. They were not combat pilots, though God knows all of them had been harassed often enough by nightfighters to qualify for some kind of medal. Neither was there anything in their contracts with British Overseas Airways that said they had to fly unarmed aircraft at zero feet over enemy territory.

"I take it you wouldn't be asking us to do this unless there was a flap on."

"You take it right. Major Browning says he's empowered to tell you that your action could alter the entire course of the war. If necessary he's willing to come out here and talk to you in person."

"Oh, I don't think we'll put him to that trouble."

The crews concurred. Many of them were married and some had children, but not one man refused to fly. They had already agreed to fly by day so what the hell was a little more danger? As *Gaggle*'s radio officer, Jock Munroe, put it: They didn't often get the chance to outshine the glamour boys of the RAF.

Masefield had one final question. "What happens when we've left Denmark behind and are over the North Sea. Are we still required to wave-hop?"

"Your decision."

"Fine. We'll probably stay low to avoid German coastal radar. I'm not too worried about Denmark. Even at its broadest it's only a hundred miles across. We'll be in and out before they know it. But a direct line to East Anglia will take us within a few miles of the North German coast, and among those nasty Luftwaffe bases you mentioned is a particularly nasty one at Jever. Bunch of belligerent bastards, they are."

If many of the pilots of JG 11 based at Jever were feeling at all belligerent at that precise moment, their aggression was directed at the Luftwaffe High Command and not the Allies, for after a morning that had promised much, all but one Staffel, Oberleutnant Knocke's, was grounded and on standby.

Hauptmann Otto Reinberger couldn't understand it. Standby for what, for the love of God? The teleprinters had been clattering away like crazy since mid-morning. It was hardly the best-kept secret of the war that something big was afoot. Scuttlebutt had it that Knocke's Staffel was on its way to Antwerp to intercept a massive fleet of B-17s on a southeast heading. Fair enough. Knocke had helped pioneer the technique of aerial bombing, which could only be carried out effectively against tight formations. He deserved to be one of the first up. But what were the rest of them doing sunning themselves? It was known for a fact that twenty or thirty B-24s were on their way to the Frisian Islands. Christ, he could *piss* that far.

It was high time he found out what the hell Group Headquarters was playing at.

Group was not able to tell him, because Group was still waiting for firm orders from Berlin, and as yet none were forthcoming.

It had taken some time for Hauptsturmführer Knobel to get through to Schellenberg in the Chancellery and it was only a few moments ago that the Brigadeführer had informed Göring that the Ju 52 had transmitted. The question was, to whom? And had the message got through? If so, did the recipients intend turning the bomber stream away from the designated target, even if that were possible? There were no signs of it up to now. All incoming reports suggested that the B-17s were still on the Schweinfurt heading, but did that mean the Americans were trying a bluff of their own? What if all the northern fighters were committed to the southern sector and the bombers changed course?

Such thoughts paraded through Göring's mind as he studied the huge wall map of Germany and the Low Countries. He had three hundred front-line fighters ready to do battle with the American juggernaut, and one word from him could put another seven hundred into the fray. He knew what Schellenberg wanted, what most of his senior commanders wanted: to commit the planes and take a chance. Well, he was rapidly coming around to their way of thinking. Schweinfurt was the target; it could be nowhere else. The B-17s had not been warned in time, possibly not warned at all. If they had, surely the fleet would have changed direction by now. If it didn't, it was going to be annihilated.

He would give it a few more minutes. If it kept on the same course, he would order the northern fighters south.

"It is not," Butler was saying in Joe Calhoun's ear, "going to be easy. Rough though Schweinfurt will undoubtedly be, there we would at least have had the protection of two-fifty, two-sixty other aircraft. Still, we have one advantage: most of us were on the Bremen raid of October eighth. You all know the way there and back. Let's get in, clobber the joint, and get the hell out. E.t.a. over the target is 1400 hours. We'll be home before the Schweinfurt boys. Good luck."

"So now you know," said Calhoun to the entire crew over the intercom. "Any questions?"

There were none.

"Okay. Jimmy?"

"Yo," answered the radio operator.

"Keep me informed of anything from Pinetree. You never know, they might let us in on the big secret before the day's out."

"Got it."

In response to a command from *Dallas Dragon,* Calhoun put *Hazel* into a long left turn and checked the new heading on the gyro. For this twenty-fifth and final mission of his tour he couldn't make up his mind whether or not he was happy missing out on Schweinfurt.

At 1327 Göring was on the point of at last committing his northern fighters to the southern sector when news came through from Zeist that a large formation of B-17s—precise numbers were being verified—had changed course. Probable target Bremen or Hamburg. What were Berlin's orders? So far the B-17s were enjoying uninterrupted passage. The northern fighters were still grounded, as instructed. Did that directive still apply?

Before Göring could answer, a flash signal was received from Frederikshavn in Denmark. It stated that coastal patrols had sighted a squadron, perhaps more, of Mosquitoes over the Kattegat, flying at low level and heading southwest. Destination and intentions unknown.

Such a minor piece of intelligence would not normally have reached the ears of the illustrious gathering in the Reich Chancellery; but anxious not to fall for an Allied trap, Göring had ordered that any unusual happenings be fed back to the operations room instantly. And this was certainly unusual. Where the devil had the Mosquitoes started from to be heading southwest?

Not that it really mattered. The Anglo-Americans were up to something, and that something did not entail sending the entire Eighth Bomber Command to Schweinfurt. It therefore followed that the Luftwaffe could not dispatch its northern fighters south.

Göring seemed almost relieved now that the decision had been more or less taken for him. If the Americans could turn one wing they could turn two. Not putting all his eggs in one basket had proved to be the wisest strategy.

Schellenberg knew what was coming before the announcement was made, and he was hard pressed not to show his disappointment. He was still not convinced that the wing of B-17s going to Bremen or Hamburg was anything more than a panicky impromptu move by the Allies, but he had no answer for the mysterious Mosquitoes. Neither had Mueller, who was already making for the exit, the profit in this exercise now nonexistent.

"That seems to be it, gentlemen," Göring was saying. "We shall now revert to conducting this air war in the traditional manner. That is, with the Luftwaffe alone taking all decisions concerning the shooting down and destruction of enemy planes. Kindly deploy your reserves accordingly. All previous instructions regarding the grounding of the northern fighter units are hereby rescinded."

Schellenberg collared him by the door. "About the experimental Ju 52, Herr Reichsmarschall . . ."

Göring looked at him steadily. While it was a Luftwaffe officer who had allowed the plane to be hijacked, it was on Schellenberg's orders. The SD and Mueller's Gestapo had also bungled things in Schweinfurt, allowing the Allied agents to escape in the first place. It would be a disaster if the radio equipment fell into enemy hands, but it would be a greater disaster, inviting Hitler's full wrath, if he were seen to be in any way culpable. In the Third Reich one pulled up the ladder as soon as one was aboard.

"You have its last reported course, do you not?"

Schellenberg said he did.

"Then I hereby authorize you to liaise with Major Busch and take whatever steps are necessary to ensure that the plane does not leave German air space. I would prefer to save the equipment, naturally, but if that cannot be achieved you may —on your own initiative, you understand—order the plane destroyed."

Twenty-two

"How's it going?" Fallon asked Travis over the intercom.

"Fine."

"No problems?"

"None."

Fallon hesitated. "Natalie?"

"Yes."

"Are you all right?"

"Absolutely. In spite of the circumstances, I have to admit I'm rather enjoying myself."

"It'll certainly be something to tell your grandchildren," said Fallon, and removed the headphones before the Swedish girl could answer.

"What was that about grandchildren?" asked McKenna as Fallon came out of the radio compartment.

Seated on the packing case, the Schmeisser across his lap, the American was keeping an eye on Alfred Lunström, though it was pretty obvious there was no fight left in the Swede, who was nursing his broken shoulder and moaning softly from time to time. Magda was still unconscious. She had woken up once and then promptly passed out again.

"Nothing," answered Fallon. "At this precise moment

I'd be happy to be in a position where I'm capable of having grandchildren. We've a hell of a long way to go before we're out of the woods."

"Still," said McKenna, "it's looking good."

And it was. In the fifty-five minutes since Fallon finished speaking to Curzon the Ju 52 had covered a further 120 miles and was now in air space between Dortmund and Münster, still flying at 5,000 feet. Travis recalled reading somewhere or being told at an intelligence briefing that an Iron Annie had a ceiling of 18,000 feet, but getting up that high was out of the question. Above 10,000, oxygen was needed and the 52 had none. He could have gone up to 9,000 without any danger of blacking out, but two factors militated against that. The first was the fuel they would burn gaining altitude, fuel already in perilously short supply; the second, the higher they went, the more chance there was of running into an inquisitive fighter.

Strictly speaking, they were not flying the most direct of lines to the English coast, but Travis had confessed earlier that he wanted to keep well clear of the Ruhr—Happy Valley as it was known to the RAF and the USAAF alike—with its heavy defenses. The others accepted this argument wholeheartedly. Up to now, no one had taken the slightest interest in them, but that didn't mean that someone, somewhere, was not frantically trying to trace their whereabouts. Avoiding flak and fighter concentrations seemed an excellent idea.

A veteran of twenty-eight bombing missions over Germany, Travis had the location of many of the Luftwaffe fighter stations fixed firmly in his head. Two crack Geschwader were based on the Channel coast. These were JG 2 (Richthofen) and JG 26 (Schlageter), and they could be considered too far south to be much of a danger until he turned to cross Holland, though rumors in England suggested that Schlageter was about to be withdrawn to the Low Countries. He had also heard an unconfirmed report that JG 3—the experienced Udet Geschwader—had been brought "home" from the Eastern

Front and was based on the Lower Rhine, occupying airfields at Deelen near Arnhem, which was on their flight path. Units of JG 11 were at Jever, but that was way up north. Besides, he was flying a Ju 52 bearing Luftwaffe markings, so who was going to bother them? They were likely to get a hotter reception from the Spitfires later.

If he were a betting man, he would have put a lot of money on the odds now being in their favor.

He would have been less sanguine had he known that within the last minute—Geschwader records would show the time to be 1331—the Jever fighters had scrambled with orders to intercept Frank Butler's B-17s. And he would have reduced his wager considerably had he realized that the course the B-17s would fly back to East Anglia after bombing Bremen was a converging one with his own.

"Hals- und Beinbruch!" Grinning fiercely, Wolf Löhr called across the traditional fighter pilot's salutation to Paul Weinrich as he and his wingman raced for their 109s. The expression meant "Break your neck and a leg" and was reputed to fool the Valkyries, those handmaidens of the Norse god Odin who selected warriors destined to be slain in battle, into thinking that the speaker and the listener had enough trouble on their hands and would be killed without any interference from minor deities.

Weinrich smiled his gratitude.

Otto Reinberger's was not the only Staffel of JG 11 based at Jever. In all, some sixty aircraft, all Me 109s of various vintages but many of them the brand-new Gustavs with the big DB 605 engines, were airborne and making for the Dutch-German border. Nor was JG 11 the only Geschwader scrambled. A total of 120 fighters were heading toward Frank Butler's flotilla.

Radio messages from the ground told the Luftwaffe pilots that the B-17s numbered between thirty and forty and were flying at 7,500 meters. Their present position was just east of the border town of Coevorden, some eighty miles southwest of Jever. There was no Allied fighter cover, and the target was almost certainly Bremen.

At the head of his Staffel, still climbing, Reinberger listened anxiously to the note of the 1,475-hp engine. It still didn't sound right, especially when he turned on the power. They kept promising him a replacement, but it had yet to arrive. He could only hope that today was not the day the old one chose to give up the ghost.

On a pad strapped to his left thigh he made a few rapid calculations. He wanted the Staffel at 10,000 meters, way above the *Amis*. In the ten minutes it took to get there the B-17s would have traveled a further twenty-five miles. Interception should therefore take place somewhere west of Bremen around 1400 hours.

He tossed a glance over his shoulder. Mahle was where he should be, off his leader's starboard quarter, and Reinberger hesitated before switching on the radio-transmitter. The earlier row with his wingman had left a nasty taste in his mouth and he wanted to put it right. They had enough trouble fighting the Allies without squabbling among themselves. Certainly Löhr was no saint when it came to making cutting remarks, but they were generally delivered without malice. Mahle would have to learn to take it, change his attitude or be transferred to another unit. He would tell him as much when they landed.

"Gray Leader to Gray One."

Mahle came on immediately. "Gray One."

Reinberger gave him the altitude they were seeking and added, "We should be on top of them in twenty minutes. Keep it tight, Heinz."

There was no need to repeat the instruction to the remainder of the Staffel. They would all be listening.

Also at 1331 the P-47 escort to the main force turned for home at the limit of its fuel between Aachen and Düren, leaving the B-17s at the mercy of the Luftwaffe. Where a moment earlier the German defenders had been hovering at a safe distance, as aware as the enemy of the P-47s' limitations, now the skies around the bombers were filled with fighters of every description. Me 109s, Fw 190s, twin-engined Me 110s, the versatile Ju 88s. Even the long-obsolete Stuka dive-bombers were getting in on the act, climbing high above the Flying Fortresses and dropping time-fused bombs among them.

The Luftwaffe was represented by so many aircraft, pouncing with such speed and fury, that they were in danger of colliding with each other. Most of the Americans had never seen anything like it, and this was but a small fraction of the strength Göring could have put up.

In their anxiety to defend themselves, the B-17 gunners ignored everything they had ever learned about conserving ammunition. It wasn't a hell of a lot of good, they reasoned, saving ammo for the return trip if there was no return trip to make.

The first Fort was seen going down at 1336. Nine parachutes were counted, indicating that one crew member, probably the pilot, hadn't made it.

But it was not all one-way traffic, and here and there a yellow canopy of a German chute was seen among the American white.

One of the first victims was Oberleutnant Knocke, commander of JG 11's 5 Staffel and the officer Reinberger had envied for being allowed to fly while the rest of them were grounded.

Attacking from the rear with rockets, Knocke was hit before he had a chance to fire, the underside of his port wing being torn away and with it the left-hand rocket rack. He continued to direct the Staffel's attack from a distance until it became apparent that he would lose the wing completely—and perhaps not only the wing—if he were forced to make a tight turn. With great reluctance he broke off and pancaked his 109 at an airfield near Bonn. Even as he landed he was given the news that the remainder of the Geschwader was now in action in the north.

From his mid-upper gun platform Bob Baker, *Hazel*'s flight engineer, saw them first. Dozens of the bastards arrowing down from the south, starboard, three o'clock high. Along with the other commanders, Reinberger had ordered his Staffel to overfly the B-17s and come at them out of the afternoon sun. It would give them only a momentary advantage, because the best way to tackle the B-17 formations in fighters armed just with machine guns and cannon, not rockets, was head on. But a momentary advantage might be enough to sway the battle in favor of the attackers before the bombers could unleash their lethal payloads on Bremen.

It was 1357, and the smoke and grime from the German seaport was easily visible six or seven miles up ahead. Joe Calhoun was about to hand over verbal command to Billy Concannon, the bombardier. From the moment he did so until "bombs gone" Concannon would be in charge of *Hazel,* directing her this way or that. Calhoun would merely drive and take orders.

"*Fighters, fighters!*" yelled Baker, simultaneously opening fire.

A split second later Max Shapiro in the right-waist aperture and Jimmy Ryan on the radio operator's gun joined in. Then *Hazel* was full of smoke and noise, the smell of cordite.

"Hold it, hold the bastard!" shouted Concannon as some reflex action made Calhoun put his foot on the left rudder.

Hazel's skipper made a supreme effort to calm his thudding heart. This was the last one. It would be all right.

"Sorry. Billy," he said. "How many and where?" he added in general, but before anyone could answer he saw for himself. There were scores, a hundred or more, and they were coming in the fucking window.

In the vanguard of the attacking fighters, Otto Reinberger selected a target, put the 109's nose down, and opened the throttle. He cursed loudly and fluently when the engine stuttered and faltered, but a fraction of a second later it picked up with a healthy roar.

"*Pauke-Pauke!*" he said into his microphone for Mahle's benefit. The word meant "kettledrums" and was used in the same way and for the same reason Allied fighter pilots used "Tallyho: I am attacking."

With the B-17 and the Messerschmitt closing on one another at a combined speed of 500 mph, it seemed as if nothing could prevent a midair collision, but the skipper of the Fort was accustomed to such tactics, unnerving though they were. There was nothing the fighters wanted more than to break up the B-17s' flying formation, destroy the defensive fire pattern where each aircraft in the stream was able to give cover to those above it and below it, those to port and starboard. It took guts from both attacker and attacked and sometimes, because of misjudgment on the fighter pilot's part, a brace of aircraft vanished in a ball of flame.

But not in this case. The Fort's skipper held his course and Reinberger, thumb over the firing button, held his fire. As he had pointed out to newcomers to the Staffel on scores of occasions, the big *Ami* planes could absorb masses of punishment. A pilot had to get close to be sure of a kill.

But not so close as to commit suicide, Reinberger reminded himself when he was close enough to see the flashes from the dorsal guns. There's nothing in the manual that says that.

At 300 meters he opened fire and had time to see the 20mm cannon shells tearing chunks from the B-17's fuselage before he threw the stick over and half-rolled out of the encounter.

Behind him and slightly to starboard to make things difficult for the gunners, Mahle pressed home the attack, happy that, for once, there were no fighters to worry about, reducing his part in the affair to that of watchdog guarding Reinberger's tail and flanks against sudden rushes out of the sun. He was still expected to fly tight, however, take instructions from his number one regarding the target, not go off hunting alone. It was basic Luftwaffe strategy when engaging unescorted bombers to select individual aircraft for a concentrated assault, usually starting with those in the van because it was there that the bombing leader and the task force navigator would be flying. Deal with the bastards one at a time, that was how to put them on the deck and make sure they stayed there. Many an Eighth Air Force crew had watched in despair when (it seemed) every enemy fighter in the sky had its sights trained on them while other bombers plowed on as though on a training exercise. "Why just us?" was a frequently heard lament.

"Pauke-Pauke!" called Mahle, and opened fire.

But the B-17's upper guns had found the range and the Luftwaffe Oberleutnant managed only a short ineffectual burst before barrel-rolling to starboard and climbing in an upward spiral to find Reinberger.

Elsewhere, successes were being registered on both sides in this first minute of the encounter.

Breaking all the rules, two comparative newcomers to 7 Staffel JG 11 chose to attack the bombers from below. Normally a greenhorn would fly as wingman to an experienced pilot for his first dozen sorties, but 7 Staffel's commander, like Reinberger, was short of experienced fliers willing or able to help break in novices. He was also under constant pressure from Group to put every aircraft he could into action as often was demanded. In vain did he protest that some of his youngsters (the Staffelkapitän himself was an old man of twenty-three) hardly knew how to fly a tight circle, let alone take on the US Air Force. The argument came back that a novice was not likely to develop latent skills flying circuits and bumps on the training field. There was a war on, didn't the Staffelkapitän know that? It was imperative that every flier and every plane answered every alert.

So against his better judgment 7 Staffel's commander let his two chicks fly every sortie. Today would be their third.

Following their Staffelkapitän in out of the sun, they both realized they were far too high to make an effective pass, and indeed they overshot the entire task force without getting in a blow. Peeling off, the leader (age nineteen, born May 1924) told his wingman (age nineteen, born July 1924) that they would try an attack on the B-17s' bellies.

It seemed to the uninitiated a logical enough decision. A B-17 of the type they were facing had eleven .50-caliber Browning machine guns: two each in the tail position and the upper and ball turrets, one in each waist aperture, the radio-room upper hatch, and either side of the nose. A head-on attack exposed the fighter to at least seven machine guns, both on approach and peeling off; a total of nine if a man was unlucky and the tail-turret gunner managed to bring his guns to bear. But going in from underneath reduced the guns to an absolute maximum of six—ball turret, both waists, and tail —and that figure could be lowered to two, providing the angle of approach was correct.

It was different when there were two or three hundred B-17s stacked dozen upon dozen, giving low group, middle group, and high group, and staggered laterally as well as vertically. Then an attacker had to run the gauntlet of hundreds of guns as well as threading his way through the bombers.

But here there were just thirty or so aircraft flying mostly straight and level, too small a task force to build itself into a stack. Instead of facing the number of dorsal and side guns multiplied by the number of aircraft, they would reduce the opposition's firepower by going for the belly.

Fine. Fine. Beautiful theory, especially when thought out traveling at 350 mph with blood being drawn away from the brain by g. With one drawback that it's hard to remember

302

when you're young, scared, and excited: standing on its tail with the propeller whining for a hold on the thin atmosphere at 24,000 feet, a 109 loses half it speed. It's facing fewer guns, but those guns have more time to bear. The attacker— who must hit and run using the two assets he has, speed and maneuverability—has lost the advantage. The ball-turret gunner has to keep his nerve, but, assuming that, it's like shooting fish in a barrel.

And so it was that George Bushman got two 109s in the space of fifty seconds, watched them pour smoke and oil and cling to the air like a man desperately hanging on to the edge of a crumbling cliff before falling away through five miles of space. There were no parachutes.

Bushman's jubilant cries of victory echoed in the ears of every man aboard *Hazel*, but there was no time to congratulate him on his achievement. The 109s were still coming in from every angle, and *Hazel* was at the beginning of her bomb run.

Traveling at 160 mph, she had covered almost six miles since the 109s first appeared, and Billy Concannon was now at the Norden bombsight. Targets of opportunity, Pinetree had said, and the very first target of opportunity he saw was going to get *Hazel*'s eggs. This was no place to be for a man who wanted to celebrate another birthday.

"Steady . . . steady . . ." he called.

"Bastard fighters aren't going home," muttered Calhoun.

Usually the fighters broke off over the target to avoid being hit by their own flak, but there was no sign of that happening today.

"If you think it's rough up there," said Don Schaeffer from the tail, "you want to see it back here."

Right in front of Schaeffer, so close he could easily make out the silhouettes of the pilot and co-pilot, the port wing of a B-17 was burning, the flames creeping closer and ever closer to the outboard fuel tanks. But there was no sign of the crew abandoning ship. The pilot was going in to bomb. That was what he was here for, what he was paid to do.

In the vanguard of the task force Colonel Butler in *Dallas Dragon*, bombs dispatched a second earlier, was making a long sweeping turn to port and attempting a count of his force as he did so.

He too could see the burning B-17 behind *Hazel*, but it was one of several in trouble and held his attention for no longer than any of the others.

Twenty-eight . . . thirty . . . thirty-one . . . thirty-two . . . Not easy to count with everything else that was happening, but if he was accurate he'd lost four planes already and there were two or three more that would not make it home.

It was madness, insanity, and not for the first time he wondered what the hell it was that attracted young men to planes, to volunteer to do this day after frightening day, week after week.

You took an airplane seventy-five feet long and crammed it to overflowing with instruments, cables, wires, circuits, machine guns, ammunition, and Christ knows what else, and then you dressed ten men in heavy flying suits, face masks, and cumbersome gloves and told them to get aboard.

You asked them to fly five miles high, where the outside temperature was sixty degrees below zero and where, because the waist guns were fired through open windows and it was impossible to heat the ship or pressurize the cabin, men disabled by frostbite outnumbered those wounded by enemy action in a ratio of four to three. You warned them about the dangers of frostbite, of course, and told them to keep dry at all costs, but you couldn't tell them not to sweat with fear before take-off, and it was the sweat freezing at altitude that was responsible for 90 percent of the amputations. Oh yes, men lost limbs, ears, noses because of frostbite. It wasn't one of those things that stood out on the recruiting posters, but it was there anyway.

To combat the bitter temperature, you introduced electric suits and then the engineers came along and told you that no more than two men in each crew could wear them, because the plane's generators couldn't handle the load.

You cautioned them that anoxia was a threat at high altitudes and gave them oxygen masks, but even the best equipment tended to freeze up above 20,000 feet, and that was where most of the flying was done.

You told them it cost $50,000 to train a pilot and asked them to fly the sort of tight formations that would scare the hell out of a display team.

You lectured them that there was no such thing as an emotional disorder and that anyone wanting to be taken off flying had better have a bloody good reason, because otherwise it was going on his service sheet as cowardice.

You told them they were the elite, today's heroes—bronzed, brave, blue-eyed, magnificent. You patted them on the head, gave them medals, and wished them luck as they went off to fight. You did not tell them how it was when one of your comrades got his head blown off and it landed in your lap, brain still functioning, eyes surprised, still *talking,* for the love of Jesus. Nor did you tell them what it was like when the skipper gave the order to abandon ship and you were the only one left aboard because your parachute had been destroyed in that last pass by a 109. You left out entirely how it felt to see a fellow crew member burning, frying in his own fat, flesh peeling from his face like leaves from an artichoke until there was only skull—but still alive and screaming. Nor did you inform them of the feeling they would experience when their B-17 plunged through five miles of sky, wings tearing off, spinning wildly, pinning them to the spot, everyone shouting and willing death because death, final though it was, had to be better than just knowing you were going to die.

You omitted it all and you were surprised when they broke down, when they wept, when they shook from head to foot at some sudden noise, when they got drunk, when many would rather shoot their toes off than be ordered aloft again.

305

Yes, sir, thought Frank Butler, it's a man's life in today's Air Force.

"Bombs gone," called Billy Concannon. "Let's get the fuck out of here, Joe."

There was no asking the Holy Mother to forgive his dirty mouth on this occasion, a fact that disturbed the rest of the crew, who were reassured by the familiar. Ken Cornelius reminded him of the omission.

"Sorry," said Concannon. "May the Holy Virgin excuse my obscene tongue. Now can we please get the fuck out of here."

"I'm way ahead of you, Billy me boy, way ahead of you."

Calhoun had felt the sudden buoyance as *Hazel* was relieved of 6,000 pounds of high explosive, and assisted by Hank Quincey was already banking the B-17 to port.

As often happened in air combat, *Hazel* had been one of the lucky ones, hardly attacked at all. But that situation was not destined to last for long. Because 2,000 yards to starboard Wolf Löhr and Paul Weinrich, with one bomber already to their credit, had lined up Calhoun's Fort as their next victim and were preparing to attack.

Two hundred miles east of Bremen, Walter Schellenberg had displayed remarkable astuteness in divining the intentions of the fugitive Ju 52 and deciding what to do about it.

After confirming with Major Busch via Knobel that it had not transmitted since 1236, when it was in the vicinity of Nordhausen heading west-northwest, he next discovered there were no aircraft available to go off on a wild-goose chase. Every fighter that could fly and was within range of Bremen and Schweinfurt was otherwise occupied. But a quick glance at the map led him to suspect that the pilot of the 52 was making for England by one of the shortest routes: Dortmund, Arnhem, the Dutch coast around The Hague, East Anglia. And by an incredible stroke of good fortune the B-17s returning from Bremen would also have to cross the Dutch coast near The Hague.

All he had to do was alert every fighter base that had planes in action against the Bremen raiders and every emergency airfield that could conceivably be used for refueling to ask the fighters to keep one eye open for the Iron Annie as they chased the B-17s over the North Sea. If at first glance it appeared quite a task, it was certainly no more difficult than dispatching pursuit aircraft now, even if they were available. The fighters would doubtless be harassing the Flying Fortresses at a vastly different altitude than the one the Ju 52 was flying, but there would be no problems over identification. It was the Luftwaffe's only three-engined plane, it was bristling with radio antennas, and he had its code letters.

He would also make his orders unequivocal. There was to be no nonsense about forcing it to land in occupied Europe. Once seen, it was to be destroyed.

"Pauke-Pauke!" said Wolf Löhr, letting Weinrich know he was going in.

Baker and Ryan in the dorsal turrets and Billy Concannon in the nose, free to act as a gunner now, saw him attacking, heading for a point somewhere between the starboard inner and outer, one o'clock level, and let fly with everything they had.

"Jesus," muttered Löhr, but kept on coming, holding his fire as long as he dared, because he was low on ammo and fuel and every round had to count before he was compelled to put down at the nearest airfield.

The manual said to open fire at 500 meters and break off at 100 meters, aiming either for the flight deck to disable the pilot and co-pilot or just beyond either outer engine, where the fuel tanks were. In practice, what you did was hold any part—*any*—of the big *Ami* planes in your gunsights, take a deep breath, and thumb the firing button. If it was your lucky day you might just hit something before something hit you.

As far as Löhr was concerned, October 14—Black Thursday, as the Americans were to call it—was about half and half.

At 500 meters, he was firing and he could see the plexiglass behind which the pilot and co-pilot sat shatter as the 20mm cannon shells punched home. But simultaneously he felt the 109 being hit and a moment later smoke and oil were pouring from the engine cowling. No pilot liked bailing out, especially at that altitude, but there was no doubt about it that his Messerschmitt had had it. There was also a grave danger of fire.

"Gray Six, I'm hit and getting out," he called urgently.

He was unhurt as far as he could judge, and as he quarter-rolled to starboard he pressed the catch which released the cockpit cover. It flew off with a roar like the end of the world.

He checked that his parachute harness was secure, flipped the 109 onto its back, and fell clear. As he did so, flames licked the fuselage. He was still close enough to feel the blast when the remaining fuel exploded and his aircraft disappeared.

Following up the attack behind Löhr, Paul Weinrich disobeyed all the rules of survival and heeded one of humanity. He should have concentrated on *Hazel,* tried to finish the job Löhr had begun, but it was only natural he should want to see whether his friend and comrade got out safely. It took a couple of seconds to verify that he had, but in those seconds Weinrich's 109 had traveled 600 meters, bringing him to within 50 meters of *Hazel* on the same lateral plane. When he looked up he knew he was going to hit the B-17.

He yanked back on the stick and stamped on the left rudder, hoping to climb clear. But it was like jumping off a moving bus facing backward.

Hazel's starboard outer engine sliced into the 109's port wing, removing it as neatly as a surgeon performing an amputation.

The impact rendered Weinrich unconscious though otherwise unharmed, and he remained that way until he and what remained of the 109 plowed into the ground and disintegrated four minutes later. Even had he recovered consciousness, he would have been unable to bail out, as after thirty seconds of downward spiral the centrifugal force which built up inside the fighter pinned him to his seat as securely as any butterfly on a specimen slide.

Aboard *Hazel* bedlam reigned until Calhoun called for everyone to kindly shut up. It took an effort. Löhr's cannon fire ripping through the flight deck had wounded him in the right thigh and he was losing blood. He reckoned it wouldn't be long before he passed out, but at least he was better off than poor old Hank Quincey, now slumped back in his harness, his chest mangled, part of his face missing. Because the German fighter had attacked from starboard Quincey's body had absorbed most of the shells. Calhoun tried not to look at it.

He quickly established that *Hazel* was still capable of flight, though the starboard outer was a goner, barely part of the plane any longer. Neither did the feathering mechanism function. The engine was going to create a drag problem before long, but he'd worry about that when it happened. He was not concerned about the wing. It was still intact in spite of being clobbered by the second fighter. They built these birds to last, did the Boeing Company.

A check of the instrument panel told him that he was losing oil pressure on the starboard inner and also altitude, but neither at any great rate. As things stood at the moment they'd make it back.

After calling for a damage and casualty report and receiving confirmation that no one else was wounded, he announced generally that Hank Quincey had been killed and asked Shapiro to come forward. It meant leaving the right-waist gun unmanned, but Max was a pilot. The way things were going he'd be the only conscious pilot aboard in a few more minutes.

"And bring some morphine with you."

"Jesus," muttered Shapiro sixty seconds later. "How's she handling?"

Calhoun told him. "There hasn't been enough time to check it out yet, but I reckon we're losing altitude at a couple of hundred feet a minute, maybe a bit less. It could be the drag caused by the starboard outer but the inner's acting up too, and there may be other damage that's not registering on the instruments. What d'you reckon?"

Shapiro flicked his eyes across the instrument panel. It wasn't good but he'd seen worse. "I reckon we'll make it. We may be crossing the North Sea at zero feet, but if I were in your seat I'd take a shot at running for home. What about you?" Shapiro had a syrette of morphine in his hand.

"Jab it in, then see if you can do anything to stop the bleeding. Just pad it up."

"Much pain?"

"Not a lot, funnily enough."

Shapiro cut through the leg of Calhoun's flying suit with his knife and bandaged up the wound as best he could, using long strips of surgical tape and a thick wad of medicated gauze. Nothing vital seemed to have been hit, but the bullet (there was a single entry wound) was still inside and Calhoun was losing a lot of blood.

"What about Hank?"

"Drag the poor bastard out and take his place," said Calhoun. "If I go under because of the dope or any other reason I want to make sure that *Hazel* and everyone else get home."

"The Luftwaffe may have something to say about that."

Calhoun squinted through the shattered plexiglass. It was hard to tell just how many B-17s were still flying, but the fleet did not appear to have lost any more since making the bomb run. The fighters had thinned out also.

Shapiro read his mind. "A lot of them will be low on fuel and ammo by now. They'll be putting down anywhere they can."

"Gives us a breather."

"Until they come back."

The battle with the Americans had occupied a hundred miles of air space when Reinberger and Mahle set down on the emergency airfield at Apeldoorn, twenty miles north of Arnhem, for refueling and reammunitioning. Both pilots had scored hits on B-17s, inflicted damage, but neither had achieved a solid victory yet. Both were anxious to rectify that state of affairs.

There were other fighters landing and taking off from the same strip but none, as far as Reinberger could see, from his own Staffel. Not that that meant anything. There were dozens of emergency fields around.

The engine of his 109 had proved troublesome several times at high altitude, especially in tight turns, and he would have given a month's pay to have had it looked at there and then. But it would have to wait. Each minute that passed took the B-17s three miles closer to England and safety.

Along with every other flier who landed here and at other bases in the Netherlands, Reinberger was handed a typewritten message from Berlin warning him to be on the lookout for a Ju 52 (identification code letters as attached) on course for East Anglia. It was a matter of priority that it be destroyed, even if by doing so a B-17 escaped.

It was 1430 before he and Mahle were airborne again. At that hour the Ju 52 was crossing the Dutch coast just north of The Hague; *Hazel* was approaching the IJsselmeer, that reclaimed stretch of water formerly known as the Zuider Zee; and the Mosquitoes from Bromma were over the Frisian Islands. All of the aircraft were on more or less converging courses. In ten minutes, although at different altitudes, they would be on top of one another.

Twenty-three

At 1439 Pinetree received a signal from the main force over Schweinfurt: "Primary target bombed." There was some cheering in Brigadier General Anderson's headquarters, but not much. That sort of thing belonged in the movies. The men and women here knew there would be no hats in the air until every plane was safely back—which was impossible, of course. They had no idea of the full extent of the mauling the US Eighth Air Force was taking today, but they knew it would be bad.

Still tuned to the Pinetree frequency, Jimmy Ryan heard the same signal and passed it on to the remainder of *Hazel*'s crew. But there was hardly time to digest the news before Ryan was again on the intercom, on this occasion with bad tidings for the Bremen wing as well as the main force.

"Message from Pinetree timed at 1440 hours," he intoned. "We're not getting any fighter cover. The P-47s and the Spitfires are weathered in."

It had happened before and no doubt it would happen again, but *Hazel*'s crew couldn't help thinking that it was always the fighters who let the bombers down, never the other way around.

"Tell 'em thanks a million," said Shapiro.

He was alone at the controls now. Calhoun was barely conscious from loss of blood, possibly even dying; they'd moved him aft, applied a tourniquet, made him as comfortable as possible under the circumstances.

"I just did," said Ryan. "Hey, here's a funny thing."

"Spit it out so's everyone can hear it," called Billy Concannon. "I don't know about the rest of you guys, but up to now this trip's lacked humor."

"Give him a break, Billy," said Shapiro. "Let's hear it loud and clear, Jimmy."

"We're to watch out for a Junkers 52 carrying Luftwaffe markings on our heading. If we see it we're to leave it alone. It's one of ours."

"If I see anything carrying Luftwaffe markings," said Mike O'Malley with feeling, "it gets both fucking barrels."

"Well now's your chance," called Bob Baker, "because here they come again."

Hazel was twenty miles from the Dutch coast now, over the North Sea. But she was also down to 8,000 feet, not all of the loss of altitude due to the drag occasioned by the shattered starboard outer.

Since Quincey was killed and Calhoun wounded, the B-17 had come under attack a dozen times, been involved in dogfights across the breadth of Holland. There were few parts of her that had not suffered damage of one form or another. She had chunks out of her fuselage and tail; and the port inner and outer engine casings, both leaking oil, looked like relief maps of the moon. The ailerons responded moodily and the instrument panel on the co-pilot's side was a mass of broken dials. The readings had to be taken on trust. The starboard wing creaked ominously, and Shapiro was more than half prepared for it to snap off without warning.

313

And that was only what the substitute skipper could actually see for himself was amiss. He had given up asking for damage reports from other parts of the ship. Unless something fell off, he didn't want to know.

But there was at least one plus in this catalogue of woe. The intercom to all gun positions was still working, and so far no one else had been wounded.

Since the remainder of the Bremen wing—those planes whose crews were neither dead nor destined to spend the rest of the war in a German POW camp—was flying 15,000 feet above *Hazel,* there was no question of keeping her speed down to cruising to take advantage of the wing's mutually defensive firepower. Or what was left of it. Shapiro had told Cornelius to plot the quickest course for home and opened the throttles as far as he dared. He couldn't give *Hazel* maximum revs for fear of shaking her to bits, but if the air-speed indicator was telling the truth they were only thirty minutes away from landfall. They'd make it all right, if they could keep that pair of 109s at bay until range forced them to turn back.

They had picked up the Messerschmitts just west of the IJsselmeer, when it seemed as if *Hazel*'s inability to maintain altitude was working in their favor. The bulk of the fighting was taking place five miles up and it was possible the Luftwaffe were so busy they wouldn't notice one tiny little Fort trying to sneak through 15,000 feet below the main event. Or so Shapiro hoped.

It wasn't to be, however, and the brace of 109s had harassed and harried them since the coast.

Mahle and Reinberger attacked *Hazel* either side of the nose, ten o'clock and two o'clock level respectively, with a two-second gap between them.

Throttle wide open and aiming at a point several meters to the left of the starboard outer, Reinberger had enough time to see what a hell of a mess the B-17 was in before opening fire. Any normal plane would not now be flying. This one was no more than a mass of nuts and bolts and wires and circuits held together by will power.

And still she wouldn't go down. He could see his shots hammering home, but they seemed to have no effect on the bomber's ability to stay airborne.

Mahle thought Reinberger's tactics all wrong and was determined to tell him as much if they failed to make the kill again, as they were obviously going to. It was only supposed to be good strategy to attack a B-17 head on when there were others in the formation. From behind and below—that was where a lone Flying Fortress was a sitting duck. That way there were only two gunners to face, tail and ball turret, and the fighter had all the advantages.

Pulling out of a tight turn 1,000 meters astern of *Hazel*, feeling the big Daimler Benz engine laboring as he did so and wondering how much more of this it could take, Reinberger heard Mahle's voice in his headphones and saw his wingman overshoot the B-17. They had abandoned radio procedure a while back. Group, who monitored all conversations between pilots, would probably haul them over the coals for it later, but it was a common enough practice when only two planes were involved in an attack.

"We are never going to cripple the *Ami* this way, Herr Hauptmann. From the stern is our only chance of success."

Reinberger was now inclined to agree. Previously he had argued to himself that as they were running low on fuel and ammunition—and as the B-17 was evidently immortal—the only method of making the kill was by hitting the pilot or the wing tanks. But as that wasn't working either, it was time to go back to the book.

"Agreed," he said. "From two hundred meters below."

Mahle found it hard to keep the satisfaction from his voice. "Excellent. The sooner we put this one into the sea, the sooner we can get back to altitude and perhaps score more victories."

"You may not have to go so high."

315

Reinberger was leaning forward, peering through the cockpit canopy. It was hard to tell, because there was so much shit on the plexiglass, but two or three kilometers up front, not that far ahead of the B-17 and perhaps 600 meters below it, was another plane on the same heading. It was too big to be a fighter. At this range against the choppy backcloth of the North Sea a fighter would be invisible. It had to be another Flying Fortress.

"Do you see it?" he asked Mahle. "Twelve o'clock low."

"I see something. Should I take a closer look?"

"I will. It might not be another *Ami* and there's no point in us both wasting fuel."

Lying in *Hazel*'s nose in the bombardier's compartment he shared with Concannon, Cornelius had also seen the other plane and at first made Reinberger's mistake in judging it to be another damaged Fort. But they were slowly overtaking it, and after a moment he made out its markings.

"Max," he called up to Shapiro on the intercom, "I think that's the Junkers 52 Pinetree just warned us about."

Those aboard the 52 were starting to believe they were going to make it. No one had shown any interest in them crossing from Dutch air space and out over the North Sea, and although they were fighting a northwesterly wind and it was far from over yet, the East Anglian coast was a mere hundred miles away, less than an hour's flying time. Then Reinberger flashed across their bows.

Aft of the flight deck Fallon and McKenna heard the roar of the 109's engine and were on their feet instantly, peering anxiously through the observation windows. There first thoughts were of RAF or USAAF fighter cover. Then they saw the swastika on the 109's rudder.

Fallon went forward.

"What the hell do we do?" Travis called over his shoulder.

"Keep going," answered Fallon. "And wave like hell at the bastard. Maybe he's just curious."

Reinberger was very curious. Making a slow 360-degree sweep to port around the Iron Annie and eventually standing off its starboard quarter at 200 meters, struggling to keep the 109's speed just above stalling, he saw that the identification letters on the fuselage matched up with those on the typewritten sheet in his pocket, and that the plane was unarmed.

The instructions from Berlin were unequivocal. The 52 was to be shot down even if it meant letting an *Ami* bomber escape. But he had never in his life shot at an aircraft carrying Luftwaffe markings, armed or unarmed, and he wasn't sure he could do it now, not when the crew were waving at him.

Whether he would ultimately have obeyed Berlin became of academic interest. He was attempting to edge closer, to see if he could somehow get a better look at the crew or the faces in the observation windows, when Mahle's voice rang urgently in his ears.

"Reinberger! *Indianer!* Two o'clock low!"

Indianer meant "Redskins" and was Luftwaffe slang for enemy fighters.

A combat pilot was trained to react instantaneously to a warning from his wingman, not ask for verification, and Reinberger's reflexes were those of a seasoned campaigner. If the Redskins were at two o'clock low—down to his right—he must get the hell out of it up to his left, seek the safety of altitude.

He dragged the stick back into the pit of his stomach, simultaneously opening the throttle and putting his foot hard down on the left rudder, attempting a power climb. He gained 500 feet in a matter of seconds, but it was then that the engine he had worried about, complained to his ground crew about, gave a single cough and cut out completely. Where a moment earlier the 109 was three tons of aerodynamic beauty, a mag-

317

nificent piece of precision engineering, now it was just so much scrap metal.

Desperately Reinberger tried a flick roll to put the nose down and prevent a stall, but without power it was useless. The Messerschmitt began dropping like a stone. Soon it would begin to spin, and then he would be trapped by centrifugal force. He heard Mahle's voice but paid no attention to what was being said. He had to get out.

There were about six seconds in which to do so, he estimated, but in spite of that he remained absolutely calm and went through the escape drill. First the cockpit canopy was released. The sudden rush of icy air chilled him to the marrow. Next he checked his parachute harness and life jacket. Both were in order. Finally he unbuckled the restraining straps and forced himself up out of his seat, pushing against the cockpit sides until he thought his arms would break.

The 109 was beginning its spin now and the cold sea was rushing up to meet him. Blood was draining from his brain and part of him wanted nothing more than to remain precisely where he was. But it wasn't the first spin he'd been in, and he recognized the symptoms, similar to those of a man in a blizzard who wants only to lie down and sleep.

He was 1,000 feet over the North Sea when he heaved himself over the side, losing a flying boot in the process. He pulled the ripcord immediately, but even so the yellow chute did not open until he was a hundred feet above water. The life jacket would keep him afloat indefinitely. It was not that he had to worry about. It was the cold, which would kill him in an hour unless Mahle radioed his position to the air-sea rescue services.

Above him Mahle had no intention of doing any such thing. He would excuse himself back at Jever by saying his radio had malfunctioned, but he was not going to save Reinberger's life. With that arrogant bastard out of the running, the Staffel was his. Now the High Command would see some scores!

As for the Redskins, the Mosquitoes from Bromma which had made the whole journey from Sweden at under 1,000 feet without coming under attack once, they continued on their way, skipping across the sea. If Mahle or those aboard *Hazel* and the 52 wondered why a force of eight twin-engined fighters did not turn to give some assistance, they were not to know the flotilla was unarmed, for it was impossible to tell at the speed they were traveling and from the distance that they were not carrying RAF roundels.

But each crew had seen the 109 crash and the pilot land in the sea, and it was left to Jim Masefield, at the head of the squadron, to have the last word. Flicking on the ship-to-ship radio he said, "I guess we frightened him to death."

Mahle was alone now and coming to the end of his fuel and ammo. He calculated he had ten minutes' flying time left before being compelled to turn for home and enough ammunition to make perhaps two good passes. All he had to decide was whether to make them at the Flying Fortress or the Ju 52.

Had Mahle ended up in the North Sea and not Reinberger, there is little doubt that the Staffelkapitän would have tried for *Hazel*. He was a fighter pilot, after all, and the B-17 was the obvious enemy.

But it was Mahle who remained aloft, Mahle who was a devoted reader of Goebbels' *Völkischer Beobachter,* who would, in Wolf Löhr's words, have the entire Staffel singing the Horst Wessel song before breakfast if he ever took command. He was no coward, Oberleutnant Heinz Mahle; that the 52 was unarmed had nothing to do with his decision to go after it. He was a good Party member and good Party members obeyed Berlin. It had to be the 52 even if the B-17 escaped in the process.

When he made his decision he was circling *Hazel* at a safe distance, out of range of her guns and at the same altitude. Everyone aboard the B-17 saw the 109's nose go down. Shapiro at the controls, Concannon and Cornelius up forward. Jimmy Ryan and Bob Baker saw it happening just as they were preparing to repel what looked like another attack. In the tail turret Don Schaeffer witnessed it, as did Mike O'Malley, hopping between port and starboard waist guns now that Shapiro was flying Hazel. And finally George Bushman saw the 109 skip across his line of vision and open fire on the 52, which was now only four or five hundred yards ahead and 2,000 feet below.

There's no doubt about *this* 109's intentions, thought Fallon, watching it swoop down from three o'clock, taking advantage of the fact that the Iron Annie was unarmed by coming in to deliver a blow broadside. But there was nothing they could do about it except hope for the best and trust in Travis.

At the controls, the RAF officer glanced past Natalie, ducking his head to see what the Messerschmitt was up to. Experience told him when it would open fire, which would be any moment now. The 52 wasn't a fighter; and with a fixed undercarriage and all those radio aerials, it had the grace and maneuverability of a fat man on a ski slope. But he had 5,000 feet of space beneath him, and the RAF did not sit back and get the bejesus shot out of it without protest.

"Hard over starboard!" he shouted to Natalie when he saw the flickers of flame that were the 109's cannon and machine guns.

They both put their weight against the control column.

Mahle couldn't believe his eyes when he saw the 52 suddenly lose 300 meters of altitude in a violent sideslip and his ammunition pass harmlessly over the top of the fuselage. Then he too was beyond it, putting the 109 into a tight banking turn to conserve fuel. Whoever was at the controls was a flier, there was no doubt about that, but it was the kind of trick he

could only use once. To ensure there was no repetition, however, he would make a head-on attack next time.

Everyone aboard *Hazel* witnessed what happened. They
were virtually over the 52 now. More to the point, they were
approaching the 109 at a high angle, except it no longer
seemed interested in them.

Shapiro came to a decision. He had begun this mission as
an ordinary crew member, but with Quincey dead and Calhoun out of action he was now *Hazel*'s skipper.

The 109 had to give up soon. It had pursued them for
thirty minutes and if it wanted to get safely back to the Dutch
coast it would have to break off shortly. It was the perfect
opportunity for *Hazel* to make good her escape, except that
would condemn the occupants of the 52 to a watery grave.
And there could be no doubt that, whoever they were, they
were no friends of Germany.

He flicked on the intercom. "What say we give the 52
some help, fellas?" he asked, and explained what he had in
mind.

Not a man demurred. They were all tired and more than
a little frightened, but not one of them raised an objection
when Shapiro suggested they drop down beside the Junkers
and give it a hand.

"I'll remain to starboard and maybe three hundred feet
above," said Shapiro. "That way, if the 109 comes in from the
right he's got to come through us, if from the left he's flying
straight at us."

"I think he's got other ideas, Max," called Billy Concannon. "Looks to me like he's coming in the window."

Mahle completed his turn a mile ahead of the 52 and
Hazel. He could see the B-17 losing altitude and at first did
not understand the significance. When he did he shrugged
philosophically. So be it. He was not worried about one semi-
crippled *Ami*.

Travis had already figured out what the 109 was up to,

but this time there was nothing he could do about it. He had lost 1,500 feet before managing to correct the sideslip, and that left only 3,500 between them and the North Sea. Not enough margin for error. They would have to sit this one out.

He was about to relay this to Natalie when she nudged him and pointed. Out of the corner of his eye he saw the huge shadow of the B-17 dropping alongside. So too did Fallon and McKenna, and they felt like hugging the skipper. Jesus Christ, it was a mess.

The three aircraft hurtled toward each other at a closing speed in excess of 500 mph. Mahle held his fire until 400 meters and was rewarded by seeing the heavy 20mm cannon shells and the lighter 13mm machine-gun bullets strike home before hearing the ominous rattle that told him the magazines were exhausted. Then he was barrel-rolling to port, jinking to get out of reach of *Hazel*'s eleven Brownings.

It would have been more sensible to flick-roll starboard, away from the B-17, but he was too close to the 52 and feared a midair collision. Thus it was that he was compelled to run the gauntlet of *Hazel*'s entire arsenal.

On the approach, Concannon and Cornelius held him in their sights, firing long bursts that punched huge holes in the fuselage forward of the cockpit. Backing them up from the dorsal turrets were Baker and Ryan, who kept on shooting long after O'Malley in the right-waist aperture opened fire. Smoke was pouring from its engine cowling and there was a suspicion of flames when the 109, losing height, came abreast of Bushman in the ball turret and a fraction of a second later Schaeffer in the tail.

Every gunner who fired a round claimed the coup de grace, but there was no coup de grace, not in the truest sense of the expression.

Although his aircraft was mortally hit, Mahle himself was unharmed when he concluded there was nothing for it but to bail out. His radio was undamaged and he had time to flash a mayday to Zeist, giving his approximate position, not appreciating the irony of it all vis-à-vis Reinberger, because he was essentially a stupid man.

Parachute harness and life jacket checked and found to be in order, he tried to release the cockpit canopy, only to find the mechanism jammed, the bolts evidently fractured by shots from the *Ami* bomber. Although losing altitude, the 109 was still capable of flying and there was a good possibility he could get much closer to the Dutch coast before being forced to ditch. But that was overlooking the flames, which were now licking the cockpit. He might survive if he were very lucky, but he would be so badly burnt as to be useless as a human being.

Mahle didn't hesitate. He pushed forward the stick and went into a steep dive.

He was still conscious when the 109 hit the North Sea with a force that broke every bone in his body. The Messerschmitt stayed afloat for less than half a minute before sinking beneath the waves.

Hazel's engines were laboring now. She was a proud member of a magnificent breed of aircraft, but she was not designed to fly at low altitude at a speed close to stalling, not after the punishment she had taken this day.

Shapiro thought he saw someone on the flight deck of the 52 give him the thumbs-up sign, but it was hard to be sure. It could have been his imagination. Certainly the transport was still airborne and seemed capable of making a landing, but the windshield in front of the pilot and co-pilot was in tatters.

He eased the throttles open and felt the engines respond. If the altimeter was reading correctly they were down to 4,000 feet, but they'd make it to England okay. The only question was: Where?

He put it to the crew. There were airfields all over East

Anglia, and any one of them would be delighted to welcome them; but he was of the opinion they could just make Bassingbourn. What did they think?

They left him in no doubt that if he didn't deliver them to Bassingbourn, skipper or no skipper, he could begin looking for a new head.

The Ju 52 landed at Bardney in Lincolnshire, home of 9 Squadron, RAF Bomber Command. Through Curzon in Bern all RAF and USAAF fighter and bomber stations had been alerted to expect a 52 carrying Luftwaffe markings and not to treat it as hostile; but it was surrounded within seconds by armed guards.

Because nothing of the sort had ever happened before at Bardney and doubtless would never happen again, someone had the foresight to bring along a camera and an entire roll of film. Much of the negative did not develop properly and most of that which did was quickly confiscated by intelligence. But the photographer managed to retain a single picture, which he blew up and had framed. When the fuss died down it occupied a place of honor in the mess, and in later years many were the legends that grew up around it.

It depicted a woman in her early thirties, head bandaged, standing next to an elderly man with white hair, who was clutching his shoulder. Behind them was a very tall individual holding—though this was disputed by some experts—what appeared to be a Schmeisser machine pistol. To his right stood a youngster in RAF blue. An examination with a magnifying glass revealed him to be wearing the rank insignia of a flight lieutenant, though there was so much blood on his tunic it was hard to tell.

In the hatch of the German transport stood a square-jawed man who seemed—again it was disputed—to be wearing the uniform of an SS Obersturmbannführer. He was carrying in his arms a young woman who appeared to be dead.

Not one of the individuals was identified by name, and

when 1943 became but a dim memory the photograph aroused much discussion and argument. Some said one thing, some another; but there was never anyone around to confirm that the dead girl's name was Natalie Lunström and that she was killed during Oberleutnant Heinz Mahle's last pass.

Epilogue

The attack by the main force on Schweinfurt did not cripple the German ball-bearing industry, though production was severely curtailed. Aerial reconnaissance photographs at first gave the impression that the southwest corner of the town was a blazing ruin, but it later became apparent that it was the superstructure of the factories and assembly plants that was mainly damaged, not the vital machinery inside.

The cost to the US Eighth Air Force was appalling. Of the air fleet that set off from England that morning of October 14, sixty planes were lost. Six hundred men. Excluding the Bremen diversion, 228 B-17s attacked and bombed the target, dropping 350 tons of high explosive and 80 tons of incendiaries, and incidentally killing 276 people, among them Major Busch and Hauptsturmführer Knobel, obliterated when a Flying Fortress released its payload short of the Mean Point of Impact and wiped out the control room of the experimental airfield.

Yet Mission 115 was termed a success. It proved once again that the USAAF was determined to carry out massive daylight bombing missions regardless of casualties. It could also have been a hell of a sight worse.

In the high-level top-secret postmortem that followed, US Air Force brass were horrified to learn that they might have lost the entire Eighth Bomber Command, though it wasn't until after the war that precise details of Schellenberg's plan emerged. Captured German documents revealed that as early as May 1943 senior German generals were considering a coup against Hitler, who had not given the Reich a military or political victory for a year and who, since El Alamein and Stalingrad, they now thought to be a liability. Through his security services, Hitler was well aware of their plot—which would come to fruition with Claus von Stauffenberg's attempt to kill the Führer in July 1944—but decided, at this desperate stage of the war, he could not afford to arrest and execute the ringleaders without causing severe unrest in the Wehrmacht. What was needed was a massive military victory over the Allies to convince the generals *and* the German people he had not lost his grip. The destruction of the US Eighth Bomber Command was to be just that.

Further proof that Hitler was concerned about his position is to be found in document number FO 371/34435, now kept in the Public Records Office. The original is a memorandum from Sir Victor Mallet, Minister in Stockholm, to the Foreign Office and is dated 14 August 1943. Part of it reads: "Since then [the Kursk offensive] he [Hitler] has been forced more and more to abdicate military control to the generals. . . . He has lost much of his control over the Home Front. . . . As a result of all his mistakes over the past year he is in a state of nervous frustration. . . . He has now lost his talent for timing which stood him in such good stead earlier in the war."

Mallet's source was the Swedish businessman Marcus Wallenberg.

To a man in Hitler's predicament, Alfred Lunström was

as manna from heaven, but for the Allies there remained the vexatious question of what should happen to him now. The legal position was complex. He was a neutral and therefore guilty of no crime for which he could be tried in British or American courts, not without bending the law somewhat. In a pinch he could be regarded as a semi-belligerent, but that was not considered desirable. He was still the senior member of an extremely powerful family whose assistance was needed and would continue to be needed until Nazism was defeated. There was also very little likelihood that Felix would allow his brother to be thrown to the wolves. Whether Alfred would have to shoulder the blame for Natalie's death was open to conjecture, but that was between the Lunströms.

At a meeting in London attended by, among others, Curzon and Harry Mortimer, it was agreed that Alfred Lunström should be returned to Sweden and no further action taken—subject to the family being a little more pro-Allies in the future and Alfred's freedom to travel restricted. He did in fact drop out of sight and seek the sanctuary of his vast estate outside Stockholm. Fallon was sick with anger when he heard the outcome of the meeting, but there was nothing he could do about it.

It was further agreed that all references to Alfred Lunström's part in the affair be deleted from relevant documents from the outset, to be on the safe side. The Official Secrets Act could be invoked if one day anyone got too curious.

Of those who survived October 14, 1943, Flight Lieutenant Travis (whose injuries were minor, the blood on his tunic belonging to Natalie) was promoted to squadron leader and transferred away from his original unit to prevent awkward questions being asked regarding how, having been shot down over Germany, he was now back in England. He continued to fly Lancasters, both operationally and as an instructor, until the end of the war. There was talk of awarding him the Victoria Cross, but such a decoration would have required explanations, and that was out of the question.

Magda Lessing settled in England, where she eventually married. (Sworn to secrecy, as far as her husband and children are concerned, she escaped from Germany at the beginning of the war to avoid persecution for her political beliefs and spent the years between 1939 and 1945 doing dull work as a translator.)

Oberleutnant Wolf Löhr returned to JG 11, where he was given command of Reinberger's Staffel. He continued to lead it until he was killed over the Ruhr in 1944. Reinberger himself died of exposure in the North Sea.

Joe Calhoun recovered from his wound, but the bullet had damaged the femur and it left him limping. He was shipped home and given a desk job, which drove him slowly berserk. Like many fliers who wanted to get their tours over and done with, he found there was a lot to be said for active service. Nowadays he runs a small import-export company in Boston, and ironically many of his best customers are Germans. Sometimes he talks about the years he flew B-17s, but not often. His wife and daughters find it boring.

Max Shapiro and the remainder of *Hazel*'s crew were separated after October 14, for *Hazel* was destined never to fly again. It was easier to cannibalize her for spare parts than make her airworthy. B-17s were no longer in short supply.

Shapiro returned to his own plane, and the rest of the crew—Concannon, Schaeffer, George Bushman, and the others—dispersed among other crews. As often happens with the survivors of a particularly dangerous raid, they promised to keep in touch but never did. October 14 became just one day among many. Neither did any of them establish who was flying the 52. Shapiro and Ken Cornelius tried, but a wall of silence greeted their inquiries.

The Mosquitoes continued to make the run from Leuchars to Bromma and back, but no one ever told Masefield, Jock Munroe, and the rest why they were asked to make a low-level flight across Denmark and the North Sea that afternoon.

G-AGEL did have an unexpected passenger one day in early November, however, when with the blessings of the Ministry of Economic Warfare Sam McKenna flew to Stockholm in the bomb bay and forty-eight hours later married Ingrid Lindahl, the Swedish girl who had shared the apartment with Kirsty Gottmar. He wanted Jack Fallon to accompany him and act as best man, but Fallon was nowhere to be found. He was on a month's leave and, rumor had it, was trying to drink London dry.

Nevertheless, he turned up in the middle of November, presented himself for duty at Baker Street, clean and clear-eyed. He told Curzon he wanted to get back on operations as quickly as possible.

Curzon wasn't so sure. Mainly from Sam McKenna's debriefing he knew how Natalie Lunström's death had affected Fallon, and the easiest way out would be to put the SOE major into cold storage, a training unit. But Curzon was never one for taking easy outs. The war was all Fallon had left.

He volunteered for every hazardous mission for which he was qualified and served with distinction in several war zones and, later, areas of occupation until demobilized in mid-1946. They wanted him to stay on, but he refused. There was no Special Operations Executive any longer. Curzon was back in banking, the shop closed. It was all MI5 and MI6 now, and it was starting to be taken over by youngsters with very superior old school ties and a penchant for belonging to gentlemen's clubs.

A couple of months later, tipped off by an anonymous informant who seemed to know what he was talking about, several left-wing and liberal newspapers in Scandinavia began a campaign against Alfred Lunström that stopped just short of libel, hinting that he had harbored and continued to harbor Nazi sympathies. It began to hurt not only Alfred personally but also the Lunström empire, and it was decided that the elderly Swede would have to emerge from seclusion to refute the charges. He wasn't keen. He had received several thousand threatening letters since the campaign began and he felt safer surrounded only by his hand-picked armed henchmen. But finally he agreed.

He chose his moment well. On October 18, 1946, two days after the remnants of the Nazi hierarchy were executed in a Nuremberg prison, he gave a press conference on his estate, attended by correspondents from all over the world. Everyone was searched by armed guards on entering the huge library, but they failed to find the German Luger with which Lunström was killed by a single shot through the forehead as he was in the process of deploring the fact that Albert Speer had drawn only a twenty-year prison sentence, not the death penalty.

His assassin was gunned down immediately, before— although many witnesses said he didn't try—he could shoot anyone else or make his escape. He was a man in his middle thirties, six feet tall, square-jawed, and in excellent physical condition. He carried no identification papers or documents of any sort, though in one of his pockets the police found a heavy gold bracelet weighing four or five ounces. The initials NL were subtly interwoven in the design.

Acknowledgments

I hope the undermentioned will forgive me if I just give their names and my thanks. As I have said on another page, this is a work of fiction. To detail how some individuals and organizations contributed to my research might lead the reader to believe otherwise.

Mr. Malcolm Bates
Imperial War Museum
Public Records Office
Fran Winward
Mr. G. Skilling, RAF Strike Command HQ
Squadron Leader K. R. Jackson, AFC, Flight Commander,
    Battle of Britain Memorial Flight
Mr. R. A. R. Wilson, British Airways
Sir Archibald Ross, CMG
Colonel Andrew Croft, DSO, OBE
Mr. Torbjörn Oaulsson
Mr. John Stride
Mr. Ralph Barker
Squadron Leader F. E. "Jackson" Dymond

Mr. D. M. Greenwood
Mr. Rick Barker
Mr. Andrew Cormack
Captain A. S. M. Rendall
Captain Arvid Piltingsrud
Mr. W. I. Scott-Hill, OBE
Mr. W. J. Goldsmith
Mr. Harald Meltzer
Staff of Tiverton Library
RAF, Hendon